SPIES AND LIES:
THE PARADOX

Also by Frederick L. Malphurs:

Meanie Mouse versus the Orlando Operators:
The Adventure Begins

Mexia: A Novel, The Memoirs of J.C.Mulkey

My Life in the VA: Lessons in Leadership (nonfiction)

SPIES AND LIES:
THE PARADOX

FREDERICK L. MALPHURS

iUniverse, Inc.
Bloomington

Spies and Lies: The Paradox

iUniverse books may be ordered through booksellers or by contacting:

iUniverse
1663 Liberty Drive
Bloomington, IN 47403
www.iuniverse.com
1-800-Authors (1-800-288-4677)

ISBN: 978-1-4759-1846-5 (sc)
ISBN: 978-1-4759-1847-2 (hc)
ISBN: 978-1-4759-1848-9 (ebk)

Library of Congress Control Number: 2012907721

Printed in the United States of America

iUniverse rev. date: 06/29/2012

This book is dedicated to Robin, our six children, and Jack.

"The aim of a superior man is truth."
—Confucius, Analects

"Truth is the beginning of every good thing, both in heaven and on earth; and he who would be blessed and happy should be from the first a partaker of truth, for then he can be trusted."
—Plato, Laws

"I never give them hell. I just tell the truth, and they think it's hell."
—Harry S. Truman, cited in William Safire's Safire's Political Dictionary

"The truth is rarely pure, and never simple."
—Oscar Wilde, The Importance of Being Earnest

"The analogy between the intelligence industry and the military-industrial complex famously described by President Eisenhower in 1961 is fitting. By 2006, according to the Office of the Director of National Intelligence, 70 percent, or almost three-quarters, of the intelligence budget was spent on contracts. That astounding figure, which I first reported in June 2007, means that the vast majority of the money spent by the Intelligence Community is not going into building an expert cadre within government but to creating a secret army of analysts and action officers inside the private sector."

—Tim Shorrock, Spies for Hire: The Secret World of Intelligence Outsourcing

CONTENTS

INTRODUCTION

The idea for this novel started rattling around in my head decades ago. In the interim, my work in health care management had to get done, the family raised, and then when I retired, other books got written, but the idea was still bouncing around. The real espionage stories of our time will be whispered about in a few settings, and among a few people for some time to come, and maybe will see the light of day. This story is based upon the notion that very able spies can read between the lines of a great investigation or even a plain report of a seemingly unrelated matter. Perhaps from those elite, in-the-know groups, one or a small few who are still alive decades from now might write the true facts about this matter if they are able.

This book is dedicated to the notion that Daniel Pearl, the Wall Street Journal investigative reporter who was murdered in Pakistan would have written a book such as this, except it would be nonfiction, in other words, the convincing truth. Courageous and dedicated to getting the story, Daniel Pearl had the intelligence, the drive, and the commitment to write this story, as it should be, based on facts. But lies led him to his death. In any war, there are the known and unknown connections, the true and the false among us who tell us what they want us to believe and/or manipulate us in ways that we may never discern. Daniel Pearl's mission was definitely a highly risky assignment, but it might have changed the course of the war and avoided mistakes that followed his death.

In this work of fiction, David Pearl, Daniel's younger, distant cousin, takes up the challenge of determining the truth by a different path, and this is the story of that journey. Please remember the Daniel Pearl Foundation, which is dedicated to the spirit, style, and principles that shaped Daniel Pearl's work and character. In the author's mind, however, the hero of the novel was always going to be David Pearl. But, the fictional relationship serves, in a small way, to keep the torch burning for Daniel Pearl and his courageous work.

PROLOGUE

The Sudden Demise of a Political Appointee, December 28

Dante Tolliver eased the unmarked police car up and over the curb, in front of the Alexandria Fitness Center, its glass exterior throwing out yellow light into the frigid early morning darkness. The uniformed officers yelled greetings at him as he got out of the car.

"Cold enough for you guys?" Dante laughed and moved languidly toward the double glass doors of the fitness center, pulling his camel hair topcoat more closely. Small patches of ice formed in crystalline patterns on the sidewalk.

The officer standing guard in front of the glass doors opened the door for Dante and his partner, Ace Greensteen, who followed a few steps behind him. "Dante, get this investigation together fast, so we can get out of this fucking cold."

"We'll do what we can, Jake. Colder than the fucking North Pole tonight, ain't it brother?"

"You got that right, typically fine December cold ass morning." The officer released the door, clapped his gloved hands together and stamped his feet.

Dante went through the second set of glass doors followed by Ace Greensteen. The reception counter was on the left, a small conversation or waiting area on the right. Ahead of them were the bright lights that illuminated a forest of athletic equipment in the main area of the fitness center. The center was still decked out in artificial Christmas trees, fake presents, tinsel, and twinkling lights. Fake green balsam garlands hung over doorways, and red and green bows were placed randomly on the windows.

Dante and Ace approached the counter. Behind it were two employees dressed in the fitness center's black and silver attire and a skinny young woman wearing black spandex shorts, athletic shoes that made her an inch taller, and a tee shirt advertising a long past Marine Corps Marathon.

"Hi guys, I'm Detective Tolliver. This is my partner, Detective Greensteen. We're here about the homicide. Don't go anywhere just yet. We want to check the body and then we'll come back here to talk to you. You might find some paper to write down what you know about this: name, rank, serial number, how we can reach you, okay? We'll get you out of here as soon as we can."

Out in the multiple rows of exercise equipment, Tolliver honed in on the tight cluster of three crime scene technicians huddled behind a long line of treadmills. A middle-aged woman among them was the first to look up. "Oh, good news, we got the A team on this one." They all laughed.

"Dante, you get dragged out in the middle of the coldest night in history, and you still look like you're fresh as a daisy." The woman cocked a hip and grinned at Dante.

"Sally, you are too kind. I owe it all to good, clean living." More laughter followed, but quickly, almost immediately, dropped off into silence.

"Well, I wouldn't know about good, clean living," Sally answered, her face sharpening into complete seriousness. "What we got here is a male about fifty, in good shape except for getting his throat cut by something very sharp. I think he was on the treadmill judging by the blood splatter. He was exercising so the heart was really pumping. Our killer stepped into the blood unconcerned about shoe prints apparently to make sure that our victim was dead. He tracked blood several feet down this aisle until the residue wore off his sneakers." With her arm she directed Tolliver's eyes to the blood splatter on the treadmill, carpet, adjacent equipment, and finally, down the aisle behind the treadmills and in front of the elliptical. The body lay on its left side, in a fetal position, with the feet spread apart.

"Sounds professional, that's what it looks like alright, Sally. You didn't find the weapon?"

"No, we pulled up all the equipment to look under and checked all the trash containers. If it's a professional, he would take the weapons with him. I'm sure the killer got a considerable amount of blood on his clothes. So, we need a search inside and outside. Maybe he was calculating enough to use the locker room to change before he went back on the street." The two younger men with her stood behind her silently, but nodded their agreement.

"No identification, and other than the clothes he's wearing, there's only the locker key." Sally held up a clear plastic bag. Inside it was a key with a white elastic band attached to it. "The fitness center has lockable lockers. Each member puts their things inside and puts the key on their wrist or pocket. Our victim kept it in his pocket. We haven't gone to the locker room yet, other than to check the trash."

"Okay, that will be our next job after we talk to the people at the counter. Sally, we'll leave you to it then." Dante accepted the plastic bag, and he and Ace returned to the counter. Ace picked up the statements, which were written on the back of green data sheets provided to the members to record their workouts, and began reading.

Dante smiled at the group. "Alright, who wants to go first?"

The woman in workout attire seized the moment. "I'm Alexis Conn. I found the body. I screamed. These two came running."

"What time was that?" Dante looked at the two employees. The male had an arm around the female's shoulder. He was a head taller than her. His shoulders and chest were disproportionately large for his head and his lower body.

"12:35. I was just finishing up my routine. When I finished abdominals, I turned to go to the elliptical and saw this man lying on the floor behind one of the treadmills. I crouched down, did a 360 to see if I was next, then went over to him, close enough to see all the blood." Alexis confidently reported.

"Then what happened, Alexis?" Dante checked his watch. The time was 1:45 AM.

"I screamed bloody murder. Can I go now?" The slender woman continued talking in her calm, but assertive voice.

"After you've shown my partner your driver's license and reviewed your statement, he'll cut you lose."

Dante turned to the employees. "Miss, why don't you go next?" The woman moved closer to Dante, leaving her work partner frowning in the middle of the workspace.

"I'm Delores Perez. I usually work the graveyard shift and then go to my classes at Northern Virginia Community College."

"Good, do you know who the deceased is?"

"Oh God, I hate to think about it." Delores sniffled and blew her nose. "It's Cardiff Shapiro. He's a regular, comes in mostly late at night. He was quiet and reserved, but always had a trace of a smile on his face. He seemed like a nice man."

Chapter 1

Shocking News, Whispers, and Shouts, December 29

David Pearl, owner and Chief Executive Officer of DRPearl, Inc., sat at his desk reading the front page of the December 29 edition of the Washington Post. He looked up when Alice Boggs appeared in the doorway. With her usual look of intensity on her charming, intelligent face, Alice stood for a moment waiting for her boss to respond to her appearance.

"Should I come back? You look like you just saw a ghost." Alice cocked her head.

David waved her to the leather chair that sat on the right side of his desk. "I wish I had, Alice. Cardiff Shapiro, the State Department's Undersecretary for Terrorism and Financial Intelligence was murdered in the early morning hours of December 28 while he was working out at the Alexandria Fitness Center. Our good friend, Ritzenheim, told me last night that some big shot fed had been murdered."

"I bet all of the security and intelligence operatives have gone completely batshit."

"Sure they have; the murder of the Undersecretary for Terrorism and Financial Intelligence for the State Department has got to have lots of possible implications. I met with him once at a briefing for intelligence contractors. He was brilliant by all accounts and seemed like a very nice guy." David returned to the newspaper article and read aloud:

"Cardiff graduated from Princeton University from which he received undergraduate and doctorate degrees in political science. He graduated summa cum laude from Columbia Law. After interning on Capitol Hill for the Senate Foreign Relations Committee, he joined Abbot, Van den Heuvel, and Sorenson, the preeminent Washington law firm practicing international law. During the last presidential campaign, Shapiro served as one of George W. Bush's principal foreign affairs advisors. After the election, he joined the State Department as a senior undersecretary."

David saw Alice's concern. She had pushed herself to the very edge of the chair. "You are really disturbed by this, aren't you?"

"We're in the intelligence business and this has to be good for business, I'm sure of it. But for me personally, to have a government official murdered, or more likely assassinated, is going to be deeply worrisome to the Washington community in general, politically first of all, and to the general public. All of the security around Washington and he gets whacked in a public place. There's got to be a fascinating back story to this."

"Does the article give any guesses as to who did it and why?" Alice squirmed in the leather chair, adjusted her skirt, flipped open her notebook, and pursed her lips.

"Not directly. President Bush is quoted: "Our nation mourns the loss of a devoted public servant. We, as a nation, are, today, stronger, more vigilant, and more secure than we would have been without the intellectual and analytical abilities of Cardiff Shapiro. He was simply a giant among all of those who serve this great nation. His warmth and quiet demeanor will be missed. His brilliant, articulate, and insightful political analysis cannot be replaced. I am saddened by this great loss. Of course, our prayers and sympathies go out to his wife, Julie, and their three sons, all of whom are serving their country with distinction. With them, I celebrate his life and his incredible service to the country he so loved.""

David listened as Alice's polished, articulate speech turned cynical. "W mourns the loss, but doesn't mention the possibility this is a terrorist attack? I bet he won't be having a press conference anytime soon. His statement just invites questions. And, I think, I would have expected him to come out guns-a-blazing." Alice sat back, a frown briefly on her face.

"No, his statement is not revealing, except it may mean that they don't know shit so far. But, it doesn't matter either, the security apparatus of this country will be checking and verifying every possible contact that Shapiro ever had. They will run down every lead, climb into every rabbit hole, until they find out. And then when they do, they'll never tell the public. W will simply tell us 'mission accomplished.'" They both laughed.

David reached for a cup of coffee and brought it to his lips, his hands holding it under his nose. "I will call our friend, Ritzenheim. I am going to have to stay on top of this one."

CHAPTER 2
Duty and Honor, December 29

Dante Tolliver watched the crowds of people quick stepping along the sidewalks surrounding the massive edifice of the headquarters of the FBI on Pennsylvania Avenue. Groups of office workers hustled into restaurants and taverns, some clutching their copy of the December 29 Washington Post. The cold front lingered, and the biting wind chill caused people to minimize their time outside, except for a few of the most hardened smokers. He chuckled to himself, smokers were the new lepers. Dante Tolliver put a hand on the shoulder of Ace Greensteen, directing him to go first through the glass revolving door entrance into the FBI headquarters.

Inside the FBI building, arriving security officials patiently went through the security process. Once there, Dante and Ace's names and IDs were verified against a security list of people permitted to enter the building, they received an FBI security ID, and were instructed to place it around their necks. Then, they were escorted to the fourth floor conference room overlooking Pennsylvania Avenue.

Dante quickly deduced that the real leader of this meeting was Burt Dingfelder, the Deputy Secretary of Homeland Security, who was standing just inside the room, meeting and greeting each attendee as if he was the master of ceremonies. Dingfelder looked to be a former athlete whose muscles and grace were sagging into middle age. A paunch rode over the front of his belt, and a layer of neck spilled over the top of his button down, blue, oxford cloth dress shirt. After a few minutes, while many in the group milled around and interacted with others, Dante watched as the FBI Deputy Director, Abner Michaels, cleared his throat and asked for everyone to be seated. The chairs around the highly polished, mahogany conference table were all taken. The only amenity present was a gunmetal grey pitcher of water accompanied by a stack of small, clear plastic cups. Deputy Director Michaels spoke when the conversations dwindled. He cleared his throat and opened the meeting by requesting a moment of silent prayer for Cardiff Shapiro.

"May he rest in peace, ladies and gentlemen. Let us be dedicated to the search for the assassin and the reasons behind Cardiff's murder. We need to find out who did it as quickly as we can and why. We need to increase the security for our leaders. Cardiff's death was a terrorist act, in my opinion. I know that the White House is very concerned that it might be a terrorist act. Finally, we must follow the leads to the people who ordered this assassination. The coroner is here, and I'll ask that he go first so that he can then get back to his business. Dr. Felson?"

Dr. Felson sullenly, but momentarily, stared back at Michaels. The large, black bags under Felson's watery eyes betrayed his workaholic habits. "I am the chief forensic pathologist responsible for examining the numerous dead bodies provided by the denizens and visitors in Alexandria, Virginia. This case is taking precedence over all the other deaths we have in the city and my other responsibilities. We see victims of stabbing, gunshot, overdose, and so forth on a fairly routine basis. We have a backlog of victims, but we understand the critical nature of Doctor Shapiro's death."

"Please, Dr. Felson," interrupted Dingfelder. "We are all under a lot of pressure about this case. Please give the specific findings."

Dr. Felson stared sullenly, but momentarily, at Dingfelder and began speaking without consulting any notes. "Our subject, white male, was in excellent physical condition, forty-eight years old, married with children. The cause of death was a deep laceration across the throat, nearly from ear to ear. This incision was made by a very sharp object. I would venture the professional opinion that the incision was made by a professional killer. I also speculate that the killer waited until he could verify death. I think the killer waited for the absolute final moment of death and to make sure that no one stumbled across Dr. Shapiro prior to his death. That may be neither here nor there, but the death was very quick, matter of a minute or two at the most. I am speculating that something like a knife for the throat, bigger than a pocketknife. A large switchblade perhaps, also for the wound directly to the heart. Questions?"

Felson recognized Liesl Konik, who sat directly across from him, her warm smile and pixie cut hairdo bobbed gently as she spoke. "Dr. Felson, assuming a professional killer, what can be the reason that the murder was done mano a mano as opposed to a sniper shot, a spray of bullets, poison, or something else where the killer would not have needed be right there at the scene of the crime?"

"My guess would be advances in forensic science. Police crime scene investigators can trace ballistics back to the gun in nearly all cases, then the gun to who sold it, then to who bought it, and so on. The more exotic the weapon, the easier it is to trace. That includes toxic substances because of DNA. Not to mention that getting these weapons across borders and into the U.S., if that was the case, would pose formidable challenges. The same could be said for making a purchase at a gun show. An evidentiary trail would be followed to the buyer. This deed could have been done with a well-sharpened steak knife, a sharpened piece of hard plastic, or a straight razor. The weapon could be disposed of in many different ways. For example, it could be back in the kitchen drawer right now. No, I think with a skilled and cunning operative, a fatal knifing is a good way to go for a highly politically sensitive murder target."

The group sat in silence, mulling this theory over; finally Dingfelder spoke. "Dr. Felson, is there anything else that you can tell us about the autopsy?"

"No, the victim was otherwise quite healthy for a man of his age. He had good muscle tone. He must have been completely, immediately in a state of shock. It is sad, a tragedy for the family and for the US. I am always available by phone or Internet for your comments or questions. Now, if I may, I should get back to work. My backlog waits." A smattering of thanks recognized the pathologist's briefing.

As soon as the door closed behind Dr. Felson, Dante watched as Deputy Director Dingfelder looked to Michaels who simply sat with a blank expression on his pallid face. After a brief frown in the FBI Deputy Director's direction, Dingfelder asked Liesl for a State Department report.

Liesl was ready, posed and with her notes and outline side by side in front of her. "Deputy Dingfelder, colleagues, we are carefully analyzing all the materials collected from the office and files of Undersecretary Shapiro. He was, of course, engaged at the highest levels of national and international police investigations concerning terrorism, especially the funding sources and financial conduits in support of terrorism. All of his work involved the very highest classification levels. At this point, we are convinced that the murder was professional. This means that we are excluding a random attack or some personal vendetta."

Dingfelder interrupted. "Simply not consistent with the nature of the man himself?"

"Right. Shapiro was loved by his family and admired by his coworkers and direct reports. He was helpful, humorous, generous, charming, tolerant, and fair by every account. He wouldn't have gotten into a verbal altercation with a street person or with a rude person in the locker room. He was, in short, extremely accomplished and self confident. We think that there has to be a reason behind the murder. We have to find out what that is."

"Okay, thanks, please continue." Dingfelder glanced at Michaels, who kept his head down doodling on a lined pad in front of him, his comb over revealing a red, splotchy scalp.

"We have begun a case review of the matters brought before him. We are starting with the most recent, and working backwards. Under his leadership, the major financial work was focused on the banks and financial institutions transacting business with or within the countries of the Middle East, and especially those countries we already know finance terrorism, like Iran. We have begun our examination of these investigative efforts, but so far we have found nothing that would point us in any specific direction. There were no recorded threats against Shapiro at all. Certainly, the nations being examined, those with funds confiscated and otherwise challenged, could not have been happy with the US, but Shapiro had a political appointment, was a top level adviser to the Secretary of State and the National Security Administration, but was still a bureaucrat. His was not a face that they would recognize, or in all probability, blame. Finally, we are examining his foreign visits. For your information, in order of most recent to the last, for the past two years, his international visits have been to: Tel Aviv, Jerusalem, Beirut, Athens, Moscow, Helsinki, Cairo, Belfast, and Rome." Liesl leaned back against her chair, pushing her shoulder length red hair away from her face.

Woggins cut off Dingfelder to ask a question. "Liesl, please tell us the nature of these visits. By that I mean, was he out wandering the countryside, acting like a spy, visiting banks under suspicion, without cover?"

Seated at the last two spaces on the west side of the table, carefully placed and ignored, Dante elbowed his partner, Ace, and whispered, "Pompous ass."

Liesl laughed softly. "Nothing like that, Robert. Undersecretary Shapiro was always accompanied by State Department Security, including while he was in transit. Except for meals and a little sightseeing where he was also accompanied by security, his work was in the embassy, the CIA station, or in official government buildings of the nations involved. He was in no way a secret agent."

The meeting droned on with each subsequent round of questions and statements of less and less merit. Dingfelder mercifully released the group thirty minutes after Felson's departure.

Chapter 3

A Most Unusual Mugging, January 3

In the Alexandria police department building, the detectives were situated on the third floor. The top brass had the fourth and final floor of the red brick, colonial—style building. In the Tuesday late morning hours, a week after the Shapiro murder, Toliver was quietly trying to sip his coffee as he sat at his desk reading the Washington Post sports section. His moment of relaxation was brought to a halt by his partner, Detective Ace Greensteen.

"Dante, we have to go to Alexandria Hospital. We got ourselves a lead." Ace was short and feisty, with a cherubic face and a head full of tight black curls that forecast his intense and driven nature.

"No rest for the weary, son. What do you have?"

"We have ourselves a mugging victim who just happened to use the fitness facilities on the night of the murder. He entered the center about thirty minutes prior to our victim."

"No shit?"

"No shit. The only problem is that he had already been admitted to the Alexandria hospital because of severe injuries that he received from a mugging. He was dining out with a date on Queen Anne Street." Toliver smiled broadly at what sounded like a real lead.

Dante let his partner drive, but since he couldn't bear to watch, he read the sports pages while Ace dodged recklessly through the Alexandria streets. Some icy snow remained from a New Year's storm. The remnants hugged the curbs, and crevices were now dirty and icy. Now, the businesses and sidewalks were back to normal, full of shoppers, errand runners, and deliveries. Normally, in the late afternoon traffic with the streets full of commuters, the drive could have taken twenty-five minutes. Ace made it in ten. He pulled their unmarked vehicle into the emergency drive, set the bubble light on the roof, and turned it to flashing.

After consulting at the information desk, and then with the nursing station, the two detectives arrived at the bedside of Jasper Reinking. The detectives introduced themselves and asked Reinking how he was doing.

"How does it fucking look like I'm doing?" His words slurred out of his mouth slowly, with effort. The man was badly bruised, with two black eyes and lacerations on his face. Both hands were swaddled in bandages. A deep cut across his cheek had nicked his left ear and the tip of his nose. The cheek on that side was covered with stitches.

"You look like you're doing bad." Dante's soft, mellow voice was friendly and concerned. He placed a hand on Reinking's shoulder.

"Thanks for that, Lieutenant. The son of a bitch also stabbed me twice in the chest. Both wounds penetrated my lungs, so I'll be in this bed for at least two more days, according to the doctor." The man tried to turn to face Toliver, but the effort quickly failed and he settled back into a prone position with his head slightly elevated on two pillows.

Ace Greensteen smiled. "Mr. Reinking, we need to ask you some questions about the mugging. What can you tell us about your assailant?"

"Jeez, I've already told this to several other policemen. Can't you just read their reports?"

"I've read their reports. We are working a different case, Jasper, a homicide. So, it's important to get as much information about your assailant as we can." Ace kept on smiling.

"A homicide, I suppose I'm lucky that I'm not dead." Jasper sighed.

Ace Greensteen nodded. "Right, we think you dodged a bullet."

Dante laughed in gentle and warm support. "Probably. The murderer may well have been a professional assassin. The murder we are investigating is a matter of national security, highest priority. Your membership card was used to access the Alexandria Health and Fitness Center shortly after midnight. We believe that the person who accessed the fitness center with your card killed our victim. We know that you were already in the ER at the time of death."

"Jesus, I guess I should thank my date, Cookie, for saving my ass then. She screamed bloody murder and that attracted several people. I think the guy would have killed me for sure if he'd had just a few seconds longer." Reinking chuckled softly, but the pain in his chest stopped him abruptly. He used a corner of the bed sheet to wipe the spittle that had collected on the edge of his lower lip.

"Mr. Reinking, could you start at the top? What were you doing on the evening of December 27?"

"I had a date with Cookie Piaggio. I met her through a dating service. She's a civil engineer with the state. She apparently facilitates the creation of these monster traffic jams that we have in northern Virginia." Reinking sighed. Ace and Dante laughed.

"I met her at the Dolce Vita Restaurante. That's right there on Queen Anne Street. She was on time. We had a pleasant dinner. She agreed that I could walk her back to her condo. We left through the main entrance and turned right on Queen Anne toward her condo. About twenty feet down the sidewalk, I thought I heard something behind me." Jasper sighed deeply and stopped talking.

"Just take your time, Mr. Reinking. There's no need to wear yourself out. You need some water?" Dante watched Jasper shake his head very slowly.

"As I was turning, I got slammed in the back of the head. I nearly lost consciousness. I definitely saw stars. I fell. I heard Cookie screaming. This guy rolled me over onto my back. The man grabbed my wallet, put it in his jacket. He stabbed me twice in the chest, as I told you already. Then, he slashed my face. I grabbed the knife, first with my left hand. I'm left handed. Then, when I couldn't stand the pain any longer, I grabbed the knife with my right hand. He was on top of me and was pounding my face with his free hand. When more people started yelling, some waiters came out of the restaurant and ran to get to us, so they could pull him off of me. But, he was too quick. He ran off. The waiters chased him for a block or two, but the guy lost them."

"From your other reports, you describe the man as older, strong, and taller than you, gray hair, and pale. Do you still agree with that?"

Jasper closed his eyes for a moment before responding. "Yeah, the guy must have been in his early sixties, pale, hair thinning, strong, and slender, but very athletic and quick."

"What else?" Dante placed his hand on Jasper's shoulder.

"Nothing else, oh, except he smelled of a strong aftershave or cologne."

"Would you recognize him?"

"No, I don't think so. Why would he pick me?"

Dante's eyes never left Reinking's face. "If we are right and he's a professional, then as soon as he observed his target's comings and goings, he knew he would need a gym membership key card. He must have seen you leaving the gym, followed you until the opportunity to get access to the fitness center."

"You mentioned that his cologne was strong. What did it smell like?" Dante watched Ace Greensteen's pale, freckled, and homely face glance over to him, seeking Dante's reassurance.

"Well, I don't know, strong, pungent. Not something I would slap on. It was a little over the top as far as I'm concerned."

"How would you describe it?" Dante had moved to the end of the bed so that he could maintain eye contact.

"I'm an actuary for the Department of Agriculture. Describing smells is not in my skill set."

"Go ahead and try."

"Overly strong, but masculine, very different from the one I use, fruity, a little punchy, like maybe, grapefruit."

The detectives thanked Reinking and departed the hospital. Toliver tapped out a message on his Blackberry covering the interview. He sent the message to Liesl Konik and Robert Woggins.

CHAPTER 4

Time Out at the Sofitel Bar, January 3

David Pearl sat at the crowded bar watching the customers in the bar and those people passing through the hotel lobby just outside the bar. His beer and a plate of cheese and olives were situated in front of him. As he sat there, he felt Alice lean her shoulder onto his.

"David, there's a little table that just opened up over by the 14th Street side. We may be able to hear ourselves talk there."

David smiled at her, glad for the company and a chance to talk to his friend, confidant, and assistant—whenever DRPearl, Inc. could afford her. "Alice, how could I have missed you? I've been watching everyone who comes in here or leaves, but I didn't see you. How are you doing? We haven't seen much of each other lately."

David waved the waitress down and ordered Alice a dry martini double.

She reached out her hand and covered his right hand. "Your hand is nice and warm. It's a frigid night out there. Did you have a good New Year?"

"As good as it gets when one spends it with their parents. How about you?"

Their eyes met. Alice had blue eyes, pale skin, dark blonde hair cut short. After a few moments, David finally diverted his eyes away from Alice out the window view of the sidewalk, 14th street, and the busy restaurants on the other side.

Alice removed her hand. "A neighbor had a small get together, nothing special. I had to do some homework. My work at InfoSystel is going really great, but I can't wait to come back to DRPearl. Still, duty calls, I'll have to go back to work tomorrow."

"We need you back too, Alice. Business is picking up. I really miss your clarity of thought and vision. I need your help, but alas finances at the moment haven't improved much. We have some proposals out that are promising. Ritzenheim tells me that the search is spreading out to find Shapiro's killer. He says that Homeland Security might bring in some contractors in the near future to work on that case."

Alice held the drink under her nose for a brief sniff and then sipped the martini. "That would be cool. No, David, I consider myself very lucky to have met you when I did. I was really in a dark place, and getting to know you and how comfortable it was to talk to you really made a difference in my life. Here's to you." Her martini glass met his beer with an inaudible touch.

"I feel that same way. At first, I thought you would be impossible to have as a friend. That night we were out with some of your college friends, I couldn't believe that they all considered you to be their best friend. What a group, they idolize you." David turned his eyes back out to the people passing by on the sidewalk.

"Oh, they just admired my independence and my hard partying style." Alice smiled and gently laughed.

David's eyes returned to Alice. "That night I took you home. I was afraid you were too drunk to get home safely after that party. And, you started getting undressed before I could get out of there. You told me that you didn't want anyone but me looking at your ass."

Alice's eyes never left his, showing no embarrassment. She smiled at him. "I still feel that way, too. I had way too much to drink. I seem to remember also telling you that the only thing I wanted in my oven, other than my shoes, was you." Alice finished her martini, caught the server's eye, held up her glass, and was recognized.

"Jesus, what a night that was." David shook his head at the thought. "I'm unlocking the door for you and when I turn around, you taser some guy who had walked up behind you. In the groin!"

"He was a street person. I had encountered him before. He should have known what was going to happen. I warn them. I still keep an armed taser in my purse. Sometimes, the knuckleheads just will not leave you alone." Her soft, southern accent was regional to her hometown of Appomattox, Virginia.

"Hey, I'm going to be good. You'll never have to taser me. I've got to run for the Metro. I have a big contract meeting tomorrow, January 5. I'm excited about the possibilities, real intelligence work for a change. I've really got to go. Even though she's retired, my mother still stays up for me. If I get the contract, I'll need you back at DRPearl." David gave Alice a kiss on the cheek. Alice ordered another martini.

CHAPTER 5

Greeks Intruding in the Night, January 9 through 19

To stay financially afloat, David had a part-time job waiting tables at a neighborhood bar called Stoney's. On January 9, the cold and wind outside kept many of the usual patrons in their apartments. Stoney's was nearly empty. David sat polishing glassware and listening to a bar regular, Demetrios Constantinos, complain about Greece's distrustful, low-pay attitude toward Foreign Service employees, especially those on contract, like him. Suddenly, the Greek put his arm around David's shoulders and conspiratorially pulled him closer.

"Hey, David, you know I like you, and I know that times are tough starting a new business. I think I can get you some work at the embassy, security stuff, it will get you more money so that you can quit waiting tables." Demetrios burped, wiping his mouth with his sleeve. He looked around and took another mouthful of gin and tonic.

"Thanks, Demetrios, I'm sure the embassy has enough talent to watch over its employees, but I appreciate the thought just the same."

"They got their own security coverage. They need additional security because one of the embassy staff has been threatened. The work would be watching their homes, driving around the immediate vicinity of the residence looking for possible security issues. I'll leave word with the Chief of Security tomorrow." Demetrios stared at his watch.

"That would be January 10." David made a note in his pocket calendar and placed a supportive hand on Demetrios's back.

Demetrios abruptly jumped up from his bar stool. "Yes, that would be great. Probably nothing too stressful, and the work would be boring, but it would put some gas in the tank." His last words slurred off into the silence of drunkenness.

David approached the bar manager who sat in the back of the bar checking receipts. "Denny, I am leaving now, if that's okay."

"Yeah, business has dropped off a cliff tonight. Walk Demetrios back to his house, will you? I don't know where the guy puts all that gin. He must have a wooden leg."

Demetrios was singing some Greek pop song quietly and was very unsteady on his feet. Built like a professional middleweight boxer, Demetrios would suddenly stop and jab away at some invisible foe. "I'm in charge of internal security, but don't tell."

At the door to Demetrios's apartment, David waited patiently while the man fished around in every pocket before finding his keys. Once inside, Demetrios went into the bathroom where he stumbled into the toilet and called out a few angry words in Greek.

Pictures, presumably of family, were crowded on a three-foot-high, dark, wood chest. The profusion of men, women, and children in the pictures with Demetrios signaled a large, extended family. Then, as Demetrios was coming out of the bathroom, David noticed the SIG Sauer, automatic pistol hanging in its holster on the back of the door.

David helped Demetrios undress down to his underwear and got him into bed. Before leaving, he easily confirmed Demetrios's identity and professional position with a quick glance into Demetrios's wallet. With that, he left and went back outside into the early morning parade of traffic and people on Thomas Circle in Washington, DC.

Later that day, after a few hours of sleep, David walked into the glassy reception area for the Greek embassy and told the receptionist that he had a meeting with Demetrios Constantinos. She hit a speed dial code. When Demetrios answered, she barked Greek at him. Then, she listened for a moment and laughed. She told David that Demetrios would be right up. After his arrival, he escorted David to the security manager's office in the basement.

The security manager looked up from his computer screen and went to greet David. "We have a contract job available. We want temporary security at the residence of our political affairs attaché, Nicolaos Polopolis. There have been anonymous threats against him."

"Super, when can I start?" David's maintained his calm demeanor, kept smiling, but wanted desperately to ask a thousand questions about the embassy, its diplomats, their issues and concerns, but he didn't.

"David, just sign these papers. Demetrios will provide the details of the assignment and show you out." The man walked around them, leaving Demetrios and David looking at each other in the chief's office.

"Is he always so pleasant? Don't answer that. I'll just take my contract and be on my way."

Demetrios shrugged. "Trouble back in Greece. His son has become an anarchist, out on the street nearly every night, throwing rocks and protesting."

"Oh yeah? I can see how something like that would be a major distraction."

"It would sure put any parent into a seriously bad mood. David, here is the address; you are taking the night shift, 6:30 PM to 6:30 AM shift. Here are all our radio codes. You are to call me at once if anything suspicious happens. Hopefully, this thing will work out for us without any problems, and you'll have a few bucks in the coffers to keep you going."

"I really, greatly appreciate it, Demetrios. We'll do a good job. Thanks." David shook hands and walked through the corridors, signed out at the front security desk, and walked out into the brilliant sunshine of another frigid January day. He'd get some sleep, or try to, and begin his work that same evening.

For the next seven days, a team from DRPearl watched the assigned house throughout the night. On the night of January 17, cold and clear, David sat in the car of Marine Lance Corporal Jose Gonzalez.

"David, I really appreciate you bringing me on. I want to save up for when I get done with my tour. I'd like to try college."

David nodded, but continued to stare at the darkened residence of Polopolis, a red brick house in the early fifties style of D.C.'s inner suburban communities, two story, white paint on the eaves and shutters. Mature trees added the darkness and shadows. Streets lights lit only the street and few of the other houses had any lights on in the front. "I'm glad you joined the firm. Business has been bad, so until I got this contract, I really couldn't afford employees."

"David, man, I can't believe you don't have a car. Is business that bad?"

"Jose, all the cash that I possessed I put into setting up the corporation, buying the town house, purchasing the panel van, and some computers. With the contract funding that we'll earn from this Greek Embassy

17

operation, I was able to get a loan to have a cash reserve that, hopefully, will see us through until contract payments arrive."

"So what were you doing before?" Jose's thick muscular neck and shoulders moved powerfully under his insulated parka.

"I worked for the CIA and got outsourced. Five years, almost all of it overseas."

Jose grinned at David. "That must've been a crock of shit, man."

"Oh, it was, it most definitely was. The government has contracted out most of its intelligence work, so many of us were expendable. I used every penny I had to get set up. I wanted to stay in the intelligence business. But still, I had thought I was on my way to a career and had ambitions to go to the top. For a few weeks after, I was out in the cold. I was devastated."

Jose's brow arched down in the middle, above his nose. "It's good to have a business. I think you're the man. It's a good thing, I guess, that they don't outsource Marines." He chuckled.

The residential street where they staked out the Polopolis home was lined with parked cars. The residential neighborhood would empty out beginning at daybreak, as the commuters departed for their worksite.

On January 17 at 2:30 AM, Jose Gonzalez gently prodded David awake. "Boss, I see someone beside the house."

Pearl was still refocusing his eyes when he saw the movement. The slender man went through the screened side of the front porch, fluidly and silently.

"Boss, he must have cut through the screen with a box cutter or something. You want me to go get him?"

"Not yet, Jose, I'm calling the man who is supposed to live there, just in case." The phone rang several times, but no one answered. "Let's go, Jose, quietly please." The two men moved silently across the yard. Both were carrying Berretta 9 MM's. When they reached the house, Jose quickly went through the same opening as the intruder. The intruder had cut through the screen and then raised the glass window enough to slip in. David followed Jose through the window.

Once inside, Jose and David stopped, listened intently, but heard nothing. Pearl switched on his micro flashlight. He could see that the room was a living room, a leather sofa, three cushioned chairs, a coffee table, and lamps. Nothing appeared to be out of order. He whispered for Jose to cover him while he slowly ventured toward the next room, the kitchen.

Pearl stopped abruptly when he saw a body on the floor. He felt himself holding his breath, and a cold shudder swept through his body. He bent one knee to the floor, felt for a pulse, instincts suddenly on high alert, his eyes searching in the darkness for movement and his ears straining to hear. The man dressed in black was lying face down. Blood was pooling beneath his head and neck. Pearl punched out 911 on his cell phone. David reported the murder, gave the address, and told the operator, abruptly, that he wouldn't stay on the line. Then he called the Greek Embassy number that Demetrios had given him, surprised when the number took him directly to Demetrios.

"Demetrios, this is David. I am in Nicolaos's house. Someone has been murdered and is lying on the kitchen floor. I called 911. My security man is checking the rest of the house. The body is still warm."

Demetrios was wide-awake, but apparently still feeling the effect of a night's drinking. He slurred some of his words. "David, who is the dead man?"

"I don't know, I will wait for the police to turn him over. He's wearing a black nylon hood over his head, so I can't even give you a decent description other than he's about six feet tall, slender, and dressed in black. I hear the sirens. I'll stay here to find out everything I possibly can."

Demetrios promised to be there as soon as he could, thanked David, and hung up. Jose Gonzalez reported back that the rest of the house was empty. "The beds haven't been slept in. Everything is clean and orderly. I think that this dude is the guy we just watched breaking into the house."

"I think you're right, Jose. I seriously didn't want any untoward events on this contract. Now we have a situation." David turned and walked toward the front door, a thousand possibilities, issues, concerns boiling in his mind.

Pearl opened the door to a DC police Sergeant. The Sergeant was followed by two more uniformed officers, bundled in heavy coats, wearing gloves, and caps pulled tightly onto their heads. David led the three to the kitchen. The Sergeant called in the detectives, the crime scene investigators, and the on-duty public affairs officer. As the three of them were staring at the body, David briefed them. "I'm a security contractor for the Greek embassy. Some of their employees have been threatened, including their political affairs attaché who owns this house. My partner and I think that the dead man is the person we observed breaking into the house. We didn't see anyone else here, and we looked in every closet, under the beds, and out back. We didn't see or hear anything as we crossed the street and followed him into the house either."

After fifteen minutes, a detective and his partner arrived. The two were middle-aged African-Americans, both slightly over six feet tall, and athletic in appearance. "Hi, we're the pros from homicide. I am Taz Washington, and this handsome devil is my partner, Neal Walters. We'll start with the Sergeant here. The rest of you go have some coffee."

The night had turned from cold to raw cold, gusting with wind. The detectives kept their topcoats on. The front and back doors opened and closed repeatedly as the official police party gradually increased in size.

David repeated his story. "Detective Washington, I need to cut Jose loose, he's an active duty Marine at the Barracks. He needs to get some sleep before he has to go on duty."

"Yeah, sure, and do me a favor, call me Taz." Taz nodded, slapping Jose on the shoulder as Jose walked past. "Right now, we have no idea who the deceased is. No one has seen the perpetrator, who seems to have vanished. How long do you think it was between the time you first saw the deceased enter the house and the time you found the body?"

"Oh, less than three, no more than four minutes—four minutes at the very outside. After we found the body, I immediately sent Jose to check the rest of the house. After that, he checked outside, but he didn't see anyone." David sipped black coffee from a thick-lipped mug.

"Right, we think the dead guy is a professional, and whoever killed him probably is, too. This neighborhood is generally considered safe. We are a few blocks from Walter Reed Army Hospital and a block from Rock Creek Park. So, we'll check with the neighbors as soon as they start to stir. David, why don't you take off? We know where to find you." Taz then ordered the uniformed police to recheck the entire house.

David checked his watch. It read 5:00 AM. "I'll leave you guys to it, then." David walked out of the neighborhood to the nearest Metro station. When the train stopped at the Chinatown Metro stop, David got off and walked two blocks to his office row house nestled at the end of a nondescript block of row houses—which also doubled as his substitute bedroom. Once there, he inflated the camping mattress and entered into a troubled sleep.

David woke at 10:30 AM to a ringing phone. He was groggy. It took him a few moments to find the phone. "Pearl this is Preston Williams, the corporate outsourcing officer with TechPro. I think you've heard of us."

"Yes sir, one of the biggest companies doing intelligence work in the nation."

"Good. TechPro has a couple of deliverables that have gotten backlogged. We'd like to see if DRPearl, Inc. can handle them. Do you have an interest in this?"

"Yes sir, definitely."

"Are you on a secure phone?"

"No. I have secure email, but not the phone yet."

"Then, you better get your ass over here. See you at one."

As soon as David clicked off, his cell phone started playing Hail to the Chief again. He answered in the company name.

"Am I speaking to David Pearl?"

"You are."

"David, this is Taz Washington. I'm the good-looking detective you met last night."

"Oh, sure, Taz, I remember. How could I forget such a beautiful face?"

"I know it's hard, but I got two ex-wives who are giving it their best shot. My partner and I need to talk to you some more and we need to re-interview your man, Jose Gonzalez."

"What's it about?"

"We think we found the murder weapon. The crime scene guys studied the backyard thoroughly. Then, one of them got the bright idea to go onto the roof. He found what looks like the murder weapon, a box cutter behind a drainpipe. The perp must have thrown it up there. We have also talked to the embassy's director of security, Georgios Kostas. He isn't too happy about your services at the moment. I'll see you at your office at five today. Can you get Jose there?"

"Yeah, I think so, Taz. I'll call if I can't."

David rushed to his meeting with Preston Williams at TechPro. David stepped out of the cab, now a few minutes before the meeting due to the TechPro building not being identified in any way. He clutched his notebook, signed in at the desk, then took the stairs two at time. Most of the offices he walked past were anonymous, as well. Card key and push button security codes were in place on every door. Preston had a corner office with a view of the Potomac River. David knocked, heard the buzzer, and pushed the door into the office.

David stepped to the front of the desk and watched Preston as he kept looking through papers on his desk. Finally, he found the one he was looking for. Only then did he look up at David, handing the one page document to David. David studied it.

"This document is a preliminary agreement and outline for the proposed work that we are interested in subcontracting to you. At the bottom, if you are agreeable, is a place for you to sign."

David read the document before signing. Handing the paper back to Preston, he quickly took his leave while Preston took a phone call, swiveling in his chair to gaze out at the river.

Taz and Neal Walters showed up about fifteen minutes late. David watched from his second story window, as they left their vehicle double-parked in one of the two traffic lanes. David quickly went downstairs and briefly looked over the squalor in the office, deciding that he could do nothing to improve it without a major overhaul, and went to the door to let them in.

"Hey, Taz, welcome. Neal, good to see you again so soon, I hope you guys are making progress on the murder. Do you want some coffee?" David poured four cups of half caffeinated and half regular and served them, along with a tray bearing artificial sweeteners, sugar, and fake cream.

Jose Gonzalez sat hunched over, his muscular arms bulging through his grey sweatshirt sporting the Marine Corps logo. He greeted the two DC detectives with, "Sorry I was late, couldn't be helped."

"Not a problem, Jose. We just got here ourselves."

David watched Detective Neal Walters's eyes widen as he surveyed the shabby surroundings. Walters looked quizzically at David. The room was clean, but the furniture was threadbare, used beyond reason and cheap when it was new. A coat of paint at the very least would have dressed up the place considerably. The one visible trashcan was overflowing. "Sorry, funds just haven't permitted us to replace this squalor with something less offensive." The men laughed.

"David, I understand that you talked to your contact at the Greek Embassy last night?" Taz had his notebook out, poised to begin writing.

"That's right, Taz, my contact is Demetrios Constantinos. He is the acting chief of internal security at the embassy. He's a retired cop from Rhodes. He said that all he knew at that point was the homeowner, Nicolaos Polopolis, is the political affairs attaché. Polopolis had been threatened through anonymous, untraceable letters that came to the embassy addressed to the ambassador. Polopolis is a womanizer. His family stayed behind in Greece. He had been forbidden to date female employees in the embassy. The embassy took the threats seriously, upgraded his home alarm system, and hired my firm to provide increased security. The intruder effectively bypassed the alarm system. Beyond that, they don't know of any enemies. The written threats were nonspecific. So, they are thinking that the threat resulted from something personal, maybe some woman scorned. And, I think the embassy really doesn't know where Polopolis is."

"Let me have Constantinos's number, then, David."

David quickly looked up the number and provided it.

"So, do you have an ID for our victim yet, Taz?"

"Yes, we do. The deceased is a reputed hit man for an organized crime gang in Greece." Taz flipped back a couple of pages in his notebook. "His name is Antonis Pelekanos. He is suspected of numerous murders in Greece. He is in this country illegally. He probably used the box cutter to slash the screen and then whoever was waiting for him in the kitchen must have had a weapon, disarmed him, and cut his throat. The box cutter was wiped clean, and it's standard issue; millions are in use. We haven't located Polopolis. We haven't found his car, if he had a car. No one's answering his cell phone. We haven't located a vehicle for Pelekanos. You got any information on Polopolis's whereabouts?"

"No, I don't, Constantinos seemed as confused about his present location as anyone, but if Polopolis was the one waiting in the kitchen, he's on the run for some other reason than killing an intruder in his own home."

"I think you got that right. Neal and I are going out to the embassy right now. Thanks for the coffee."

David returned to the second floor to continue briefing the two Arabic-speaking temporaries that he'd hired to assist with the TechPro contract. "We need expert Arabic speakers to analyze the taped recordings under our subcontract. I speak only English and Russian. My assistant, Alice, speaks English, French, and Spanish. You have both received emergency top-secret status. The contract requires that we analyze transcripts of spoken Arabic."

"So, what are we looking for?" said Mike Hamooush, a Ph.D. candidate at Georgetown, who spoke English without a trace of an accent.

"In a word, intelligence, anything out of the ordinary, finances, plots, anything that sounds suspicious."

"Abdul and I can do that." Hamooush indicated the young man sitting beside him, a slender and dark man with a heavy thatch of black hair.

David looked back down at his notes. "We also need a list of words that might be triggers for further investigation. Alice has installed a program translator on the computers that you'll be using and on-line Arabic dictionaries. Once we have the translations, we'll run it all through another software program that will run correlations, regressions, and other statistical analysis to find word and text patterns and hopefully anyone speaking in a code."

Abdul sat back. "It sounds really cool. When can we get started?"

"As soon as possible, let me show you the work stations. If you find you need anything else, just let Alice know."

At 8:30 PM, David received a call from Denny Van Pattin, the night bar manager. "Hey David, can you come over here? It's Demetrios Constantinos. He's passed out. We hauled him into the back room."

"I'll be right there."

Stoney's was crowded with visitors, refugees from the much higher priced hotel bars in the area. The customers were in a party mood, buying flowers for good-looking young women at other tables, raucously shouting, and telling stories. David made eye contact with Denny who then led him to the back room. Demetrios was lying in his own urine and moaning. At five feet, ten inches and heavily muscled, Demetrios now was pale and helpless, lost in a drunken fog.

David and Denny pulled Demetrios to his feet and dragged him outside. Denny flagged a cab for David. Demetrios was solidly unconscious throughout this maneuver and the cab ride back to the office. Pearl had decided that Demetrios was far too drunk to be left unattended in his own apartment. At the curb, he paid the driver generously and then dragged Demetrios out and parked him on the steps. Demetrios couldn't be brought to his feet. David ran inside and got the Algerian-Americans to help get Demetrios inside, where they managed to haul him up onto the sofa, his limbs half dangling off. David slipped Demetrios' shoes off, tossing them onto the floor.

Pearl left Demetrios on the first-floor sofa. The young Algerian-American temporaries went to back to their computer screens and David settled himself in front of his own computer screen where he worked for two hours.

David then went up to the third floor, where he found Alice passed out on his inflatable mattress. She was naked, and from the overpowering smell of booze, obviously drunk. David gently covered her with a sheet and a blanket. He set his cell phone to ring in an hour and settled himself down on the floor to catch a quick nap.

When Pearl woke up, he was sweaty and had a sour taste in his mouth. He brushed his teeth in the tiny bathroom. Alice's clothes were hanging on the shower rod. He laughed; this was one small positive sign that Alice had at least been functional when she took her clothes off. David took a quick shower, brushed his teeth, dressed, and went downstairs.

David started the coffee brewing and then went to Demetrios. Demetrios was sleeping, snoring softly. Pearl woke him up, shaking his shoulder gently.

"Good buddy, I need to check on your health. Give me a sign. Say something. Do you know where you are?" Pearl sat down on a chair that he had dragged over from the desk.

"David, what the fuck?" Demetrios then mumbled something under his breath that Pearl thought was probably a Greek oath of some kind.

"You had a bad night of drinking, Demetrios. Stoney's called me to come get you. I brought you back here, so I could monitor you. This is my reception office and occasional spare bedroom. I just didn't want you to get up and go outside to pee or fall down because you didn't know where you were. Are we okay with that?"

"Yeah, I think so. I need to talk to you anyway, David. I need some help with this situation at the embassy. It's about Polopolis. If you are interested, I think that I can get you a new contract. You'll need to be briefed by the deputy mission, Theo Gliniadakis. I won't spoil the surprise now. Show me where the bathroom is and where I can get some cold water. Then, if you don't mind, I'll go back to sleep."

CHAPTER 6

Greeks Intruding in the Night, Part II, January 20

Theo Gliniadakis was a tall, pale man with thinning hair. He greeted David and Demetrios warmly. Gliniadakis's office was carefully appointed with four Grecian urns, each holding a brilliant array of fresh flowers. Beautiful oil paintings of Greek beaches and islands were artfully posed on the walls. A picture of the last Greek Olympic soccer team was framed and hung over the sofa upon which Pearl and Demetrios sat. The team and coaches signed it.

"That's a great picture, Theo. How did the team do?"

Theo smiled. "They made it to the Olympics, but lost the first game quickly and were sent home. I blame the coaches. They approached the training in the wrong way, letting some of the team treat the Olympics as a vacation. Regardless, I love soccer and the National team, even when my National team suffers defeats when they should have won."

"I guess that's the way it is with being a fan. I worship the Redskins myself. It's been a long time since we had a championship season."

The coffee arrived on a silver tray, carried by a young woman with an athletic figure and an angular, but cute and intelligent face.

"I like the Redskins, as well." Theo's voice was warm, fluid, and toned like a professional radio announcer "Sometimes, I am able to get tickets to go to the games. I enjoy American football, but don't understand it all the time. They seem to keep changing the rules, or maybe it's the interpretation of the rules." Theo took a sip of his coffee from the crystal teacup.

As the secretary closed the door, Demetrios spoke. "Theo, my apartment was ransacked last night. I have a feeling that I would be dead now, but for my friend here, who took me to his office to sleep."

Theo lost his smile. "You need to quit drinking entirely, Demetrios. As soon as your drinking gets you in trouble or in the news, you know your contract will be ended. But, we can save that discussion for another day. We need now to talk about our missing friend and colleague, Nicolaos Polopolis."

The desk phone rang. Theo excused himself and answered. Pearl got to his feet, but Theo motioned him to sit back down. "Yes sir, absolutely sir. We'll take care of that. That was the ambassador. He has decided that he needs to be briefed again on Polopolis. The Greek National Police are investigating every aspect of the man's life. I think that the little problem of womanizing was a strong indicator that Polopolis was a security risk, but I was overruled." Theo's face hardened into a stern expression when he looked at Demetrios. "Also, Demetrios, getting drunk two or three times a week means you are also a security risk. Let me remind you of this. But, I digress. David, I need your services. Demetrios will work out the terms of the contract. We know and trust you. Our Canadian friends have reason to believe that Polopolis is hiding in the Greek community in Montreal. That's obviously a problem for the Greek government. We cannot send any of our people, that is to say, Greek citizens or any Greeks that can be alleged to have ties to the Greek government, in case something goes wrong. Therefore, David, we want you to perform a specialized service for us."

"And what would the specialized service be, Theo?" David knew he would do just about anything that paid. He wasn't totally desperate yet, but he felt that he was only one shaky level or two above it.

"We want you to go to Montreal. We want you to find Polopolis and bring him back to the embassy. We don't want you to go armed. We would prefer if you drove across the border so that when you find Polopolis, you can bring him back, hopefully at an unmanned border crossing. We will have an intelligence agent get in contact with you at the Queen Elizabeth Hotel, where reservations have been made for you. We have taken the liberty of reserving one room for you with two double beds. We think you should take a trusted associate to watch your back for security reasons. Once you and an associate are in the hotel, our agent will get in touch with you. Polopolis can be gracious and charming, but remember this: his presumed friends in Montreal are suspected drug dealers, sex slavers, gunrunners, and, among other things, smugglers for hire. They are affiliated with the gang once ruled by the late, unlamented Spiros Velentzas of Queens, New York. The gang is ruthless and has branches in Greece, Turkey, Armenia, the U.S. and Canada, among other places."

David, for a moment, simply stared at Theo. No weapons, armed criminals, probably take a person against his will? "Sounds like there is a high potential for danger." This kind of assignment was far beyond his expertise or experience. His perilous financial situation drove his decision to accept.

"It will be, my friend. It will be. But you, we think, can deal with the danger with intelligence and cunning. We don't want anyone hurt and the chances go way down if you and your associate aren't armed. The threat is diminished, you see. The contract will be cost plus. We have already arranged an increase to a $50,000 credit limit on a new corporate credit card in your name. We have a dossier of Polopolis's friends, family, and possible contacts. We want you to reason with him and convince him to return on his own. We want him back here or failing that, in Greece, but in any event, in our custody. Demetrios will provide you with $5,000 in Canadian funds. Who will you use as your backup?" Theo began to glance at his Rolex watch every thirty or forty seconds.

"I'll take Jose Gonzalez if he can get leave from the Marine Corps. He's tough, trustworthy, and intelligent. I think that he'll be very good in a fight, if there is a fight."

"The embassy prefers," began Demetrios, who paused to breathe through some sort of hangover pain, "there be nothing that requires local police intervention, but I know what you mean, and I agree."

"Why should Polopolis agree to come back? What's the motivation for that?" David was already putting the requirements for the job in a mental priority and developing strategies and contingencies.

Theo turned slowly to the credenza behind his desk, briefly searching through the neat piles of paper. Through the window behind the dark walnut credenza, David could see the bright sunshine of a cold, late, January day. Theo searched briefly for the file that he sought. "Here it is, David. We want to know what happened. We want to know how compromised the embassy is or was. We want damage control and a thorough post assessment. In return, we will exercise diplomatic immunity for Polopolis. Here's a statement of intent from the U.S. State Department that says in effect, I should say guarantees, safe passage out of the country for Polopolis. When he gets back to Greece, he can be with his family, if that's what he wants. He'll get an early retirement and not have to go to jail, so long as he agrees to cooperate and fully inform us of any crimes he's aware of and name his criminal associates.

We'll have to determine if he's telling us the truth. If that goes well, he'll be on probation for a few years after, maybe house arrest for a year or two. So, David, go find him, talk to him, knock some sense into him if you have to, scare the shit out of him, I don't care. Tell him this is his last, best hope. Get him back here. Demetrios is your contract technical representative. You'll need a satellite phone. Demetrios will get you one that cannot be traced back to the embassy. Demetrios will be in the embassy 24/7 until the DC police can find his burglars." Theo walked over to David, signaling the end of the meeting. Theo patted David on the back on his way out.

Once outside, David called Alice. "Business has perked up. Give notice, and come back to DRPearl as soon as you can. Thanks."

In the rented, Volvo, eight-cylinder, all-wheel drive, SUV crossover, David and Jose drove north as rapidly as they could. Dave picked a car that would handle well in any conditions. They switched off driving. At a rest stop on the New York State Thruway, they stopped to make a final check before driving on to the Canadian border and the border inspectors that would be waiting for them.

"Let's go over this again, Jose. I have a security conference. You decided to come along because there's a jazz festival in Montreal. We've been working hard and wanted some downtime before returning to Washington." It was ten degrees and spitting snow. David had not bothered to put on his coat and began to shiver before he got back into the warmth of the car before the final push to Montreal.

"Security conference, jazz festival, downtime before heading back for another hard push on contract deliverables. I think this is the coldest I have ever been." Jose kept his parka on as they slid back into their seats.

The pavement was mostly white, encrusted with salt and sand from snowplows and salt trucks. Most of the trees were only gray branches connected to naked trunks. A few evergreens were clumped here and there. Once in a while, a speeding car with Canadian license plates would accelerate past them. When they finally arrived at the border, there was only one lane in service, and it was open. The US customs official jotted down the license plate number and checked their ID's. He quickly waved them on to the Canadian border crossing.

"Hello there. What's your purpose for entering Canada today?" The officer was smiling while working his eyes over the entire interior of the car.

"Business and pleasure," David said. "I have a conference on computer security in Montreal. My friend and I want to go to the jazz concert, maybe sightsee a little." David smiled back at the young customs officer.

"May I see your passports and drivers' licenses, please?" David and Jose handed them over.

The officer took the documents into the office. He entered their numbers into a laptop computer, and then wrote something down on a small pad of paper. He returned the documents to David. "Sir, I see that your friend here, Jose, is an active duty marine. Is that correct, Mr. Gonzalez?"

"Yes, it is."

"And, Mr. Pearl, what exactly is the nature of your conference?"

"Physical and internal security to prevent computer hackers or terrorists from hacking into sensitive and confidential data bases, and the like."

"Who do you work for?"

"I am CEO and owner of a small company that performs contracted services for security and intelligence organizations. Jose works part time for me. We just finished a big job, so the trip is mostly to relax and enjoy ourselves."

"Where were you born?"

"Bethesda, Maryland."

"And you, Mr. Gonzalez?"

"El Fuerte in Sinaloa State, Mexico."

"But, you are a U.S. citizen, correct?"

"Correct, my family moved to San Antonio when I was three years old."

"Mind if I search your car?"

"Not at all." David smiled as the agent motioned for him to step outside of the car.

"Just step inside here until I'm through, then." The inspector went through their luggage and the interior of the Volvo with a thorough and intense search. He looked through the glove box, under the seats, in the engine compartment, and under the car. Apparently satisfied, he returned to the office, but not before looking them over once again as if he was calculating the odds that these two were who they said they were.

"Gentlemen, you may be on your way. I am required to remind you that you have no work permit, and no commercial activity of any kind may be transacted. Is that understood? Enjoy yourselves in Montreal and stay out of trouble."

"Yes, sir."

Chapter 7
Greek town, January 22, 23 and 24

David and Jose checked into the Queen Elizabeth Hotel, which loomed large in the Montreal skyline, with more than 800 rooms. Its vast lobby stretched the length of the front of the building, a city block lengthwise. Diverse groups of visitors, guests, and business people filled seats in nearly every conversational furniture arrangement available in the lobby. The furniture was dark green, upholstered loveseats and wingback chairs surrounding square coffee tables made of a light yellowish wood.

David and Jose declined bellman assistance. Their room overlooked a massive, recently shuttered department store. It and the streets were covered with Christmas lights. The Queen Elizabeth Hotel sat over the largest transportation hub in Canada. Trains and subways interconnected between the Queen Elizabeth hub and dozens of intercity and outlying points. David lay down on one of the double beds, closing his eyes to rest, but he was not sleepy. Jose sat at the desk and tinkered with his laptop. They were to wait in the room until they were contacted by their Greek coordinator.

Their Greek contact called from the lobby at 6 PM. Jose answered the phone. "I will be at your room in less than two minutes." Jose winked at David, then got up from the desk chair and splashed some water on his face.

The knock on the door came two and a half minutes later. Jose ushered the Greek embassy representative into the room. She shook his hand and David's. She was, thought Pearl, the most attractive, fit woman that he had seen in a long time. She was dressed in a beige pantsuit, black high heels and a gold chain with a small jade stone hanging from it. She wore a white silk blouse that revealed a generous bosom. Her long, brown leather winter coat was draped casually over one arm. Whatever her real job was, he guessed that she was highly professional and thorough. She found the radio and turned it on. She located a French pop music station and increased the volume.

"I'm Sophia Vogiatzis. I am your point of contact, point of reference, if you will, while you are in Canada. My cover is cultural attaché at the Montreal consulate. The embassy is in Ottawa. Hopefully, you will not need the embassy. You have your report from our embassy in Washington?" Pearl waved it at her. "Excellent. I have done some additional research, which will be of some assistance."

Sophia pulled the report out of her large Hermes handbag. "Polopolis is definitely here in Montreal. He has an uncle named Ike Zisis with whom he stays when he is in Montreal. You have the cousin's address in Mont-Royal in the report file. The house is easy to find. The uncle has a legitimate furniture business in Laval, but is widely rumored to be involved in smuggling and anything else that makes him money. Polopolis has been spotted drinking at Gus's Bar, a somewhat seedy hangout for college students, bikers, and assorted lowlifes in an area of Montreal called Greek town. He is conspicuous there, so maybe there is a reason that demands that he hang out there. I am suggesting that you two check it out this evening, after dinner. It is rumored that Ike is a part of a Greek criminal gang that operates here in Montreal. It is an offshoot of the old Velentzas gang, but here it's called the Stella, for reasons that aren't clear, maybe somebody's girlfriend or grandmother. The names, photos, and addresses of the known gang members are in here." She flipped the folder over to Pearl.

"You don't know anything about official Greek government involvement in this. You are freelancers. If you are caught for any criminal activity at all, we will not help you. We don't anticipate that you will be caught, but if so, we will encourage the U.S. Embassy to protect you. My guess is that they probably will. My understanding is that you are not armed. My order to you is do not acquire weapons in Canada. That may well help you stay alive. Any questions?"

David looked up from the folder that she had given him. "Yes, Sophia, is there a number where we can reach you?"

"Yes, here's my business card. Everything on the card is phony, except for the cell phone number. You can call me at any time. But, I am only available to provide local information and insights. I will also be pleased to use our resources to research any questions that you might come up with." Sophia stood up, straightened her pants and jacket, shook hands with them again, and left the room in a quickly departing blur.

"Jose, open that folder and write down the address of Gus's Bar. I think we should walk to the bar for a little watching and learning."

"You got it, boss. I want to do some eating and drinking, too."

David laughed and gave Jose a thumb's up.

The temperature had dropped to fifteen degrees. Greek town consisted of storefronts in an area slightly away from the main downtown. It was shabby and looked comfortably familiar, like some of the changing urban areas in DC or many other cities across North America, but with fewer people moving at street level because of the extensive underground in Montreal.

Greek businesses had sprouted up widely in this area. The area was full of restaurants, cafés, bars, and boutiques. There was a travel agency that specialized in trips back home for the hundred thousand Greeks who had settled in Montreal. David could clearly see, outlined in the blackness, the elevation called Mont-Royal rising above Greek town to the west. Pearl guessed that this Greek town had a high crime rate and frequent police presence. He and Jose entered the bar, found a booth near the middle of the place, and sat down.

Pearl assessed their location. The bar was decorated with faded reproductions of Greek settings of farms, ruins, and the seashore. Several neon signs advertising Molson and other Canadian beers hung above the bar. The bar was nearly full, with close configurations of men and a few women sitting at tables or booths or at the bar, chatting amiably and drinking amid the occasional laughter or boisterous statement. The nearest television, elevated on a wall, was showing highlights of the NHL games underway. Polopolis was not among this crowd.

The waitress sashayed her hips as she walked, like a model vamping on a fashion runway. "I'm Odette. I'm your server. I haven't seen you guys in here before. What's it to be?"

They gave her their order. Odette snapped a wink in David's direction and stepped briskly away to the kitchen order window.

"Boss, I am going to check out the men's room."

"Good idea. See if there's a back door while you are at it."

After a few minutes, Jose ambled back to the booth and slid into the bench gracefully. "There's a back door, but it's not open to the public; apparently they use it for deliveries. The men's room is clear. They have a communal trough for urinations that can serve five or six guys at the same time. It's the perfect pisser for drunks, makes it hard to miss."

"I helped myself to a sip of your McAuslan's, excellent choice. I think I'll order that next."

At 11:30 PM and after three more beers, David decided they should close shop for the evening. He settled with Odette, tipping her generously. The cab ride back to the hotel took six minutes. The call light was flashing when they entered the room.

The message was from Sophia. They listened. "You absolutely must call me as soon as you're back in the room." David retrieved her business card and dialed.

Sophia answered quickly. "Photosi's."

"Photosi, this is Pearl, what can I do for you?"

"How was your evening, Pearl?" Sophia's articulation was smooth and appealing with its soft femininity.

"Sure did. We spent the evening at Gus's. The place is busy, lots of traffic in and out, like a walk-in communication hub. Many of the patrons simply come in, say a few words to someone, often to the bartender, and then they're out as quickly as they came in."

"Sounds interesting. Before you get started in the morning, we want you to look at some photographs for us. A situation has come up. We need you to go over to the furniture dealer's home in Mont-Royal tomorrow. We've learned that Mr. Zisis is leaving Canada tomorrow afternoon, ostensibly on a buying trip back to Greece. We have reason to believe that the trip is more about gang activities than anything else."

"Affirmative. Will do."

"Please report back as needed. The photographs will be slipped under your door during the next few hours. Sleep tight." He wanted to talk to her some more, to listen to that sultry voice. Pearl had a momentary fantasy of the two of them in bed, with her telling him all about herself in that sweet, sexy voice.

Jose was in his boxer shorts, standing at the window taking a last look at the eastern vista of nighttime Montreal before he went to bed.

Pearl set the alarm for 5 AM. He would check his email, drive by Zisis's home in Mont-Royal, go register for his conference, and be back to pick up Jose at 9:30. Jose was already asleep when David turned the lights out.

The next morning at 9:55, having studied the photos, Pearl and Jose walked purposefully up the front walk of the house in Mont-Royal. It was clear and ten degrees above zero. Jose rang the doorbell. When there was no immediate response, Pearl rapped on the door. They stood there, listening for any sounds or movement from inside the house, and looking around the neighborhood at all the well-maintained homes on manicured lots and at the mature trees. The houses looked buttoned up, prepared for the intense cold, by closing tightly against the frigid air.

Finally, there was a slight opening of the door. A small, chubby woman of maybe about sixty-five, showed her face reluctantly in the gap between the door and the frame. "What do you want?" she asked in heavily accented English, in a scratchy and weak voice.

"We would like to speak with Mr. Zisis, please." Pearl aimed to sound cheerful.

"I'm sorry, he's not here. Anyway, he never does business at home. You English?"

"No, we're Americans. We have an appointment." Pearl thought Zisis was probably still at home, given that his flight was in the middle of the afternoon. He had seen him earlier that morning walking a brown, longhaired mutt. He gently pushed open the door. The old woman simply stepped back.

"We won't be any problem, Mrs. Zisis. We simply need to talk to your husband about a mutual friend. I'm David Pearl and this is my associate, Jose Gonzalez. We won't take but a minute. We know how busy Mr. Zisis is."

Mrs. Zisis disappeared into the kitchen. Pearl could hear her breathing hard, possibly trying to calm herself or dealing with the emphysema-like condition that sounded from her lungs. They sat in the living room and waited. The small room was forest green, with matching cushioned chairs and sofa. The wood trim was tan, and the pillows on the chairs and sofa were, to Pearl, a motley collection of mismatched sizes and colors. The glass-front collectibles cabinets were jammed with Hummels and an incredible array of ceramic and crystal angels. The room barely had enough room to walk around.

"Yeah, I thought I recognized the Volvo." The voice was gruff and challenging.

"I told them to leave, Ike. I told them. They said they had an appointment," said Mrs. Zisis, wringing her hands.

"My dear friends, you know you don't have any goddamn appointment." Zisis stood at the edge of the living room, rocking back and forth ever so slightly. He was sizing them up. Pearl stood, and so did Jose, who stared at Zisis.

"Sit, sit, gentlemen. You come up here on a ball-busting, cold morning, you deserve to sit. You want coffee?"

Pearl and Jose nodded.

"Stella, get us some fresh-brewed when you get a chance, sweetie," Zisis said.

David wondered if this 'Stella' had any connection to the 'Stella' gang that Sophia had mentioned.

"So, gentlemen, you got some ID? You guys look like the fucking police, but they don't drive Volvos, at least not in Canada and I bet not in the states either. Governments got to buy from the home country, don't they?"

"Right, Mr. Zisis, the Volvo is rented," said David. "We aren't cops, and we don't work for the government. We work for a private company that does security work." He sized Zisis up as a formidable, self-confident man, well versed in facing challenges and challengers.

"Oh? I see then, you're not my long lost cousins from Crete? The ones who were lost at sea? My Stella still prays for those boys every morning. But, you're not here to answer her prayers." Zisis laughed.

"We aren't. As you can see from our ID's, we work for a firm named DRPearl, Inc. I'm that Pearl. We do security analysis, consulting, and really security work of all kinds. Right now, what brings us up to this particular house is we are looking for your nephew, Nicolaos Polopolis. We need to talk to him." Pearl leaned forward, looking intently at the furniture dealer. He agreed with Sophia's estimate that Zisis was much more than a furniture dealer.

"Nicolaos, eh, I'm glad that you want to talk to him. I'm tired of talking to him, myself. The man is my Stella's late, lamented, sister Ruta's oldest. Nicolaos has been a challenge these last few years. Ruta died from a broken heart because of Nicolaos. What do you want with him? Please try to explain it all to me. Stella, you got that coffee yet?"

A moment later, Stella slowly strolled in with an insulated pot and three mugs. She sat all of this down on a little, highly embossed, flip-top, wooden table that she pulled out from behind the sofa. She told the men to help themselves, that she'd be right back with the cream and sugar.

David had already decided to level with this man. "Nicolaos is involved in an uncertain situation with lots of downside. Important people in the U.S. and Greek governments want to talk to him. The DC police need to talk to him. Jose and I are by far the best people for Nicolaos to talk to. We have confidential communications that guarantee him a safe passage to wherever he wants to go and a flexible way out of being accountable for the situation that he left back in Washington."

"Those fucking Redskins going to cover the spread next season? They have played like they're being paid to flop. All that talent, all those highly paid geniuses in the front office go for shit. I suppose you two would know something about the Skins that would cheer up an overworked, tired football bettor?"

Pearl laughed, puzzled by the sudden shift in topic. "I'm afraid not, Mr. Zisis. My advice is quit betting on them. They are not even consistently bad."

"That's the ticket, they're not consistent. You can't depend on them one-way or the other. You guys know my bar, Gus's, in Greek town?"

"Yes, we do. We spent three hours there last night." David had his elbows perched on his knees, leaning forward, carefully studying Zisis.

"That's interesting. What made you pick that bar?" Zisis's tone went hard, and his clear, cold, blue eyes stayed on Pearl. He kept smiling, but his eyes narrowed.

"Mr. Zisis, we were told to go there by a highly placed informant who told us we could find Polopolis there."

"You guys be very careful with my backside because I got a very bad side that goes right along with it. You might even call it a mean streak. Be at Gus's tonight at 10:00. If I can contact Nicolaos, he'll be there; if not, the night after that. I'll have him there. Now, if you don't mind, I have a flight to catch."

David and Jose excused themselves and went back outside into the frigid air.

When they returned to the diner that evening, Odette broke into a wide grin. She casually put one hand on the Jose's hard, muscular shoulder and left it there for a few seconds. He didn't have to pretend to be physically tough; his steady, devotional workouts gave him a muscled and toned physique. The students and other habitués of this bar were either pale and reedy or pasty and fat. Those few that weren't reedy or fat still looked like denizens of the night.

Odette brought their beers and the pretzels. "How much longer you guys going to be en ville?"

David smiled at her, admiring her cheerful attitude and soft, casual beauty. "I guessing that means here in Montreal. We have a few more days at the most. While I'm up here enjoying myself, the work is piling up back home."

They were interrupted by two Montreal police officers entering the bar. The noise level dropped low enough that David could actually hear the bar man washing dishes and the refrigerator running. The two officers had the manner of cops in big cities: suspicious, wary, prepared. They scanned the people in the bar from front to back.

One of bar patrons yelled to the shorter of the two policemen, "André, what brings you out on a freezing night like this?"

"Eli, we need to check to make sure you are holding down your place in the universe." This exchange was spoken in French. Many in the crowd laughed at this exchange.

The officers walked to the back door, checked the men's room. They summoned the bar manager with a curt word at the end of the bar, far enough away from customers that they could not be heard.

Jose and David had kept talking. Odette was in the front replenishing beers for a rowdy group that looked like they could be university students: sweatshirts, two to three days growth of beard, and loud and ready to party. "David, I think that the bar manager just sent the police officers in our direction."

"Keep smiling, Jose. I doubt this is a random bar check; maybe someone wants to know who we really are, or someone wants to make sure that the coast is clear before Nicolaos shows up. I'm getting the feeling that Zisis set us up."

"Bonjour." Officer Andre Vimont then turned to Odette and spoke quietly to her. David and Jose kept smiling and said hello.

"David, Jose, the nice officers would like to see your identification, please. They would like to know why gentlemen such as you who do not speak French would come to a bar like this. I am afraid they share the Quebec attitude of antagonism against Americans."

"Please tell the nice officers that a friend of ours who lives in Montreal recommended this bar as inexpensive with decent food." David said, as he and Jose handed over their passports.

Officer Vimont took their documents over to the bar. The bartender helpfully handed him a flashlight. Vimont got on his radio. Once connected, he began to read their names and information.

Odette began translating again. "Officer Vimont says it will take a few minutes, gentlemen. They want to make sure that you are who you say you are." The officer with them, Corporal Malouda, had stopped smiling. Vimont walked back to their booth and spoke to Malouda.

Odette translated again. "The officers request that you pay up and leave. You are creating a distraction in the bar. They would like you to leave before there is trouble." David and Jose readily agreed. David now had confirmation that Zisis had set them up. Nicolaos wouldn't be in the bar as long as they were, and hanging around in the bar wasn't going to be an option.

After they had settled the tab, they were given their ID's and passports. The officers escorted them outside, with grim expressions, and didn't offer to shake hands. David was surprised and anxious about the encounter. He and Jose walked down the street and then turned toward their hotel. They then ducked into the first bar that they came upon. Once inside, David called Sophia.

"Yeah, hi, Sophia, I need a quick consultation. Two of Montreal's finest just escorted Jose and I out of Gus's bar. What do you make of that?"

"Sounds like somebody at the bar wanted you two to leave, but it could be anything. Find a place across the street where you can safely watch the front door of Gus's."

When they got back, they went into an all-night diner almost directly across the street from Gus's. This place was darker, more dingy, and lacked the steady strum of conversation of Gus's. The customers coldly and deliberately stared at the two. David felt even more out of place in this establishment and saw Jose looking anxiously around. The waiter eyed them suspiciously. Dave and Jose just kept smiling. They ordered draft Molsons.

The waiter tried French with them first. They figured that he would know the word "Molson." He did, but he couldn't leave it at that. "I am sorry you do not speak French. You come here; you should speak French." He stood there as if waiting for something else.

David said, "I speak English and Russian. My friend here speaks English and Spanish. I know we need to learn French. I'm going to start working on it." He smiled.

The waiter stared across the street at Gus's bar. David and Jose turned to look. A team of uniformed police all in black was running into Gus's bar just like a SWAT team in the U.S. The SUVs belonging to the police blocked most of the scene. A police commander was standing in the middle of the street barking commands into a radio.

After a few minutes, the police commandos began bringing men out of the bar in handcuffs. Those arrested were taken away in a special van designed to transport prisoners. This van was white with the light blue striping and lettering of the Montreal Police Department. David thought the men and women in civilian attire who entered must be detectives.

"This raid can't be a coincidence," David muttered to Jose. Jose nodded.

With the arrestees secure in the transfer van, the SUV's and the van roared off. For five minutes, there was relative quiet.

Dave heard the semi-truck grinding its gears to slow down and begin to climb the street. When it came into view, the cab and trailer were a reddish color with bright yellow, block letters covering nearly the entire side of the trailer. The name on the side was BOURASSA. The truck stopped immediately in front of the bar. Their view of Gus's bar was now totally blocked. The crowd that had gathered beside their table, to check out what was going on, now dispersed.

In a few more minutes, Odette came running around the truck and into the diner. She had no jacket. She was shaking and crying. David got up quickly to comfort her. He placed his jacket around her shoulders and brought her to sit down with them. He ordered her some hot tea.

She sat there quietly, tearfully, trying to catch her breath.

"Boss, I'm going outside to check out the Bourassa truck." Jose walked casually outside and down the sidewalk.

"David, I just can't go back to work there," Odette said. "I need to work to finish school, but I am so afraid. There are gangsters going in and out of there all the time. They hit on me, pinch me, slap my rear. I don't know what I am going to do. Tonight, I thought I was going to be arrested. And, when I wasn't, the bartender accused me of informing on the bar patrons." Odette cried between deep, wracking breaths.

"Odette, calm down. You are safe now." Before David could finish all that he had intended to say to Odette, his cell phone rang. "This is David."

41

"David, this is Sophia. Get out of there right now. The evening has only just begun in Greektown. Go back to the hotel. Do not get involved with whatever is happening at Gus's bar. We think Ike Zisis tried to set you up. Go right now."

"We are on our way." David glanced at Odette. "Odette, please come with us right now. We have to leave right now." He put his topcoat around her shoulders.

They walked outside and immediately moved toward a yellow cab waiting at the taxi stand. David saw Jose walking back toward them at a brisk pace. David told the cab driver to wait for him. At the same time, a tall man in a hooded parka came around the rear end of the truck. The man stood in the middle of the road, shaking his head at the cab driver. The driver nodded agreement at the man and turned around.

The cab dropped them off at the Queen Elizabeth Hotel. The threesome walked into the nearly empty lobby. The security guard eyed them and followed them into the elevator. He got off at their floor, but walked slowly in the opposite direction. In the room, Jose threw himself into the recliner and kicked off his boots. David went to the window. Odette flopped on the bed.

For a few minutes, David stared out the window, lost in thought. "Odette, I think this situation here isn't likely to improve for you. That means you will have to apply for temporary status as a "person in danger" when we get to the US. I think you need to stay with Jose and me for the time being. We will help you get a visa and you can work for DRPearl. I'm alarmed that I don't know what exactly is going on. But, for you to go back to your apartment now could be dangerous. Based on what my Montreal liaison person told me, it seems very clear that Zisis set us up. After the Montreal police asked us to leave, they expected that we'd come back to the hotel, where some gangsters would be waiting for us. My contact says that we would probably have been killed. Fortunately, we were advised to stay in Greek town. Then my contact in concert with the Montreal Police arranged for the gambling raid. They arrested five men and confiscated $12,000 Canadian. Unknown to us or my contact was the tractor-trailer delivery. Jose, you got any idea what they were unloading?"

Jose sat slumped on the recliner, casually, with his hands behind his head. "Better than an idea. The boxes were labeled in English. They contained cigarettes, which must have been untaxed. A metal door for supplies opened into the adjacent space, a furniture store, I think. The smugglers were dropping the boxes right into the basement. When they caught sight of me, the tall one put his hand inside the parka pocket and motioned like he had a pistol in the pocket for me to clear out. I did. I'm sure that he had a pistol. He's the same guy who was standing in the middle of the road when we left."

"Odette's asleep." Dave walked over to the bed and pulled her sneakers off. Then he put the comforter over her and turned out the bedside light.

"So, boss, do we have marching orders yet?"

"Indeed, we do. We are to hang here and await further instructions. Sophia says that her intelligence sources believe Polopolis is still here in Montreal. They think that he's involved with Greek organized crime and in deep debt to the gang, and that his involvement is a necessity to escape punishment for not paying them back."

"What kind of gambling were they doing in the restaurant?" Jose lay on the floor doing stretches.

"Sophia told me that the gambling was under the restaurant by means of a trap door with attached steps, in the manager's office. The gambling was Barbut, a dice game approximating craps. The Greek mob cheats the customers blind, gets them into debt, and then has willing collaborators in other criminal ventures."

David's cell phone chimed. It was Sophia. He listened intently for several minutes.

"David, leave the hotel at once. The Stella gang is out looking for you. The police are back at Gus's bar again, this time for those cigarettes. They've made more arrests. Ike Zisis must be furious. The police have told my sources that his number one enforcer is among those arrested." David hung up and turned to Jose and spoke softly, but urgently. "Sophia says there is a massive search for us going on. Sophia says we are to leave the hotel at once. Pack up!"

Just then, there was a knock on the door. David looked through the peephole. Whoever was out there had blocked the view. David stood without making a sound. The person at the door knocked again. David didn't answer again. The person outside the door used a passkey to open the lock, and at virtually the same time, pushed the door open violently, breaking the chain lock. The interior locking device on the side of the door was pulled out of the wall. David absorbed the full impact of the forcefully opened door and fell back into the wall. The taller man advanced into the room first, and a stocky man with a deep frown closely followed him. The two men, with pistols drawn, entered cautiously.

Jose had been standing unseen, just to the left of the door, flush with the wall inside the closet. As the first man entered, Jose grabbed his arm and shoved him back into the frowning, stocky intruder. Jose disarmed the tall intruder by grabbing his wrist and twisting it violently. His left foot kicked the stocky intruder's gun hand upward causing him to momentarily lose control of the pistol. Jose slammed his fist into the taller man's face, leaving him unconscious on the floor and bleeding profusely from his nose. The stocky intruder hit Jose's leg with his foot and kept kicking at Jose, but he was off balance and using his gun hand on the doorjamb to stay upright. Jose grabbed the man's arm that held the pistol, slamming his hand into the wall and held it there. He then swiveled his torso, at the same time bringing his knee into the man's face. The second man's head kicked back into the doorjamb. As his head ricocheted off the wall, Jose hit him in the side of his head with a hard, left hand punch. Both men lay still on the floor.

Jose searched the men while David stood guard with their weapons. Jose pulled their wallets, car keys, and one Leather man tool. The wallets and car keys went into the toilet. With the Leather man tool open to the blade, he went to the drapes and cut off two lengths of cord. He tied the men's hands and feet. He pulled the first man into the stairwell. He pushed this man down the flight of stairs. Jose then dragged the other man to the stairwell. He rolled this man down the stairs. The second man landed partially on top of the first. Jose went down to the landing where they had fallen, took off the socks from one of them, and stuffed one into each of their mouths.

When David and Jose returned to the room, they found Odette sitting upright, crying again, and shaking uncontrollably. "We have to go, Odette. You are going to be safe with us. We got people who are going to take care of us. But, we must go now."

David and Jose packed up quietly and departed the Queen Elizabeth hotel as fast as Odette's tired, shaky movements and terrified state of mind would allow. They drove toward the airport, and as soon as they reached that area, they checked into a motel on a side street about four blocks from the main entrance to the airport. David decided on the motel, Le Parisienne on Cote-de-Liesse Street. The hotel was a three-story building that looked to be from the early fifties, built with bricks that were now painted white. The young man at the front desk quickly checked them into the two rooms that David had requested. Figuring that the gangsters or police might check all the hotels, he used Jose's credit card.

The next morning, David drove to the Montreal airport rental car agency and exchanged the Volvo for a dark green, Ford SUV. Then, he and Jose drove to Mont-Royal to stake out Ike Zisis's house.

After surveilling the house and the neighborhood for a few minutes, David's cell phone rang. It was Sophia. "Do you know anything about two men who were found bound and gagged in the Queen Elizabeth Hotel early this morning?"

"Yes. They broke into the hotel room. Jose managed to get the better of them. We thought it would better if we didn't kill them, but we did want time to escape."

"The Montreal Police arrested both of them. They are members of the Stella gang. Even so, the police are now looking for the perpetrators of the crime. They told the police that you jumped them. When they checked with the front desk, the police found your room empty. So they are looking for you. And, the Stella gang is seriously searching for you." Sophia's tone was cold and urgent, her words clipped as she rushed them out.

"I figured. We changed motels and rental cars."

"Remember if they find you, there's nothing we can do."

"Yeah, I don't need reminding. I'll call the American Embassy if I have to. We were accosted. They used a master key to break into the room. If Jose hadn't jumped the gunmen, we would all be dead. You got any news for us?"

"No, we've run into a brick wall. Our usual sources are quiet, laying low, afraid to talk. The intelligence units of our friends in the CIA, the Royal Canadian Police, the Quebec Provincial Police, our own Greek Embassy political attachés, and the Canadian government are not picking up anything on Polopolis. The police are grilling the gangsters that they have in custody, including the two guys found at the Regency. That's making the criminals paranoid and our informers deaf and dumb."

"Has the Greek Embassy filed a missing person's report yet?"

"No, and they won't. All their chips are on you at the moment, David. What are you going to do?"

"I'm going to sit tight. We will drop in on Mrs. Zisis later on this afternoon. Please watch our backsides, Sophia."

"I'll try."

"Jose, that's a comforting thought, 'She'll try to watch our backsides.' I am seriously beginning to wonder about that."

"Yes, seriously, I think we are better off knowing it's up to us to stay safe. I'd feel better if we had a few more of my Marines here in the foxhole with me." Jose's dark brown eyes roved the streets and the road behind them.

"Yeah, I guess me, too. Let's get up to Stella's house, and see if our boy is there."

The SUV sat two houses past Zisis's home, facing up Harvard Street, sloping upward. "Jose, sit tight here for ten minutes; don't take your eyes off the house. If I'm not back in ten minutes, turn the SUV around, and back into the Zisis driveway. I'll call as soon as I'm able, or I find something. I think Stella is a lot more involved in this than we gave her credit for on our first visit. Maybe she's more than just the namesake of the gang."

David knocked on the door and rang the doorbell. He heard footsteps of people moving around inside and indistinguishable voices moving about inside. When no one came to the door, David tried the knob, but it was locked, so he tried the garage door. He was able to push the door up enough to squeeze under. He opened the door to the house and found himself face to face with Mrs. Zisis. She stared at him with a sneer on her lips. She brushed past him and locked the door behind him.

"Where is Polopolis?" David scanned the chapel-like living room and the dining room. He walked into the kitchen. Two coffee cups sat on the dinette.

"I don't know. I'm calling the police." Mrs. Zisis said, and walked to the telephone that hung on the kitchen wall.

"Please do. I'm just going upstairs to check out your visitor." David bounded up the stairs, grabbing the banister at the last moment to assist in his spinning turn to the right. The upstairs hallway ran the length of the house. Its walls were covered in framed family pictures. A large-as-life picture of a Greek Orthodox bishop looked solemnly down from his perch at the end of the hall. David tried the first door. The door opened to a bedroom that overlooked the driveway in the front of the house. He saw Jose standing outside the SUV, studying the area. He searched the closet and looked under the bed. No one else was in the room.

David went back out into the hall, opening the door immediately across from the room that he had just searched. This door was locked. He heard the sounds of the window being unlatched and the harsh grating noise of that window slowly, and with difficulty, being shoved upward. David kicked the door open in time to see a man jump from the window. David looked down and spotted a man scrambling to his feet on the ground below. The man could be Polopolis, David realized: same height and build. David took a deep breath and then jumped from the window. The bank of snow cushioned his landing, but the uneven landing forced him to fall forward, throwing snow into his face. He felt a stabbing pain in his back. As he got to his feet, he heard Jose yelling.

David came around the corner of the house in time to see Jose chasing the man down the street. David tried the door to the SUV. It was open. The keys were in the ignition. He quickly pulled out of the driveway and headed down the street in the direction that Jose had gone. At the end of the block, he found Jose sitting on top of a man who was kicking and screaming. David pulled up beside them. Jose jumped up. The two of them wrestled the squirming, resisting man into the backseat of the Ford. Jose pushed the man into the seat, pulled the man's hands behind him, and put plastic tie handcuffs around his wrists.

"Stop resisting, Nico. We aren't going to hurt you on purpose." Jose was still regaining his breath after the foot chase. Jose added, "My lungs are hurting from sucking in the cold air too. Slow your breathing down and take deeper breaths."

They were stopped at a traffic light at Terrebonne when a Montreal Police car turned and passed them, heading in the direction of Mrs. Zisis's house. David drove calmly but urgently toward the airport and their motel. He watched Nicolaos in the rear view mirror. His face contorted and ranged through some kind of silent, internal turmoil.

David pulled into the parking spot immediately in front of the entrance, nearest their motel room door. He got out, went inside, found their room, and knocked. Odette opened the door. She was freshly showered and wore a towel around her wet hair. The hotel's robe was wrapped around her tightly, and she quickly stepped back as the frigid air reached her. David closed the door and went back to the car, motioning Jose to bring their guest inside.

"Who are you?" The slender Nicolaos Polopolis slumped awkwardly, but casually, in the room's recliner chair. His black hair was carefully barbered into a swept back cut on the sides and the top. His brown eyes opened wide and flitted from one person to the other.

"I'm David Pearl. This is my associate, Jose. The young lady is our friend, Odette. Who are you, just for the record?"

"I am Nicolaos Polopolis. I'm a consular officer for the Greek government. I wish to be taken to the Greek Embassy."

"Not going to happen, Nico. They don't want any part of you at the Greek Embassy. They do want you back in Washington, however, and have asked me to arrange that."

"That wouldn't be suitable, I'm afraid. Really, I demand to talk to an embassy official here, to the Canadian government if I must, but I do not want to go back to the United States. My life would be in danger. I would be killed. I want to request political asylum." Polopolis was attempting to assert himself. His voice rang with authority and confidence.

"I don't think that is going to happen, Nico. You got into Canada illegally. You aren't safe here. If we found you, your enemies could have found you. If you contact the authorities, you will be arrested for murder and extradited back to the U.S. You wouldn't be safe in jail or prison in Canada. Your aunt's gang couldn't protect you. If you don't cooperate, we might not be able to protect you."

"I demand to be taken to the consular office in Montreal or, preferably, back to the house where you found me."

"Not going to happen. Accept that. This is your new reality. You can protest all you like, but please do it silently. Jose, if you have to, stuff a sock in his mouth. I've got a call to return. I'll be outside for a few minutes. Then, when I return, Odette can go for some food and more coffee. Agreed?" David stared into Polopolis's black eyes, searching for any clue as to what the desperate man would think of next.

"I agree, David, but I also think that we need to be on the move. I'm getting antsy." Jose began to stretch in the middle of the floor.

"I think so too, Jose. Our plans may be changing rapidly." David went out the door, closing it softly behind him. It was another cold, slate grey day in Montreal. He watched an airplane landing at the airport and then made his call to Sophia.

Sophia answered the phone with a cheerful 'Bonjour, monsieur.'"

"Madam, we need to talk. I need some assistance. I have accepted delivery of the package. It became a little unwrapped in transit." David hoped that would be vague enough to confuse any listeners, if there were any.

"I will be at the Café Bar Le Metropole at the Trudeau International Airport in thirty minutes. Please take a cab. I will meet you there. I would like proof of delivery. I will wait no longer than five minutes." Sophia abruptly disconnected.

David proceeded back to the room. Tall convenience cups of coffee, donuts, and bagels were spread out on the desk. Jose had opened the connecting door between their rooms. David noted that Polopolis's hands had turned a dark shade of red.

"Jose, get our friend a new set of cuffs, give him a little more room to maneuver, and take the laces out of his shoes."

"I need to call my roommate, David," said Odette.

David responded quickly. "You can use my phone when we get on the road. We need to get out of Montreal as soon as possible."

"I need an overcoat," Polopolis whined. His lean body lay unmoving in the room's recliner. Jose had thrown the bed's comforter on top of him.

"You should have remembered your coat before you went out the window, Nico.

Boss, get going. I'm more than ready to get back to the states." Jose was now on the floor doing pushups. He began alternating the pushups with abdominal crunches. Odette put on Jose's leather jacket, and despite the fact that it swallowed her torso, she tugged it around her and sat by the window.

David departed the cab at the Air Canada arrivals' egress. Once inside, he carefully checked the cars arriving behind his cab to see if he was being followed. He located a directional sign for the Café Bar Le Metropole. He walked circuitously to the area of the bar. Only after he spotted Sophia did he meander casually into the bar.

"I took the liberty of ordering you a beer." Sophia was perched on the tall bar stool at a bar built along the outside wall. David could see the airplanes taxiing on the runway. Sophia sat erect with her short brown hair fluttering softly in a breeze wafting into the bar from the busy corridor. He thought that she was being very professional and appropriate, but he also thought, damn she sure is attractive.

"No problem, beer is always on the menu at my place. I got the package. The package is unhappy. We need to get him away from all of this as soon as possible." David kept looking into her eyes, wondering if there was a spark there somewhere for him, too. He casually took out his cell phone and clicked to a picture taken of Polopolis just after he had been settled into the motel room.

She looked at the picture and smiled. "I agree. More importantly now, we need to get you and your associate back home as soon as possible, of course, with the package intact. Mrs. Zisis convinced the Montreal Police that you kidnapped her nephew. She didn't give his correct last name, of course, and played the complete innocent victim with them. Our intelligence division thinks that you may be right about her. She may not be the power behind the throne of the Stella gangsters, but if she isn't, then she's the first lady. More to the point, she has her minions out looking for you. I have made arrangements to sneak you out of Canada." She adroitly slipped a small piece of paper from her palm into his palm. The maneuver was made effectively with the appearance of a completely innocent touch. To anyone looking on, it looked as if they briefly and accidentally brushed their hands together.

"Thanks, I'm anxious not to overstay my welcome." She smiled in his direction, but David figured it for a professional smile rather than a flirtatious one.

"I have communicated the full report of your accomplishments and encounters to Demetrios. He has a copy of your instructions. As soon as you are safe and secure in the U.S., you are to notify both of us." Sophia had stopped smiling. Her eyes appeared to search for something in David's eyes.

He returned the inquiring look. "Will do, and thanks for all of your assistance, Sophia. You have been a real pro."

Sophia held her beer, peering at the bartender. "Please stand up. We'll walk toward the exit and then to short-term parking. I will follow behind you. When we get to the escalator, I will drop a set of car keys and a parking ticket into your jacket pocket. The Mercedes E63 AMG wagon is parked on level 3, row J, about two thirds of the way back from the airport side. The row and aisle are written on the parking ticket. The Mercedes is dark green and has Ontario license plates. I will stay behind you about thirty feet until you reach the car. Someone will pick it up tonight. Do not call me again until you are safely out of Canada. Unless, of course, there is a mega—emergency. Like you've been shot, something like that. We don't want our host country to get to feeling abused."

David was sorry to have to leave her. He loved her smell that reminded him so much of his first love, a freshness with sparkling champagne, and he wished he'd asked her the name of her perfume, anything to keep the conversation going. But he knew his duty and pushed those thoughts out of his mind. He wanted to know her better and hoped she would not be lost to history.

David drove slowly out of the parking garage, checking carefully and continuously to make sure that he wasn't being followed. He called the rental company and told them where they could pick up their SUV. He wheeled into the hotel parking lot fully alert and, at last, not thinking of the woman who had so impressed him.

David alerted Jose on the short trip back to the hotel to prepare to leave. When David parked, Jose was casually escorting Polopolis outside and then to the Mercedes, though he shoved him roughly into the back seat. His hands were cuffed discretely behind him and to the metal hook securing the middle seat belt. Jose rode behind David, who drove. Odette took the front passenger seat.

The snow had begun while David was at the Café Bar le Metropole. It was now snowing hard, so David drove the Mercedes very carefully. The streets had yet to be plowed and the wind was driving the hard snow crystals into every crevice and corner.

They traveled south on Canada Highway 401. At Cornwall, they stopped at a Tim Horton's donut shop. Jose escorted Polopolis inside after removing the handcuffs. After using the men's room, the two of them sat at an empty booth closest to the front door. David remained outside, at the back of the restaurant, where he paced back and forth. Sometimes he stopped to stretch or brush the snowflakes out of his hair. Odette, after buying a large coffee and mixing in her sugar and cream, went back outside with David's cell phone to call her roommate. Odette stood beside David, using him to shield her front the wind.

David listened to the conversation.

"Rosaline, it's me," Odette said.

Rosaline's voice was loud enough that he could hear it from where he stood. "Oh, Odette, I thought you must be dead. The bar manager wouldn't tell me anything. Are you all right?" Rosaline sounded scared and partially out of breath.

"I'm fine, Rosaline. What has happened there?"

"First, these gangsters came looking for you. They threatened me. They tore the apartment apart looking for you. They said I must call them as soon as I hear from you." Rosaline was clearly frightened.

"I'm not coming back, Rosie. And, you must tell them that."

"What? What about your mother?"

"I've left a message on her work phone, but tell her that I will call her when I am safe and settled. In the meantime, tell the gangsters that I am not coming back."

"The police were here, too. What do I tell them?"

"Tell them that I am innocent of any crime. I left the bar because I am afraid of the gangsters, and I knew the police raid could only make things worse for me. The gangsters will be looking hard for whoever set them up. That's not me, but the criminals have no reason to believe me. The bar managers will look for me to testify on behalf of the gangsters. You be brave, Rosie. Everything will work out fine. I love you." Odette ended the call, held the cell phone to her chest, and appeared to be saying a silent prayer.

Jose escorted Polopolis out to the car. Polopolis nodded vigorously, over and over. In the donut shop his eyes had become vacant and fearful.

"He's decompensating," Jose whispered to Dave.

"Nico, let's settle down. We don't have time for your antics." Jose pushed Polopolis into the middle seat and secured him. Snow dusted their hair and was collecting on all parts of the car except for the hood, which was still warm. The visibility greatly restricted anyone inside the donut shop from clearly seeing anything that went on in the parking lot. Jose went behind the shop and motioned for David to rejoin the group.

David pondered the weather. He figured he still had about an hour before they would arrive in Kingston, which according to the note written in tiny print was their destination. He read the note again. "1. Go to Kingston. 2. Proceed to the Kingston waterfront. In the inner harbor, there is protected docking for pleasure boaters. This time of the year, the marina should be vacant or nearly so. 3. You will be looking for a forty-foot cabin cruiser with U.S. registration and the name, Athena. 4. Stow your packages on the boat. The captain will assist you. He will not tell you his name. Don't ask. He is a Greek family friend who helps us at a substantial personal risk. 5. You are to drive the car away from the waterfront to the Hotel Dieu, the name of the largest hospital in town. Park the car in the hospital's parking lot on the third level. 6. Place the parking ticket under the right side floor mat in the back seat. Then electronically lock the doors. 7. There is a strong magnet attached above the tire in the front right wheel well. Place the car keys there. 8. Run back to the boat. As soon as you arrive, the captain will depart for New York. He will only wait one hour with his packages. 9. In the event you don't make it back or any member of your team doesn't make it to the cruiser, use your own resources to make it back to the U.S. 10. The Canadian police will investigate your departure. 11. Completely destroy this note. It should not leave the Hotel Dieu parking garage. May the force be with you." David crunched the note and put it in his coat pocket and began the journey to Kingston.

As they neared Kingston, other traffic had vanished. The heavy snow continued to fall. As David turned onto the route identified by signage as the direct way to the waterfront, the Mercedes skidded on the icy road. David reacted by turning into the direction of the skid and taking his foot off the accelerator. The powerful car partially corrected, but still slid gently into the curb, narrowly missing parked cars. David slowed the car down to ten miles per hour and gritted his teeth. From that point to the waterfront, the trip was more like skating than driving.

David helped with the bags and with escorting their detainee to the boat. Odette quickly settled into the cabin. Jose seated Polopolis across from her. The captain of the Athena was a middle-aged man with a deep tan and a weathered face. The captain's movements were quick and jerky, as though nervous, though he was agile and confident on the boat. Despite his obvious nervousness, he facilitated the loading, directing Jose where to place the baggage.

The captain placed blankets around Odette and Polopolis. Polopolis grabbed at the captain. "Captain, you need to take me to the police. These people have kidnapped me. I'm freezing and starving. Just call the police, please. There's a reward."

"Save it for your memoirs, son." His voice was authoritative and definitely American, no trace of an accent. The captain went back to the bridge, checking and rechecking the instruments and the nautical map.

Jose made himself useful on the deck, sweeping snow, clearing the windshields, and keeping a watch on the surrounding area.

Driving up the hill to reach the Hotel Dieu was slow. David tacked the big car from one side of the street to the other, trying to maintain speed. He ran a red light rather than stop. The Mercedes slipped into the ticket device as he tried to enter the garage. This accident left a ding in the rear passenger door on the driver's side. On the third level, now nearly empty, he parked, hid the ticket and the keys as instructed. He walked as fast as he could with the snow and snow-covered ice patches, sometimes sliding as much as he walked, to the bottom of the hill. On the flat surface of the waterfront, he jogged toward the boat, no longer worried about risking a fall.

When he reached the boat, he found the captain and Jose wrestling with Polopolis.

"The dumb fuck tried to escape," Jose said. "All he managed to do was to get us both wet, and now I am freezing."

David watched him lift the back of Polopolis's head and slam his forehead into the deck. Polopolis was shivering and moaning.

"Captain, if you please, let us get the hell out of here." David then bent over to help Jose pull Polopolis to his feet.

The captain removed the lines holding his boat to the pier. He drove the boat slowly out of the marina. When the boat cleared the harbor, it quickly picked up speed. The town of Kingston rapidly disappeared from view. They found themselves completely enfolded in a dread inducing world of black water, white foam, and snow.

The captain stood stoically at the wheel, gripping it with his bare hands and staring hard at the water ahead. He wore a heavy blanket around his shoulders. David stood in the bridge, holding on tightly. Jose had changed clothes and resumed sweeping snow off the deck. Odette and Polopolis were in the cabin. Polopolis was now tied with rope provided by the captain. His hands were tied together, his feet were tied together, and his upper arms were tied to his torso. From a loop around his neck, the rope led to the anchor well at the interior of the bow where the line was firmly secured. Odette and Polopolis were bent forward over white buckets, into which they periodically threw up or tried to.

"Put on the life jackets." The captain's voice was strong and confident. David and Jose complied.

The radio cackled. "Calling Athena. Calling Athena. This is Rochester Harbor Marina. Come in. Over."

"I can barely make you out, Rochester Harbor Marina. This is Athena. Over." The captain tried adjusting the radio frequency.

"Athena, we have hostile visitors, FBI. Repeat FBI. Suggest alternate destination imperative. Over." The strong male voice rose and fell amid static and brief absences of sound.

"Roger that, Rochester Harbor Marina. Athena out." The captain reached into a drawer and pulled out a map of the Lake Ontario shoreline which he carefully studied.

He turned toward David and asked, "Does it matter to you where in New York you are put ashore?"

"No, but how about someplace warm with palm trees?" David was sorry immediately when he saw the tired, frustrated look on the captain's face. David waved his hand at the captain in apology and suddenly realized how cold he was. The captain had changed clothes and pulled on yellow waterproof pants and jacket, but still had to be suffering, but was showing no signs of it.

"Good, then I'm going to Oswego, a small college town that is a lot closer than Rochester. I may have to stay there myself if the weather doesn't let up." The captain spoke without ever turning away from the water in front of him. Silently now, he went back to his business of guiding the boat safely through the rough water and the blinding snow.

The captain altered course more directly due south now. The Athena bucked the waves, plowing steadily toward Oswego. The snow was coming from the west. It piled up on all of the flat surfaces of the boat where Jose couldn't risk sweeping because of the waves and wind.

CHAPTER 8

A Small Town in Snowy Upstate New York, January 25

When the tired and battered group finally reached Oswego, the early winter evening had already settled over the landscape. Beyond the snow, nearly everything was black. The few lights that they could see blinked feebly on and off, briefly clear when the snow abated somewhat and dark when the snow smothered their glow. The captain docked the boat at Wright's Landing Marina. The marina was empty and locked tight. "All the boats were pulled out by the end of October," the captain told David. "The marina is locked up tight. My docking here will be the talk of the town."

"It looks like a ghost town, all right." David was glad to be anywhere safe and sound.

"The marina is quite busy in warm weather. The New York State Canal System meets Lake Ontario right here. That was originally the Erie Canal. Oswego is in the heart of the Snowbelt. I suppose they must get 300 inches of snow in a bad year. I'm sure the harbormaster will be writing me up. I'll probably have to pay some penance, but I'm docked. We're safe; that's the important thing. I'll find someone to get my boat out of the water here and transport it back to Rochester on a trailer. I'll get it winterized again." The captain's weary face never lost its look of resolute determination, but he chuckled gently as he talked. David thought that the man would be driven for success in whatever his business or ventures were.

"Captain, I sure appreciate the chances you have taken in picking us up. I'll tell our mutual friends what a stand up guy you are."

The captain smiled, but shrugged. David could tell this was not a man who needed any references or testimonials.

"I think there's a ma and pa motel up the street about three blocks. Go three blocks and then turn right on Seneca Street. I'll sleep here in the cabin. You guys need to get clear of me and my boat as quickly as possible. I'm sure the police will be by here soon, and they'll be wondering who the nutcase is that had a boat out this long after the season closed, and in this weather." The captain's pointed the directions out as he talked.

"Jose, you stay with our cargo. I'm going to find us some rooms and transportation." David headed out by himself to find the motel and, he hoped, a cab. Odette and Polopolis were in no condition to walk very far. As he trudged up the street, the snow was finally slacking off.

David walked from the marina past a marine engine repair shop and a sailing store. A little further up Lake Street, there were two bars, a pizza joint, a donut shop, barbershop, newsstand, antique store, and dress shop. Only one of the pizza joints was open. As soon as he made the right turn onto Seneca Street, he thought he could see a wooden sign with gold lettering advertising the Oswego Motel. The buildings lining this street were large houses, some still residential and some law, insurance, or medical offices.

David was very glad when he arrived at the motel to see that the lights in the office were still on. He marched in, grateful for the warmth and the smiling desk clerk.

"May, I help you, sir?" The desk clerk looked like a college student. There was an open text in front of him on the counter top.

"I hope so. I need three rooms, if you have them available. My friends and I have been put ashore here instead of Rochester because of the storm."

"You were out on Lake Ontario in this weather? You are lucky to be ashore, sir. We are empty at the moment. Can I see your credit card and ID, sir?"

The negotiations required for the three rooms were soon completed. The office had cherry paneling and comfortable, home-style, maple furniture with dark green cushions. David hoped that the rooms were as cozy.

David asked, "Could you call a cab for me? I need to get my friends and our gear off the dock." The clerk quickly made the call. In five minutes, the cab pulled to the front of the motel and David hopped in.

Jose had all their bags lined up on the sidewalk. He had given his coat to Odette, who sat on a bench that faced out to Lake Ontario. She looked forlorn and abandoned. Her face was red, raw from the abuse of the hard, cold breeze. Jose's coat was covered with remnants of snow. She sat there, arms clenched around her stomach. David felt a deep sympathy for her. Her elopement from Gus's bar and the gangsters who frequented it had, so far, been urgently stressful for her.

The cab driver helped to load their luggage into the trunk of the cab. Polopolis had been freed from his bindings, but he was too sick and feeble to try to escape. He wasn't even whining or complaining. Jose steered him into the middle of the back seat as usual. David walked Odette around the opposite side and got her into the cab. David offered the captain a warm room at the motel, but the captain declined with a wave and a smile.

Inside the small, but comfortable rooms, David and Jose settled Polopolis into the middle room. They re-cuffed him and used the rope the captain had given them to secure one of his ankles to the wall-mounted, metal stand holding the television. They left enough slack in it so that Polopolis could reach the toilet. They agreed on pizza and salad, which David ordered for delivery.

Jose and David worked on their email until 1 AM. David looked outside at the crystalline blanket of snow covering the darkened, almost black green of the abundant fir trees that lined the town. A beautiful little town, he thought. He read email until he couldn't concentrate any longer. He accomplished some of the most urgent tasks. Then he called Alice's cell phone.

Alice picked up immediately. "Hi David, you're up late.'

David laughed. He sat rubbing his forehead with his free hand, and wondering when he would be able to get a full night's sleep. "Yeah, well, you, too. We can catch up when we're dead, I suppose."

"Like they say, when you can't get your work done in 24 hours a day, it's time to start working nights and weekends." Neither one of them laughed.

"Give me a quick rundown on the most important stuff. We both need some sleep."

"TechPro has changed the deliverables. They bought an Arabic translation super program and have run all the stuff they had already provided us through it. Now, they want us to review the garbled English translation, looking for the same things: terrorist financial arrangements, sources and applications, plots, anything that looks potentially sinister, really. I've started the guys on this, but it's slow going. They think that the computer has made some awkward, and in a few cases wrong translations, so they have to go back to the original, make corrections. It's incredibly tedious."

"Listen, Alice, get with our contract guy, what's his name?" David was now standing up, swinging his torso from way to the other in order to be more alert.

"Her name is Suzy Stordahl."

"Oh? Sorry, I'm a little woozy from lack of sleep."

"Have a stiff drink and go to sleep then." Alice was using her brassy, 'I'm-in-control-here' voice. David had learned long ago to accept her unapologetic directness.

"Not a bad idea, Alice, but we have no refreshments on board at the moment. Get with Suzy and get a bill out to TechPro. I'll work on the embassy for a payment."

"One more thing, David, we've got visitors out front. They come and they go, but they seem to be monitoring us. Seriously, they are making me quite nervous."

"What do they look like, Alice?"

"Pardon the stereotype, but they look like movie gangsters, Eastern European, maybe, or Mediterranean. To me, they look like professional killers. We need to do something. I feel like something bad's going to happen."

"Call Taz, and ask him to stop by every so often. If he spots them, ask him to talk to them. I'll get Demetrios on it in the morning."

"Will do. Thanks for that. I feel a little better. Go to sleep, David."

David woke up at 5:30 AM. There was a determined knocking on his door. He struggled out from under the covers and opened the door. The cold air rushed in. Standing in front of him were two New York State Police troopers. Dave froze for a second, chilled to the marrow. He invited them in then ran to the bathroom to put on a flannel shirt and trousers.

The female trooper spoke first. David took her to be in charge. "I'm Sergeant Marsha Gagnon of the New York State Police. This is Trooper Manuel Ruiz. We'd like to ask you a few questions."

David needed to get to the bathroom. "Excuse me one second, I have to go to the bathroom. David went to the toilet, urinated and splashed water on his face. When he finished, he opened the door to find Trooper Ruiz gazing down benevolently at him.

"I didn't want you escaping out into the cold, sir," Ruiz said with a charming smile.

"I needed to pee, really. Go right ahead then, ask me your questions."

The woman sat in the desk chair, her partner in the recliner. David sat on the bed. Trooper Gagnon wore little makeup, and her prominent ears stood out through thin, brown hair. She placed her gray Stetson on the floor and opened up her memo pad. Her demeanor was serious, and her jaws clenched repeatedly as she talked.

"What's your name, sir, and state your business here in Oswego?"

"My name is David R. Pearl. I have no business here in Oswego. I'm just passing through on my way back home to Washington, DC." David's stomach was growling. There was leftover pizza in the next room. Just the thought made his mouth water, but he would wait.

"What is your business then, sir?"

"I am CEO of a small security firm in Washington. We do security consults of various types and some communications systems intelligence work for the government." He pulled his identification out of his wallet along with a business card. Ruiz got up to accept them and passed them along to the sergeant.

"We understand that you landed in Oswego on the New York State registered power boat, Athena, last night."

"That is correct."

"What was the purpose of your boating expedition?"

"Sightseeing, though we could have picked a better day for it."

"So, the boat didn't pick you up in Canada?"

"Actually, the boat did." David didn't size up this situation as a likely friendly visit, and he didn't like where this line of questioning was going. He hoped that Polopolis would sleep through it.

"You had some associates who traveled with you, did you not?"

"Yes, my business associate, Jose Gonzalez. Odette Lacoursiere is traveling with us. She is a Canadian citizen who will apply for a U.S. visa. And, we are traveling with a Greek citizen, an officer of the Greek Embassy in Washington, whom we are protecting."

"Thank you. I will want to interview them later. Did you pass through the U.S. border legally?"

"As far as I know." David grinned, but anxiety made his right leg tremble slightly.

"Do you have any weapons in the room, on your person, or in your car?"

"I don't have a car. I need to rent one today. We need to get back to Washington. We have no weapons either."

"Please get Mr. Gonzalez for us, Mr. Pearl." David went through the next room where Polopolis was still sleeping. In the next room were Odette and Jose, sleeping in twin beds.

"Wake up, Jose." Jose was awake instantly. He sat up. He looked behind David to see the tall state trooper, Ruiz, smiling down at him.

"Boss, what the fuck?"

"I don't know, Jose. Two New York State troopers want to talk to us. You're next. Just get dressed and answer their questions."

Trooper Ruiz escorted Jose into David's room and closed the door.

David turned his attentions to Polopolis. He pulled the comforter back and cut off the plastic ties, untied the rope, putting the rope in his duffle bag. He advised Polopolis of the situation. Polopolis smiled for the first time since they had met.

"Don't pull anything, Nico. I will follow you wherever you go. You've made this personal for me. Please don't forget that I'm your best shot at living." David turned away from him and made a pot of coffee in the motel-provided automatic brewer. He ate a slice of leftover pepperoni pizza. He took a shower, shaved, brushed his teeth, and waited for whatever happened next. David was studying the state map of New York when Jose interrupted him.

"Boss, I got to go and go fast. The troopers have cleared me, but they say that they will be in contact with my commanding officer to verify what I told them. I will have my leave canceled immediately when that happens. They'll know I'm not where I said I'd be and assume I'm in some kind of trouble with the law. Can you rent a car for me?"

"Of course, Jose, I'll get right on it." Dave called the office and asked the man who answered the phone for a recommendation.

The man's voice was mature and friendly. "Oh yeah, my son told me that you might need a car rental. I'd use National Auto Air. They are located at the airport. It's a family business like us, so they probably won't be in the office, but I'll call them if you'd like."

David said he would appreciate that.

"By the way, we have a charge on the room for a long distance call to Greece. My son let it go through since it was at 3:00 AM this morning, and he didn't want to wake you up to approve the call. It's $151. I hope that's okay."

"Sure, it's okay. My friend here from Greece needed to talk to his family. The time difference, you know."

Polopolis had stopped smiling, but he stared at David, a smug look on his face. David hung up the phone.

"Who did you talk to, Nico?" David got immediately in front of Nico's face. "You may have put us all in danger if there was a tap on the line of whoever you called."

"My wife." Nico smiled, seemingly unconcerned about any adverse event arising from his telephone call.

"I'll find out. You know the people who want you dead are already looking for all of us. Maybe you should talk the troopers into arresting you. That's probably your best bet to go on breathing in the long term."

The phone rang. It was the motel owner, who identified himself as Lou Lampley. "Hi, Mr. Pearl, I have the car rental manager on the line. Can I transfer him over to you?"

"Sure, thanks very much. Oh, and can I get the number of that call to Greece?"

"Yes, the number will be itemized on your bill. I'll have it ready for you when you're ready to leave." The motel manager clicked off.

"Mr. Lampley? I need two rental cars. I need one immediately and the other possibly in an hour or two. Could you tell them to come here to the Oswego motel? That'd be great." David gave his credit card number, terminated the call, and turned to see Odette, walking to her room after her interrogation, red-eyed as though from crying.

Ruiz escorted Polopolis into the room where Sergeant Gagnon stayed seated. David watched her working on her notes. The smile never left Ruiz's face.

David put his arm around Odette. She collapsed against him, sobbing. Jose left in the first rental car.

"It's okay, Odette, tell me what happened."

Odette moved away from him and flopped in the leather recliner. "They threatened me. They have reported me to INS. I have to go to some kind of administrative hearing in two weeks. They think that I'm part of a gang, not that I am running away from criminals. Some break for freedom, don't you think?"

David sighed and shook his head. "Yes. I'm sorry about all of this, Odette. I really am. We'll get you a lawyer. Don't worry."

Polopolis came sauntering into the room. He was smiling. He went directly into the bathroom and closed the door. Trooper Ruiz came to the door and motioned for David to enter.

Sergeant Gagnon looked up at David as he walked in. She motioned him to the desk chair and then stood at the window, looking out.

"We need to ask a few more questions based upon what Mr. Polopolis just told us. Is he really a diplomat?"

"Yes, he is really a diplomat. I'm working for the Greek Embassy who wants to talk to him. He's been on some kind of sick leave. By the way, he called Greece this morning, so his criminal associates may be on their way here already. He made that call at 3 AM."

"What is your relationship with Mr. Photios Burstos?"

"I don't know him, so no relationship."

"Let me clarify. He's the nice man who provided his boat and navigation skills to get you safely from Kingston, Frontenac County, Ontario Province, Canada to Oswego, New York."

"I never learned his name."

Gagnon pursed her lips, shot a glance at David charged with hostility and disbelief. "I see. It's kind of a cloak and dagger story we have here. Why don't you know his name? He went to a lot of trouble on your behalf."

"He didn't offer his name and I didn't ask."

"Well, just for your future information, Photios is a rich car dealer in Rochester, very active in Greek-American affairs. I think he was probably doing the Greek government a small favor. What do you think?"

Pearl pursed his lips, looked up at the ceiling and said. "I wouldn't know."

"I see. Why isn't there a warrant out for Mr. Polopolis?" Sergeant Gagnon cocked her head to her left, waiting for his answer, in a pose suggesting that whatever it was, she wasn't going to believe it.

"He's a diplomat. The embassy is deeply embarrassed by his recent actions. The Greek government needs to talk to him to see what breaches of its security and confidential information there may be. And the Greek government and our State Department want him out of the country as soon as feasible."

"Your friend, Odette, has a date with INS. My contact in Albany with the New York State Police, Colonel LaPierre, tells me that the

State Department is interested in getting you and Mr. Polopolis back to Washington as quickly and safely as possible. I think you crossed the border illegally with a Greek national and a Canadian national. Unfortunately, Albany isn't interested in that. We aren't going to hold any of you. Were you holding Mr. Polopolis against his will?"

"It's a love/hate kind of thing for him. We had to protect him from himself. You see what happened with the phone call. He's his own worst enemy. He's not thinking straight, and he might get himself killed, or worse, might get me killed before I can turn him over to his embassy."

"I see. I'm sending a copy of my report to the State Department and to the INS. You may be interviewed further when you get back home. Goodbye, Mr. Pearl."

The two troopers walked outside into the intensely cold, clear, bright sunshine. David worried while staring out at the winter landscape. He wanted the trip to Washington to be over and Polopolis delivered to the embassy. So much had happened. All of it new to him. He was used to mentally juggling assignments, tasks, and challenges, but juggling the responsibility for people—that was a new one. Maybe he could get used to it. Still, the fear of what Polopolis, or a Greek gang, or somebody else would do next moved beyond worry to actual fear.

CHAPTER 9
Almost Heaven, January 25

The UPS truck headed up the steep hill in Dunbar, West Virginia, its driver facing another of the difficult delivery routes in the hills above the river. The driver shifted the gears as he carefully steered the big truck on the narrow, paved road. The big brown truck was too wide to be safely accommodated on the narrow roads, so the utmost caution was required. The driver frequently had to steer the right tires onto the narrow shoulder, dangerously close to the steep drop on the valley side of the road, to let cars coming down the rugged hill pass him.

Reaching the address for his next delivery, the driver double checked the house number, then jogged to the front door because of the biting cold on this early March day. The value of the delivery required him to wait for a signature. At the door, he sat the big cardboard box on the small concrete porch, just to the side of the door. Then, he rang the doorbell and knocked. He had been at this address before. This person, Victor Nevzlin, usually answered within less than a minute. He heard dish-stacking noises from the inside. After a couple of minutes, the man opened the door. The man was slender, but wiry, dressed in expensive slacks and a yellow dress shirt with the top two buttons undone. His receding hairline showed a prominent forehead, cold dark eyes, and a mouth seemingly unable to smile. The driver, for the first time, became in fear of this pale skinned man. His customer, who seemed to be offended by the delivery and his own presence, then signed for the package. The driver nodded and handed over the package. The door closed in his face.

The driver headed back down the hill, carefully negotiating the many tight curves in the road. As had happened once before, when he turned off Skyview Road onto Briarwood, he had to stop. The old lady was out in the street again, blocking his route. He had reported her to his bosses the last time. The driver rolled down the window.

"What did you deliver to the Communist?" She was about sixty and barked out her question.

"Hi, Mrs. McKay. I can't tell you that."

"The police will want to know. You want to tell me, or do you want to talk to the state police?"

The driver kept on smiling. "Mrs. McKay, that's none of your business, but if you won't tell anyone, it was a gift box from Harry and David."

"Who are Harry and David?"

"Harry and David is a gourmet food catalogue store in Oregon."

"I see, the Russian is getting rewarded for something then. That's interesting. You know he disappears in the night, comes back a few days later. Well, can't talk, got to go." The woman marched into her small frame house before the driver could deliver his 'have a nice day.'

Mrs. McKay dialed the state police. They wouldn't take her call, so she left a message. Then, she called the FBI in Charleston. The person who answered the phone listened politely.

Mrs. McKay told her story once again. "I have resented this guy, Nevzlin, from the moment he moved in. I welcomed him with a homemade cherry pie. The cherries were from my back yard. The man didn't smile, didn't thank me, and he slammed the door in my face. My neighbors have told me that they have tried to converse with the man and failed to get any kind of response. The man just walks away from them without speaking. Sometimes, when he yelled at some of the children in the neighborhood, his accent sounded Russian. The children don't like him. I think the younger ones are actually afraid of him. He's up to something. He needs to be investigated."

CHAPTER 10
Mistakes Were Made, January 26 and 27

David spent much of the long drive back to Washington, DC, talking on his cell phone to Alice Boggs. "Alice, I want you to work on a tactical plan for the next six months. We need to hire a financial type, someone with a top secret clearance and drive."

Alice's voice boomed through the cell phone, which was secured to the console with Velcro. "I agree. We need new revenue sources. We probably should get into a little discreet advertising. What do you see as the next steps?"

David and his two passengers were now crossing over the state line into Pennsylvania on route 17. "The next steps are getting our receivables paid. Secondly, getting more talent on board. Thirdly, get some strategic direction. It seems our focus is now too much on security and not enough on data analysis. The more we do in security, the less time I have to really provide leadership in the analytical part, which is what I would personally prefer. I think we need to write out the next steps on each of our contracts. We also need to find a mathematician. With all of the initial translation work being done by a computer, we need someone who can write algorithms and programs to do complicated, specific searches and analyses."

"That makes sense: have algorithms that track and link key words, phrases, and names. We'd have proprietary software that would probably fast track the work and improve upon what amounts to manual cross searches using spread sheets. So, I start recruiting a mathematician and a financial person."

"That's right. Thanks, Alice, hopefully I'll be there in a few hours."

Several hours later, as they entered DC, David drove straight to the Greek Embassy. The receptionist escorted Polopolis and David into the ambassador's office and asked them to wait. Polopolis, who had been silent, now became quite fidgety. He paced, stretched, and cracked his knuckles. David had watched his moods change in seconds, in an erratic repetition of facial movements and tics. David sat quietly, pretending to read a Greek tourist publication, one of several piled on top of a side table, but he watched Polopolis constantly.

When the door flew open, the deputy mission, Theo Gliniadakis, walked in. He was followed closely by Demetrios and a robust, tall man with a forceful, military bearing. Theo hugged Polopolis and with a quizzical facial expression, gently tapped Polopolis's cheek with his right hand. Then, Demetrios put steel handcuffs roughly onto Polopolis's wrists, whose face had now gone blank.

Theo turned to David. "Thanks for the timely delivery. I hope my friend Nico wasn't too much of a problem. Let me introduce you to our military attaché, Anastasios Dimantidis." David stood and shook hands with the military attaché. The man had a handshake made of steel; David's hand hurt for a few seconds after Anastasios had taken his hand away.

"David, we received many positive comments about your work from our mutual friends in Canada. I have your check somewhere here." Gliniadakis briefly looked through papers in the in-box and pulled out an envelope. He handed the envelope to David.

"Thanks, Theo. It's been interesting."

"I'm sure. We will be finding out what our bad boy has been doing behind our backs. Anastasios will be Nico's constant companion until Nico is safely returned to Greece. I've put a small bonus in the amount you were due on our contract for a job well done. I hope it's satisfactory."

David shook everyone's hand except for Nico's. He slapped Nico gently on the back and whispered, "Get with the program."

Nico turned his head quickly upward toward David. "We'll see who gets with the program, David. I won't forget the hurt you've caused me and my family."

"Don't be bitter, Nico. Let the embassy help you. Thanks again, Theo." David walked out of the office and outside where Odette was waiting in the rental car.

The first day back in the office passed uneventfully for David. He and Alice worked productively on the backlog of contract updates. They met with their part-time financial person and their contracted lawyer. They met with their new employee, a linguist named Frankie Ballinger. She was a petite, red-haired dynamo David found compelling to watch her energetic movements and darting, bright green eyes. They set up progress meetings with their customers. They polished the final deliverable due to TechPro. The three of them worked through a pile of contract amendments and bids for additional work at 8:00 that evening, Odette volunteered to pick up their order from the Chinese restaurant, Chung's Buddha Belly. The Buddha Belly was about two blocks away from Washington's small, struggling Chinatown, but conveniently at the end of DRPearl Inc.'s block. When she returned, she was carrying a shopping bag full of food and a large manila envelope.

David was in the front reception area talking to Taz Washington and his partner, Neal Walters. "Taz, I appreciate you talking to those guys that were hanging around the office."

"Like I said, David, they answered my questions and complied with showing their ID's, but they are trouble beyond a doubt. They were armed. I figure them for hoodlums. As far as I know, they haven't been back. I think the ID's were fake, but if so, they were convincing fakes. They said they were couriers protecting a jeweler in the neighborhood, but the jeweler's name they gave us was an obvious fake. We notified the uniforms patrolling this area to keep an eye out for them."

"I sure appreciate it. Let's eat some dinner."

"David, we already ate. Neal has to watch his waistline. We've already been called to another homicide, so we gotta go. The devil never rests here in DC."

"Nowhere else, either." David walked the two detectives to the front door.

David was more than halfway finished with his plate of lo mein when he remembered the envelope from the Buddha Belly. He opened it and read: "David, my friend, please pardon this note. My uncle in China has asked me to introduce you to my cousin, Jiang Gao. Jiang is mathematical genius, very knowledgeable about computers and statistics. Jiang studied in USA on a student visa. Now, he is back from China and has applied for citizenship, but needs a job. His English is very good, much better than mine. To stay in this country, he needs a job. You have computers and do analysis, so Uncle Vern is hoping that you can help him. Let me know, I get in touch with him. Your Friend, Vern."

David handed the note over to Alice and finished eating. As he ate, he smiled about Uncle Vern's note. His company definitely could use a mathematical genius. The contracts were finally coming in at a decent rate, but the deliverables were backing up. "Alice, why don't you tell Vern that we'll take a look at Jiang Gao tomorrow?"

"I will. We don't want Jiang wasting his talents at the Buddha Belly, do we?" Alice was in a long sober period. This translated to peak efficiency that not many analysts could match. Tonight, if she stayed on form, she would work until 2 AM and then be back at it at 7 AM.

"What else has come in for us this week?"

"MagnaMeta has called us, emailed us and sent us the outlines of a proposal that they have marked urgent. They want a response in five days. Apparently, one of their senior analysts has gone missing in Baghdad. They would like us to examine all of her files to determine what could be missing, copied, or otherwise transferred without authorization or their knowledge. They are proposing an open-ended contract, which is good. We don't have anyone with a skill set on board that could do all of this. I wanted to pick your brain to see if you were aware of anyone out there that we could tap on short notice."

"No, I don't. The kind of analyst we need is already gainfully employed in one of the intelligence shops. What information do they provide us about their missing analyst?"

"She's an Arab specialist. She's forty years old, not married, and speaks five languages. The family is originally Lebanese, but with some French ancestry. She was born in this country in Shreveport, Louisiana. She has three brothers, all physicians. She received her Ph.D. from the University of Cairo. They have searched her condo and found nothing of interest to report. She passed her annual physical with no issues noted. They have found nothing to be suspicious about, and there have been no demands, no threats, no videotape, nothing."

David had been studying the resumé of Jiang Gao, which had been included with the note from Vern, manager of Chung's Buddha Belly. He looked up at Odette and said, "I think we should give this guy a flyer at the MagnaMeta project if he passes the interview. I don't know of anyone else who could even attempt to navigate their way through the software programming, analyze the data files, and interpret the intelligence loss from that. Ask around with our other employees, Odette, but let's get Jiang in here to start the project."

"So, it's a go then, David?" Alice frowned.

"Yeah, put my name on the response to the proposal. Leave Jiang out of it. If we have to, we can tap into other corporate expertise, or put the word out in the intelligence community for someone with the skill sets and the security clearance we need to acquire."

"Okay, David, let me get back to work on the TechPro contract. We don't want to slip the drop dead date any further than we already have." Alice stood up and started clearing the remains of the meal.

"That new employee, Frankie Ballinger, looks like she's going to be a spitfire. She's a good catch for us. How's Odette doing?"

"Fair to middling, I'd have to say. I think she's got potential. I'm working with her on contracts, PERT charts, and the like. She's worried silly about her immigration requirements, but I think she's got a good chance to stay in this country. She's a willing worker and committed to learning everything she can about everything. And, everyone including me loves her soft French pronunciations." Alice finished the clearing, started the dishwasher, and headed up the stairs, back to her computer.

David decided to take a walk. He went out the back door, crossed the tiny, bare-ground backyard, and opened the back gate. He turned right down the alley, again at the corner, slowed his pace, and edged to the corner of the storefront at that end of his block. He studied the parked cars, looking for the two presumed Greek mobsters who had previously staked out his office. He didn't see them.

Still searching cautiously, David walked the perimeter of the block in front of his townhouse office. He avoided the normal pedestrians, swinging wide of the beggars and drunks. He hesitated as he caught a glimpse of two men, slouched in a rental car driving slowly by, but it was too dark to be certain. He decided to walk to Stoney's for a nightcap and then return to work. He hadn't been to Stoney's in two weeks. It would be good to get caught up on the bar's gossip and get some new jokes from the bartenders.

David walked into Stoney's with the confidence of a regular. The place was packed with chattering customers. The bar was full, the booths fully occupied, and the tables were swarming with noisy groups of drinkers. He walked to the bar and asked for a draft. The music was rocking as he went outside where one of the five tables was empty. He enjoyed listening to the bantering and boisterousness coming from the groups that occupied the rest of the tables outside.

Sipping his beer, he felt a tap on his shoulder. It was Demetrios, eyes furtive, puffy bags under his eyes, and the skin on his neck sagging. Demetrios indicated with the flick of a wrist that he should follow him inside, which he did. Demetrios found two places open at the bar. David noticed the two Greek gangsters sitting side by side in a booth along the far wall. They seemed to be listening attentively to a man sitting across from them who was dressed like a professional: wearing a shiny, silver suit, a loud, maroon-and-white, wide-collar, dress shirt, and a silver and maroon, regimental, striped tie.

Demetrios sat hunched over the bar. "David, I so totally miss my ten-year-old daughter. Missing her so much I'm homesick. I have two more years on the contract and because of this Polopolis mess, my planned trip back to Greece has been canceled."

David was straining to listen when he felt a tap on his shoulder. The man standing behind them was smiling, overweight, and wearing a silver suit—the man who'd been sitting with the Greek gangsters. He was smiling. "Gentlemen, please join me over there." He pointed to the booth where he had been sitting. The gangsters were gone. David and Demetrios looked at each other in affirmation before agreeing.

Once they were settled into the booth, the man leaned toward them. "I am Harry Markos, an attorney in town, representing the business interests of Ionnis Zisis in this country. I have a proposition for you, if you are willing to listen."

"Yes, Harry, go right ahead." David was suspicious, but the atmosphere at Stoney's made him feel as though he were in his own living room. He waved off the young woman in black who stopped by the table trying to sell bouquets of roses. She was frequently in the bar and had a good market with the male drinkers, who probably needed something to appease the spouses or girlfriends waiting back home.

"Good. I would like to contract with you both, individually, on a 'word is my bond' basis for any information that you may collect concerning Nicolaos Polopolis. Now, before you object, let me just say that we have a common community of interest here. We are interested in his safety and in getting him treatment." Harry Markos continued smiling. He was about fifty, with salt and pepper hair, which was trimmed closely to his skull.

Demetrios spoke first. "Why do you need us, when the Greek Embassy already has Polopolis in their custody?"

Harry laughed and took a sip of his beer. "I need you because at 3 AM this morning, our Nico escaped at Dulles International Airport. Despite what appears to be more than adequate security arrangements, he managed to elude his handlers. He was in a stairwell with two Greek Army officers in plainclothes. Due to the narrow stairwell, Nico was able to pull one of the men over him and down the stairwell where this guard was knocked unconscious. Nico pulled the man's weapon and shot the other one in the knee. This man tumbled to the landing where Nico was. Nico got the handcuffs key, took one of the Berettas, their cell phones, and their car keys, and fled. However, he did not take their cars. Of course, from Dulles, the possible travel arrangements and directions are almost impossible to track. And, the Greek secret police came a-calling on me this morning, but I had no knowledge of where Polopolis might be, and I told them so."

"We owe first allegiance to the Greek Embassy. They haven't called me, but if they do, we will work for them." David shot a glance at Demetrios. From the tight jaw and intense stare on Demetrios's face, David figured that he had been alerted and probably had been at the scene when Polopolis escaped.

"Completely understood and agreed to. What I want is information. We lost time and assets in trying other methods. Mr. Pearl, you were too shrewd and clever by far." Harry was still smiling. He sat slouched comfortably, as if they were guests in his home.

"Harry, I have to tell you that I strenuously object to your other methods, using those thugs to watch my office. I run a business, not an escape and evasion training course. Do you have any idea where Nico is at the moment?" David was growing concerned that Demetrios was about to punch Markos. Demetrios was openly sneering at Harry.

"As I told the Greek investigators, no, we have had no contact from him or anyone else. I think the Greek government has something to hide. Nico hasn't been in custody long enough for anyone to find out. He is running from something, and it appears that he has had some kind of psychological break. He has gone from being a dutiful, loyal, Greek government employee to being paranoid, running from something we don't know, and maybe to something we also don't know. At times, he seems to be afraid of everyone, including his own family. He needs treatment and he needs to be debriefed. He needs to be placed in a safe and secure environment so that he can be properly medicated and get treatment. I'm afraid that none of us realized the extent of his mental condition." Harry adjusted one of his ostentatious silver cufflinks.

Demetrios slowly and unconsciously rubbed the back of his head. "Could you be more precise in what your concerns are relative to Polopolis?"

"The family is concerned for his safety as well as wanting to maintain control over their trust fund. With Nico is operating like a misguided missile, the family is worried that he might create liabilities for the trust fund."

David finished his beer, catching the waiter's eye while he lifted his empty glass to get a refill. "What kind of resources does Nico have at the moment?"

"That's a good question. The truth is we are not sure. His uncle, Ike Zisis, says that he gave him $3,000, when Nico was in Montreal, but as you know, he didn't have more than pocket change when you picked him up. He has his credit cards, but I am sure that the Greek police are monitoring the activity on the cards. Nico, as you know, can be smooth, clever, and charming when he wants to be, so he is capable of just about anything: stealing cars, romancing women, talking his way into friendships and homes. The possibilities are many."

David got his beer. "From the sounds of this, Demetrios and I will need more information from you than you'll get from us."

Harry laughed. "This may be true, but we are counting on the embassy to contact you. When, or I should say, if, they contact you, they will want you to use your sources to get information as to Nico's whereabouts, and then to secure him, and finally, as before, make the safe retention and delivery of their employee." Harry reached into his interior jacket pocket and pulled out a thick envelope. He placed it on top of the table and pushed it to David. David picked up the envelope and glanced inside. The noise in the bar had subsided somewhat and now had a few empty tables.

"Think of that as a small retainer. All of my contact information is in there as well. I practice here in the District, mostly immigration law for my fellow Greeks, but also some maritime law relative to the Greek shipping and international trade."

David stopped the man from leaving with a hand on his arm. "Harry, how did you come to represent Uncle Ike, as you call him?"

"He's my actual uncle. This is a family matter, not a legal one."

"The two men you were talking to when we came into the bar tonight, who are they?" David shifted uncomfortably on the bench, worrying about what Demetrios might do.

"Gangsters from Montreal. I met with them and pulled them off your case after I convinced Uncle Ike to go in a different direction. You won't be seeing them anymore." Harry stood. He threw a fifty dollar bill on top of the table, slapped David on the shoulder, and walked vigorously out of the bar.

Demetrios was intrigued. "What is in the envelope, David?"

David counted the money. "$1,000. I guess now we need to sit tight and wait." David instantly regretted taking the money in the first place. "Call me as soon as you hear anything, Demetrios?"

Demetrios shrugged. "I think you just made a big mistake, David, in taking the money."

"I think you're right, I'll make a record of it and use it as a cushion against further damages that might result from Uncle Ike. You need to get some rest. Why don't you knock off for the evening."

"Not going to happen, I am too miserable."

David stood and walked back to the office. Inside, David typed out a complete account of the conversation with Markos and the cash he'd received. He sent the message to Alice and copied the part-time attorney. Then, he sealed the envelope, signed and dated it, and stuck it in the safe.

Upstairs, the next day, David and Alice hammered their talking points home to the two contract auditors from MagnaMeta. David spoke of the need to make accountability a clearer objective of their contracts. "Guys, as you can see, DRPearl Inc. has provided you with detailed accounting of the personal service hours put into the analysis requirements of your contract. Our software makes this assignment as soon as each individual analyst logs onto the secure files provided by MagnaMeta. I doubt that any of your other subcontractors have this kind of detailed record, which can track back to each analyst from whatever part of the file that they are examining." David felt the vibration from his cell phone and checked the screen. It was Odette, texting him that two FBI agents were waiting to talk to him downstairs.

The senior of the two accountants, a small man of about fifty, with wire rim glasses, and a combed straight back haircut, spoke. "Your accountability and analyst tracking software does look interesting. We will include in our report a recommendation that our software folks take a look at it. When will you have your final deliverable of action items from the contract?"

Alice responded. "We are polishing our draft report at the moment, and we need to tie up some loose ends. So, it will be ready on time, two weeks from today."

The senior accountant spoke up abruptly. "Any chance that it could be ready before then?"

Alice laughed, but quickly said, "For a price, anything's possible. Tell your technical rep to call me." The group stood and made small talk on their way down the stairs.

The FBI agents watched the group come down the stairs and go to the door. David saw the two auditors outside. He returned to the FBI agents and introduced himself.

"I'm Brian Ridgewood. This is my partner, Juan Montoya. We'd like to ask you a few questions about one of your clients, Nicolaos Polopolis." Ridgewood picked up his notebook. He was a tall, slender man, with a blonde crew cut, and a cold, blue-eyed stare. His partner was dark, older, and had a nervous tic in his left eye.

"Brian, Polopolis is not one of my clients. I feel like my life's being consumed by Polopolis, who is quite a pain in the ass. I'll tell you what I know. Come on upstairs, guys." David indicated the direction and followed the two agents up the stairs.

The FBI agents and David went upstairs to the conference room. Alice disappeared to her work station on the third floor. The men sat down. The agents accepted coffee.

"Mr. Pearl, Nicolaos's family has contacted us, and alleges that he has been kidnapped. His wife says that you kidnapped him at some point. Any truth to that, sir?" Ridgewood was smiling, but maintained hard eye contact with David.

"Oh, my God, I'm sorry that I ever met that asshole. No, I didn't kidnap him. I'm in the security and information intelligence business. I did some security work for the Greek Embassy, where Polopolis is or was some kind of political affairs officer. He got into some kind of personal trouble, and I think had a mental breakdown. While I was watching his house with one of my security people, an intruder broke in. The intruder was found dead in the kitchen with his throat slashed. There was no sign of Polopolis in the house. After a few days, the embassy calls me and asks me to go to Montreal and find him. I do that. After a several days in Montreal, I find Polopolis in his uncle's house. He tries to escape. My partner and I detain him and bring him back to the Greek Embassy here in Washington. The uncle has ties to a Greek gang that does gambling, smuggling, and other assorted, illegal activities."

Ridgewood raised his hand. "Mr. Pearl, that's a fantastic story which leaves out myriad details. However, I would like to know where Polopolis is now."

David's jaw tightened, and his neck stiffened, but he hoped these physical changes weren't observed. He smiled at the agents, gaining control over his anger. "I don't know, and I don't care. I've been told that he escaped custody of the Greek government's agents at Dulles airport about 36 hours ago. That being the case, he could be anywhere. Polopolis is wanted by his government and by the Greek gangsters. He is extremely paranoid, but functional most of the time, and quite elusive."

Ridgewood smiled but remained focused on David. "If you should hear from him, you will contact us immediately." He handed David a card with his name and telephone number on it.

"Sure. With any luck, I won't hear from him."

"Right, but if you do. What's the nature of your intelligence work, Mr. Pearl?"

David poured himself another cup of coffee, wondering where this line of questioning was going and what, if anything, it really had to do with the missing Polopolis. "We are a full-service intelligence and information security business. We do mostly subcontracting for the major intelligence firms, the ones that have the telephone, internet, and cell phone communications capture abilities. We then analyze what they give us to find patterns, particularly financial trails, economic transactions, or funds tracing that might lead to specific individuals. Our physical security work began as an attempt to make some money, any money at all to keep the lights lit and the heat on."

Ridgewood laughed. Montoya remained stoic. "How do you identify those patterns?"

"The major intelligence outfits have software that captures communications transmissions, and then they translate from any language and phonetically search texts and audio recordings. We look for similarities, gaps, or curiosities in those data sets provided to us using our own software products as well as those that are available to us commercially. We might run the data through as many as twenty different programs to find the connections that we are looking for or that we see, but weren't looking for."

"Sounds tedious. How did you get into this business?"

"It is the business we're in, and we are very good at it. Finding a hole in our security or zeroing in on a bad guy's bank account is hard work. We have a number of analysts we have trained and who have security clearances to work at the different tasks. I was at the CIA for five years until they decided to contract out my work. That was a bad time, but I came back to the states and decided to go into the business for myself."

"Where were you overseas?"

"That's still classified."

"What language were you proficient in?"

"That's still classified. Our work is completely confidential. I'm sorry, but if you know the credentials of our staff, then you could make assumptions about our work."

Agent Ridgewood laughed cynically. "Assumptions about your work? Seriously, give us a call if hear anything about Polopolis." The agents stood, closed up their matching notebooks, and waited for David to respond.

"I would be delighted. Here's my card." David walked them to the door. It was an obvious fishing expedition. As soon as he returned, he noticed the tall, thin, Chinese man of about forty sitting on the sofa looking nervously around the room.

"Dr. Gao?"

"Yes sir, are you Mr. Pearl?" Gao had a deep voice with a very slight British accent. He carefully pronounced each word and maintained direct eye contact.

"I am. Come on upstairs. I'd like to talk to you."

Gao squirmed in his loose-fitting, new, navy blue suit. His white socks and brown shoes and a solid black tie and a white, short-sleeved shirt completed his attire. His jacket rode up his long arms almost to the elbow. His head bobbed up and down slowly, but his Adam's apple moved irregularly to a different beat. "Mr. Pearl, I, I, I am so happy to have the opportunity to meet with you."

"Dr. Gao, I am honored to meet with you. You have a most impressive resumé. Can I offer you something to drink?"

Gao smiled and sputtered, "Only if you have green tea; otherwise water would be fine."

"Water we have. I think that we have a job for you. Let me explain what it is that we do, and you can tell me if it's something that interests you, all right?"

"I can do it, whatever it is, sir. As my cousin Zhen, or Vern as he is called now, may have told you, I am a hard worker and have a strong mathematical background. I want to stay here and work."

"Please relax. Vern has been a good friend to me and the company. Here's what we do. We analyze data, tons and tons of data, communications intercepts, computer databases, and we do security analyses for a variety of top secret activities for our government and other agencies as well. Our work is totally confidential and meeting our deadlines for contracts is a hallmark of the firm. Right now, we have agreed to analyze the computer of a corporate analyst who has been determined to be missing. I want to hire you right now as a temp and put you to work on that case. Interested?" Gao's evident sincerity and eager enthusiasm endeared him to David almost immediately. The Ph.D. in econometrics earned at MIT would be a great asset, as well.

Gao expressive face gleamed, and tears rolled down his cheeks. "I am so glad we met, Mr. Pearl. I won't let you down. I was so afraid that my wife and I would have to go back to China. I will stay with Cousin Zhen Chung and work here to get the job done. Thanks so very much."

"Let me get you introduced to the project. My vice-president, Alice Boggs, will provide everything you might need. We have a work station for you up on the third floor. We are so happy that you will be joining us."

"Let me get right to work then, Mr. Pearl."

"Please call me David. I need to talk to Alice for a moment, and she'll be right up to get you oriented and get the information we need for a security clearance."

"Alice can you tell me what the FBI visit was all about? They left me with a bad feeling." David searched Alice's soapstone, grey eyes.

"On the one hand, it was a big nothing, and on the other hand, I think it might have been an opening salvo from an unknown enemy, from somewhere within our intelligence community." Alice quickly ran up the stairs in search of Gao.

CHAPTER 11
The Velocity of Suspicion, February 7

On a cold, rainy day, David answered his office intercom to hear Odette proclaim, "Two FBI agents tell me they need to talk with you, David." Less than a week after the previous visit by the FBI, David found himself with another unannounced visit by the FBI. He resolved to get as much information, this time, as he gave on the last visit. He went downstairs and met them in the reception area with a big smile on his face.

"Hi, I'm lead agent, Robert Woggins." Woggins had deep set eyes, a prominent chin, and ears that protruded outward. His partner stood a few feet apart from him and was younger, slender, and wearing a mild look of curiosity on his face.

Woggins avoided David's proffered hand. David stared back at Woggins's dark eyes. He asked Woggins if he wanted coffee. He did not get an answer.

"Pearl, do you have a private place where we can talk?" Woggins's eyes surveyed everything in the reception area. He waited with what appeared to be a natural sneer on his face and rigid stature.

"Sure, let's go to my conference room. It's right down this hall." David yelled at Odette to hold any calls. Without further polite chatter, David sat abruptly in one of the chairs and began to write himself notes on questions that he wanted resolved about his firm's performance on the various contracts. He thought that it must be one of these contracts that brought these FBI agents into his workplace.

Woggins didn't smile. His forehead was deeply furrowed, as if he was utterly determined about something. He looked David over. David felt like he was being judged and not passing the mark. David watched Woggins visually check out the conference room. When he got to the chair that he had evidently picked out for himself, he dropped his pen. Bending over to pick it up took far longer than it should have. David figured that Woggins was checking for recording devices.

"This conference room is completely secure. We have an outside communications security company that regularly tests our rooms, computers, telephones, and offices." Woggins nodded, then took out his cell phone and took a picture of David. Then he pulled out a small recording device and tested it for recording this interview.

Next, Woggins sat down and opened his notebook. His partner sat at his side with a pad of paper and a poised mechanical pencil. Woggins looked through his notes and, after two minutes of silence, began his interrogation.

"How long were you stationed in Helsinki?"

"Five years, plus or minus a week or two. What is the nature of your investigation?"

"I'll explain that later. What were your responsibilities with the CIA?"

"I'm not permitted to talk about that."

"I am cleared for top secret and beyond."

"Show me."

Woggins laughed. "I don't have to show you shit, Pearl."

"I'm sorry to hear that, Mr. Woggins. If you want an answer, you'll show me."

"I want a list of all your official contacts with the CIA and Department of State."

"You want a lot of things." David put a smile on his face and leaned back in his chair, confident, but curious about where this was going.

"Let me rephrase that so you can understand it, Pearl. Get me a fucking list of all of your official contacts while you were in Helsinki." Woggins leaned toward David suddenly and aggressively. His partner leaned away from Woggins.

David scratched his chin for an itch that didn't exist, then he did a brief drumroll with his pen on the table top. "Go fuck yourself, Woggins."

"This is a matter of national importance. We can take you back to the office, where perhaps you'll be able to be more responsive."

"I'm not going anywhere. I'm not going to accompany you on your quest for volumes of information you may not be cleared to hear, either."

"Get up. Let's go."

"You don't understand." David felt his temper warring with his natural instinct to stay calm.

Woggins smiled a tense smile. "You like giving the orders, don't you, Pearl? Stand up." David did so, but in slow motion. Woggins put handcuffs on David's wrists. Then, he shoved David out into and down the hall. As he was pushed out the front door, David yelled to Odette to call Alice.

At the FBI Regional office in Washington, DC, David sat in an interrogation room for two hours before someone checked on him. He asked for a cup of black coffee. That was quickly delivered.

Right after the coffee arrived, Woggins entered the room with an older man dressed in a dark brown suit, yellow shirt, and tie. The man's suit fit him perfectly, a sharp contrast to Woggins's appearance. The man in the brown suit reached for Pearl's hand and shook it warmly.

Then Woggins and his apparent superior settled themselves into the metal chairs across the small table from where David sat. Woggins stared at David. The man in the brown suit was smiling and carefully examining a small file containing about twenty sheets of paper that he held in his hands. Finally, he looked up.

"David, I'm Fred Winstead. I'm in charge of the Washington Regional FBI office. Special Agent Woggins has been working the highly sensitive case of the murder of Cardiff Shapiro. What he is doing is cross checking all of the contacts for the past three years with the late undersecretary of state for terrorism and financial investigations, Dr. Cardiff Shapiro. You and Dr. Shapiro were in Helsinki for a few days at the same time."

"I was in Helsinki for five years. I worked for the CIA as a listener. I listened and sent reports of anything interesting. I was in charge of nothing and no one. If Cardiff Shapiro was in Helsinki, I never saw him and certainly had no dealings with him. Prior to reading his obituary in the Washington Post, my only awareness of him was due to my firm's contracts in the national security arena." The FBI and everyone else must be scouring the records, searching for any possible link between Shapiro and the reason for his assassination. If they are talking to me at this point, they must not be making much progress.

"We are aware that your job was outsourced, so you would naturally have an attitude that you were betrayed by your former employers, the CIA."

"That's because I was betrayed. A lot of us were. I decided to continue my career in intelligence as a contractor in the national security and intelligence fields. I think that anyone whose job is outsourced would feel disowned and lied to. And, that's how I feel."

"You are working in the same business that Cardiff Shapiro was engaged in. Do you hear any rumors out there?"

"I have contacts in the State Department, NSA, Homeland Security, and the CIA. I have friends in other firms and agencies. What I have heard is that Dr. Shapiro's murder leaves a huge void in intelligence leadership. By all accounts, he was a fine human being. If I do hear anything, I'll let you know without a doubt."

"We don't like coincidences, nor do we believe in them, Mr. Pearl." Winstead leaned forward, his eyes fixed on David.

David considered a moment before responding. "I don't like them either. But, if you are insinuating that I had anything to do with Shapiro's murder, you are wasting your time and mine."

"Anything at all could have happened between you and Dr. Shapiro in Helsinki, unofficially of course, off the record kind of thing."

David tilted his head and raised one corner of his mouth in a small sign of annoyance. "I understand that I will remain under suspicion, but the reality is this: I worked for the CIA. When I was in Helsinki, my status was somewhat lower than that of a junior gremlin. There would be no reason for Shapiro even to know of my existence. I didn't see Shapiro in the rest room, or the hall, or outside the shop."

Winstead had closed his eyes. Woggins still stood at attention in the corner of the room.

"Your associate, Alice Boggs, is waiting for you outside with a solicitor. You are free to go, but of course, our investigation into this matter is only just begun." Having said this, Winstead huddled with Agent Woggins. David walked out of the office, unescorted. Alice was waiting for him on the sidewalk with Suzy Stordahl, his contracting officer. Suzy Stordahl was skinny in a black sheath dress, bag, shoes, and big brown eyes that seemed to take everything and everyone in.

"Suzy, are you my solicitor?"

"She's all we could get on short notice, David." The three of them laughed and hugged as they walked toward the van.

Chapter 12
Tempest in Tarpon Springs, March 2

David was sleeping on the office sofa on the first floor reception area. He had been working hard to complete the analytic review for the MagnaMeta contract. His dreams were troubled with all kinds of mistakes in the data, missing deadlines, and fitfully waking up in sweaty panics. This time, he was awakened by the office phone ringing incessantly. He fell off the sofa trying to get his limbs coordinated after twenty hours of office work and what amounted to about three hours of sleep. Fumbling the receiver out of its niche, David finally brought the phone to his ear.

"Thank God. I need to talk to someone. Somebody's got to help me." Ike Zisis's unmistakable voice was harsh and demanding.

David's brain started to clear, the images of Zisis and Polopolis eventually coming to the forefront in his mind. "Mr. Zisis, this is David Pearl. What can I do for you?" It was 5:25 AM. David walked to the front window and pulled the drapes back. The open space in front of his building revealed that this part of the world was unchanged from the day before: The cars were parked in every available, conceivable space. The Hispanic construction workers were already walking along the sidewalk on their way to a job site, toting their large coolers of food and drink for what, for them, would be a long day. Homeless people were gathered over a grate for heat.

"Pearl, I need your help. Polopolis has been staying with us down here in Florida. I woke up this morning to find him gone. Also gone are all my cash, my credit cards, my Lexus, and my lap top computer."

"I'm sorry for all of that, Mr. Zisis, but I am not aware of how I can help."

"You know the crazy son of a bitch. You tracked him down once, and you can do it again."

"I had a contract to provide protection and security for Polopolis. You know he's mentally disturbed. He's very paranoid. He escaped from the Greek government security as he was about to be put on a plane back to Greece. As soon as he showed up down there, you should have notified the Greek government."

"Bullshit. He's family. My wife always wanted to help him because he's family. That was a big mistake. My guys are occupied with business at the moment. Can you help me or not?"

"That depends, Mr. Zisis."

"On what, for Christ's sake?"

"Money, time, and what it is you want."

"I want you to find him and get my stuff back."

"I assume you want the utmost in discretion. You won't contact the local police and have no intention of notifying the Greek government."

"You got that right."

"Give me your fax number." David wrote it down. "I will fax you my standard agreement. On it, I want you to state exactly what it is that you want DRPearl, Inc to accomplish. My fee is $3,000 per day, plus expenses. You are contracting with the DRPearl, Inc for security services at that rate. Fax that agreement back to my office right now. Write down your address, license plate number, and the registration number and description of the computer and anything else that's missing. Cancel your credit cards. I'll be down there this afternoon. I'll come to your house, and we'll talk some more then."

David called Demetrios. Demetrios's voice was soft and slow, which David knew meant he was depressed or hung-over. He'd have to carefully state his concerns. David explained the situation. Demetrios called the embassy security director for guidance. He was advised to sit tight for the time being.

David was pacing at the gate for the flight to Tampa when his cell phone rang.

"Hi, David, this is Sophia. Please meet me at the Tampa airport." She provided David with the flight number. Then, she clicked off.

After striking out with his Marines due to the short notice, David carefully considered his remaining options. When approached, Abdul Choudri, the part-time translator and analyst, jumped at the chance to accompany David to Florida. David knew that he needed backup to deal with Polopolis, and while Abdul was not trained in surveillance or physical security, he was solidly muscular, a quick learner, and intuitively intelligent.

They had two hours to kill while waiting for Sophia. David and Abdul casually walked through all of long-term and short-term parking. Ike Zisis's Lexus was not there. Abdul waited in short-term parking in the rental car. David waited at the exit that Sophia's flight's passengers would use to get to baggage claim. He spotted her athletic, self-confident strides before his eyes connected with her face. She smiled. He smiled back, realizing that this woman had emotionally attracted him in a way that he had not ever experienced before.

She walked up to him. They hugged. Her lips gently brushed his cheek, thrilling and momentarily stunning David. She brought her right trigger finger to her lips in the 'silence please' gesture. Without talking, they walked to short-term parking.

Once in the car, David briefed Sophia. "I am going to Ike Zisis's house in Tarpon Springs. You want to ride along, or should we drop you off somewhere else?"

Sophia was no longer the aloof and cold special agent. Her smile radiated nearly continuously, and she made frequent glances in David's direction. "Of course, I want to go with you. I want to find Polopolis as much as you."

"So, are you here officially?"

"Sure, but Zisis doesn't need to know that. It'll go better if I'm a mystery to him. All Zisis needs to know is I'm Sophia."

As soon as they entered Tarpon Springs, David called Zisis to let him know that they would be there in five minutes.

Zisis gruffly answered, "Finally."

They soon pulled into the circular driveway. The house was a sprawling, ranch style, concrete-block structure. Like the rest of the houses on the short street, it was painted in loud, tropical colors. Zisis's house was banana yellow. David asked Abdul to stay outside, to walk around, but be ready to roll out on short notice.

David pushed the bell. Zisis threw the door open and motioned them to come in. At the same time, his eyes thoroughly reviewed Sophia, slowly reviewing her curves. He led them into a glassed-in room in the back of the house. The windows revealed a large swimming pool and beyond that, the waters of Tarpon Bay. They were asked to sit. They declined a drink offer. Zisis drank from a green beer bottle.

"Very nice house, Ike. This place is quite a contrast to your home in Montreal. This is my partner on this case, Sophia."

"Sure, pleased to meet you. Yeah, we get down here every chance we get. The fucking winters in Canada are too long and cold for an old man. Here's the inventory you wanted, Pearl. He's got my gold and silver coins, so the bastard can run for a long time. Just pull into a coin shop and sell one or two. No questions asked. Nico may be crazy, but he's not stupid. Listen, you got to find him and fast."

David nodded as he scanned the list. "Where do you think Nico will go?"

"I think he'll go to some resort and spend my money. He kept saying that he just wanted to chill out."

"Did he have any friends while he was here? Did he hang out with anyone in particular?"

"I don't know. All I do know is that he bought golf clubs, an expensive bag, and a few hundred golf balls on my card before I got it canceled, so I'd say he's planning on playing golf."

"Okay, great, that gives us a place to start. Where did he buy the clubs and when?"

"Two days ago, at the Inverness Golf Club and Resort. That's not too far from here."

"Okay, let's start looking for Nico, Sophia." They got up and left Zisis sulking in his white wicker chair, nested in his tropical paradise themed Florida room.

After checking out the Inverness Resort, David, Abdul, and Sophia went to the Greek sponge diving tourist area along the Auclote River. They settled into a bar that fronted the river. They sat staring out at the water and the boats lining the retaining walls. They discussed and planned their next move. David relaxed and briefly recounted his personal history with Polopolis. Once in a while, an intrusive thought would pop into his mind that he wanted to get to know Sophia a lot better. He would need to explore this undesired diversion from his ordinarily sharply focused mind. For David, this was a pleasant, new, and slightly unsettling development.

Sophia was quiet. She seemed to be content to listen to them talk and watch the other people in the bar.

Abdul stayed focused on David. "I'm excited. We graduate students don't often get to stay at a real resort area." He nervously played with the plastic straw, tying it into ever-tighter knots.

"Abdul, business takes us to where the client needs us to go. Remember, last time it was Montreal and freezing." Sophia sat in such a way that her hip brushed against David.

Sophia turned her head toward Abdul. "What are you studying in graduate school, Abdul?"

Abdul returned her smile. "I am working on a doctorate in applied financial research." He went on in some detail to explain his thesis and its importance.

David, Sophia, and Abdul went walking in the tourist area of Tarpon Springs. David enjoyed Abdul's fresh exuberance and Sophia's charming observations, but he worried and tried to strategize the fragments of Polopolis: the known, the unknown, and the conjecture. And that left him feeling like he was on a mystery tour of, perhaps, grave consequences.

David's small team returned to their suite at the Inverness Resort. The suite was spacious, with two bedrooms, kitchen and family room. He asked Abdul to call golf courses and coin shops the next day. Sophia and he would start at the pro shop at Inverness, and from there, improvise.

CHAPTER 13
A Narrow Escape, March 4 and 5

The occupants of the office townhouse of DRPearl Inc. worked into the night of March 4. Gao and Alice labored away on the third floor. Odette was making copies on the first floor. The other employees had, over the last few hours, drifted out, heading home. The knocking at the door surprised Odette, who felt a cold shiver throughout her body. She went to the door and peeped out.

Outside on their little stoop, stood the flower lady. She was smiling and holding out a bouquet of roses, indicating the roses were for someone in the office. Odette opened the three locks on the front door. When she opened the door, two men with pistols in their hands burst in, knocking her to the side. She ran out and saw the flower lady had her skirt up in one hand, sprinting away. The bouquet lay on the sidewalk.

Odette ran to Stoney's Bar. "Please, call the police," she begged the bartender. His eyes widened, but he did as she asked while Odette huddled in her seat. When she heard sirens, Odette walked back, stopping behind a panel van, so she could observe the front door of the office. She crouched down, nervously watching everything around her for a minute or two. Her breathing had become gasps for air, and her arms were wrapped tightly around her chest.

Suddenly, Odette watched Taz Washington and his partner, Neal Walters, sprint down the sidewalk and burst through the front door. She quickly ran after them, watching Taz lunge into a man, knocking him backwards. A second man stopped and held up his hands. Walters relieved the man of his PK Walther pistol.

Neal Walters slammed him into the wall. "You two are under arrest. My partner will remove everything from your pockets. Do you have anything that might hurt him?" Uniformed officers arrived and immediately moved to secure the building.

With their hands cuffed behind their backs, one man sat in the first floor conference room, and the other was separated from him on the reception area sofa. The uniformed officers brought Alice and Gao to the kitchen. Odette nervously stood at the kitchen counter, sipping hot tea, slyly looking around. Gao offered everyone green tea which they all declined. With watery eyes, Odette looked from Gao to Alice and back again.

Taz and Neal walked into the kitchen where the employees were huddled. Taz hugged Odette, and she began to cry softly.

Taz gently pulled away from Odette. "I know you've had quite a scare. Are you guys doing alright?" Taz motioned for Neal to get coffee.

Alice held her hands in front of her on the table. "We're fine. I didn't see them. They grabbed Gao and kept asking him 'Where is it?'"

Taz looked to Gao. "That's right. They kept asking, 'Where is the agreement? Where is it?' They threw me to the floor and sat on my chest. I spoke, but only in Chinese, pretending that I didn't know any English. When they heard the siren, they ran down the stairs. But before they reached the second floor, I threw a cardboard box full of copy paper at them. It hit the second one on the stairs, and he fell into the other one. Both of them fell, but they quickly scrambled up, and that's when you came in."

Alice looked up. "Gao, here, is our hero. The office has been under surveillance by Greek gangsters before. We worked on a contract from the Greek embassy, and that's when we encountered this Greek mob, but we were told whatever concerned them had been resolved."

"Yeah, I certainly agree the guys we talked to out on the street that day were mobsters. Okay, we're glad you're doing all right. Nothing is missing. I think we should call this a home invasion, of sorts. How'd they get in?"

Odette nervously told them, "Okay, we should be looking for the neighborhood flower lady. She rang the doorbell and saw her through the peephole, standing there with a bouquet of roses. When I opened the door, the gangsters burst in, the flower lady took off, and I ran to Stoney's. We really appreciate you guys getting here so fast."

We were in the neighborhood when we heard the call. I don't know if we'll stay on this case, but rest assured, we'll follow up on it." Taz looked alert and excited. Neal Walters appeared to be about to fall asleep.

"We are fine, Taz. Thank you so much." Alice was now shaking. "We are so glad you got here so soon. I shudder to think what would have happened."

A uniformed police sergeant came into the kitchen. "We are hauling these two to jail. They are under arrest for breaking and entering and resisting arrest. According to their identification, the two are Andreas Chitzou and Vassillis Gadis." He handed a piece of paper to Taz.

"Thanks for your statements. We'll be back in touch. If you see these two guys again, call us immediately. Sleepy and I have a long night ahead of us."

Odette called David and relayed the evening's crisis. David listened to Odette for a few moments. "Oh my God, those fucking Greeks, Harry Markos promised me that he had pulled them off my case. I'll figure out a way to pay that bastard back. I'll go back to see Zisis tomorrow. I'm so sorry, Odette. Tell the others we are going to proceed much more carefully now." He carefully wrote down the names of the two men who were arrested. "Thanks, Odette. Get one of our marines to sleepover in the office for the next few days. Thanks for calling." David went out into the night, walking and thinking that he needed to get tougher and smarter.

CHAPTER 14
Still Life with Flamingos, March 6

In the morning, at 7:30, David and Sophia quietly got ready, drank coffee, and left Abdul working the phone.

David and Sophia parked in front of the pro shop. Inside, the golf gear, shirts, and other clothes and accessory displays cluttered the available space. The sales clerk was talking on her cell phone. When she saw David and Sophia, she jumped down from her perch on a high stool behind the counter.

"Hi, we are private investigators. We're looking for a man named Nicolaos Polopolis. He's about six foot, one inch." Sophia spoke softly, but authoritatively in her, quite nearly, unaccented English.

The clerk cut her off. "I remember very well. He's a flirt, flamboyant, and seemed to be refreshingly friendly and nice. He was well-spoken and polite."

David interrupted her. "When was he in here, and what did he say while he was here?"

The young lady across the counter from David frowned. "Yesterday afternoon, about 1:15 or so. He said that he was going to sign up for lessons, but he didn't. I gave him a tee time." She peered at her computer screen and hit two keys. "As a matter of fact, he should have teed off fifteen minutes on the Hibiscus Course."

"And where would be the first hole for the Hibiscus Course?"

"As you go out the front door, turn right, follow the cart path. The first hole is located immediately behind this building." David flashed a quick smile and a wave of his hand as he and Sophia headed out.

On their way to the golf course, Sophia took David's hand. He felt a wave of warmth come over him along with the pleasant surprise. They followed the cart path to the first hole. David studied the group just then reaching the green. "Nico is not in that foursome. Let's walk along the path to see if he played through them or started out early." David and Sophia studied the golfers. After they walked five holes, they became convinced that Polopolis was not on the course.

David playfully suggested a break. "Coming over yesterday, I saw a sign for Honeymoon Island. I'd like to check it out, if you agree."

"Sure, sounds like fun." So, David drove them to Honeymoon Island. His priorities were now a little jumbled by his emerging feelings for Sophia. They took off their shoes and walked in the surf. When they stopped to examine some shell or a passing boat, David looked into her eyes and thought how unbearably grateful he was to have this beautiful, intelligent woman at his side. After an hour on the beach and a brief romantic kiss, Sophia pulled away from David. David felt a surge of wonderment. Could one brief kiss mean everything like it felt right now to him?

Sophia turned toward the ocean. "I think that we should revisit Ike Zisis."

David agreed.

The Tarpon Springs residential areas nearest the water are bounded by bayous and creeks meandering to the river or the bay. David pulled into Zisis's driveway, and they went to the front door. No one answered the bell or David's hard knock on the door. They separated, each going around one side of the house, meeting in the backyard. David tried the back door. When it didn't open, he stepped aside, deferring to Sophia, who pulled out a thin-bladed pocketknife and quickly slipped the lock and the bolt. No one was inside. They decided to investigate the house and wait for Zisis to return.

After finding no one home, David made a pot of coffee and systematically searched the kitchen, dining room, and the garage. Sophia began her search in a room clearly set up to be an office. She made numerous copies, and downloaded files from the computer. David searched the rest of the house, three bedrooms, and the Florida room. He found two Ruger SR9C pistols, one in a nightstand in the master bedroom and one in a kitchen drawer under the hand towels. He found nothing else of interest other than the photographs that crowded the hallway walls and sat on top of many of the dressers and chests. He studied the family photographs while sitting on the white wicker couch in the Florida room. There were no pictures of Polopolis, but he did find Zisis and Markos in several. He slipped several photographs of Zisis and Markos, in various social groupings, out of their frames and into his notebook.

The bay, forty feet behind the house, was dark blue, with an occasional whitecap forming as a result of the wind blowing in from the Northwest. The aquamarine pool glistened in the direct sunshine. There were numerous plastic flamingos on long pink metal legs, stuck in the grass and landscaping.

They heard a car enter the carport, a door open and close. In the next minute Ike Zisis came walking into the Florida room at 3 PM. "What the fuck are you doing here?"

David firmly responded, "Sit down, Ike. We need to talk."

"What about? How did you get in here?" Ike stood at the glass door leading to the pool. He was angry. David got up and firmly led him to the chair opposite the sofa.

"What have you been doing?" Zisis twisted out of David's grasp.

"Playing golf, like I do every day when I am in Florida."

"Where did you play?"

"At the Inverness Resort, like always. Today I played the Hibiscus Course, not well. For some fucking reason, I started topping my drives. I need to get more practice, maybe some lessons."

"See anybody you know?"

"As a matter of fact, no. I played with two guests staying at the resort. Sometimes I match up with people. What does this have to do with anything? You can quit this star chamber routine right now. You're supposed to be looking for my nephew, Polopolis."

"You'll be pleased to know that your nephew was supposed to be on the Hibiscus Course this morning, as well."

"Really?" Zisis didn't look too shocked to David.

"Really. Why don't you level with us, right now?"

"I don't know what you're talking about! I'm paying you to find him. Why would I do that if I knew where the fuck he was?"

Sophia interjected, "Ike, tell us slowly and carefully everything you know about your nephew. If I get the feeling that you are leaving anything out, I'll arrange for the Greek government to put a hold on all your funds in Greece. That wouldn't do much good for your shipping fleet."

"Who the fuck are you? Really?" He glared at Sophia.

"It's way better that you don't know, but please understand that you must not make a mistake with me or David. If we walk out of here without answers, we will report what we have learned to the authorities."

Zisis laughed. "Fuck the authorities."

"Now, Ike, you know you don't mean that." Sophia laughed gently, and she was calm and successful in staring Zisis down.

"I don't get it." Ike attempted to get to his feet. David, far quicker, reached him, put a hand on his chest, and pushed him back down.

"Ike, you've paid me for three days' work. Yesterday evening, my office was broken into by two of your thugs. They're now under arrest for breaking and entering. Your nephew has cost me a lot of time and money. Your man, Harry Markos in Washington, told me that your thugs were no longer on my case. You can begin your tale with why the thugs were in my office and what they were looking for."

Zisis's brow furrowed with deep worry lines, and his eyes tightened into slits. "Those assholes. I wanted that agreement I signed back. I was having second thoughts. I told Harry you weren't there. All I wanted is that agreement canceled. Nico called me late last night and said he wanted to make things right between us. So, I talked to Nico at the course this morning. He seems more composed. He just wants to play golf. He has that bug, along with whatever else is wrong with him. He says he wants to get his pro card. He had the golf bug before his nervous breakdown, or whatever it was. His wife argued with him all the time about it. I thought he would grow up. I don't think that's going to happen." Ike laughed again.

"Is he good enough to be a pro? He's almost fifty." Sophie said.

"No, a fool and his money, or my money, or our money, are soon parted. He lives in some delusional fairyland. I guess that's better than reality for him. To give him his due, he shoots in the mid to high seventies for eighteen, pretty consistently. I think he'd be wasting his time, and I told him that."

"Living the dream, huh? Now, Ike, I need some damages money. Why don't you write me a check for about fifteen thousand? That'll give my three employees enough bonus money so that maybe they won't file charges. We will find Polopolis, Ike. You can count on that." David threw Ike's checkbook into his lap.

"I need something to drink." Ike looked downcast and began slaping his checkbook against his thigh.

Sophie responded, "I'll get you a cold beer."

"You bastards know where I keep my checkbook? Fuck this." Ike's face reddened, and the vein above his right eye suddenly became more visible.

"Write the check, Ike. And, while you're writing the check, tell me about your missing assets. Did your golf buddy return your money, car, and the rest of it?"

"This is blackmail. I'm not telling you shit."

"No, it isn't. And you damn sure better tell me. What happened in the last twenty-four hours that changed your mind about getting your stuff back?"

Ike waited until Sophia returned with the beer. He took a big swallow. He had started sweating and clenching his jaw. "Nico arranged for a transfer of funds to pay me back. He has plenty of money; he just doesn't like to spend it."

"Where is the Mrs., Ike?"

"She's at the Greek Orthodox Church. She is lay presenter, or some shit like that. Counsels the heathens and the sinners. She likes to hold their hands and see the dying off to the promised land."

"Where is Nico?"

"Honest to God, I don't know. The son of gun knows that I play golf nearly every day at Inverness. He moves around. He is paranoid as hell. I told Stella to forget about helping him. I could buy a yacht for what he's taken us for." Ike slowly wrote the check. When he finished, he pursed his lips and waved it at David.

"Something doesn't add up, Ike. You just said there was a transfer of funds. And what about your car and coin collection?"

"I told Nico that he could keep the car. He promised to return the coins. Nico needs his wife to co-sign, or Harry Markos. Most of the time, his wife won't, and Harry won't sign unless she agrees."

Sophia stared down at her notes. "We took the liberty of copying some of your files, the financials mostly, and copied everything on your computer. In fact, one of your corporations appears to own a yacht. Let's see, the Kirie Pondiki. And you just said you could buy a yacht for what Polopolis took you for. Do I have that right? But, you already have one. And it seems like Nico is a shareholder in your shipping line, a large shareholder."

"He is, but those dividends go into that trust fund bank account in Greece. He doesn't want to go back there, and I think he'd just as soon live off other people's money. Find him, and kick him in the ass for me." Ike was now looking pale and smaller, slipping down further into the cushions. He seemed sad and worried. David and Sophia stood up.

"Ike, we have to go now. Why don't you call Harry Markos and tell him to expect me? Don't stop payment on that check, or I'll be back. And, Ike, just to let you know, I don't think all the interest in me is about your nephew. Maybe you can think real hard and tell me what that is?"

"You got information that I need."

"What information would that be, Ike?"

"We lost a man, a good man, and maybe you did it."

"Pelakanos? I didn't do it, and I don't know who did. Your nephew is our leading suspect."

"He didn't do it."

"Okay, then, what else could there be? Maybe when we go through your records in detail, we'll find out." David leaned forward, holding his hands together, pointing to Ike.

Sophia sat at the edge of the sofa, alert and defiant. "And then, after we have given all our intelligence to the various governmental entities that would be interested in some of your shadier business affairs, we might even come back to continue our discussion," Sophia added. She and David went out the back door, walked to the edge of the bay. They stood there briefly, enjoying the view. When they turned, they found Ike staring out at them. They didn't bother waving.

They drove back to the Inverness Resort and their suite. Walking into the building housing their suite, David put his hand gently on Sophia's shoulder. "I think we should go to dinner at one of the Greek restaurants along the river.

Sophia glanced at David. "No, I think we should let Abdul pick. He's been inside all day, talking to strangers on the phone."

They found the door to the suite slightly ajar. They cautiously entered the suite. Sophia pulled a small pistol out of her purse, dropping into a shooter's crouch, with the pistol aimed in front of her toward the floor. They waited at the door for a few moments, listening carefully for any sounds of danger. David began to slowly edge into the suite, turning just his head around the wall blocking the view of the kitchen. He saw Abdul tied to a kitchen chair, with dried blood on his face and in his hair. He had also wet his pants.

"Abdul, I am so sorry. I feel terrible about this." David genuinely felt hurt and responsible for what happened to Abdul.

Sophia cut the plastic cords off him. With a wet towel, David gently washed his face and hair. Sophia massaged his wrists. They led him to the shower. Abdul took off his clothes and gratefully stepped in.

Washed, in clean clothes, and with a cold beer in his hand, Abdul told his story. "Well, guys, I was chatting with a nice man at the biggest coin shop, according to him, in Tampa, when at about 11:30 AM, the doorbell rang and I went to the door and opened it. Standing there in front of me was, I was pretty sure, Nicolaos Polopolis. Polopolis had a pistol, pushed me back, and tied me to the chair. He wanted to know where you were. After I refused to tell him, he pistol whipped me, like almost for kicks."

Sophia listened intently. "So we can add sociopathic to the list of Nico's traits."

Abdul placed the cold beer bottle up against his cheek. "Yeah, I would agree to that. Anyway, all of the calls were fruitless. Nico isn't known by any of the coin dealers that I talked to. Maybe we should try to pawn shops."

David leaned back on the sofa. "No, that isn't necessary now. Zisis told us this afternoon that Polopolis had promised to return the coins and everything else, but I think Zisis is a fool if he believes him."

"Polopolis said several times that he wanted to talk to you, David. That's it." Abdul drained the remainder of his beer. "I'm starving. Let's go to this Columbia restaurant in Ybor City, in Tampa."

In the living room, there was a large mirror between portraits of a stork, stalking along a riverbank, and a heron hunting fish, while wading in a marsh. Written, with a blue, felt-tip, marker, in an unsteady hand, were the words, "Quit screwing with me," and a telephone number. David called the number and left a message for Nico to call him back. David thought, right then, that this was getting a little too personal for comfort.

During dinner, Odette called. "David, all your credit cards are blown." David pulled out his wallet and saw that the cards were still there. "Somebody stole the numbers, David, so I have canceled them. Also, MagnaMeta wants a face-to-face. They are insistent and say that it's urgent."

"Odette, I know it's Polopolis. He's a slippery devil. How's everybody?"

"All is well, except for Alice. She's been drunk for two days. She's upstairs now, hopefully sleeping it off."

"I'm sorry to hear about Alice. When she wakes up, make sure she eats something decent, and make her drink plenty of non-alcoholic fluids. Abdul had a rough day. I'll fill you all in when I get home. You should see me tomorrow about noon. Set up that meeting with MagnaMeta. Thanks again."

On the drive back to the suite from the restaurant, David took a call from Demetrios. David briefly explained their lack of success. Demetrios could barely be heard because of electronic noises clicking and clacking in the background. David figured those for the sounds of the embassy's recording and encoding system.

"David, I'll brief the embassy tomorrow. Maybe, they'll want me to come back to Florida to try and find Polopolis. Anyway, the embassy wants to meet with you and discuss a contract." David clicked his phone off, discouraged at his lack of interest in another contract from the Greek embassy, and his feeling that Polopolis still posed a threat.

CHAPTER 15
Nevzlin v. McKay, March 6 and 7

Mee Maw McKay sat at her dining room table. She was plotting her evening and enjoying this moment at dusk, when she would look at the view out of her rear picture window. Tonight, there were, as usual, three white-tailed deer that came stealthily out of the bordering woods, to eat the apples that she left there for them. Mee Maw patiently watched the three does step daintily out onto her lawn. They munched contentedly as the shadows deepened, but they were vigilant in their surveillance for possible danger.

Mee Maw was vigilant also. She kept her Browning 22 rifle and Mossberg 20-gauge shotgun locked in a broom closet by the back door. She wouldn't shoot a deer, but she would shoot a wild turkey, or a wild dog, or someone attempting to break in.

She was a retired elementary school principal, a widow now for more than twenty years. Her only son had retired from the Navy and lived with a friend in Key West. He didn't visit very often, but she wrote letters to him often, sent clipped articles to him to keep him up to date on his hometown, and loved him with a quiet, but fierce resolution. She didn't have any grandchildren, but she doted on the children in the neighborhood, and they on her. She would often do little favors for them. Favors like making a Halloween costume, or baking her special chocolate chip cookies, or helping them with their homework. Sometimes on a cold winter day after school, she would make her special hot chocolate for them. And sometimes, she would make them read to her.

Mee Maw had plans for that evening. She would be going out into the woods. She would follow the trail that she had been making. The trail followed along the inside edge of the woods. She had marked the trail with little strips of pink, fluorescent cloth. The ridgeline where she lived dropped off sharply to a creek far below. She needed the trail to be marked because she would be using it in the dark. The little housing development where she lived followed the very top of that ridgeline. Her plan was to walk the trail until she arrived behind the Russian's house. Then, she would climb the persimmon tree until she was eye level with the Russian's windows. Once there, she would spend a couple of hours spying on the bastard.

Mee Maw left her house shortly after dark. She left the kitchen and dining room lights on, so she would have a beacon to guide her return back. She took with her a small, pen flashlight, her new, powerful binoculars, a granola bar, and a small bottle of water. She walked deliberately and quietly, and without any delay found her persimmon tree. With her items in a backpack, she climbed the tree. Mee Maw was pleased with her health and grateful for all the years of Tai Chi and Yoga.

The Russian was in his back bedroom, the one that he used for an office. He sat steadily working at the computer, gazing intently at the monitor. Mee Maw used the computers at the senior center for fun, but the Russian seemed to be actually doing some kind of work on his. After about thirty minutes, he got up, went to the kitchen, and poured himself a cup of water, put a tea bag in it, and microwaved it. He returned to his computer.

Mee Maw enjoyed the evening despite not being able to determine what it was that the Russian was actually doing. He was reclusive, a loner, hiding something, and she was determined to find out what. After an hour, comfortable that she had seen enough of his routine, she slipped down the tree and walked boldly to his trashcan. She took out the two bags of trash and carried them back down the trail to her house. Tomorrow morning, she would go through his trash. Maybe that would provide the hard evidence that she needed to convince the authorities to investigate the man.

The next morning, she backed out her ten-year-old Toyota, parked it in the driveway, and closed the garage door behind her. She went back outside to supervise the loading of the school bus. Sometimes she would talk with mothers about their children, the school, or the town. Today, the mothers stayed inside their homes, watching the kids through their living room windows. Once the kids were off to school, she returned to the garage to sort through the Russian's trash.

Mee Maw set up her card table and placed her white, plastic, kitchen trash can beside it. Wearing clear plastic gloves, she gently pulled items from the bag that were of no intelligence value. She carefully placed the garbage into a plastic bag. In addition, however, there was a lot of shredded paper. Mee Maw carefully set these paper strips aside. She pulled out a window envelope with the return address of the BB&T bank branch in Charleston. She found Styrofoam peanut packing materials, plastic that once shrink-protected some device or other in shipping. She completed the search through the two bags, put the trash out in her bin, and returned to work on the shreds.

At 2 PM, she took a break. As was her usual routine, she walked the length of Skyview Drive. She turned left out of the front of her house and then after a half block, onto Skyview. Skyview meandered along the ridge top for a mile and a half. She fast-walked through this thoroughly familiar group of houses, the smaller ones side by side and the larger ones set on a half-acre or an acre. She noted any changes in the houses or the yards. She waved to anyone whom she saw watching her. She kept walking, her sneakers marching briskly along the road. At the end, she would abruptly turn around and repeat the process in reverse.

She was about halfway back down Skyview when she saw the Russian's black SUV pull out of his driveway and motor away, down the hill toward town. When she got to his house, she decided that she might as well look around. She found all the doors locked. She realized that a neighbor might be watching her, and while she did not fear that they would talk to the Russian, they might confront her. So she went to the back of the house, safe from view of any of the neighbors who might be looking out their window, and looked into the house through each of the windows in the back of the house.

Not seeing anything out of the ordinary, she next looked around the separate, free standing, double garage. She tried the back door and found it unlocked. She entered and looked around. He had lots of tools, including power tools, neatly arranged on the walls and on the open, wooden shelving. She found a stack of magazines on the workbench. They were issues of the house journal of a company called InfoSystel. She pulled out the waistband of her skirt and stuck three magazines beneath her skirt and sweater. Then, she went back outside and was quickly on her way to finishing her walk.

The InfoSystel house journal was entitled, Intelligence We Trust. She spent the rest of the afternoon reading the journals and trying to figure out what exactly was being said in its highly technical articles.

But, she found the most important detail: the man's name on the address label, Viktor Nevzlin. She drove down to the senior citizens' center and Googled the name. There were a couple of Nevzlins that popped up in her search, but she quickly determined that neither of them was her detested neighbor.

She fixed her supper, a tuna casserole with green peas. She made enough for three meals, eating one portion and freezing two. She watched the news on television. She went back out into the garage and began sorting through the strips of paper piled on top of her card table. She sorted all of the strips into two piles, one for Russian and one for English. When that was done, she allowed herself a glass of red wine, read a few pages in her latest English murder mystery, and went to bed.

The next morning, Mee Maw was eating a banana nut muffin, when her doorbell rang. She went to the door and opened it. Before her stood Viktor Nevzlin, who had a stern, disapproving look on his face.

"Hi, there, what can I do for you?" Mee Maw kept her tone strong, though her legs trembled. She wondered how she had been caught.

Nevzlin stood back from the door. Mee Maw came out and closed the door behind her. At five foot, six inches, she had to look up at the tall Russian. She figured him for about six foot, two or three inches, and in his late fifties or maybe early sixties. They stood facing each other, three feet apart, their eyes in constant contact. He wore a potent, cloying cologne.

She frowned at Nevzlin. "What can I do for you, neighbor?"

"You can quit sneaking around my house. And, you can return the journals that you stole from my garage," he said. His accent was not thick.

"What makes you think I sneak around your house?"

"Because I have you on videotape inside my garage."

"Why do you have security cameras? Are you afraid of your neighbors?"

"I live my life the way I choose to. I want to be safe. Why does it matter to you?"

"Okay, I won't sneak around your house. But, I don't trust you."

"That simply doesn't matter." The Russian abruptly walked off Mee Maw's porch and back to his house.

Mee Maw took down the West Virginia flag from the pole that angled off from a column on her tiny front porch. She put up her tan and brown cookie flag. The neighborhood's children knew that meant they could have one of Mee Maw's cookies when they got off the bus, and maybe another one later, after their homework was done.

Chapter 16
Dirty Lowdown, March 7

David walked from his office to K Street, where lobbyists, powerful law firms, and a few of the intelligence corporations kept offices. The rich and powerful associations and corporations doing business with the federal government also located most of their government operations on K Street, or as near to it as possible. He quickly found Markos's office and joined a group of people who were collectively marching back into the building.

He knew he looked like he belonged with this crowd, wearing the uniform that signaled membership in the club of highly-paid executives, lawyers, and lobbyists: a paisley, striped, silk tie, worn with a long-sleeved dress shirt, and a crisply tailored dark suit. The highly polished shoes and the confident expression were also found on many of those whose incomes provided ample security and financial comfort. He got off on the third floor.

Markos's office was inside a frosted glass front that ran along the outside corridor of the building. The gilt lettering boldly printed on the door announced the firm of Markos and Associates. David tried the door and found it open. No one sat at reception. After waiting for a couple of minutes, he jumped onto the counter, then slid to the edge before landing softly on his feet, on the inside of the reception area. He looked around on the countertop. He found the office schedules and learned that Harry should be in his office. He placed the stack of documents awaiting the shredder into the trashcan liner he pulled from the dark grey metal can.

David saw he had three doors to choose from. He tried the middle door. It led into an empty conference room. The door on the left opened onto a corridor. He stepped into it. Smiling and looking confident, he passed a young lady who looked at him quizzically, but kept on walking and entered the open corridor on the right. Alone, David slowed his pace and looked at the office sign identifiers. At the end of the corridor, he turned left and stopped to read the name of the corner office occupant. Markos would have floor to ceiling views on two sides.

David opened the door and stepped into the office. Markos sat in his high-backed leather chair, leaning back and gazing out the window toward a building some thirty feet away. He was studying a legal sized file that he held up in front of his face. He did not appear to have heard David come in and hadn't yet sensed his presence. David took this opportunity to look around. He studied the art on the walls. Expensive, but unremarkable, he thought.

"Excuse me?" Markos asked.

David walked quickly to Markos, slapped him on the back, pumped his hand vigorously, grinning like they were the dearest of friends who hadn't seen each other in a long time. "You remember me, Harry. It's David Pearl. I was just talking to your uncle yesterday in Tarpon Springs, and he was telling me how much he missed you."

Markos's eyes popped open wide in apparent shock. "That's funny, I was just talking to him and he complained about you extorting money from him."

"That's not funny, Harry. Let's not get off on the wrong foot here. It was a business transaction, and now I am here to transact some more business." David watched the man very closely.

"What the fuck do you want?" Markos's jaw tightened, and his face tensed.

"I want you to get into your head that you should not screw with me again, Harry. You and your fucking cousin are interfering with my business. Do you want me to start taking this personally?"

"Listen, we made a mistake. Some wires got crossed. I apologize for the trouble. But, you are on my personal enemies list, fucking with Uncle Ike like you did. Our business is private. We don't want you or anyone else sticking their nose into it." Markos was firm, but sweat glistened on his forehead, and David latched onto this potential sign of fear.

"We need to reach an understanding. My guys are studying the information your uncle so graciously let us download. When we find out what's on it, we'll know better what that information is worth. I hope you understand that DRPearl Inc. is in business to make a profit, while inspiring confidence in our customers. We have numerous clients that we have maintained effective partnerships with for years. But, we only have one group of people that tries to interfere with our legal business. That would be you—your uncle and your associates. I'm calling that organization a criminal enterprise. You are—how shall I put this—a threat to my firm and its progress."

"Fuck you. If you have said your piece, get your ass out of here."

"How are your boys, Chitzou and Gadis?"

"Out on bail and safely back in Montreal."

David watched Harry push the panic button under the edge of his desktop. David had locked the door behind him as he came in. In seconds, a concerned male voice asked Harry if everything was okay, while pushing against the door.

"I think you should tell him to relax, Harry. You wouldn't want a confrontation in your office. That would be messy, hard to explain."

"Ernie, it's okay for now. Wait outside the door." His voice reverted to its previous, low, conversational tone. "You broke in here five minutes ago, remember?"

"Now, Harry, let's try to stay rational here. I walked right in, and you really don't want the police to know why I need your cooperation, do you? I'd be happy to tell them, on behalf of the Greek government, that I'm looking for someone who is fleeing justice. Why don't you tell me everything you know about Nicolaos Polopolis?"

Markos swiveled his chair to face the window, sitting there in silence for a few moments, gently shaking his head as if trying to make up his mind. "Nico graduated from prestigious universities. Normal childhood, more studious than the rest of us, he didn't cause any trouble and was a likeable person. We have some relations who are in criminal gangs, smuggling, and gambling. Like Ike, who owns a bar or two, takes in trade in return for favors, solves gang problems, and gets paid a percentage from all the rackets operated by affiliated gangsters. I represent them sometimes, or I find a criminal lawyer, if that's what they need. We're a big family. Some are in the shady activities, and some, like me, are on the legal side, but we are still family, understand?"

"I understand, but what happened to Nico? You know he attacked one of my employees and damaged his hotel room, don't you? Not to mention that he's suspected of murder."

"No, I hadn't heard that. I think the old expression, 'middle age crazy,' applies to Nico. He has a beautiful family and had a good career going. He has plenty of money of his own. I truly do not know of any of his connections to the worst elements of the gang. We have them, but I don't think Nico was into gambling or, for that matter, anything that would cause him to have contact with anything like that."

"What about women?"

"I guess so. I don't personally know of Nico's romantic exploits. I guess I'd have to say that I believe some of the stories. But, I also think that he's a stupid ass if he compromised himself in that way." Markos stood up, walked around his desk, and stood facing David with an intensity that popped a vein out in his neck. You need to leave my firm, Uncle Ike, and me alone."

"Is that a warning or a threat?"

"It's a plain, simple statement of fact. Now, get out."

"Harry, I'll see you around." David opened the door and motioned for Ernie to enter Markos's office. David ducked into the men's room on the way out. Ernie followed David, and he quickly caught up to him. David opened a toilet stall, reached behind the toilet and retrieved the plastic bag of documents. He smiled at Ernie and said, "I almost forgot my lunch."

Ernie grabbed for the plastic bag. David danced out of his grasp and seized Ernie's neck, pinning him to the wall. Ernie was shorter than David, maybe five feet, ten inches, but he was thickly muscular from his neck down to his ankles. Ernie tried to kick David.

"That wasn't very nice, Ernie. I'll keep you here against the wall until you can convince me that you will behave when I leave. Otherwise, I will hurt you enough now, so you will behave." David thought he saw a glimmer of retreat in Ernie's eyes.

Ernie took his hands off David's shoulders. His face was dark, his eyes bulging. He nodded his agreement.

"That's cool, Ernie. Have a good day." David let Ernie go. The man fell to his knees and grabbed his throat. David calmly left and headed back to the office.

David found the office in the midst of a small celebration. Both Gao and Hamooush had made breakthroughs on their assigned tasks. Alice, back on her feet now, but still looking a little shaky, had gone to the nearby Cuban-American bakery and purchased a birthday cake to mark the progress. David joined in the celebration.

Alice escorted a middle-aged, slightly overweight man in a grey pinstriped suit into the conference room. When everyone had sat down, she introduced him. "Everyone, here is our newest employee. This is Yacob

Fleischmeister. We waded through a lot of applications to find him. Since most of us are here, I wanted to take the opportunity to introduce him."

"Welcome, Yacob, we seem to be getting deeper into financial issues than we had anticipated. You will have plenty of work. We are very glad to have you on board. Gao, why don't you lead us off?"

Gao smiled and nodded. "I have written and programmed an algorithm that searches all of the analyst's data. Essentially, the algorithm determines patterns in the data. As we step from slide to slide, you will find an increasing level of deception from the missing analyst."

David lifted his head from his note taking and asked. "Gao, so let me interrupt here for a moment. Your judgment then, considering her entire body of work that's in the files and what you estimate is missing, is that her own work was honest and accurate?"

"Yes, yes, that's a good determination. Yes, that's what I think. Her logic is applied carefully and is consistent in every case that I have examined, in that she treats individual data, or facts leading to conclusions, or intelligence consistently, and, I believe, within the boundaries of what the data really indicates, using her own logic and expertise."

Alice, who was sitting up straight and drinking strong black coffee, asked, "If that is the case, and I accept that it is, what is the bottom line?"

"Here is what I found: first, there are emails in electronic folders erased on purpose. These emails must have been erased by the operator, or in this case, our missing analyst. I have recovered them. Alice and I will independently review them tomorrow. I have a casual opinion, but will save that for now."

"Excellent. Go ahead, please, Gao." David found himself smiling. Gao, he thought, was turning out to better than he had anticipated.

"Secondly, it appears that, based on my findings, there is a glaring deficit in the data provided by our customer, MagnaMeta. The analyst dealt with files that concerned all of the Middle East, the Arab countries, plus Iran. My determination is the files for Lebanon are missing. As all of you know, Lebanon is a major banking center for the Arab world and throughout the Mediterranean. There might be other omissions, but I think they would be minor."

"Just how can you be sure of that, Gao?" David wanted to prepare himself for the looming showdown with MagnaMeta.

"Yes, pointers in the programming indicate where data would go, and it would go automatically. For Lebanon, however, the programming has been altered for no logical reason that I can think of. Plenty of raw data, but no aggregation, so one can only guess at her real intent. Of course, it's probable that MagnaMeta doesn't know what files are missing." Gao talked slowly, looking at David for support and confirmation.

"That's quite a condemnation right there." David had already thought that MagnaMeta was at risk, but now his concern elevated.

Alice spoke first. "So, she was working on Lebanon as well, but her supervisors were not aware of it."

Hamooush added, "She found something and was determined to hide it. Something of value or perhaps, a vulnerability, something that could embarrass her or her firm is a possibility, I think."

Gao responded. "Yes, both could be true. That much is logical. But, she could have been trying to hide her own mistake. Or, she could be in a collusion. Is that the right word?"

"Yes, a conspiracy to defraud, provide information to competitors, that sort of thing." David smiled at Gao. He admired Gao's fresh thinking more and more.

"Okay, thanks. I think that there might be a conspiracy because of the missing link, and my third finding."

Alice gulped from a fresh cup of coffee. "I can't wait to hear the third finding."

"Number three finding, I believe and I know that I can prove that within the company's email software, a deliberate, malicious program has been inserted that sent copies of the chief executive's messages to this analyst. The facts are simple: emails to him, Douglas Antonopoulos, are included in the recovered deleted files. Furthermore, this fact leads one to believe that the systems security personnel were fooled somehow or are not doing their job."

Alice was getting very interested in this now. "And, what would your educated guess be?"

Gao paused for a moment, seemingly trying to come up with the right words. "The security people aren't working hard enough or critically enough to see what's happening, and for some reason, probably complacency, their intellectual assets were no match for the hacker, or motivational corruption, or whatever. They were blind to the unauthorized activity inside their computers. A clever analyst programmer created a screening shield that obscured what she was doing from MagnaMeta's computer security personnel."

"Good point, Gao, what's next? This is great information, but remember, we need to get a final report that is irrefutable." David checked his watch and then looked over at Alice whose tiny nod of her head told him she was in agreement.

Gao recognized David's time crunch and spoke more rapidly. "Fourth, there is an apparent innocent glitch in their software that was exploited by the analyst. She exploited the glitch to get regular data dumps on financial arrangements of these shipping corporations. For some reason, she was mostly interested in Lebanon and Greece. I have found no official reason for her to be interested in Greece, and as I previously mentioned, her Lebanon files vanished."

"This is an important point. Our client, MagnaMeta, is confronted with a glaring internal loss of critical intelligence. They will defend themselves vigorously. So without an official reason, why would this analyst be doing unauthorized work, people?" David's face showed his concern with the looming magnitude of MagnaMeta's problem.

Alice shrugged. "Money, the second oldest reason in the world, is probably the reason. But, somebody has done somebody wrong could also be the reason. Money and resentment, both, would be my guess. Powerful enough reasons for someone to desert their comfortable nest and profession and start running."

David was lost in thought for a moment. "What does Greece being involved mean to us?"

Alice said, "They are the biggest shippers in the world. And smuggling is the oldest and most traditional profession in Greece. Yes, even before prostitution, in Greece there was smuggling." Alice laughed. "Plus, by history and possibly culture, some smuggling for profit is all right with the authorities, provided no one gets embarrassed. If our analyst, here, was doing intelligence involving shipping, there can be no doubt that getting information on the Greeks would have to be included. They are shipping's numero uno."

"Good, let's forge ahead. Gao, please continue." David looked up from his notes, thinking for MagnaMeta, this is going to be a bloodbath.

"Finally, I see deliberate, subversive, software programming. Somebody successfully hacked into MagnaMeta's computer systems. Someone with great talent. This malware programming routinely retrieves financial data and internal reports. The missing analyst got all of the financial reports, but someone else, as yet untraceable, did the dirty work. This is not a fault of their security staff laxness. Experts did a masterly job at copying these financial files and seamlessly replacing them with pseudo files. The company needs a comprehensive, internal systems audit of all of their computer systems. I see evidence of the fraud, but I haven't figured out where to start to try to quantify it."

David smiled, nodding. "Gao, great report. MagnaMeta won't be happy to hear any of this. They must have deluded themselves about the missing analyst and her work. Now, they are exposed and compromised. Their bread and butter are contracts for intelligence work from the CIA, DOD, and the National Security Administration. I'll bet any of you a cup of coffee they have not notified their customers at all about the missing files, let alone of the severity of the potential loss. Yacob, you will be a big help with this job if we get it." Yacob smiled and made one brief nod.

"I agree, David, and they won't be happy to hear about the situation from us," Alice said. "I'll work with Gao, and we'll make our report airtight." Alice smiled, and her bright eyes met David's. David knew that between Alice and Gao, the MagnaMeta report would be irrefutable.

"Okay, Hamooush, your turn." David turned the page in his notebook and entered a new heading under Hamooush: Tracking of Zisis/Markos Clients' Financial Transactions.

Alice responded. "Hamooush and I had a discussion before he began plotting out his approach. As a result of that discussion and the information that you provided him, David, we felt like we needed additional data. So, we secured transactions to and from the identified banks, brokers, and other financial institutions with both Greece and Lebanon to and from the U.S. As a result, Level 8, our dear, greedy friends, are charging us $100,000 and have demanded to see the results of our analysis. We couldn't get it any other way, without, that is, having to produce a work order from some government entity, which we couldn't."

"That's fine, Alice. We will send them an executive summary, without the detail, which would enable them to do their own intelligence gathering. Then, if they want the data files, they will have to pay us. So, we will get our money back eventually. Hamooush, let's get this show on the road."

Hamooush smiled and returned to his papers and the slides on the screen from what appeared to David as a prayerful position, head down and fingers of each hand touching in front of him. "Thank you, David and

Alice. I know the time is slipping by us here. Let me remind everyone that the initial data proceeded from the information that was recovered from Zisis's computer files and the paperwork David secured from Markos's office. We had to contract with Level 8, as Alice has described. Mr. Zisis owns or controls, with his wife, Stella, a number of corporations. These corporations are in Montreal, Canada, Tarpon Springs, Florida, and in various locations in Greece. Other than the bars and furniture stores, these businesses are engaged in the marketing or trading, if you will, of furniture, decorating accessories, certain commodities such as sand, gravel, limestone, olive oil, wine, and liquor. His businesses, in essence—from examining thousands of invoices—tell us that Mr. Zisis will trade in anything for a buck." David and Alice exchanged glances.

"Accordingly, we have to be suspicious based on what we already know about Mr. Zisis and Mr. Markos. That suspicion leads us to a clear conclusion that one of the product lines of Mr. Zisis's shipping line is definitely smuggling. Five ports of call are of the most interest: Montreal, Canada, Beirut and Tripoli, Lebanon, Al Hudaydah, Yemen and Brindisi, Italy. The shipping line, Nicolaou Kasos, of which he is ten percent owner, is a moderate size firm, approximately 100 ships, but that number varies with the vagaries of the maritime economy. Of course, the ships go anywhere and everywhere, but the five most prominent stops are as I just stated."

David was perplexed about these ports because nothing seemed to be consistent about them as destinations for illegal activity. "Hamooush, what are the commonalities, the correlations among the five ports? What are the linkages, if any?"

"We were able to acquire a software program from a New York firm called CoSense. This software enables us to quickly analyze, from cell phone records, in graphic visualizations, to see if there are correlations between formal legal business in each port and the records that we have from Nicolaou Kasos Shipping. In other words, is reality being served by what, officially, is shipping into those ports? We can say with a very high confidence level that the volume of these calls is unrelated to official business, so something else is being done."

"What's next?" David asked.

"Ideally, we would get some video at each stop. Get something set up unobtrusively that would monitor what comes on and off the boat, 24/7."

"Costs too much and too complicated, so let's skip that. We don't need hard evidence. What's next?"

"We analyzed time in port. It's significantly longer in the five ports. There could be many reasons, but it supports our hypothesis that smuggling is important revenue stream for Nicolaou Kasos, or rather, Zisis and his confederates."

David interjected again, "Right, we don't need to prove this in a court of law. We just need to collect our intelligence and determine what the market is for it."

Hamooush paused to sip some water, but he kept up the briefing pace. "Now, and Alice was a big help with this step, she suggested that we begin with the appropriate websites, then pursue all the linkages. The links led us to blogs and carefully concealed chat rooms, from which we have managed to capture a tremendous amount of intelligence. Alice spent some time last night examining the language in the blogs, using our Greek language translator. This yielded the proof, David, as you said, not legal proof, but highly, statistically, confident proof that what we have is smuggling on a huge scale."

Alice spoke next. "There you see it, David. This is what pays for the multiple homes, the muscle, and the probable payoffs, when necessary."

"Oh, this data shows that arms smuggling is the big ticket item, followed by highly expensive, rare metals."

"That's right, David. I think Zisis and his companies are like ticket scalpers, but instead of concert or game tickets, they buy medicine, arms, minerals, and rare metals in bulk from smugglers and hold them until the price is right."

There was a quiet pause in the entire group. Alice was the first to speak. "David, with the millions of dollars involved in these illegal transactions, I think that our Greek friends, Markos and Zisis, and maybe Nicolaos, are playing us. Markos and Zisis are not going to allow us to keep digging. It seems clear to me that we are a threat to them. That knowledge should guide our actions from here on. We were attacked once. I think they were looking for you or Nico. That wasn't about some stupid contract."

"Alice, you are probably right. Call Taz and Jose Gonzalez tomorrow. Ask them to provide us, this building, and me with additional security. Based on this briefing today, we must ask ourselves what Zisis's motivations are. A, they don't have a plan yet in regard to managing us, and are therefore, simply protecting their business interests; B, they are making plenty of money and are concerned about us somehow screwing it up for them; or C, they are doing multiple illegal activities for a huge payoff and will, under no circumstances, tolerate further intervention from us. Since our answer must be all of the above, we must adapt our strategy. I'm a fool for confronting Markos and Zisis. There simply must be something more to this. Alice, you and I must think harder."

Chapter 17
Love Assumes, March 10 and 11

David sat in Faber's Coffee Shop at Ronald Reagan National Airport. David was positioned, so he could clearly see the exit where Sophia would come walking out at any moment. He could also see a small sliver of the Potomac River. He watched as the crowds of travelers ambled, jogged, rolled, and stumbled to or from their destinations. He wondered what brought them to the nation's capital or what was taking them away.

Suddenly, there she was. Sophia was wearing a tan trench coat over a black, slinky skirt and a burgundy sweater set. David thought she was simply ravishing, the most stunning woman in the world at this very moment. He rushed to her. They embraced. When they let go of each other, David felt almost giddy.

"Sophia, how was the trip?" David was elated. He hadn't realized just how much he had missed her.

Sophia pushed up against him, giving a kiss on the cheek. "It was fine. The few hours before the plane took off seemed like the longest in my entire life. That was excruciating. This is our first long weekend together, and already I can't imagine leaving you to go back. I realized that I must, simply must, do some long-term planning. I can't imagine being without you."

"We are here now together, and we have a beautiful day. We'll make the most of it." David wheeled her suitcase and, still holding hands, walked to the short-term parking lot. The firm's plain, white surveillance van was still David's only means of automotive transportation.

They ate a late lunch at the Café on the Potomac in Georgetown. From the outside seating, a broad series of steps led down to a sidewalk that ran along the Potomac. Boats were tied up alongside; sailboats and more pleasure craft were further out on the Potomac. All of the diners were chatting and seemed to be energized, enjoying the beauty and the day. The early spring day had just a slight chill in the air. The lightest green on the early leaves contrasted beautifully with the Potomac's dark, blue-black water. David was happy to be part of the tableau with Sophia. It seemed so natural.

They were shown to a table by the outside railing, protected by an overhead, plastic awning extended out from the building. As they were sitting down, David asked, "Would you like to visit my parents?"

She winked at David. "Of course, I'd love to meet them. I'm sure they are anxious to find out about me."

"Great, what else would you like to do?"

"There's a show of paintings by Monet at the National Gallery of Art. I would love to see it."

"You got it. There is always something to see in DC. Sometimes, I just sit awhile after lunch and wonder what the other people are doing. Are any of them spies like me?" David watched Sophia's eyebrows arch, and she laughed.

"Nearly all of them are normal people, not like us, David."

They ate their warm bacon, spinach, mushroom, and green pea salads slowly. When the table was cleared, they held hands and finished their red wine before walking slowly, closely, back to the parking garage.

The couple moved slowly through the Monet exhibit, pausing at each painting to share in the glory of the art. They lost track of time, wandering through the various rooms, captivated by the genius of a fabulous artist. During all of this viewing, they bumped hips, held hands, and rubbed shoulders, or Sophia's arm was hugging David's while her soft, ample breasts pushed gently into the back of his upper arm. Standing at the last Monet painting, David clutched her hand.

"Will you marry me, Sophia?" He pulled her hand in front of him, but he focused upon her eyes, waiting for an answer.

She stepped to him and they embraced. Stunned, she kept looking into his eyes for seconds before she could respond. "My answer is yes. I never expected this. You've swept me off my feet, my love."

"Let's go meet my parents." They embraced again.

David navigated the way to Silver Spring. As they approached the compact ranch house, they saw his parents standing outside on the steps, grinning and waving. David's father, Ben, stood with his arm around his wife, Alexis. With a voice full of love and excitement, David whispered, "There they are, Sophia."

The couple got out of the van and stepped into hugs from David's parents. David's mother gave a strong hug for such a small woman. After several moments, she reluctantly released him and turned her attention to Sophia.

"Mom and Dad, this is Sophia. We met in Montreal where she works. We just got engaged. I wanted you to meet this delightful creature who is the love of my life." His mother grabbed Sophia's hand and lifted herself up slightly to kiss Sophia on the cheek. David imagined his mother's pure pleasure of anticipation: a wedding, a daughter, a grandchild.

He was too well aware of the characters, values, and personalities of his parents to have missed the blazing ray of excitement from his mother's eyes or his father's grinning approval. "Now Mother, Sophia and I have much to talk about and careers to arrange and other things to plan before you are getting that wedding or the granddaughter that you've always wanted."

His mother laughed and said, "What are you talking about? Just because most of the ladies at the mall already have grandchildren in tow doesn't mean that I've been jealous of them." They all laughed.

His father, Ben, added, "Not much, she isn't."

David's mother turned to go in the house. "Dinner is nearly ready. Ben, get the wine served, and I'll finish setting the table."

Sophia followed her to the kitchen to help. David put his arm around his father's shoulder, and the two of them slowly walked into the house, settling in the warm comfort of the living room that was so filled with memories. He got up and helped his dad open the bottle of Cabernet. His dad splashed some into each wine glass. At the table, at his mother's urging, Sophia talked about life in Montreal and growing up in Greece. At his mother's insistence, the couple spent the night together in David's old room. David and Sophia quietly made love and fell asleep spooned closely together.

The next morning, David woke up first and gazed at Sophia. Her hair was tangled, and her arms splayed at girlish angles. She was the most beautiful woman in the world. Today, he would tell her again that he loved her and that he wanted to be with her all the time for the rest of his life.

CHAPTER 18
The Jimmy Bimini Tour, March 20

Jimmy Blitchford found himself assisting a late entrant into the Jimmy Bimini tournament in Naples, Florida, at the Naples Country Club of the Sun. "Yes sir, you can sign up for the tournament. Just let me see some ID, and give me the $500 entry fee."

"Thanks, Jimmy. What does my competition look like?" David Pearl was wearing dark blue, finely tailored pants and a light orange, tropical shirt. He pulled five one hundred dollar bills from the roll he had stashed in his front, right pants pocket.

"David, it's the usual assortment of guys who have tried and failed to make the PGA tour, or they couldn't get through the "Q" PGA tour qualifying school, or they couldn't find a sponsor to allow them to simply play golf, or any of other reasons that have led them to try and keep their golf hopes alive."

Pearl grinned at Blitchford and asked, "What about you, Jimmy? How did you end up sponsoring a golf tour?"

"I got tired of the family business of selling cars. I cashed out, moved to Florida. Running this little tour is a great way to meet new people, women, party, and maintain that Florida lifestyle. I'm actually Jimmy Blitchford, but for professional reasons, I prefer Bimini."

Both men laughed.

Blitchford gave a careful appraisal of the charming, handsome golfer in front of him. "Well, David, you certainly look the part. What's your story? I haven't heard your name before."

David Pearl shifted his gaze out to the golf course. "I was on the European tour for awhile a few years back, then family reasons caused me to drop out to take care of the family business. So, now that I've retired from that, I decided to make a comeback."

"That's great. I think you'll like this tournament. After you finish your round for the day, come on up to my suite. You'll get to know the other players and meet some businessmen who provide financial support for the Bimini tour."

David Pearl reported to the first tee at 9:15 AM. On this April 10, spring was long past in this part of Florida. He was waiting at the first tee when his playing partners for the day dragged themselves up. They were burly twins from North Dakota, Mike and Mark Englemeier.

Mike proved to be a talker, with his brother not far behind him in full-throated loquaciousness. "Howdy, David, where did you play your college ball?"

"I didn't play college ball. I went into the service, played the South Africa tour and then the European tour. I came to the states for family business reasons. Now that's taken care of, I want to make a comeback." David continued to warm up by stretching.

"Yeah, my brother and I grew up and played in North Dakota. You only get three or four months to play golf up there." They all laughed. They were called to tee. Mike teed off first, hitting a screaming straight arrow of a ball that traveled three hundred yards, landing in the middle of the fairway. David shook his head. Mark hit his driver into an adjacent fairway. David hit his driver straight down the fairway, but was still about fifty yards behind Mike's ball.

Mark Englemeier pounded his driver into the turf. "Now, I'm further away from the green than I was here on the tee." David played slowly, taking plenty of practice swings before every stroke. His recoveries from errant shots drew praise from the Englemeiers. Mike Englemeier fell a few strokes behind David. Mark Englemeier was all over the course, scrambling to an eventual eighty-one, mostly as a result of errant drives. Both of the Englemeiers played quickly, walking up to their ball, addressing it, and then swinging away.

As the trio waited for the group in front of them to clear the fifteenth hole, David Pearl led the golf tournament. He hadn't yet had one of those mind-wandering moments where his round would be ruined. Mike was at par. Mark was five over par and furious with himself.

At the end of the day's golf, David had the lead by two strokes. By virtue of his 67, he was pleased, happy, and satisfied. He went to his room and cleaned up for the reception.

At Bimini's suite, the bartenders and servers wandered through the crowd providing champagne and hors d'oeures. David Pearl stepped up to the bar for a gin and tonic. Bimini was enthusiastic about the day's play, making an impromptu announcement the moment David Pearl entered the room. Then, he toasted David, the women in the room, and finally the golf course. Mike Englemeier had sneaked into the top ten. He was out on the small deck area, drinking a beer and chatting with one of the young women. David stood out on the deck for a few moments watching Mike's brother on the driving range, hitting balls with one of the club professionals.

Back inside, David grabbed a second gin and tonic. He sat on the couch, which provided one aspect of a four-sided conversational grouping with other matching pieces of plushly cushioned, black, leather furniture. Bimini came over with two older men at his side. He introduced them to David. They owned car dealerships in Naples. The men chatted amiably.

One of the businessmen, a bald, rotund man of about sixty, patted David on the shoulder. "That was some round you played today, son."

David grinned. "Thanks, I played on the South Africa tour and then in Europe. When my father died unexpected, I had to come back to run the family business in Greece. That eventually brought me to the states. Now that I have a good management team in place, I wanted to see what I could do playing fulltime. If I can keep my game together, I hope to get to the qualifying school."

"Man, the way you played today, you can do it. Whenever you are in Naples again, give me a call. I'd like play a round with you."

David listened politely as the men talked about golf. Eventually, he wobbled back to his room.

Chapter 19
Risk: A Term of Art, March 25

David had just finished reviewing the final version of their report to MagnaMeta. Leadership would be the issue. Would they accept the report and its findings, hard and realistic or would they be in denial? He was reviewing the slides when Odette knocked on his open office door.

"David, I hate to interrupt your prep for the MagnaMeta meeting, but I have learned something strange that I think you need to know about."

"Sure, Odette. Fire away." David enjoyed the company of the cheerful young woman.

"Two weeks ago, while monitoring our blog, someone left a strange comment complimenting your golf game. I thought it was like a wrong number. I've never heard you mention that you play golf."

"Right, I don't. I don't have time for it. Too much time for too little benefit."

"Three days ago, I read another message from some car dealership in Naples, Florida, asking for your schedule and what tournaments you are playing and wishing you luck in something called the Q-school. I dismissed this as a peculiar coincidence. But, this morning, I get a call from a very angry club professional in Howie in the Hills, Florida. He said you ran out on a huge bar bill, food bill, and pro shop items. I told him you have been in the office here in Washington the whole time, and you couldn't possibly have done it."

David momentarily looked downcast. "Odette, I smell a dirty rat named Nicolaos Polopolis. It wasn't enough to steal my credit; now he's stolen my identity."

"Right, so I asked the man for a description of 'you,' and it fits with Polopolis, alright. I gave him Uncle Ike's name, address, and phone number."

"That's right on, Odette. Call Abdul Choudri, and see if he can start tracking Polopolis down. Tell him the golf angle. When we definitively locate the bastard, we go get him. Make a copy of the bills. Don't pay them, but send the bills to Uncle Ike and our friend, Harry Markos. I have to scoot to the MagnaMeta meeting. You did good." David grabbed his files and headed out.

This time the meeting was in a building on New York Avenue, a slice of pie shaped building filled with law firms and anonymous sounding firm names, whose real business was in no way revealed by their names. Immediately inside the door was an escalator that took its passengers to the third floor, the first level of executive offices. David expected Alice to meet him outside the office space in the community reception area, but she wasn't there, so he went inside.

The tall, officious, African-American receptionist led him immediately to the conference room. A long, highly-polished, mahogany table on the opposite side filled with MagnaMeta staff. Alice was not there, either. David tried to push down his annoyance and concern about Alice, and began by introducing himself. Quickly dispensing with his own small talk, the chief of contracting from MagnaMeta told David to begin.

"Thanks, Carl. Before we take a look at the first slide, I need to caution all of you. What I am about to present to you will be difficult for you to hear and perhaps harder for you to accept. I want you all to know at the outset that our finest analysts have pored over these data. The resulting intelligence has been thoroughly scrubbed. I have personally reviewed all the data sets and the resulting report."

Carl frowned, but casually waved David to begin. "I think we can determine for ourselves the impact, and as professionals, we can leave our emotions out of it. But thanks, anyway, for the warning."

"I understand. This first slide depicts the actual damage or loss to your files. Those are identified in the circles. These are definite security issues. Outside the circles are triangles. These triangles are there to show the suspected gaps or deficiencies that we have determined from carefully examining your programming. Then, outside the triangles are boxes where malicious, deliberate subversion was done to your files and email. The next slide will focus on the circles."

"Stop right there. You are telling us that our analyst, Yvonne DeLorme, made copies of the data, some of which is intact and some of which is missing." Carl's voice was gruff and bossy. He was well known to David for his desire to maintain the upper hand in contract meetings, particularly where a relatively unknown and much smaller firm like DRPearl Inc. was involved.

"That's what I'm saying, Carl. The mathematical analysis is fully included in the attachment to our report. All of the copies we have provided include the attachment, which is entitled Algorithms. Our econometrician has outlined all of our conjectures, proofs, and analysis there."

"Who is your econometrician?" Carl asked, his words clipped and harsh.

Just then, Alice Boggs slipped into the room. Alice dropped her trench coat, purse, tote bag, and umbrella onto one of the chairs lining the wall of the conference room. She looked around the room and flushed with embarrassment at the silence and David's look of surprise. She dropped into the chair next to David, quietly apologizing.

David returned to the briefing. "I'm very sorry, that's confidential. Get your people to go over it. The facts are that your firm has been severely compromised. As a result of that, some of your work for the government may be compromised. MagnaMeta didn't provide us with any customer information about your contracts, so we can't elaborate. Other than the names of corporate entities mentioned in email and those identified in your financials, DRPearl cannot be sure of the totality of this . . . security breach."

"Oh, come off it, David. What you are hyperventilating about? What is this all about? You were asked to do a risk assessment on the work of one analyst, not on the entire company." Carl then abruptly directed the staff from MagnaMeta to go into a small huddle away from the conference room. When they returned to the conference room, they appeared downcast and anxious.

Carl resumed. "David, we were expecting your report to be an assessment of risk relating to our missing analyst, not this programming review."

"We went where the data took us, and we went where the missing files led us. Would you like for me to continue?" Each of the MagnaMeta staff was now carefully studying their copies of the Pearl report.

Carl sniffed and said, "This is a damning report. My bosses aren't going to like it. In fact, I am going to tell them not to like it."

Alice responded before David could respond. "I suggest you get them into a briefing as soon as possible. David and I have another meeting immediately after this on Embassy Row. If you want us to participate in a briefing, we will need an amendment to our contract."

"What if you're wrong about all of this?" Carl sighed heavily.

David looked around the room briefly before responding. "First of all, we are not wrong. Let me use the analogy of the levees protecting New Orleans. Your information levee has been ruptured. You just didn't know it until now. Your financial system has a significant breech of undetermined proportions. Your email communications system is leaking because every message that your CEO sent or received for months was copied to Ms. DeLorme. Your required confidentiality firewall has a huge puncture in it. Instead of water rushing in, I'm afraid that it's your intelligence work and your finances that are rushing out. This is incredibly bad news, but it hasn't started raining yet. By which I mean your government contract managers haven't found this out yet. If and when it starts raining, your firm's continued existence could be in doubt."

The staff of MagnaMeta sat in a chilled silence. The only one maintaining eye contact with David was the contract auditor, a woman who had spoken very little, and with a strong German accent. In this woman's eyes, David recognized the beginning of understanding.

David continued. "We don't know what will happen. We do know that your firm is vulnerable. I do understand something about risk management. But understanding the risk doesn't mean that we know what will happen. Our understanding of risk management tells us that based on what has happened and what appears to have happened, what could still be happening is a very significant, storm-of-the-century type of crisis. That concern, in other words, is that you and your colleagues have a shit storm of unknown proportions that potentially could bring your firm down. My consequences of being wrong are that I lose some business. Your consequence of being wrong is ridiculous. And, let me remind you once again, it is not yet raining. No one outside of this conference room and my econometrician know the full extent of this."

Carl was now giving David a cold, blatant, and threatening stare. David would not have been surprised if the man had invited him outside to duke it out.

"Any more questions, people? Alice and I must be going to our next meeting. You have our report. You have our slides. On the last slide are our recommendations for actions, which MagnaMeta should undertake immediately. Sorry to be the bearer of the bad news. Thank you for your time. Alice and I are overdue." Alice and David collected their materials and left the room.

"I think we managed to suck all the oxygen out of that room. Looking at those faces was getting unbearable." Alice breathed deeply. They both continued to step quickly down the moving escalator.

Once in the cab, David turned to Alice. "What was that all about? You coming into the briefing late."

Alice turned her head toward David, her eyes searching his face. "Well, I'm very sorry, David. I could blame it on a lot of things, but to me, getting there late is simply inexcusable. I let you down. I'm not what I am determined to be, and that's sad."

"Alice, for God's sake, what's wrong? You don't have to have a pity party for my sake. Just own it. Own your behavior. You got drunk, you overslept, but on a day when I really needed you there."

Alice looked away from him, her face reddening with anger. "Okay, that's good enough for me."

The cab delivered them to the Greek Embassy twenty minutes later. The security guard carefully checked their drivers' licenses against the list that was provided to him for expected visitors and guests. He searched Alice's canvas tote, which carried about five inches of files, her handbag, and her lap top computer. With that done, the officer escorted them to a door at the far right of the main embassy building. David held the steel security door for Alice. Once inside, he heard the guard lock the door behind them. They followed the hall to an intersection marked with an arrow. They went in the direction indicated by the arrow and came to a Greek Army sergeant seated at a small desk. They again showed their identification. The sergeant checked their names against her list. The sergeant led them to a receptionist, who smiled and asked them to be seated.

After about five minutes, Demetrios appeared from yet another unmarked door and beckoned them to join him. Demetrios hugged both of them.

David stood back and looked in Demetrios's eyes. "I think you are looking better than you have for weeks."

Demetrios grinned and shrugged before leading them to a conference room where upon David, seeing the array of communications equipment along the back wall, immediately pegged the room as the embassy's most secure meeting room, its command and control center. It was a large rectangle with a long dark redwood table in its middle. The table was surrounded by chairs upholstered in the light blue color used on Greece's flag. Along most of the room's walls were more chairs and pictures of Greece. David noted the outlines of cabinet doors along the opposite side from the entry door and at each end, and speculated that behind those doors were almost certainly the key information: contacts, must do's, and problem lists arranged in clearly marked binders, along with the specialized equipment necessary to maintain communications under any circumstance except oblivion.

David recognized the military attaché, Anastasios Dimantidis, and the deputy mission, Theo Gliniadakis. The two of them greeted him warmly. Anastasios provided both David and Alice with a cold bottle of water from a carefully disguised mini-refrigerator set into a wall. Demetrios sat at the end of the table. David and Alice sat side-by-side facing the two Greeks.

Gliniadakis opened the conversation. "David, let me say that we have become more troubled by the activities of our mutual friend, Nicolaos Polopolis, than when we last met. Demetrios has educated us about your firm's extraordinary skills in identifying problems with data base security. As much as it does embarrass me to elaborate, I have been instructed by my government to get our leaders clear, accurate answers to what they see, and we see, as a remarkable series of coincidences that have occurred since Nico departed our premises. Of course, letting the damn fool escape is an incredible embarrassment. I personally spent several hours with your State Department and your Homeland Security Department explaining, reassuring, and frankly—what's your phrase?—eating humble pie."

"I'm sorry, Theo. I really am. Nico has a way of making things personal for us all." David kept his pen poised over his small notebook, ready in case there was an assignment or a follow up.

"Not nearly as sorry as we are, my friend. We want your firm to examine our computer systems, email, and our computer files. We will give you remote access to all our communications traffic, except for a few we consider to be requiring utmost confidentiality. Of course, all of this will be outlined in the contract proposal that should be ready in a day or two for you to examine. Frankly, you already know some of the mess that Nico created, and that's another important reason for us to want your firm to do this business. We have no desire for our dirty laundry to be aired out any more than it already has."

"May I ask a few questions, Theo?" David imagined that the verbal hostilities within the Greek State Department must have been epic.

"Of course. Anastasios, do you think that you can find the coffee pot and get us some coffee? Angela should be still on duty. Thanks."

"What were the findings from your own internal review of the situation? Were there any other investigations?"

"The Greek government is also a bureaucracy, Mr. Pearl. Of course, there were numerous investigations, after-the-fact post mortems, but the most compelling and damaging was an audit report from our National Security Service. As a result, my personnel file, and that of Anastasios, is red-flagged, and we will probably be sent to a less complex and, I hasten to add, less desirable assignment in the near future. Both of us join you in your personal ill will toward Nico."

"I am truly sorry, Theo."

Theo Gliniadakis gestured with his left hand as if to signal that it was a small matter and to be expected. "Of course, at my stage of career, it doesn't matter in any big way; still, there is some sting. One doesn't want to be regarded as a less than stellar diplomat by colleagues. For Anastasios, however, he will be shipped back to the real army and, maybe if he is lucky, make another rank or two before it's over for him."

Anastasios came in bearing a small silver tray with an insulated coffee pot and four china cups. He was accompanied by a small, dark, very young woman who carried the condiments. She sat them on the table in front of Demetrios and disappeared without making a sound. David and Alice quietly conferred. There was a small, uncomfortable silence before Theo resumed speaking.

"We owe you an apology, Mr. Pearl. Had we provided more background on Nico and the situation he has left us here to deal with, we might have all been better off." He paused after speaking each of the last few words, as if he was searching for the strength to go on.

"No you don't. Polopolis owes me more than an apology, but you don't." David interjected this comment more loudly and fiercely than he had intended.

Again, Theo waved David's comment off with his left hand. "Sadly, we do. Polopolis comes from a well-connected political family in Greece. He owns twenty percent of a small, family owned shipping company, Nicolaou Kasos. He inherited the shares and lots of other assets from his late mother, who had married a Eugeniades Polopolis, one of four siblings deriving from the founding patriarch. Eugeniades died shortly before Polopolis's mother did. Nico is wealthy, but his wealth is tied up in a trust fund to which he must apply for funds. That trust fund is controlled by a Washington attorney named Harry Markos and by Nico's wife. Now, Nicolaos joins the Greek Foreign Service. Blah, blah, blah for the next several years, marries one of his coworkers and she quickly produces two sons. First ten years, clean reports and a steady rise in the Foreign Service. He gets stationed in Istanbul, Turkey, where his grandfather's nephew, Ike Zisis, probably contacted him about the family business. Nico, because it's family, does some favors for Ike. Nico helps out with intelligence. Not only intelligence, but with actual participation from time to time, I am most sorry to say. The next stop for Nico is Great Britain, where Nicky's wife begins to smell something rotten, confronts Nico, and because Nico is Nico, she goes home to Greece." Theo paused and took a large gulp of his coffee.

"Nico stays in London, does a good job and gets promoted to the embassy in Washington. Our profiler tells us that Nico began to enjoy the danger, the action, and the thrill provided by doing illegal activities successfully. But, still at this point, he's held in good stead by his superiors in the Foreign Service. In other words, the illegal stuff hasn't caught up to him or us. He's here in Washington for two years. I wondered about his family not accompanying him. I wondered about Nico's expensive house. I wondered about a lot of things with Nico, but I never acted on any of my wonderments, unfortunately so. About six months ago, I received an anonymous complaint. Literally, some typing on a piece of paper, folded neatly, and slipped under my door sometime between when I left work and the time I returned. The note said, 'Polopolis is helping the Greek mafia.' I confronted Nico. He appeared to be stunned. But, he never provided a believable answer to my question of what he was doing that would lead to someone in the embassy getting that idea. That's when I asked Demetrios for a recommendation for someone to provide additional security, specifically, someone who we could trust implicitly and that Polopolis would not recognize." Theo sunk back in his chair, pale and lost in thought for a moment.

Anastasios leaned on the table. "From there on, you know one aspect of the case. What we did not know was that our own internal security service had picked up on Nico somehow, some way. We don't know why or how. They are independent and don't report to me or the ambassador, for that matter. And, we can't ask, because we know they won't tell us anything and that it will only make them more suspicious. What we do know is that they had one of their agents following Nico. What we don't know is what they learned. From our other reports, we know that Nico facilitated some organized crime members in this country by letting them stay at his house, probably by providing cash and concierge type services. We now think that Nico caught a whiff that he was being watched, felt the weight of his career and life coming down on him, and bolted. What we don't know is the damage. We don't know how badly the embassy is compromised."

"Knowing Nico a little bit, I can see how he could easily gain the trust of those in the embassy. I think he probably had a mental break somewhere along the way, and your physicians or his physicians didn't know or think to report it." David stayed at the edge of the chair, intensely engaged in the briefing.

Theo bestirred himself again. "Mistakes were made pure and simple. I have come to believe in your vice-president's infamous one percent doctrine: 'If there is only one chance in a hundred that a scenario is threatening the U.S., the U.S. has the obligation to go on the attack.' We don't know what our chances are here. But, my job is to disrupt, displace, and remove the threat. Of course, your vice-president also talks about total information awareness. In Nico's case, there is no one with total information awareness. We were not monitoring anyone's emails, personally or professionally. As a result, I am now charged by my own government to review all of Nico's official emails, from here in the embassy and his personal accounts. And I have my own emails monitored by our security service. We have reason to believe that, just as your vice-president gets copies of cabinet officials' emails on a blind copy basis, all of my direct reports are having their email reviewed, as well. And, without a doubt, our phones are being monitored, too." Theo paused with a swelling moistness in his eyes. "I neglected to find out the real truth. I didn't connect the dots between what we thought we knew and what our vulnerabilities might be. We all thought that Nico was family. He'd watch our back as we watched his. But, it's like one of these computer virus worms got into his brain when we weren't watching him nearly closely enough. David, if this work is of interest to you, we will have Demetrios provide the proposal as soon as we can finalize it. Any questions?"

"No, sir, thanks for the briefing. We will do a great job for you." David stood up, assuming that they were about to be dismissed.

Theo got out of his chair, turning his back to David, and gazed at the large map of Greece on the wall at that end of the conference room. "I don't need to add that my government is furious, and in order to keep this matter totally secret, especially within the official Greek family, my superiors agreed to contract with you based on my recommendation." Theo turned around to stare directly at David. "And so, David, you and your associates will keep this matter your very own little, precious secret, or else."

CHAPTER 20
Duly Noted, April 2 and 3

All of the employees of DRPearl Inc. were frenetically working on various contract deliverables due to various parties from the captured signals intelligence. Subcontract deliverables on several interim requirements were coming due by the end of April. David was consumed with revising and editing various interim reports and the related briefing packages.

Into this intense atmosphere of sustained work and long hours, the National Security Agency's Inspector General's audit team walked in unannounced on April 2. Odette met the four men and one woman at the front door, and after learning of the purpose of the visit, she requested their identification and charge letter. She sent a text message to David and Alice before makinge copies of the documents. She then sat them down at the conference room table and served them coffee. She got Hamooush's attention, and by his immediately wide-open eyes, Odette knew he comprehened the situation. He went upstairs to warn the others.

David and Alice guided Gao, with his laptop, out the back door. His work site was abruptly changed to the back room of Buddha Belly. David then went to meet and greet the five officials, who sat primly at the conference room table, looking solemn and stern.

"I think you all know the drill. We need summaries of all of your intelligence contracts with the Federal government. We will also need to meet separately with every employee according to this schedule, beginning in fifteen minutes. Here is a list of the files we require." The Chief of this IG audit team, Conrad Shiflett, slid the list and interview schedule across the table to David. The rolls of fat pushed down his collar, and his jacket strained tightly across his shoulders and chest.

David smiled, accepted the documents, glanced at them, and turned the schedule and list of files, and coordination of their work over to Alice. Alice was well practiced in the care, feeding and management of external auditors. "I'll be your contact here at DRPearl. What else do you require at this time?"

The surly, bald, fat man who had said he was in charge responded, "Just keep the coffee coming."

"You got it, Mr. Shiflett." Alice checked on the coffee before she left the conference room. She quickly arranged for fresh fruit, bagels, and cold juice in the morning, deli sandwiches for lunch, and fresh cookies in the late afternoon.

Alice was the first employee to be interviewed. When she was excused after ninety minutes, she went to David's office, walked in, and when David looked up at her, she did a couple of dance steps. "You got time for the debriefing? Of course, this is confidential stuff between them and me. Their goal seems to be you. I was asked: 'How long have you worked for DRPearl? How did you come to know David Pearl? What are the working conditions like? Tell us about your internal security.'"

David had a little smile on his face and shrugged. "It's good to be popular. So, they asked nothing about any contracts?"

"In a word, no. This seems like an internal security type visit. Are any of us security risks, are we maintaining internal controls, how are official government secrets handled?"

David leaned back in his chair and sighed. "Well, we are the good guys, so we should just act naturally. But, this inquisition couldn't have come at a worse time. Everyone is busting their tail to get product out."

Alice turned her head back toward the door. "Yeah, right, time for me to get back at it."

At 3 PM, David met with Abdul Choudri. Abdul had been surfing the Internet for leads to the phony David Pearl and the real Nicolaos Polopolis. Abdul scheduled the meeting immediately upon receiving his first lead.

"Hi, Abdul, what's up?" David greeted Abdul warmly. His personal concerns for Abdul's mental and physical health had all been satisfactorily resolved.

"I have a lead on Polopolis, David. He has entered a golf tournament in Brunswick, Georgia. The hotel operator put me through to a room registered to David Pearl. I hung up before anyone could answer. I then talked to the lady taking registrations for the tournament. Based on her description of David Pearl, Nico, pretending to be you, will play in a pro-am on Wednesday. And the regular professional tournament starts Thursday and concludes Sunday."

"Excellent. You and Jose fly to Brunswick, rent a van, and go collect Polopolis. Tell Jose to keep him locked up, contained, and secured at all times." David reached in his drawer and pulled out a corporate credit card and handed it to Abdul.

"Thanks, boss. Anything else?"

"One of you must keep an eye on him at all times. Call me at any time; he's tricky, I don't need to tell you that, but don't trust him at all. Keep him away from telephones. Call me when you are an hour away from Washington so that I can inform the embassy. Good work, Abdul." David got up and swung around his desk to give Abdul a pat on his back as he walked out of the office.

Alice came bounding into his office at 4 PM. "Problem, David. The Inspector General is demanding to meet with Gao. Our own schedules show him in the office this week. I told them that he had to return to China because of a family emergency, but they are suspicious."

"I can't think of a better lie, so let's stick to it. Promise them that when Gao returns to this country, we will call them. In the meantime, get to the National Security Agency, and find out what's taking them so damn long on his clearance."

"Yeah, I agree. You can't produce somebody who's out of the country." Alice laughed. "By the way, Frankie has the access to the Greek Embassy files. It's a lot, but she needs the kind of help that Gao brings to the table. Fleischmeister might also be able to help. He can do the systems work for her."

"Right, so talk to Gao and Yacob about that. Gao must be swamped, but put the question to him. If one of them could format the systems work, then Frankie would probably be able to take it from there. We also need to put an ad in the secure intelligence jobs online and see what that brings us."

David watched as Alice departed the office and quickly punched the cell number for Demetrios who answered on the third ring with his first name. "David, what's up?"

"I have a possible concern I need your expertise on, Demetrios. How are you doing?"

"Oh, as good as can be expected, provided your expectations are very low." They both chuckled. "What can I do for you, my friend?"

"I need your help in making a belated full disclosure. I am having a romantic relationship with the person who was our Greek contact in Montreal."

"Uh oh, well, let me have her name, and I'll run that by Theo. And, to be on the safe side, I'll suggest that he talk with our attorney. What's the name?"

"Sophia V-o-g-i-a-t-z-i-s, Vogiatzis."

"Okay, that doesn't ring a bell. Meet me at Stoney's about 8:00 this evening. I'll have our attorney's guidance and hopefully the actual status of Sophia V-o-g-i-a-t-z-i-s, and then we'll go from there."

That evening shortly after 8, Demetrios finished his second beer and motioned for another. David drank one beer to match Demetrios until the fifth beer, when Demetrios ordered another, along with a shot of whiskey. Demetrios carried himself like a former athlete. He was quick, agile, and had a grace of movement that marked him as someone who had, at one time, been a natural sports competitor. For a retired police officer and heavy drinker, Demetrios had maintained himself quite well. David wondered how long the fitness could last with Demetrios's drinking regimen.

Demetrios had just started to hesitate over his word choices when he confessed how much he missed the Island of Rhodes and his family. Turning to David, Demetrios sat up straight. "How about your family, David? I've been telling you all about mine."

"My mother and father live right outside of DC in Silver Spring. They are in good health. I'm an only child. I have a few cousins scattered from here to Boston, but no one that I am really close to. Daniel Pearl, the journalist, was a distant cousin. He's the only famous one."

"What a shame, Daniel's murder was an atrocity. He was an incredibly brave person, who deserved a better fate. You Americans seem to handle the family business with careers better. Being away from family, I mean. Sometimes, I think you are like gypsies, moving and moving, always searching for something more, some place more perfect than where you are at." David sensed his friend's sadness in his dark watery eyes and uncharacteristically soft voice.

"I think home is where the heart is, Demetrios, and for most of us, Americans included, that's where we grew up."

"It's a dirty business we are in. Take that fucker, Polopolis, for example, he's got it all: money, family, great job, and yet he's so fucking crazy that he's willing to risk anything, including his own life. Anyway, as I was saying, the investigators keep circling. I talked to two more today. Sometimes, I get confused about what it is they are after. From the first one's questions, I get the feeling that they want to get the proof on our own intelligence folks and not just here in the Washington Embassy. Then, the next one wants to know everything about Theo, rumors, thoughts, anything. It's bad, David. I'm telling you, it's bad. And, they are probably asking others about me. They're almost begging—we know you know the dirt, so just give it to us."

"Come on, partner, I better take you home."

Demetrios rubbed the back of his head. "I guess so. What am I forgetting? Oh yeah, there's no one in the Greek security in Montreal or the US, for that matter, with the name Sophia whatever it is."

The friends leaned on each other as David walked Demetrios back to his apartment.

The next day, the DRPearl staff, at the end of another long day, slowly dispersed to their usual Friday evening destination, beginning with Frankie, who saw David in the reception area and waved. "Got to go. I have a date."

David gave her the thumbs up. Alice and Odette invited David to meet them and some friends at the Legalistic, a bar on Capitol Hill, but David declined.

David rode the Metro to Reagan Airport. He waited outside security, around which Sophia, or whatever her real name was, would come walking briskly toward his waiting arms. That image was so real that he could almost feel her touch, sense her smell, and the comforting return of her embrace. The memory of her smile and her voice came to his mind as clearly and truly as if he was actually holding her. His mood shifted uncontrollably to anger and back to hope from one moment to the next. Maybe what she had told him, that she loved him, was the truth, but could he be forgiving? He didn't know. While waiting, one time, he got up to walk away. She must have known that, sooner or later, he would find out. What kind of asshole am I?

He saw her in the back of the exiting crowd. He watched her expertly picking her way through the mass of people without being noticed. She moved with the quiet grace of a ballerina. That's what David was thinking when she reached his waiting arms. They shared a long, pressing kiss. It didn't end until a clumsy jostling, from a frantic woman trying to control her child and luggage, ran into the back of Sophia's legs. Sophia and

David smiled and helped the woman get her luggage upright and her child calmed, then watched her continue her voyage to her next destination.

David, Sophia, and her small black suitcase traveled back to the office via Metro rail. They were simply one of hundreds seated and standing in the train as it zipped over the Potomac. Sophia looked out the window at the lights and the beauty of the Capital City. David held her hand. He suspected they looked like a couple in love, innocent and earnest, strong and committed. But, he wasn't sure of anything in their relationship. He doubted now his commitment to her, but still he hoped. The elderly, Hispanic woman who had finished a long hard day cleaning some government office, or other, stared at them with a slight smile on her lips. The overweight, black woman dressed in a flowery, green, party dress with green, medium heels, pearls, and a matching green purse could not take her eyes off them. David felt the stares and the quick, almost furtive glances. Sophia smiled at David. "What would you like for dinner?"

"Anything. There are a number of fine places to eat in DC. The Chop House is famous and historical with a big menu."

"Oh, I don't think so. Let's get some groceries, and let me cook something up. Pasta or Greek grilled chicken?"

"There aren't many grocery stores in DC. And, that would take too long."

Sophia frowned. "Really?"

"Really, with the traffic, we'd be starving by the time we prepared dinner and ate. We can grocery shop tomorrow and get the office kitchen completely stocked up. I promise. Let's get off the Metro at George Washington University. We'll go to the Pantheon, a Greek restaurant of some renown. It's only about three blocks away from the Metro stop."

They sipped drinks at the bar after being told that the wait would be an hour. David could wait with Sophia for a long time if need be. Still, he worried about the conversation they would have to have over who she really was? Was she the person he thought she was, or was he just naïve or worse? His head began to throb, and he felt as if he was becoming a third party looking at him critically and at her with anger.

The seating at the bar fronted a glassy, blue, plastic counter top with chrome edging. The young bartenders bustled around a teak and steel square-shaped rectangle center island, expertly making drinks and chatting up the customers. The bar was crowded with jocular, chatty, after-work groups.

She told him of the latest news from her extended family back in Greece. He talked about the team from the NSA Inspector General's office. When he had finished the story of the office celebration upon the IG's departure, Sophia laughed. David watched the lights play off her soft, brown-gold hair, the beautiful muscles in her neck and her firm, graceful face.

Seated at a table for two in a nook that provided some privacy, David gazed into Sophia's eyes. "Remember, I want to marry you. But, we have to, I have to have complete honesty from you first."

Tears filled Sophia's eyes. Briefly, she looked away. "We need to talk. There are some things that I need to tell you."

"Sophia, we've landed another contract with the Greek Embassy in Washington. As a result of that contract, I informed the embassy that I was in relationship with a Greek government employee in Montreal."

Sophia's eyes widened and her facial expression shifted from elation to sadness. "Oh, dear, what a mess I've made." She turned to her purse and pulled out a handkerchief, gently blowing her nose and patting her eyes.

"So, whoever you are, I'm in love with you. Who are you?"

A long pause ensued in which the noises of the other diners, the background music, the tinkling of the silverware and china washed over them. Sophia sighed deeply, frowned, and rubbed the side of her head, pushing the golden brown strands of hair back over her ear. "I am Zoe Papaloukas. Everything else about me that I've told you is true. For awhile, I didn't know if I could trust you or not. Then, I was afraid. I should have told you before now, I'm sorry."

David smiled. "I love you, Zoe Papaloukas. I want to marry you." But, David felt the bile in his stomach rising. Was that a reaction to his restated commitment? He knew their relationship would never be the same, but would either of them trust each other completely again?

CHAPTER 21

Without A Hypothesis: The Facts Dangle and Dart, April 2-5

During her chunky, chocolate, cookie party for the children of the neighborhood, Mee Maw McKay took sixteen-year-old Brent Bickford aside. "Brent, I need a little help with a personal project that I'm working on. Would you like to hear about it?"

Brent Bickford, an open and earnest young man, nodded rapidly. "You bet, Mee Maw. Whatever it is, let me help with it."

"Brent, I need you to help me on a computer project, a kind of investigation, but it's completely confidential."

"You mean, I can't tell anyone. Could I get into trouble?" Brent's scalp slid back on his skull and his eyes briefly widened.

"No, it's just that this is a serious matter involving one of our neighbors, Mr. Nevzlin."

Brent's eyes widened. "Oh yeah, he's kind of a freaky guy. What do I have to do?"

Mee Maw looked around to make sure that no one was listening. "You need to tell me what kind of computer and other stuff I need to buy to make it work, then you need to teach me how to use the computer."

"No problem, Mee Maw. I wish I had my own computer, but I've learned a lot in the lab at school." A small, tentative smile emerged on Brent's face.

"I know your parents can't afford to buy a computer for you, and I know very little about computers. I want to pay you for your help, and I'll get you a computer too because you and I need to be linked up, somehow."

"Like a network." A look of gratitude and amazement covered Brent's face.

"Exactly."

"I'm willing to do all that. What do I tell my parents?" Brent's face fell for a moment.

"Don't worry about that. I'll talk to them tomorrow."

Two days later, after the school bus had dropped him off, Mee Maw let Brent inside. Brent simply handed over the list of computers, peripheral equipment, and related requirements. He then shrugged. "I got to go, Mee Maw. I have lots of homework." He pointed at the list. "That should be all you'll need."

"I'll call if I have any questions, thanks Brent."

A day after he had delivered the list to Mee Maw, Brent was back at her front door. "Hi, Mee Maw. Did you get all of the stuff?"

"Yes, Brent, I have everything. The customer service at Best Buy was really very helpful. And, the assistant manager told me you did a very good job of picking the necessary equipment."

Brent grinned. "I'm glad that I didn't leave anything out. Show me where it is and where you want it, and I'll get it all set up."

Brent worked until Mee Maw sent him home at 11:15 PM. She handed him the box holding his computer. The box was really too big and heavy for him to carry easily. Brent grinned excitedly and wobbled off toward his house with it.

She next went out into the garage and worked for several hours piecing together the English-language shredded strips of paper. When she had managed to reduce the pile of English-language shreds by about one third, she went to bed.

The next afternoon, she briefed Brent on what she considered the next steps. He quickly found the user name and password for Nevzlin's email accounts. He explained that they should search through the list of all possible internet email providers because often, people have more than one email account. They did that and found two more. Most of Nevzlin's email correspondence was in English, but some was in Russian. When Mee Maw told Brent that she had ordered a Russian-English dictionary and self-instruction book, he showed Mee Maw how to use the online Russian-English dictionaries.

As Brent had to return home for dinner, Mee Maw told him to tell his parents that she was having Happy Hour on Friday and for them to please come. On that Friday at 4 PM, Mee Maw went out to her flagpole where she flew her special flags, took down the blue and gold West Virginia University flag, and put her martini glass flag up in its place.

CHAPTER 22
Naked Bootleg, April 5

Abdul was driving the white, rented, panel van. Jose slept on a sleeping bag rolled out in the storage compartment. Storms had delayed their flight to Atlanta, causing them to miss the connection to Brunswick. As a result, they didn't arrive in Brunswick until midnight on May 2. When they finally found the resort where Polopolis was staying, they were both tired and hungry. The White Marsh Golf Resort bordered a large marsh with tidal streams that fed into St. Simon's Sound.

Abdul told the security guard that the golf tournament had requested his company to service their malfunctioning computers. The security guard sleepily allowed the vehicle through the gates. The two men checked in at the guest center. While the attendant was in the office looking for faxes and packages for them, Abdul quickly deduced the keys to push for room numbers and found David Pearl's. With the room number for Polopolis in hand, they ventured forth in the van once more. Abdul parked the panel van near the balcony of the unit where Polopolis was staying. Each building was set into the edge of the golf course, with its landscaping blending in and accentuating that of the course itself. Abdul ran inside to verify the room number, listened at the door, and hearing nothing, returned to the van.

The Polopolis hotel suite stayed dark for an hour and half. At 4 AM, Abdul noticed movement. The sliding glass door opened and Polopolis stepped out onto the balcony . . . naked. Abdul reached back and shook Jose awake. Jose eased himself into the front passenger seat. They both watched as Polopolis urinated into the azalea and holly bushes below. Then Polopolis leaned on the balcony railing, apparently enjoying the coolness of the early morning. His face turned toward the direction of the gentle breeze coming in from the sea.

Jose opened his door, quickly moving toward the second-floor balcony. Polopolis immediately tensed, but remained where he was. Jose asked him to jump down. Polopolis shook his head. Jose pulled an outdoor table over to the edge of the first floor patio, stood on it, and jumped up. He used the iron railing to pull himself up to the second floor balcony. When Jose reached the balcony, Polopolis was already back inside the unit. Jose found the sliding glass door closed and locked.

Jose whispered, "Abdul, find the crowbar, and hurry." Abdul flung open the cargo door and immediately grabbed the crowbar, tossing it to Jose. Jose jammed the pry end into the sliding glass door, and broke the lock. He cautiously slid the door back. Jose looked around the room. He walked to the bed and pulled back the covers, revealing a naked woman soundly sleeping. Jose heard the front door close, so he ran out into the hallway. He spotted Polopolis running down the hallway.

Polopolis ran down the cart path that wound throughout the golf course, with Jose closing the distance between them. Polopolis was wearing a white, knee length robe, which billowed behind him, and a golf cap snagged tightly on his head. Polopolis ran with high knee action and was not nearly as fast as Jose. When Jose tackled him, the two men tumbled into a sand trap. Jose rocked Polopolis with several blows to his head. Polopolis gave up, put his hands in the air, and looked wildly around. Jose shoved Polopolis to his feet and pushed him back in the direction of the hotel suite.

The two men climbed the stairs to the second floor. An elderly couple was in the vestibule waiting for the elevator. They gasped when they saw Jose and his bathrobed companion, both covered with sand and breathing hard. The elderly man immediately grew red in the face. He yelled. "What on earth are you doing?"

Jose responded, "My friend gets very confused when he is off his meds."

"Goddamn immigrants! I'm calling the cops." The old man got his cell phone out. Before he could dial 911, Jose let go of Nico and took the phone away from the old man. Polopolis took off running again. Jose quickly followed, dropping the man's cell phone on the stairs as he exited the building. This time, Polopolis ran the opposite direction on the golf course. Abdul saw them running and he quickly got into the van and began to follow them.

An early morning greens keeper stood on the eighth green, moving the pin placement. He looked up as he heard the sounds of Jose wrestling Polopolis to the ground. The greens keeper pulled out his radio. "I called security!" the man yelled.

When Jose looked toward the voice, Polopolis broke free and ran. Jose and Polopolis were in the middle of the eighth fairway when Jose again tackled Polopolis. They went sprawling in the dewy, slick grass. This time, Jose hammered Polopolis in the gut, until he was sure that Polopolis wouldn't be doing any more running for a few hours. He put a hammer lock hold on his neck and dragged Polopolis toward Abdul in the van, which had just pulled onto the verge of the course.

Before Abdul could back out from where he had parked the van, three police cruisers had blocked his way. Jose was in the back with Polopolis, having just placed plastic ties on his wrists. Abdul quietly told Jose about the police, and Jose cut the ties off Polopolis's wrists.

The three police officers got out with guns drawn. Abdul eased his way out of the van with his hands up. One of the officers slammed him against the hood of a police cruiser, patted him down, and placed him in the back of a squad car. "We'll take you to the station. Sit there quietly, and we'll get this figured out."

"Come out with your hands up!" the officer in charge yelled. Jose pushed Polopolis out of the van's cargo door. Polopolis was exhausted from being pummeled and from all the running. He fell limply to the pavement. Jose jumped out and got slammed onto the squad car's hood, frisked, and placed in a vacant back seat. Polopolis was gingerly placed into the back of the resort's security vehicle. The police search of the van yielded nothing.

The cops drove Abdul and Jose to the local station and placed them in separate interview rooms. The detectives grilled Jose for about two hours. When questioning ended, the lead detective leaned over the table toward Jose. "We are cutting you loose, Jose. I think it's mostly because you are a Marine, and the Chief was, too. Your pal, Pearl, escaped custody about two hours ago. Without him, we can't press charges. Semper fi, now, get out of here."

When they were returned to their van, Jose called David. "Good morning, David. Sorry about waking you up."

"No need to apologize. I can sense the bad news in your voice, Jose. What happened?"

"Polopolis ran. I caught him twice. The second time I secured him in the back of the van, but the police arrived and took us in for questioning. Sometime soon after they began questioning Abdul and me, Polopolis pretended to be sick, pretended to pass out, and when the detective ran for help, Polopolis boogied away."

"Oh, man, what a con artist that guy is. Well, stay where you are, and continue the search. File a missing person report for Nicolaos Polopolis, AKA David Pearl. And, get something in it about his mental status and flight risk."

Driving back to the resort, Jose and Abdul checked into their hotel suite. They slept for two hours, cleaned up, got back into the van, and went cruising through and around the resort looking for Polopolis. They checked with tournament officials, who told them that he had no-showed for his tee time and had been disqualified. They went back to Polopolis's room, parking the van far back in the parking lot that was reserved for the building. Jose reentered via the balcony and let Abdul in through the front door. The room was still filled with Polopolis's garment bag, clothes, golf bag, computer, and brief case. They carefully searched the room, looking under the mattress, opening every drawer, and checking under everything they could move.

Abdul sat at the desk making meticulous notes on all the information in Polopolis's wallet, briefcase, and computer. They took all the credit cards, the Florida driver's license, and anything else that bore David Pearl's name, then waited in the dark with the drapes closed. Abdul tried to hack into Polopolis's computer. Jose napped on the bed.

At 8 PM, they heard a noise from the hall. Abdul hid behind the bathroom door. Jose eased himself into the closet, pulling the slatted French doors closed after him. The front door opened, and a man walked slowly into the room, carefully looking around. Jose burst out of the closet and knocked the man to the floor, and he fell on top of the pin from the 13th hole, which Polopolis was using as a walking stick. When Jose could see him clearly, he knew for sure it was Polopolis.

Jose grabbed the hair on the back of Polopolis's head and slammed his face into the carpet three times. "Let's play nice this time, Nico. What did you come back for?"

Polopolis lay on the floor, breathing heavily. "I thought you'd still be in jail. So, I came back for a change of clothes."

"Where is the woman?"

"I don't know."

"Why did you run?" Jose still had his knee in the middle of Polopolis's back.

"Because I knew that I would be arrested before they let me go. I was hurting, so I walked away. Listen, I think I got some cracked ribs."

"Tough, we ain't going to the doctor." Jose kept his knee pressed in the middle of Polopolis's back.

"You are killing me," Polopolis groaned.

"You are going to cooperate, or I will." Jose stayed where he was. "Abdul, carry some of that stuff to the van and bring back the plastic ties for me, if you would."

When Abdul returned, he assisted Jose in lifting Polopolis to the bed. They placed plastic handcuffs on his hands and his feet. They searched through all his clothes in his suitcase, and removed everything: keys, coins, brass knuckles, a switchblade, and a cell phone.

Abdul asked, "Nico, what's the user name and password for your computer?"

"Oh, fuck it. The name is 'greektown.pop' and the password is 'NICO9393.' Take me to a doctor."

Jose grunted. "We'll do better than that. We'll buy you some aspirin. Now, cooperate or you'll soon be hurting in some new ways. Now, it's quiet time." Jose used duct tape to cover Polopolis's mouth. Abdul moved the van to the front lobby of the building and began to ferry Polopolis's possessions from the hotel room to the van. When the only thing left in the room was Polopolis, Jose lifted him off the chair, put him over his shoulder, threw a sheet over him, and took him to the van. They pulled out and worked their way to I-95, heading for Washington, DC.

At 11 AM the following day, Jose called in to report on their progress. Abdul was driving the van, impatient in the slow moving traffic in northern Virginia. David asked to speak to Polopolis. Jose crawled into the open space, pulled the duct tape off Polopolis's mouth, increased the volume on the phone, and told Polopolis to talk.

David's voice came through the phone with strength and authority. "Nico, I need to ask you some questions. Are you up for that?"

"Your employee here, the Mexican creep, beat the crap out of me. I have a headache, and my ribs are killing me. I need to see a doctor."

"Be nice, and that will be done in due course. Why did you kill the intruder in your home?"

"I didn't. I wasn't there. I was already in Montreal."

"Who did kill him, and why?"

"I don't know. Greek diplomatic security is my guess. Pelakanos was trying to shake me down for money. Greek security probably used his services, too, so maybe they were following him. Uncle Gus told me that Pelakanos was a vicious killer. I talked to him once, and that was a big mistake. If I had been there, he would have killed me. He was an assassin. I would be dead if I had stayed in my house."

"What did you do to compromise yourself with the Greek mob?"

"Listen, David, I am seriously hurting. I need to see a doctor right now. I'll tell you in confidence. Swear to me that you won't give any of this information to the embassy." Polopolis's speech was slow and coarse. "Your man, Jose here, belted me in the throat. It's painful to talk, and my ribs are killing me."

"I promise. Let's just get this over with. As soon as we have you settled somewhere safe, I'll get a doctor to take a look at you."

"You'd better not be lying. I mean it. I let three of their women go. They were set up in a house of prostitution in DC. I went there a few times. These were Albanian women who had been smuggled into the U.S. and forced into prostitution. The pimps called Pelakanos about the missing girls. He couldn't find them. He then started calling the johns from their address book, which led him to confront me. I paid him $5,000, but that wasn't enough. I knew he could easily sabotage my career, which was on shaky ground already. My Aunt Stella was furious with me. I decided to end the diplomatic career myself. I was tired of the rat race and the pressure. I didn't need the money. Aunt Stella took me into her home and called the wolves off. But some of the wolves decided that I had to pay. Pelakanos had friends, people who basically don't give a shit about anyone's authority, including Aunt Stella's."

"Do you know who killed Pelakanos?"

"No, I do not, but it had to be State Department or Greek diplomatic security. Seriously, somebody from the Washington Embassy or the fucking FBI. When I heard about the murder, I went further over the edge. I thought I was the target, and I might be next. I still might be. I needed a sabbatical anyway, and I didn't want to wait for the paperwork to get processed or worse, denied."

"Sabbatical? You've got to be kidding me! I am still obligated to notify the embassy that we have you in custody. Why didn't you tell us all this before?"

"It was better for me. You tell the embassy that I'm running from Greek gangsters and why, I would have been immediately under suspicion. The Greek State Department wanted to take me back to Greece for questioning. That gave me the opportunity to escape. I just want to play golf. I am so tired of all this bullshit." An audible sigh completed Polopolis's statement.

"We have to stay focused here on reality. I need you to tell me all you know about Stella's gang, about Ike, and about Markos."

"Stella and Ike tried to protect me. Markos is a piece of shit. The gang is into smuggling anything. They've used the Nicolaou Kasos Shipping Company for years. It is a well-oiled machine. They've greased the politicians in Greece, Lebanon, Turkey, and Canada for decades. Markos is the 'go-to' man for all of it. I am a dead man if you let Markos know you've got me."

"Jose told me that they found your medications, but that you won't take them."

"I jumped off that medication train, and I'm not going to get back on it."

"Nico, we are going to try to protect you. But, you have broken quite a few laws. You know that we have no reason to hurt you. I'm not sure about anyone else. We'll protect you, but you've got to promise that you won't try to escape. Maybe the safest place for you is jail."

"I promise, but no jail, I wouldn't be safe there. I want to play golf."

"We'll see about that, my friend. Can I notify your family that you are okay?"

"Sure, but talk only to my son, Mihalis. He's the oldest. My wife is a witch that I prefer never to talk to again. I don't think she tells my boys that I call to talk to them."

"Put Jose back on the phone."

"Jose, loosen his ankle cuffs. If he tries to escape, put him in a straight jacket after you've cracked a few more of his ribs." Jose laughed.

CHAPTER 23
Changed Elements, April 7 and 8

David Pearl listened patiently to Nicolaos Polopolis's estranged wife, Dima. He was sitting in a secluded alcove of the massive lobby of the downtown Hyatt Regency in DC. He focused on the conversation, but his eyes took in the ebb and flow of the foot traffic across the ornate space where Washingtonians and visitors mingled, met, and passed though, on their way to or from something important. Mrs. Polopolis refused to let him speak to their sons.

"You get Markos to get my bastard husband off the trust fund. As far as I am concerned, you are just one more cocksucker that makes my life miserable."

David moved the phone further from his ear. "I'm sorry, Mrs. Polopolis. I have no control over your trust fund or Markos. I'm sure that your husband will be returned to you safe and sound."

"You aren't listening to me, asshole, I don't ever want to see that no-good, crazy-ass, unfaithful, lying ass, stupid, conniving, shit for brains, jerk ever again."

David interrupted her. "I'm sorry, Mrs. Polopolis. I know you must have been through a lot. Thanks for your time." He hung up.

Such a marriage must be part of the explanation for Polopolis's strange behavior, he thought, although he was confident Nicolaos was himself the root cause of his own trouble. So much for staying faithfully married in such a vengeful relationship. He was more grateful than ever for his stable, loving parents, and the caring environment they created for him to grow up in. Instead of going directly to the intelligence conference in the back room of the Library Bar in the hotel, he would call his parents to tell them how much he loved them.

After speaking briefly to his mother, David purchased a draft beer at the bar before entering the room that the Association of Security and

Intelligence Organizations (ASIO) reserved monthly for their meetings. Several of the people in the room lifted their water glasses in mock salute to David as he entered the room.

Nora O'Brian, one of the CIA's representatives, grinned and winked at David as he sat down. "You'll be, no doubt, pleased that the business part of the meeting is nearly over." He widened his eyes at her and smiled in acknowledgement.

The treasurer of the group continued speaking in a dull monotone. He finished with a small flourish. "The accounts as of this date, April 7, are in good shape. Members' dues are paid in full with one approved exception. I'll be happy to take questions at this time." There were no questions.

David carefully surveyed the twenty-one people in the room. There were three CIA representatives, one from the National Security Administration, one from the White House, and the rest were from intelligence and security companies. These reps were mostly the B team of corporate, governmental executives.

David whispered to Nora O'Brian, the CIA Public Affairs Liaison. She was tall, slender, with frizzy brown hair. "Did I miss much?"

She smiled and whispered back. "Only the happy talk, David. Business is good, life is good. It's all good and getting better all the time."

"If only the world realized what fanatics we really are," David whispered back.

The chairman spoke. "David, Nora, if I could have your attention please." The two of them smiled and nodded back.

"Thanks, David. Since you have our attention, why don't you give your report? How's business?" The chairman was VP of a world-wide intelligence firm, WaveLinks, headquartered in Bethesda, Maryland. Within the intelligence community, WaveLinks' claim to fame was the clustering of retired admirals that comprised their board. The chairman was a retired Navy captain, full of confidence and bluster. David had yet to be impressed.

"Business is good. We are busy, adding staff, looking to hire more qualified analysts, and submitting proposals that hit our skill set. In addition, we are engaged in analyzing the internal security of two major organizations. This is certainly a niche that we will exploit more in the future as the firm grows. Thank you, Mr. Chairman."

"Now, Miss O'Brian." The chairman's words trailed off with the strongest and highest notes for 'now' and each subsequent word descending lower.

"It's Mrs. O'Brian, Nora O'Brian, Captain Fulton. The CIA will be requesting proposals for three interim tasks in areas of information analysis. All three need professional analysts, proficient Arabic speakers, and absolute compartmentalization. Because of that, the contract awards will go to three separate bidders. Once awarded, these contracts will have a high and tight deadline. The CIA's technical representatives will be assigned this week."

A small woman with thick glasses and wide open eyes suddenly looked up. "What's the money on these, Nora? If you want 'pedal to the metal' work, then that requires internal adjustments, and those cost money."

"I think you should look at the published requirements. You know I can't talk about the assigned funds, but I think that many of you should be interested, provided that you have the available talent to match up with these requirements."

Without asking further, the chairman moved to the woman sitting beside Nora. "Becky, what's new with the ProTech Corporation?"

"Thanks, Mr. Chairman. We are fully involved in our major work in Iraq. So fully involved, in fact, we need more Arabic speakers and computer systems analysts. We have complained before about the lack of systems interfacing that we were promised in writing from the Army. We have to do work-arounds frequently, which expends unplanned resources. We think that our association, here, should go on record to the oversight committees, as well as the Secretary of Army, about this problem."

The chairman replied, "Consider it done, Becky. And while we're at it, we'll drop a line to the White House." The chairman continued on around the table. There were no additional business possibilities that David could detect in any of the subsequent reports, but he and Alice would carefully examine the CIA's requests for proposals.

The meeting broke up. Most of the attendees walked away quickly in order to get to the Metro rail or their parked cars to begin their journey home. Before he could get past the bar, Anthony Ritzenheim, a confidential assistant to the Secretary of Homeland Security, called David over to the booth where he was sitting.

Ritzenheim, a polished bureaucratic operative with more than thirty-five years in the federal service in Washington, DC, had taken a liking to David the first time they met, more than two years before. They had almost immediately established a friendship and often confided the most sensitive of rumors and intelligence to each other.

"Hi, Tony, how are you?"

"Pissing and moaning as usual, so not too bad, considering. Sit, and let me buy you a drink. Alice told me you had gone to the ASIO meeting, so I thought I'd take a chance."

David sat down, nodding in agreement to the drink. Ritzenheim would be drinking single malt scotch. He knew from Ritzenheim's previous storytelling moments that two divorces had resulted in him becoming a loner, married to his work and colleagues. His three grown children had little to do with him. Ritzenheim was definitely in the last few years of his career. David thought sadly that his friend would probably move reluctantly and regretfully toward retirement.

Ritzenheim leaned forward and spoke loudly enough to be heard only by David. "I was tipped by our internal security that you have interests with the Greeks, the embassy, and Greek criminal organizations doing international smuggling of arms to terrorists, my friend. I mention it only because the source wasn't discussed, and I don't ask, not in my sphere of interest, of course. It does mean that someone is talking about your business in a much too casual way, however." Ritzenheim took a sip of his single malt and smiled.

David frowned. "I'm puzzled, Tony. I trust you and all of your friends. Where could that kind of accusation be coming from?" David leaned back as the bartender set down his drink and another for Tony.

"This means that the intelligence on this has gone to the National Security Agency. What else are you working on?" The few strands of silver hair on his pale skull waved in the breeze with each passing customer. Ritzenheim looked older than he was, weak, tired, and stooped. Only the lively, alert, pale blue eyes revealed his intrinsic intelligence.

"That's fascinating. We just had an unannounced visit from NSA's IG. Makes me wonder. We've done some work relating to Greek gangsters and met some crazy Greeks. That's for sure. Alice and I were debating our Greek connection. I'll call it. Your news gives me real concern."

Ritzenheim peered around the bar. "You must track the leak down and eliminate it."

"Oh, how I wish I had never become involved with the Greeks." David's head dropped and his lips pursed outward ever so briefly before he fully recovered to face his friend again. "The Greeks are more than annoying, and the fact that they could be talking about us is suspicious. I have this thought, every once in a while, that Polopolis and the embassy is playing my firm. Still, I can't imagine the embassy would bother to tap our phones. I can imagine the Greek mob and its lawyer doing that. I think our internal security with our staff is very strong."

"Don't rationalize. Fix it. Absolutely fix it, and soon. What else might we be hearing about?"

"We have an internal review that we just delivered to one of the top ten firms. They have a missing analyst, missing data, almost certainly stolen money, and they did not like hearing about it. I expect to be called to brief the CEO. If I don't, I'll give you the particulars. This is a major security breach. If the company doesn't report it in a few days, I'll be compelled to. But, the Greek thing, I'll figure out."

"Good for you. I wish I had made the move to the private sector when I was younger. David, just keep your ears and eyes open with this administration. They are impulsive, insecure, decisive, usually wrong, or at best superficial—but always insistent. Once they make a decision, it's virtually impossible to get them off of it. They value loyalty and command structure discipline above all else. Anyone speaking a truth that isn't in keeping with the party line gets frozen out of the inner circle and ultimately chooses or is forced to leave. Just one example—there's been a mass exodus of career lawyers from the Department of Justice. The old hands, and some of the new, just can't stand the perversions of logic and the predetermined strategic decisions the administration wants backed up by bastardized legal opinions. As a result, our government has lost real talent and years of experience. The question is why no one's leaking any of this stuff?" Ritzenheim held a cigarette that he kept twirling in his fingers. Occasionally, he would look at it wistfully, then sip at his scotch.

David knew the administration's public persona of one big, well-oiled machine couldn't be further from the truth, but the seasoned observations that led to the truth were limited to the minds of a very few veteran watchers like Ritzenheim. "Ritz, you know the value I place on your opinion. What can you tell me about Captain Frank Fulton, our illustrious chairman?"

Ritzenheim gave the room a swift glance-over. "Are you sure the cretin left?"

David nodded. "His WaveLinks firm is comprised of retired Navy admirals and captains. They founded the firm in search of personal profit through insider connections in the navy and the intelligence establishment. They have never been mission-driven. By that I mean, they rely exclusively on their contacts in the administration. Sometimes they have their board members on various intelligence and data capture committees. They have hired lots of top-secret operatives, but from what I hear from our experts, their work is mediocre, except for one very important quality: they are good at figuring out the desired objectives and providing information that fits, or perhaps better put, rationales, to support those objectives. They also have some valuable contacts in the United Kingdom and Australia. The bottom line is: let them be. Don't do any work for them. They keep a wet finger in the air at all times to make sure their politics are right. They would cut the wedding band off their grandmother's finger to make a profit. If one of their contracts blows up, you can depend on them and their lawyers blaming the subs and filing lawsuits."

The bar had cleared out. The only other customers were a middle-aged man and woman. Their heads were bowed over the tabletop, their faces pressed almost together, reflecting some kind of mutual pain. David imagined perhaps it was a final sorting out of a parting of the ways, an end to a romance, not a beginning. The bar staff were cleaning up, washing, and stowing away the glassware.

"Ritz, let me get going. I've got a lot of meetings and work facing me tomorrow."

"Yeah, me too, David. Let's share a cab."

Outside, the men climbed into the backseat of a ReadySet cab that they spotted idling about a half a block away.

As the cab started to glide to a stop in front of the DRPearl townhouse, Ritzenheim patted David's arm. "I'm going over to my divorce attorney's house. It's my poker night. I'm going to introduce you two someday. Maybe you can sit in with us sometime."

David nodded.

"My attorney friend is quite a character. Hopefully, you'll never need his services. His name is Mike Finegan, and he is the kind of tough SOB divorce attorney every guy needs. But, he's a good friend. I've learned a lot about negotiating and frankly, life, from him."

The cab pulled up in front of David's office, and he began to pull out his wallet. The older man waved it dismissively away.

The next morning, the office was in a full, active work mode when David finally appeared at the kitchen for a cup of black coffee. He looked into the refrigerator for some remnants of something to eat. He unfolded some aluminum foil. Two slices of pepperoni pizza were inside. David briefly considered microwaving them back to warmth, but decided against it. He was sipping coffee and chewing cold pizza when Demetrios came walking through the front door.

"Morning, David, what's up?" Demetrios always tread with an athlete's springy step, his smile firm. Only his eyes seemed to reveal a sad pathology of the soul.

"Hi, Demetrios. Want some coffee or morning pizza?" David was feeling fairly well, considering the late-night drinking.

"No way. I want a progress report on our contract."

None of the other DRPearl employees were on the first floor at the moment. "Follow me outside. We'll get to that." When the front door slammed behind them, David continued. "We have our mutual project stashed in an apartment near the Marine Corps barracks. Jose and one of his Marine friends are with him 24/7. My instructions are to keep him there. Tomorrow, a team of Greek security begins the interview process, which we have been reliably informed could take weeks. I know the embassy must be extremely concerned about Polopolis, but I want to get him off my hands as soon as possible."

"I don't have an answer for you on that. Because of what happened the last time, I really don't think Theo is in the loop on Polopolis. I am here at his direction, for a progress report on the contract."

David and Demetrios stopped at a new restaurant and leaned on its impressive brick planter. David resumed talking, holding the paper coffee cup in front of his lips. "So, the Greek State Department is getting antsy about their communications all over again. Well, we are cranking away on it. We downloaded all the files and programs. Our best guy is making headway in his analysis of what's been copied, who's been into the secured files. We should have a full report available in two weeks. I can tell you that certain files have been erased completely. The records of embassy visitors for an entire year, ending four and a half months ago, are gone. You might want to verify the physical security of all of your log books and security videotapes. Somebody visited the embassy that doesn't want any evidence of their visit to exist."

"Really? That's curious." Demetrios pulled his little notebook out and jotted notes. "How's our boy behaving?" Demetrios smiled expectantly, apparently anticipating a lively story.

"Actually, so far, so good. We have the SOB taking his meds in front of Jose every morning, and we will continue meds supervision for as long as he is in our custody. We have an unbreakable electronic bracelet on him, so we can track him if he escapes. There are some legal problems that have to be resolved. He was playing in a golf tournament in Georgia under my name and broke a few laws."

Demetrios laughed. "I think you're going to need more than an electronic bracelet."

"Go ahead, laugh. The police charged him for public nudity, resisting arrest, and escaping from police custody. Or, to be more precise, they charged me for public nudity, resisting, and escaping from the police. When he was previously in our custody, Polopolis stole my credit card numbers and ran up some bills. My lawyer is going to take care of it, hopefully, without getting Polopolis's name on the docket."

Demetrios couldn't restrain himself from laughing.

"I know, Demetrios. I know."

Chapter 24
Some Loose Ends Seek Solutions, April 10-14

David Pearl sat in his office staring at the computer screen. The first of the analysis and justifucation to support the CIA contract proposals seemed to have a loose thread somewhere he could not yet identify. Perhaps a proposed solution without a stated problem. He would have to read the proposal again. He was about to read the document again when he heard a faint tapping on the open door to his office. He looked up to find Frankie Ballinger standing in the doorway, hugging a document to her chest.

"Oh, hi David. This is probably nothing . . ." She paused, bit her lip and shook her head. "No, I think it is something. May I bother you for a moment to get your thoughts?" Frankie nearly did a curtsey in her hesitancy to move closer to his desk.

"Frankie, come in and sit down. I need a break from reviewing proposals, so this is an excellent time. What have you got?"

"Congratulations, by the way. I hear you are getting married."

"Thanks. In two days. It's hard to imagine. Maybe I'm too focused on that to get my work done, but so far I'm not getting cold feet. So, what do you have for me?"

Frankie sat primly in the leather chair beside his desk, looking somewhat like a waif in the much larger chair. "Anyway, we are all thrilled with the news of your marriage and can't wait to get to know the lucky woman."

"Thanks, Frankie. Zoe is a very special woman."

Frankie took a deep breath and handed a copy of the document that she was clutching over to David. David began reading immediately. "Two days ago, on May 10, I received an intercept from a ship to shore radio. The ship is a Greek freighter, the Ileana Iazarou. The caller was unidentified, but was evidently on the bridge, so probably is one of the ship's officers. The recipient of the call was a company engaged in the shipping business located in the Greek port city of Pireaus. Freight forwarders, I believe they are called. No names were exchanged, but the transcript is as follows: The Ship: 'Ajax here, I have urgent news.' The company: 'This had better be that Russia has started World War III." The ship: 'I'm sorry. I have no other means to contact you and don't know when or if I'll be back in Pireaus.' The ship: 'Like I said, your balls better be on fire or else.' After this statement, there was a hard, guttural, laugh. The ship: 'I have no choice but to report. I don't have much time on the bridge. So listen, the Greek navy has seized the ship, discovered illegal arms, and there's a mystery crate on deck that is now under heavy guard. Moschos left the ship in Tripoli.' The company: 'What?' That's when the transmission concluded."

David turned to Frankie with his full attention, writing a note at the bottom of her briefing document. "So, this may be our Greek smugglers in action. Find out everything you can on this ship, the Ileana Iazarou, and this Moschos character. What else?"

Frankie leaned forward and started to speak. David motioned for her to take her time. "I requested all the calling information from this location in Pireaus. There wasn't a lot, but in the next minute after the call from aboard the ship, a person in Pireaus, using a commercial phone card, called a number in Washington, DC. This number is the private cell phone of Harry Markos, attorney-at-law. The caller from Pireaus simply reiterated the information from the ship and immediately hung up."

"Well, well, well, that's a tidy package and an outstanding pickup, Frankie, really excellent work. Let's put this in our database, along the input from Montreal. Let me know immediately if you get anything else along this line." Frankie stood, clutched her papers to her chest, and walked vigorously out of the office.

David called Alice on the intercom. "Alice, you have email I need you to read."

She read the email, "We need to talk about this CIA proposal and the Greek security contract." Alice instantaneously sent a reply. "We need to do both. I agree. I will be right there."

In two minutes, Alice walked into the office, stood there for a moment. "Wait, David. We need to do something else. Come with me." David followed her into the reception area and watched as she dropped to the floor and began to carefully inspect the baseboards. She pointed that David should get the ladder. The two of them searched the room with meticulous precision, overturning furniture, carefully inspecting every surface, and pulled up the carpet. "Let's throw this out. We really should get the floors redone, but I think that this room is clear. Let's do the kitchen next. I have a feeling."

"Fine with me. I'm so tired of writing notes and being ultra self-conscious saying anything outloud about this." David began emptying the cupboard, ferrying the dishware, food items, and paper goods to the conference room. Alice went along the baseboard, now using a magnifying glass. Finding nothing out of the ordinary, David got the ladder and inspected the ceiling and the crown molding. When he got to the open space above the cupboards, he found a signaling device, a tiny, three inch tall antenna, painted white, carefully positioned, and flush with the wall. He motioned Alice to take his place at the top of the ladder.

David dragged the ladder outside and propped it up to the second floor windows above the kitchen. As he began the ascent, he almost immediately spotted the silver relay device embedded into the exterior wall. Then, he turned and studied the rest of the side of the townhouse. He spotted the receiving device at the same level, at the very front of the building. Using a large, long screwdriver, he removed both devices. Back inside, he placed the listening equipment on the top of his desk and waited for Alice. His palms were sweaty, and his mood shifted quickly from embarrassment to rage.

Alice entered about five minutes later, her eyes glaring and her teeth clenched. She stood in the doorway for several seconds, her one hand on her hip and her files tightly clenched in the other, before she chose her usual seat, a wing back chair next to a small round table. David picked up his files and settled onto the sofa.

"Alice, we need to get another security firm here today. I want them to go over every inch of our office. This is embarrassing. We need to get our lawyer in touch with the firm that we used before."

"I agree, and I think the Greeks who burst in here that night are responsible. This is so upsetting. I'll use my most unhappy voice with our old security firm."

"Good, I'd like to scream at someone myself. Alice, I think that we are missing something on this CIA proposal. They want analysis of the Islamic underground in Europe. I can't think of an angle that would permit us to do this effectively. There's the potential for a lot of work, and to me, there's no pony under the huge pile of shit. I think we should let someone else try to be the star on this one."

"I totally agree. You wanted a proposal, so we came up with one. I don't think any other company is going to do better than we could, but let them wrestle with it." Alice trilled out a laugh.

"Good, that was nagging me. Now, Frankie tells me that there's a mystery on board a Greek freighter named . . ." David consulted his notes. "the Ileana Iazarou. The Greek navy has seized it. It was smuggling a lot of weapons, probably destined for the Middle East. The captain ran off when the ship was docked in Tripoli, Lebanon. The apparent gang leader, who took the call from the ship advising him of all this, got hung up on, and then called our dear friend, Harry Markos."

"No shit. That's fascinating." Alice scribbled notes onto the legal pad perched on her thigh.

"I think that confirms that Markos is up to his neck with our friends in the Stella gang. Too bad, we have all this evidence on these gangsters and no market to peddle it. Have the new security firm look at this stuff and demand a debriefing from the ones we will fire as soon as you get them on the line." David waved at the wireless listening and relaying equipment on his desk.

"Right, we don't want to fall into the single error conjecture trap. I don't think there's another bug, but far better to be safe than sorry. If we can prove it was Markos, then we can talk damages. Anything else?"

"What do you think about this wedding?" David peered intently at Alice.

Alice pursed her lips and nodded. "I think you two are in love, and you should be married, but it seems rushed. And I'm not convinced that you are convinced, and that makes it somewhat problematic, but you have my sincerest wishes for the best of everything."

David frowned. "Tell me about the Greek Embassy work."

"Sure, we'll have it in your inbox when you get back from your honeymoon. Abdul and Mike Hamooush are making good progress under the tutelage of Gao. The report will include a list of internal control recommendations that will further embarrass our friends at the embassy." She paused to look at David.

David wriggled his lips. "Fucking contract deadlines just don't give us enough time to develop educational approaches for the findings. Maybe we should request an amendment? So, what's the good news, or should I say, is there any good news?"

Alice glanced down at her briefing sheet. "Actually, there is. Here's my news. The jackass, Polopolis, cannot be accused of theft, mismanagement, or messing up much of anything at the embassy. Apparently, he had some kind of loyalty after all. His professional records are meticulous and don't appear to be hiding anything. He did abandon his job. He's copped to a few personal issues for which he could be fired, but he hasn't admitted to helping his Greek criminal buddies yet, and on that the jury is still out."

Just hearing the name made David cringe. "So seriously now, the former diplomat, Polopolis, simply walked away from his job because he was afraid of the Greek mobsters and in search of a second career as a golfer. Does that work? No evidence of his gang involvement?"

Alice arched her eyebrows. "I see where you are going, David. Polopolis is so smart he has us hoodwinked."

David's fist softly punched the arms of the sofa. "My god, I cannot accept for a moment that Polopolis is smarter than us." They both laughed.

Alice had one hand propped under her chin. "I don't think that's the situation, but it may look like that to the Greek embassy. So, I propose that we give them a sniff of what we have on the Greek gang, like connecting the dots where we have them between Polopolis and the Stella gang."

"Good idea, maybe they'll pony up for another contract. Thanks, Alice. That was quite helpful."

As Alice left the office, Yacob Fleishmeister stuck his head through the doorway. "Are we still on?" Yacob possessed a New Yorker accent, the 'ars' and 'ers' pronounced as 'ahs,' and a rapid fire delivery.

David glanced at his watch. "Yeah, definitely, I need some fresh air, though, so get your jacket. We need to take this conversation outside."

Fleischmeister walked beside David. He wore a light blue windbreaker and pinstriped suit pants with a Baltimore Orioles cap on his head. "So, Yacob, how's your team going to do this year?"

"Bad as usual, I think. Spring training is great for us fans. We get to raise our hopes and look forward to the season. But, right now they've won three and lost three, so we shall see."

"Let's go into Union Station, get some coffee, and sit in the train arrival and departure area."

"Great, are we having a security problem in the office?"

160

"I think we've eliminated the bug, but I'm not quite ready to test that hyposthesis. Just to be safe."

Once inside, Yacob settled his laptop on top of the little round table and set his large container of coffee on the floor. "First, I have reviewed all the bid estimates on the proposed contracts. I think we're rock solid, even with the increase for capital improvements. So, that's good. Now, let me review my work with Gao on the Greek gang, Stella. They use a lot of off shore accounts, in the Caribbean, Central America, and Eastern Europe. What data we have is very sketchy, so we are focusing on the sources of revenue, where the cash comes from, and the uses, what the gang is buying. But they own or control numerous restaurants, bars, hotels, travel agencies, etc., so all we may ever get is an educated guess."

David sat watching the steady flow of foot traffic, but his mind actively worked the information from the report "That's cool, Yacob. Just get us a list of all the businesses you think are involved. We'll give that to the embassy, and the Greek government can do with it whatever they want."

"Alright, now about my other duties as assigned, Polopolis."

"Okay, let me have it straight."

"I spend about an hour every evening with him. He's tired. The Greek investigators are working him over intensely every day. My assignment is to assess, supervise, counsel, and control him. I am using my guilt tripping, quiet persuasion, and Jewish mother inspired psycho-karate on him, so far to good effect."

"I'm a little surprised, but not quite convinced. Now, I am not questioning your judgment at all, Yacob, but are you sure?"

"No, but his presence is continuously been accounted for. I have given him some simple assignments, translating stuff that we have already translated. The Marines are taking good care of him. At least two are there every night and don't leave until the interrogators get there."

"Seriously, any worries about him at all? This is too good to be true." David sat back, his eyes questioning Fleischmeister.

"I think there will always be the potential for Polopolis to escape. With a little help, it wouldn't be impossible. Maybe he has orders from a higher power, like his gangster friends, to cooperate for the time being."

David grimaced. "Hmmm, that's an interesting thought. He can't call out, can he?"

"No, the Marines have stripped the apartment of phones and computers. Except for their personal cell phones, which they assure me, Polopolis can't use, he hasn't been in contact with anyone."

*   *   *

Wedding day eve arrived with Taz Washington and his partner Neal Walters dropping in with a case of scotch. Taz grinned at David. "Our very best wishes for your happiness, David."

David silently appraised the pair before speaking. "Thanks guys, take that on into the kitchen. You look like you're sleep deprived."

Neal held the case of liquor up on one shoulder. "You're a good judge of sleep deprived. Taz and I have been going for about forty hours now. The murder business is too good to us at the moment. Could we crash here for a few hours?"

"Sure, wherever you can find a place to get horizontal, go for it."

Taz settled on the couch in the reception area. Neal drank a full tumbler of scotch and went off to the third floor to find some space where he could stretch out for a few of hours.

At 4:00, David left the office to pick up Zoe at Reagan National Airport.

Zoe was a vision in blush rose pink. Oblivious to the passing crowd, the stares and brief second glances from the travelers parked in the cafes, or the bustling air commuters running to or from their planes, they tenderly caressed. For David, the moment, he thought, would live forever in his mind. When David looked into her eyes, he saw love and pure joy and happiness. All his doubts vanished for the time being. Alice was right. It was rushed, probably too soon, but David just kept thinking: keep your eyes on the prize.

Zoe was decked out in a short skirt, twin set, black leather jacket and high heels. The blush rose attire drew the attention of people in the restaurants bordering the main corridor, some were staring, and some were clicking their cell phone cameras in her direction. Both Zoe and David instantly shielded their faces and turned in the opposite direction.

Back at the office, David initially intended to guide Zoe around to meet everyone who was in the office, but Yacob Fleischmeister met them just inside the door.

"Welcome, my dear Zoe. I'm Yacob Fleischmeister. I was not fortunate to meet you on your last visit. Let me get you an alcoholic beverage and escort you upstairs to where we are playing poker. Pearl has a guest who needs to talk to him." Yacob led her to the kitchen, where he poured her a white wine.

David set her luggage down beside the stairs and peeked into the conference room. Sitting there, sipping scotch, was Anthony Ritzenheim. Ritzenheim jumped up and delivered a bear hug. Tony Ritzenheim had tears in his eyes.

"David, I am so happy for you. I can't wait to meet your fiancée."

"Tony, she's just gone upstairs, so we'll do that before you leave." David sat down at the table across from Ritzenheim who was, as usual, looking tired. The bags under Ritzenheim's eyes seemed to have darkened since the last time the two met, just a few days before. His bloodshot eyes completed a picture of a man teetering on the edge of physical collapse.

"David, I brought you a bouquet of roses. I couldn't think of anything to give you, other than my love and admiration, of course." Ritzenheim smiled, his eyes wet.

Speaking in the barest of whispers, Ritzenheim leaned forward to David, their faces inches apart. "David, I've also come to deliver some intelligence, which I believe is valuable to some of your work. It's also highly confidential, classified to the max, and still playing itself out."

"You know your information is safe with me, Tony."

"David, there is a situation in the Med, which I think will require your services. My contacts in the CIA tell me that they are preparing requests for proposals now for intelligence tracking services and analysis in regard to this situation. In as few words as possible, let me set the storyline. Fifteen days ago, a Greek-flagged freighter loaded cargo in Istanbul. This freighter, the Ileana Iazarou, was captained by one Andreas Moschos, a seasoned, respected, and veteran captain of the Nikolaou Kasos Shipping Line. The first officer, Alexandros Stratakis, a twenty-year employee of the line, and for the past three or four years a confidential informant of the Greek Federal Police, worked side by side with Moschos for a few weeks before Moschos abruptly disappeared. We believe that Moschos had come under suspicion for illegal activity, principally the smuggling of illegal aliens, women, and arms."

"I see. Where does the Ileana Iazarou make its next port of call?"

"Pireaus, Greece. This is where Stratakis began to be suspicious of smuggled cargo being taken on board. Pireaus is a large port, and there are past reports of a large volume of smuggling in and out of this port. The next stop was Tripoli, Lebanon. In Tripoli, the harbormaster delays the loading of the Ileana Iazarou. This delay is at the request of the Greek Federal Police. This delay alerts Moschos that something is up, and he is proven right, something is up. Stratakis had contacted his handler with the Greek police about his concerns. The Greek Police and Navy arrange the delay, so they can get a ship in place to intercept the Ileana Iazarou."

"What you're saying is that Moschos vanished?" David had immediately remembered Frankie's report.

"He bolts and disappears. There are no reports on him, except for a cab driver who took someone of Moschos's description to Beirut. The CIA is turning over every rock in Lebanon, Syria, and Israel looking for him, but at the moment, he's nowhere to be found. What happens next is the Ileana Iazarou finally leaves port and is met by the Psara, a Greek F-454, Meko Class Frigate. The navy frigate stops the Ileana Iazarou and searches it." Ritzenheim paused to take another sip of scotch. As he swallowed, he raised the glass to David in a silent salute.

"And, what, pray tell, did the Greek Navy find?"

"A double shitload of Russian arms: rifle propelled grenade launchers, AK-47's, mines, grenades, and copious amounts of ammunition. But, all of that was expected, given that this stuff is a high value cargo in the Middle East. The Greek intelligence services are convinced that these armaments were intended for Palestine. They were probably coming through Turkey and bound for the port of Al Hudaydah in Yemen. From Yemen, the arms would have gone through Syria to insurgents in Iraq or possibly, via Egypt, to the Gaza Strip. The Greek Navy also arrested three women who insisted they were to go to the U.S. to work as seamstresses, but almost certainly, they'd be used in prostitution. They have requested diplomatic asylum." Ritzenheim paused to slug back some scotch.

"What else?" David smiled at his friend.

"There were other items, according to Stratakis, the captain must have taken with him, but the central problem revolves around a very heavy steel container secured on the deck. Inside were some packing materials and a lead container. The Greeks contracted with one of their radiation consultants. The radiation consultant was flown in via chopper. He discovered the lead box was leaking low levels of radiation. There is ongoing discussion between our radiation experts and the Greeks about what to do next. The president, and therefore the CIA, wants to know for an absolute fact who was the shipper and the source of the radioactive material. You already have a track record with the Greek smugglers. Polopolis can possibly help, if you can keep him contained and motivated. I think you should get your guys a head start on finding out."

"Tony, thanks for the heads up. We definitely have some leads that we can pursue. Let's get you upstairs so you can meet the crew, drunk and disorderly though they may be, and the lovely Zoe." The two men walked up the stairs to find a Texas Hold 'em poker game going on. Zoe looked up from her cards with an artfully raised eyebrow and wiggled in her chair. Everyone shook hands and made small talk. David was impressed with the pile of chips in front of Zoe. Frankie Ballinger was writing out a check in order to get more chips. Ritzenheim warmly greeted them all, poured champagne, toasted the bride-to-be. Then he excused himself and wandered away.

At 9 PM, David, Zoe, Odette, Alice, Yacob, Frankie, Jose, Demetrios, Gao, and Abdul went to the Pantheon for what Zoe called the rehearsal dinner. The owner, Sandor Theoharis, hugged David and Zoe. He told the waiter to get two bottles of Greek red as his personal compliments to the happy couple. The group spent some time drinking and toasting before they ordered from the menu.

Gao was speaking of fractals and the potential application to the analyses and investigations that the company worked on. "Numbers and data sets create dimensions. That is, the numbers can be placed into shapes through applications. Asimov said, 'Scientific knowledge has fractal properties, that no matter how much we learn, whatever is left, however small it may seem, is just as infinitely complex as the whole was to start with.' I believe that since our work must have a beginning and end because of cost limitations, we can use fractals to predict which of the tangents or angles that we have not pursued would be the most likely to yield further information of value."

Yacob lifted his glass. "I propose a toast to Asimov and Gao. I am too drunk to comprehend the fractal possibilities, but I think I know a really smart guy when I hear one."

The entire table clapped enthusiastically.

David was still smiling about the fractals comment when he felt a tap on his shoulder. He looked up to see Harry Markos peering down at him. "What's the happy occasion, David?"

David stood up. The others remained sitting. "Hi, Harry. This is my rehearsal dinner. This is my fiancée, Zoe Papaloukas."

Harry's laugh was huge and too loud. The maître d' stopped discreetly at the back of the room to watch the interaction. "David, congratulations. Please permit me to kiss the beautiful Greek bride." Zoe allowed herself to be assisted to her feet and received the sloppy kiss from Harry Markos. She sat down as quickly as she could disentangle herself.

Markos waved the maître d' over. "Ted, I want to buy brandies for this entire table after they have finished dinner." The maître d' nodded and hustled off. "Now, if I may, dear friend, I'd like a word with you, outside." David kept smiling, but resented Markos's intrusion. Harry Markos marched out into the damp of the Foggy Bottom late evening. David followed. He always tried to anticipate what the argument or the speech would be about. He guessed that it would be about either Polopolis or the smuggling aboard the Ileana Iazarou.

The two men stood in the restaurant's service entrance. It was in the back, small alley that permitted access to vans and hand trucks to deliver food and booze into the restaurant. The back door was propped open with a wood wedge. The garlic, Greek spices, and olive oil smells wafted out to them, nearly covering the stench of the food waste emanating from the dumpsters.

"David, one of my clients has a problem. I think you know about it. In fact, I'm certain that you know about it." Harry stared David down.

David shrugged and smiled before speaking. "You'll have to tell me a lot more than that, Harry. I have a lot of clients, and I can't think of any one of them that would like for you to know about their confidential business."

"Oh, thanks for that, you self-righteous prick. The Ileana Iazarou is stopped in the middle of the Mediterranean. I know you were doing some work tracking smuggling by Greek gangs, so don't try to bullshit me. Did you provide intelligence to the Greek Navy?"

"Of course not. I have no contracts with the Greek Navy or with Greek intelligence. I have heard some tall tales about the Ileana Iazarou and its smuggling operation. But, I have no direct information about it.

I suspect that I may have a bid opportunity coming up, judging from the international security implications involved."

"What international implications?" Harry Markos asked.

"Let's just say that multiple governments are on high alert because of issues with a portion of its unofficial cargo. There are serious homeland security implications, which I know that our government and the Greeks, and possibly others will be investigating on a priority basis." David was pleased to provide this alert.

"Son of a bitch. Just one more thing, do they have Andreas Moschos?"

"Not that I know about, but my understanding is there are a lot of people looking for him." Zoe sidled up and put her arm around David.

"David, we are neglecting our guests. It's nice to meet you, Harry. Thanks for the brandy." Zoe then led David back to the table where the guests were trying to rally from their quiet state of too much food and too much booze. Gao was delivering a dissertation on 'single error conjecture.' No one was listening to him. David was sorry that he'd been unable to focus on Gao's dinner table lectures. When time permitted, he would invite Gao to repeat them for him. Suddenly, Gao stopped his lecture, a broad embarrassed grin on his face. "Here's to Zoe and David and much happiness in their life together. Please excuse my rambling dissertations, but folks there will be a quiz tomorrow." Everyone laughed or groaned.

"Thanks so much, Gao. Sometimes it's hard to believe that later today we'll be married." There was more laughter, and Zoe went to Gao and kissed him on his broad forehead. "We are very happy, and Gao I think you can put us all down for a zero on that quiz." After the laughter died down, David reflected that he really wanted to remember to follow up with Gao when his own head was not tired or over stimulated. It was now past midnight. David and Zoe stood and thanked the assembled group for their hard work and for sharing this precious moment with them, and toasted their friendship. He found himself gazing too often at Zoe in wonderment and apprehension.

*　　*　　*

The following morning was quiet. Gao worked steadily at his computer. Alice and Frankie decorated the first floor with flowers and twinkling lights. Odette worked the phones and prepared the backyard, where the actual service would be held. Odette adhered carefully to Zoe's instructions, which she had written down on a long, yellow, legal pad. When she had finished the preparations for the backyard, at 4 PM, Odette rechecked the weather service online, still zero chance of rain. Most of the crew straggled in late on Saturday to regroup and organize their work before the wedding.

When the Greek Orthodox priest arrived, he insisted on speaking to Zoe and David alone. His accent was so thick that David couldn't understand very much of the priest's advice on a happy, loving marriage. Zoe stopped him after about five minutes and asked him to begin speaking in Greek. "I'll translate later," she whispered to David. The priest happily obliged.

At 6:30 PM, the wedding mass and prayers began. Everyone who worked for DRPearl Inc. was squeezed into the small backyard of the townhouse. Some contracting officers were in attendance from Nanotech, TelTech, Level 8, and TechPro. Carl Mimbs, the obnoxious Chief Contracting Officer from MagnaMeta, had invited himself. Denny Van Pattin, the night manager of Stoney's, was there helping Odette with the last minute preparations.

Several people from the Greek Embassy were at the very back of the yard, including the deputy minister, Theo Gliniadakis, the military attaché, Anastasios Dimantidis, and several of Zoe's Greek State Department security associates. Demetrios was seated in the front row. Tony Ritzenheim sat beside him. Nora O'Brian from the CIA was there with her husband, who worked on the Senate Intelligence oversight committee. Taz Washington stood in the open doorway that opened onto the alley. David's parents sat squeezed together, right beside David.

When the priest began, a complete silence fell over the crowd. Odette was quietly crying. David looked around nervously, until he heard the priest sputter his heavily accented and unintelligible words. David quickly gave up on understanding anything the priest said. His voice was too soft and his English too garbled to be understood even by those nearest him. The evening sounds from the streets and neighbors went crackling into the backyard like a noise soundtrack. The crowd was wedged uncomfortably into the small backyard.

David looked at Zoe as the priest finished his blessing for them. Zoe wore a wan smile. Tears filled her eyes, and she stood as still as a Buckingham Palace guard. Then, the priest placed the wedding rings on the third fingers of their right hands. David touched the flowered crown that was now perched on top of his head as the priest joined it to Zoe's flowered crown with a white ribbon, a symbol of their unity. Following the crowning, the priest delivered a gospel reading, which, David knew from Zoe, told of the first wedding performed by Jesus where Jesus turned water into wine. But his main thoughts had drifted away to Zoe. Odette handed the crystal wedding cups to the priest and poured wine into each of them. David and Zoe each took three sips. Because there was no room in the backyard to do the traditional ceremonial walk, the priest led David and Zoe back into the townhouse. They walked to the front door, turned around and walked back through the back door. As the couple reached the small landing, a barrage of rice hit them. David watched the priest raise his Bible to defend his face. Then, after fifteen seconds, the rice supply was exhausted. David and Zoe kissed, and the crowd erupted with cheers and applause.

The reception party began at 9 PM, at Stoney's. Most of the crowd went there directly after the wedding. David's parents excused themselves to return home. David put them into a cab after kissing them both. David knew how much his parents were already looking forward to the trip to Greece that he had promised them. No date had been set, but they planned to remarry in front of her parents, relatives, and friends at some undetermined time in the future.

David and Zoe finally got to the reception at 10:15 PM. Stoney's erupted in applause, yelling, and screaming. Drinks were forced into their hands. Two chairs had been placed on top of the bar. Folded towels had been placed under each leg. Denny Van Pattin escorted them to these chairs. He and a bartender carefully assisted Zoe to her assigned seat. Opposite, at another table, Yacob Fleischmeister was holding court. Yacob banged a fork on his glass; soon others joined in. When the clatter stopped, Yacob arose from the chair and began to speak.

"This happy couple makes us all jealous. But, allow me to toast them to a long and successful life anyway. Those of us who have married and divorced know the trials and tribulations that might lie ahead. I believe with all of my Jewish soul, and upon my Jewish mother's heart of guilt, that this couple will make it. I truly believe that David and Zoe are in a deep and permanent love. I can recognize this because I am so experienced in the temporary kind of love, the 'I was just kidding' love. The two women that I married were shallow, mistaken loves that quickly turned into a passionate hatred. I hate them to this very day, precisely to this very moment, and I know my hate will last forever. I want the first child to be named Yacob, and I personally want to do the circumcision." A small outbreak of laughter ensued. Yacob paused in a drunken desire to find the next words. During the brief delay, he was dragged off his stage, and Demetrios was appointed for the next speech.

Demetrios was so intoxicated that he wavered back and forth in keeping with a beat that only he could hear. He stood on the table to toast the happy couple. "Dear lovely couple, a toast to you and your love." Demetrios paused for a moment. He swayed as several men at the edge of the table prepared to catch him. He caught himself in time and resumed. "David and Zoe, what a fine pair. They are truly a match that the Greek gods would envy. They are part of my family. I wish them every happiness." The last sentence was completely slurred. Demetrios was assisted from the table, taken to the back of the room, and laid out on the floor.

David turned to Zoe. "Demetrios, I think, wants us to be happy. He misses his own family so much."

Zoe replied softly, her lips caressing his ear. "Demetrios thinks you walk on water. He really loves you like a brother."

Ritzenheim was helped to the table. He was holding a large tumbler of single malt scotch. "For those of us privileged to be here at this lovely union, I want to congratulate you all for having the good sense to work with David or be friends with David. I count myself very fortunate to be among those friends. I recognized David's innate intelligence, sound reasoning, and drive several years ago. I was amazed to learn that David had started his career as an intelligence operative with the CIA. After five years, almost all of that time overseas, place still classified, doing highly classified work, his job was outsourced! Instead of changing careers or moping or whatever, David started his firm. I know it has grown every year since then and is uniquely placed to far exceed in its field. And dear Zoe, what a wonderful wife you will be. I have nothing but the highest praise for your very astute feminine qualities that allowed you to reel him in." Ritzenheim paused, motioning to a bartender for a refill.

"I am also a two-time loser in the martial, I mean marital wars. I feel for brother Yacob. He and I are losers in the love game. Losing at the biggest game of life does provide one with some insight." Ritzenheim paused to let the laughter die down. "All of us are friends to David and Zoe and want nothing but the best for them. Now, let me tell you a story that might help you get married, stay married, and survive the hurdles that will confront every happy marriage. A young married couple in the third year of their marriage discussed the issue of the husband wanting a night out with the guys. Finally, the wife relented. The husband returned home at four in the morning, whisky on his breath, and lipstick on his collar. The wife didn't confront him. She helped him to undress and put him to bed. The next morning, she called his office to say that he would be late. She then called his work associates and friends to ask if he had spent the night with them. Eight of them said yes. The other two said he was still there." A huge burst of laughter filled the bar. Ritzenheim sipped his scotch.

"Now, listen up, gentlemen. The wife decides she's going to have a night out. She stays out all night. The husband has to go to work. He stops after work and buys her a dozen roses. He walks in and the wife greets him, kisses him, and they sit down to dinner. While he was at work, he called ten of her closest friends and not one of them admitted to being out with her!" Another great burst of laughter.

"This is a tough town. Nothing comes easy here. Those who run with the wolves can never slow down. David now has a partner in life who can run at his side. Now dear friends, in closing, let me toast the happy couple to have all the joy in the world." With those words, Ritzenheim was assisted off the table. He weaved through the crowd to where David and Zoe sat. Both got to their knees on the bar and leaned over to kiss him. Ritzenheim wandered toward the front door and through it to find a cab.

The Greeks from the embassy put Greek music on Stoney's stereo, ending the speeches and blessings. Theo Gliniadakis and Anastasios Dimantidis jumped onto the bar and started dancing. Dimantidis's wife danced on the table on the other side of the room where the speeches had been made. David watched as Alice Boggs and Nora O'Brian joined her there, the three of them shaking their arms in front of them, swaying their hips, and throwing their heads back and from side to side. Frankie Ballinger's frenetic dancing included stylistic moves with high kicks and holding her dress up past her knees.

David hugged Zoe and got down from the chair and the bar. The two of them casually chatted with the remaining guests. David felt an unpleasant roiling of the food and alcohol in his stomach, when four DC police officers walked in the front door at 3:30 AM. Taz walked over to meet them. When Taz turned the stereo down by half, David breathed easier. The officers nibbled on the leftovers, then went back out into the night. David, now, was leaning on the bar for support. The few stragglers started to move toward the door. David put his arm around Zoe. They went to check on Demetrios and found him snoring loudly, sleeping under a tablecloth.

Back at the townhouse, the couple found Odette cleaning up the kitchen. Her face was flushed. David couldn't remember seeing her at the reception. She happily waved at them, and blew kisses at them, and continued to unsteadily cleanup the kitchen. David had a sudden eerie sensation; where was Polopolis? He was too tired to pursue the matter. He went up to the third floor, found Zoe, and dropped to her side, and fell asleep.

CHAPTER 25
Creative Dissonance, April 21

After a quiet week on the beaches of Aruba, David was back that Monday. He walked into his office at 7:30 AM to find Alice was waiting for him in his office, head down, pen poised. When she finished the line she was editing, she looked up at David. "Hi, David. I've got some things that we need to talk about, before you do anything else. I went to that ASIO meeting, and everybody treated me like a leper. We've stopped the leak, but the damage is done."

David held up his hand. "I get it, Alice. I really do. I understand your concern. We need some damage control, or should I say, spin control."

"You have five contract proposals in your in-box, ready for your signature. Since you didn't read email and didn't return calls, you should also know that there are three in-depth analyses for the MagnaMeta contract. MagnaMeta is the biggest decision point. The Greek embassy has been strangely silent, and frankly, that worries me. We are babysitting Polopolis, and they seem to have forgotten about him. The final deliverable on the Greek contract is due at the end of this week."

"Okay, Alice, it sounds like I've got a lot of work to do this week. What else?"

"More work." Alice delivered a half smile in his direction and retreated from the room.

David followed her out with his eyes and saw that Gao was waiting. He motioned Gao into the office and excused himself while he went to the kitchen for more coffee. Gao waited, sipping his personal blend of green tea.

Gao was conscientiously thorough. "David, the data base that I have established has provided linkages from the missing MagnaMeta analyst, Yvonne DeLorme, and the missing Greek captain, Andreas Moschos. By the linkages, the telephone numbers, and financial transactions, I can say with a high degree of certainty that the woman is in Beirut, Lebanon. I can say with some confidence I believe that Andreas Moschos is in Beirut, Lebanon. What I can't do, at this point, is say with any confidence that the two of them are together or allied in Beirut, Lebanon."

"Excellent work, Gao. Alice tells me that MagnaMeta has not yet asked us for a briefing. But, if we can confirm the two of them are working together, we have a big leg up on potential CIA contracts. I will send someone to Beirut to try to find both of them. Do you have any addresses?"

"Not yet, but I am still working to obtain more financial records. These might reveal addresses. One of my former students is working at MagnaMeta. He tells me that all budgets have been slashed, and he's afraid that analysts may be furloughed next. Management isn't talking. The interesting thing is that the Chief Executive Officer, Douglas Antonopoulos, has been away from the office, overseas, for the last two weeks. A strange phenomenon during a budget crisis, wouldn't you agree?"

"I certainly agree, Gao. I hope your friend stays employed over there. Tell him that we could always find some work for him over here. How's Uncle Vern?"

Gao laughed. "Uncle Vern has a bad case of the flu. I assisted in the evening the past few days, so he could get some rest, but he came in anyway. I'll help out until he's back on his feet."

"Tell him to get well, for me." David looked into Gao's eyes. Those deep brown eyes gleamed with evident intelligence, amiability, and curiosity about the world.

"I will. Uncle Vern thinks the world of you." Gao chuckled and shrugged.

"He's been a good friend. When you get a chance, polish up those financial pro formas that we did on MagnaMeta. Maybe when Antonopoulos gets back, he'll demand to be briefed."

As Gao was heading out the door, Yacob Fleishmeister was coming in. Yacob held a spiral notepad and was anxiously flipping pages back and forth while walking. He continued to do so as he sat down.

"How's it going, Yacob?"

"Not bad, not good, could be worse. That was a great reception, David. Everyone had a blast. How was the honeymoon?"

"Really great, both relaxing and romantic, both of which are just what I needed. Zoe is fun and hard to keep up with. She's in excellent physical shape."

"That's great. I think you two are a good match."

"I agree. What do you have on the Greek Embassy?"

"Not much, I'm afraid. The few security breaches that could have been created by our friend Nicolaos seem to be timed out, for the most part. When he left, the possible breaches were effectively sealed. I have verified that they have changed all of their security codes, so Nicolaos couldn't break in or do damage if he tried, not without some kind of inside help. I am also following the gang's telephone communications, but that's slow going. They talk in code, in some kind of gang slang and in Greek, so translations have to be carefully worked by multiple iterations of the computer programs and our best translators. I am piecing together bits and pieces, but there are plenty of indications already that Harry Markos is kind of a central nervous system for the gang. Ike and/or Stella Zisis call the shots. They are clever, but whenever a thread of thought or process needs a firm decision, it seems to end up with one or the other of them and usually through Markos. Markos works the phones constantly. I don't see how he has time to ever go to court, so he probably doesn't. Ships at sea and ports all over the Mediterranean frequently get calls from him. I have downloaded their financials from the annual reports, plus public shipping records. If nothing else, I think I can prove that there are black market reasons for the decision making. I hope."

"Keep at it, Yacob. I keep hearing reports that one of their captains, by the name of Andreas Moschos, is missing. Keep a look out for that name. Of course, there is almost certainly more than one rotten apple in the Kasos barrel. Thanks again, my friend." David turned to his computer screen filled with unread emails. Forcing himself to concentrate, he had only read two when the office phone rang on his direct line.

"David, this is Carl Mimbs from MagnaMeta. My big boss, Antonopoulos, wants to meet with you. Are you available this afternoon?" Carl sounded loud and confident.

David flashed to his schedule on the computer. He was heavily scheduled all day after a week away. And, he wanted to talk to Polopolis, who was not on the calendar. He felt the need to personally verify that Polopolis was continuing to cooperate. "Carl, this is a bad time."

"Antonopoulos wants to meet this afternoon. After the turd blossom you and your boys laid on us, I'd think that you'd be over here at the drop of a dime. I'm not telling him otherwise."

"I think Antonopoulos could use his time studying our report. I've got nothing to add to it. If Antonopoulos still wants to meet, it will have to be at the end of the week." David felt the mounting pressure of workload and the nagging worry about Polopolis.

"I'm sure you realize you are cutting all ties with MagnaMeta."

"Read the report. You have no ties left to cut with anyone." David clicked off the phone. He pulled his in-box over and began grinding through the documents.

After thirty minutes, David had cleared a few of the documents that needed his signature. When the nagging thought of Polopolis returned, he grabbed his jacket, told Odette where he was going, and drove to the apartment where Polopolis was receiving protective custody. David pulled the van into a driveway of the apartment complex, found an open space, and slapped the metallic signs for Quality Plumbing on each side. When he reached the apartment, the door was ajar, and he cautiously entered.

"Nico, stop right there." Nico looked up with wild, wide open eyes.

"Nico, give me the pistol." Nico looked at the gun, looked at the severely pistol whipped Jose Gonzalez lying on the carpet, moaning, and then back at David.

"Oh, hi, David. You've caught me at a bad time. I was just leaving." Nico pointed the pistol directly at David's chest. "Jose was getting on my nerves, and it was time for me to leave. I've told everyone everything I know."

"Where are you going?" David began to edge toward Polopolis.

"Surely, I don't know. Seems like I've worn out my welcome everywhere I go. Anyway, did you bring wheels? Toss me the keys, gently. Thanks. Now, tell me where I can find it."

"Downstairs, the white panel van. I'm sure you'll remember it."

"Ha, ha, get over by the window." David slowly walked to the window. As soon as he stopped, a bullet went buzzing by his head, shattering the glass. David whirled around to see Polopolis running through the door. David knelt by Jose, checked his pulse, and dialed 911.

By the time he got back to his office, it was 9:30 PM. He was tired, emotionally drained, and feeling like someone had worked him over with a rubber mallet. Someone was still working upstairs, and the lights were on in his office. As he walked in, he saw a man lying on the sofa. What now, he wondered.

"Oh, my God." Antonopoulos abruptly sat up. His elbow sent a china tea cup flying to the carpet. It survived, but Antonopoulos did not seem to notice. "Pearl, we have to talk. Tell me what's going on."

"I'm guessing you are Douglas Antonopoulos. I'm exhausted. One of my employees was beaten to a pulp. I just came from the hospital. Now, I have a multitude of issues with my own firm needing my immediate attention."

"I'm sorry, just give it to me straight up." Antonopoulos's immaculately tailored suit was now heavily wrinkled, his eyes red, and his posture sagging.

"We know that thirty-five days ago you received a message from your internal auditor requesting outside assistance with a cash audit. You emailed her back with a message to go ahead with her plan and to prepare a briefing for the board. The missing Ms. DeLorme was copied with every one of your messages, so she knew that it would only be a matter of time before she was caught. So, she activated her escape plan, but left in place were these electronic siphons sending MagnaMeta's incoming cash to the fictitious bank accounts that she controlled."

Antonopoulos put his head in his hands, the gold Rolex slipping down his arm.

"Now, Mr. Antonopoulos, on the last page of our report, we listed the actions you must take today. Call your lawyers, shut down your financial and email software immediately, and call an outside accounting firm to audit and reestablish a true accounting of all funds."

Antonopoulos remained with his head bowed, hands supporting his face.

David sat down at his desk, grabbed the top folder from his in box, and began reading. Antonopoulos stretched out on the sofa and was quickly asleep.

Chapter 26
Confidentially, Bankruptcy, April 23

David was sleeping fitfully when his cell phone began to rattle, and then fell off the nightstand. He swung his legs to the floor, found the phone, and gave a whispered 'hello.'

"Tony Ritzenheim, David. I have urgent, confidential information that will not wait. How soon can you get over to my place?"

"Maybe, thirty minutes." David splashed water on his face, got dressed, found the keys to his dad's car, and drove straight to Ritzenheim's condo.

As David was about to knock on the door, Ritzenheim pulled the door open. Rizenheim put a hand on David's shoulder and guided him to a chair at the kitchen table. Ritzenheim settled a cup of black coffee in front of David, grabbed one for himself, and sat down across from David.

"David, one hour ago, I got a call from Martha Graham, the publisher of the Washington Post. She was livid, apologetic, and had a fascinating tale to tell. It seems that in the business section of today's . . ." Ritzenheim glanced at his watch. "Or rather yesterday's Washington Post, the pending bankruptcy of MagnaMeta was listed in with all the others."

"That's not good." David was tired and especially tired of hearing the name, MagnaMeta.

"Not good? It's really, really bad. So, somebody, somewhere in the bowels of the bureaucracy reads the bankruptcy listings. I've never given it a moment's thought to reading the list of financial failures, but yesterday, it was truly 'must reading.' Anyway, word spread throughout the day like wild fire, maybe like nuclear fusion. Martha gets calls from the Vice-President, Secretary of State, Douglas Antonopoulos, and MagnaMeta's law firm, plus the Inspectors General from NSA and the CIA. Martha said she allowed herself a good cry for two minutes, then she called the appropriate staff into her office and chewed them out. So, that's part one, anyway. Part two is the Post's CIA desk asks the assembled group in Martha's office if anyone has heard anything about the Greek navy holding a ship with a dirty bomb on it."

"Yikes, when do we get to the part where I'm involved?"

"Don't worry, its coming. The veep creep, in response to her question about how could this happen, responded that a company named DRPearl Inc. has been asked to operate the MagnaMeta business until it completes bankruptcy proceedings. Now, that's another mystery we need to solve. Probably, a spur of the moment covering of his ass, but now that means you'll be contacted today, probably to close the loop. And, the worst part is, David, you can't say no. The bankruptcy is bad enough, but now the administration needs to protect its flanks because the bankruptcy is public knowledge, but what MagnaMeta was working on was and still is totally classified at the highest level."

"Can I get some more coffee? I suppose it's of paramount importance for national security that DRPearl take MagnaMeta on, but I know what kind of mess it is. Probably beyond the comprehension of most people in the administration. Oh, let's see. It's now 3 AM, so this is just another example of how bad news travels fast in DC."

Ritzenheim returned to the table, pushing over David's refilled cup. "You can understand the potential political embarrassment, but the intelligence agencies have legitimate concerns. Your firm has the best insight into MagnaMeta and Greek criminal activity, and you have the knowledge and assets to understand any linkages or vulnerabilities to other issues."

"I wish I could say it's nice to be wanted, but this job may kill me. We have too much work for the staff already."

"Hire some more, consider this open checkbook work. The intelligence losses have to be identified and contained immediately if not sooner."

"How come Martha is so chummy with you?"

Ritzenheim shrugged. "Martha and I once kicked the can down the road together, and she values my input."

David laughed. "I'm sure she does. I'm going to work now, Ritz. Thanks for the info and the coffee. I'll keep you posted."

Chapter 27
Roma, April 24

Nicolaos Polopolis slept little, throughout the flight to Rome. He marched up and down the aisles continuously, stretching his arms to the ceiling and, once in a while, bending to touch his toes. His flight landed routinely at the Leonardo da Vinci-Fiumicino Airport. As the plane taxied to the gate, Nicolaos pulled out his cell phone and sent a text message about his arrival to Uncle Ike.

As soon as Nicolaos walked into the gate area from the airplane, he found a quiet space inside the terminal. He called David. "David, I'm in Rome."

"Why did you escape, Nico?"

"I was tired and angry, and I wanted to go home."

"Join the club, asshole. You may be pleased to know that Jose will be released from the hospital today." David's voice was firm and sharp.

"I'm angry at being held a prisoner for so long against my will. I was tired of that cub scout, Gonzalez, threatening me continuously, telling me to keep my mouth shut, and ordering me around. It's a long flight to Rome, but after all we've been through, I still thought I owed you a call."

"Listen to me, Nico. When you get to Greece, stay there. I hope you get your life straightened out. I really do. And, we were protecting you from yourself."

"Are you in trouble with the embassy, David?"

"No, Theo seems almost relieved. And, when he finds out that you are on your way back to Greece, he will be overjoyed."

"I'm glad. Theo deserves a break. And I didn't say I was going to Greece."

"Here we go. Where are you going, Nico?"

"Oh now, it wouldn't be prudent to tell. I might have to elude the authorities again. You still there, David?" Nico stood in the terminal, looking around.

"Yeah, I was thinking what an ungrateful, selfish prick you are."

"It had to be done; the investigators were threatening me with prison. And besides, I think I can be of some assistance."

"Please, whatever you do, Nico, don't try to help me. I don't need it. Why do I have the feeling that you're lying to me. Try to remember our conversation about how you need structure, stability, and boundaries in your life? When you get too many choices, you make bad ones. Other people depend on you. Life isn't just about screwing and playing golf."

"Well, that's a crying-ass shame." Nicolaos hung up on David. He strolled past the gates until he was inside the main terminal. He stood off to one side with tears slowly rolling down his cheeks. He pulled a tissue from his pocket and gently dabbed his eyes. He had a few more hours to kill, so he wandered through the shops and lobby.

When he got to the gate from which his flight to Beirut would depart, he sat down next to an elderly, Asian woman.

He asked her how she was doing. She eyed him cautiously.

"I am fine. How are you?"

"Thirsty and tired." The woman reached into her large tote bag and pulled out a bottle of water. She insisted that he take it. Nicolaos felt his face redden. At first, he tried to wave off the bottle before accepting it.

"Do you live in Beirut?" he asked the woman.

"No, I am visiting my daughter and her family. I live in Orlando, Florida, with my husband. Our other children are in Orlando. My Beirut daughter insisted on studying international relations at Georgetown, and sure enough, she had relations with an international and married him."

Nicolaos laughed. "I am visiting too, but I know no one. My family is in Greece, and I will be seeing them soon."

"I am so glad, Nicolaos. How long has it been since you saw them?"

"Too long, about six months. Business has just been too good, so I've been driving myself to make my corporate managers happy, but I need a break."

"I am Mrs. Wong, but everybody calls me Tootsie. Will you watch my bag while I go to the lady's room?

"I'll guard it with my life, Tootsie." Nico watched as Tootsie entered the lady's room, then he rifled through her tote. Finding a small notebook, he located her cell phone number and quickly wrote down her daughter's address and telephone number, then Tootsie's ATM number and password. He was sitting beside the tote when she returned. He gave her a big smile.

"You don't look like someone on business, Nicolaos."

"The need for the trip came up suddenly. Our business demand shifted, and the boss wanted somebody on the ground in Lebanon. I happened to be available, so here I am." Nicolaos smiled at her. She looked at him with a wrinkled brow and a very slight smile.

CHAPTER 28
An Abstruse Spy, April 25

The night sky was black with a few light dots from stars. On the ground, there were vivid banks of lights illuminating Beirut. The plane bounced heavily on the tarmac, startling most of the passengers. Then, the pilot slightly overcorrected to the right, causing more comments from the passengers. A flight attendant came on the intercom. "Our entire team apologizes for the bumpy landing. We regret any inconvenience. Welcome to Beirut, Lebanon." Nicolaos reset his watch to the local time of 9:35 AM.

Nicolaos was summoned from the line of passengers waiting to get through customs. The customs officials frowned at his Greek passport and studied his visa. They huddled briefly away from the table where Nicolaos waited. They then directed him to a closet of a room, where he waited for twenty minutes before an interrogator showed up.

"I am Officer Rafiq Abdelnour, Mister Polopolis. Your passport states that you are a Greek diplomat." The interrogator was a fragile-looking man, no taller than five foot six, with a bald head that had blotchy red spots and thick black-framed glasses.

"I was a Greek diplomat. I am on approved leave at the moment."

"Why did you come to Lebanon?"

"I wanted a vacation, to play some golf. I've never been here before." Nicolaos's voice sounded tired, even to himself.

"There are many places closer to the US or Greece where you can play golf. What made you choose Beirut of all places? That makes no sense. Even though you have a visa, I must be sure that you are really in Lebanon for legitimate reasons. I will contact your embassy." The interrogator jumped out of his ancient, wooden chair and left the room. Nicolaos got up and tried the door. It was locked. Nicolaos then slumped into the metal chair and closed his eyes. He jolted upright when the interrogator came back into the room.

Nicolaos asked him for a glass of water. Rafiq ignored him. "I have spoken with your embassy, and they say that you are a fugitive without government protection and that we should send you back to Greece on the next flight."

"Rafiq, I need a drink of water. You can do whatever you like. As you can see, I brought my golf clubs. I intend to mind my own business and play golf. And, you can plainly see the approved work visa."

"I can see. We are not known for our golf. In all my years in this business, you are the first person I have heard of that comes to my country to play golf."

"I didn't know that."

"You think that we believe that story? How did you get your Lebanese visa approved?" Rafiq's squeaky voice rose even higher.

"My friend and I went to the Lebanese Embassy in Washington, DC. There was no problem. I have some business to transact for him while I am here."

"Why didn't you say that?"

"Because I am here to play golf. I don't even know what my friend wants me to do while I'm here. He told me he would brief me after I got settled."

"You don't know what business it is? Are you some kind of damn fool?" Inspector Rafiq stood rigidly in front of Nicolaos, grinding his teeth, fidgeting while he waited for a response.

"Maybe, but he is a good friend who I owe some favors, so I told him that I would do it. Why don't you call him? He will verify my story."

"I will do that. Give me his name and number." Nicolaos pointed toward his wallet, which the inspector had placed in a plastic bag held in his hand. The interrogator quickly pulled out a DRPearl Inc. business card, fingering it with a sneer on his face. Again, the man jumped up and left the room. Nicolaos put his head on the table and quickly fell asleep.

He woke up as the little inspector came back into the room and noisily resettled into the metal chair. The little man didn't look up, but studied notes that were made in a file. "Nicolaos, you say you are here to do some business and play golf. Mr. Pearl tells me you are a fugitive from the Greek police. That would make you most definitely not here on business, and you are not a Greek diplomat. Isn't that the case?"

"No, Rafiq, it wouldn't. I am on leave from the Greek Department of State. I am part owner of a shipping business, and I hope to talk to clients while I am in Lebanon."

"Yet another story for me to think over. I must talk with our embassy in Washington." Rafiq jumped up and walked briskly out the door. This time, as the door swung shut, Nicolaos grabbed the door handle and kept the door from relocking. He glanced around and then walked out of the door down a long corridor, where he took an emergency exit to the outside. The alarms began to clang away immediately.

Nicolaos casually, but quickly, walked to the line of traffic about half a block away. When he reached the arrivals area, he jumped into a cab out of turn, ahead of the twenty, or so, people waiting for one. The cab driver appeared confused and looked to the dispatcher for guidance. The dispatcher frowned, but waved him clearance.

"Where to, mister?" the driver asked in English.

"The Hotel Intercontinental Phoenician on the Minet El Hosn."

"That's a nice place. I get a lot of business from them."

When the driver stopped at a light a few blocks from the Hotel Intercontinental, Nicolaos opened the cab door, got out, and sprinted away from the cab. The cab tried to follow him, but the traffic was heavy and Nicolaos frequently changed directions, stopping often to see if the cab or the police were following him. The hotel lobbies had security at their entrances, checking identification and occasionally searching bags. After he finally reached the Intercontinental Phoenician, he blended in with a returning group who were waved through security. Nicolaos went to the conference level, found a restroom, and settled himself onto a toilet behind the closed door to plan his next move. He had left his wallet, luggage, cell phone, and golf clubs in customs. He had only some loose change in his pocket, along with Tootsie's ATM information and her daughter's phone number and address.

CHAPTER 29
A Radiation Revelation, April 26

David had gotten up early, gone for a two-mile run, and as soon as he got to the office, he sent a passionate email to Zoe. Then, armed with a mug of black coffee, he attacked his inbox. When he heard the Washington Post hit the outside steps of his building, he got the paper and his second cup of coffee.

David's eyes were drawn to the front page headline: "Radioactive Shipment Sent to the Bottom." He hurried to read the story and then he called Alice.

Alice answered on the second attempt to call her. The first call went to her voice mail. "Alice, are you okay?"

"I think so. I had a late night . . . of working, David."

"We got the second piece of confirmation about the information Ritz told me about. Listen to this. The Washington Post today is reporting the Greek Freighter, the Ileana Iazarou, was seized by the Greek navy. It was smuggling weapons, explosives, illegal aliens without papers, and US currency."

"Uh oh, I can feel the sparks flying all over Foggy Bottom." Alice's voice was now vibrant and intense.

"The Secretary of State is probably in the situation room at the White House already. The Ileana Iazarou had sailed out from its last port of call, Tripoli, Lebanon. While in Tripoli, the captain of the Ileana Iazarou, Andreas Moschos, left the ship and resigned via email. He has not been located. He is believed to have in his possession a large amount of U.S. currency that was being smuggled out of Iraq and Kuwait. Unverified accounts place the total amount at over $3 million. The two ships spent several days in the Mediterranean while the Ileana Iazarou was being carefully searched. The weapons and armaments were off-loaded in

Greece. The three women are being detained in Greece where they have applied for political asylum."

Alice interrupted. "Okay, so heads are spinning in Greece, Lebanon, the US, and elsewhere?"

"Absolutely, and the hunt is on for who's responsible. Interpol almost certainly is working the case already, and Israel is intensely aggravated because of what else was being smuggled. The last item of smuggled cargo, a steel, lead-lined container was determined to be leaking radiation. A radiation specialist, flown in from Greece, tested and recorded high levels of radiation. While the discussions over what to do with the radioactive material were underway in Greece, the United Nations and Interpol requested information from the Greek government. With both requests denied, the UN and Interpol turned to the United States for assistance. The U.S. State Department requested information and was told affirmatively that it would be immediately forthcoming, when the next major event occurred. Sometime during the night of April 15, the steel cargo container, with its radiation-leaking steel box inside, was pushed over the side of the Ileana Iazarou. At this point, all parties involved, the Greek government, its Nuclear Safety Service, the Greek Navy, and the shipping firm, Nicolaou Kasos, have stopped talking publicly. The U.S. Embassy in Greece has registered a formal protest."

"Oh là là. And into this mess, the intrepid agents of DRPearl Inc. will be stepping."

"We got the charge letter from State yesterday, Alice. We'll wear our rubber boots, but let me go on. Intelligence services from the European Union and its individual member nations, the United States, Turkey, and several Arab Nations, are actively trying to determine what happened. Several Mediterranean fishing associations have already begun protests in Athens and the Greek port of Pireaus. Mediterranean cruise lines have already noticed a drop-off in new business and a large increase in cancellations. The Italian government has requested convening the UN Security Council."

"The plot thickens. I'll be there in an hour." David sat back in his chair. He clipped the article and scanned it into the office computer system. He sent it to the team of Arab specialists and Alice. Then, he called Ritzenheim.

CHAPTER 30
Someone to Listen To, April 26

Mee Maw finished her research on where to go next in her search for further clues about Nevzlin. After searching through the faculty at all of the State Colleges in West Virginia, she settled on three resumés, reviewing each of them carefully. She then called a former student who was in graduate school at Marshall University, and after receiving a sterling report, she opted to first contact a Marshall University Russian history professor, Dr. Reginald Roach. She called his secretary and got an appointment on June 4. She drove from her home in Dunbar to Huntington, West Virginia and the campus of Marshall University.

As soon as she found the building where Dr. Roach was located, she went into the rest room, where she retightened the bun containing her silver hair, straightened her new navy blue dress, and reapplied her red lipstick. Then, she marched to his office, where the secretary looked up at her in surprise.

"Hi, are you Mrs. McKay? I'm Annie Treadway, Dr. Roach's assistant."

"Yes, but please call me Mee Maw. Everyone at home does. After I retired, I just decided that I was going to be a grandmother even if my son wasn't going to cooperate. I brought you some mocha fudge that I made last night. You were so nice to me on the telephone." Mee Maw's long fingers easily pulled out the gift wrapped box of fudge and presented it to Annie.

"You are so nice to think of me. The students aren't here this week. If they were, this would all be gone in about five minutes." The two women laughed.

"Oh, I know what you mean. I've been retired for two years and I know my high school students could disappear baked goods in the blink of an eye. I am so grateful that Dr. Roach agreed to talk with me."

As Mee Maw walked decisively into his office, his eyes displayed some surprise at the attractive woman in a tight blue dress and matching medium heels who stood before him. He shook her hand with both of his. "Mrs. McKay."

"Call me Mee Maw, Dr. Roach. I sure do appreciate your taking the time to meet with me."

"The pleasure is mine, Mee Maw. But due to our age, I think I would prefer to call you by your given name if I may?"

"Well, if you insist, I answer to Margaret too."

"Outstanding. Margaret, I understand this has something to do with translating some Russian documents you believe have some intelligence value for the U.S." Dr. Roach relaxed in his leather, executive chair, tipping back, and carefully considering the woman in front of him.

"That's right, Dr. Roach, and as I have told your secretary, Annie, I have been unable to get anyone in an official position, like the FBI, interested in this. I have written my Congressman, as well, to no avail. I think that it's too complicated, and maybe too absurd, to get anyone to take the time for what they see as an intrusion upon their time."

"Well, I see that you have an impressive volume of documents. What do you think is going on there in Dunbar that's illegal?" Dr. Roach leaned back in his chair and stuck an old pipe in his mouth, which he did not light.

"I think I have a Russian spy living two houses away from me. You aren't going to smoke that thing are you, Dr. Roach?"

Dr. Roach laughed. "I'm afraid not, Margaret. My doctor has made me quit. So, now I just chew on the stem like a kind of pacifier."

"Good. Here is my story. Three years ago, a man moved into the neighborhood. He kept to himself, ignored all the neighbors, including me. He acts like he is hiding something all the time, disappears frequently for days at a time, has an elaborate security system installed in his house and garage. Through my own snooping, I have found that he works for a Washington, DC, firm that specializes in communications intelligence. I have learned that he's Russian. I have learned that I won't learn Russian fast enough to ever be able to translate the materials that I have."

Dr. Roach stuck up a hand in a gentle request for her to stop. "How did you acquire these documents, Margaret?"

"Illegally, but I want to assure you, Dr. Roach, that I am a very serious person, and I know this situation is serious and worth the risk. Besides, the teenagers in the neighborhood call it 'hacking,' which sounds so much better. So, I searched his garage, his trash, and have broken into his email accounts. I have tried all of the police agencies, and they are just not interested." Mee Maw smiled at Dr. Roach and resettled herself into the seat of her chair.

Dr. Roach laughed in spite of himself. "I don't mean to imply that this is funny. And, I don't want to be dragged into any illegalities. I realize that it could be a serious matter. Let me see those files."

Dr. Roach started reading the first section of the files that Mee Maw had neatly filed in a notebook. He read for several minutes in silence before speaking. "Mee Maw, I think that you may be onto something here. It appears that this man, Nevzlin, is working for an intelligence firm in Washington, DC. It sounds like he is a kind of mid-level analyst. He works on translating financial documents and information from Russian oil companies, among other business entities, for a Washington, DC based firm, Infosystel. But, he also works with a company in New York, an export-import business named European Design Systems. I think that he gives some of the information that he has translated to the design company. After just a few minutes of reading, I can also tell you that some of this is in some kind of code. I'd like to keep your file and ask my colleagues in the math department what they think. Do you mind?"

Mee Maw thought about that for a few seconds. "I think that sounds fine. The files you have are copies. Please call me anytime if there are questions, Dr. Roach."

"I promise. Your new friend for life, Annie, controls all my work and my teaching schedule, and I'll ask her to help me stay on top of the case of the strange Russian in Dunbar." Dr. Roach laughed pleasantly while looking directly into Mee Maw's vibrant, blue eyes. "Margaret, before you start back to Dunbar, let me buy you a cup of coffee."

"I'd like that, Dr. Roach."

Professor Roach drove his ancient Land Rover to the donut shop, where the employees greeted him with affection. "Please call me Reg, Margaret. I'm a regular here; the coffee is great, and the staff is very friendly."

"Oh, I'm sure I'll like it as much as you do, Reg." She looked over at him, and the professor caught her glance.

On their way inside, Reg put his hand on her back, gently steering her to a table. "What would you like?"

"I think I'll go with the hot chocolate with crème topping."

The Hub Place for Coffee was designed and decorated in a mid-50's collegiate theme, with pennants, pictures of old football, basketball, and baseball players from Marshall University dominating the walls. A tall, slender, blind man in a business suit sat in the corner, slowly sipping his coffee while maintaining a perpetual smile. Dr. Roach said hello to him and then went directly to the order section of the counter where a grinning young woman greeted him. "The usual, Doc?"

"Please, and a hot chocolate with crème for my friend."

Reg picked up their order and returned to the table. As he sat down, their knees bumped. Mee Maw didn't pull her knees back, so they sat there, knees touching. "Margaret, I am intrigued by the materials. I look forward to working on it."

Mee Maw smiled. "Who's your friend over in the corner, Reg?"

"Oh, that's a retired mathematics professor, Ed Miles. Ed gradually lost his sight over the last four or five years due to macular degeneration. He's a real brain, and I might call him to study your materials. He can crack codes as good as anyone. How's your hot chocolate?"

"Just fine, Reg. This is a nice place. I like it, and I'm glad you brought me here. Everyone seems to know you, and it's got a very comfortable, relaxed feel to it."

"Yes, Margaret, I've been coming here for more than twenty years." Dr. Roach looked out the window, momentarily lost in thought.

"I enjoy seeing you so comfortable here. I'm afraid that I haven't found a café where I would feel so much in tune with the people back home in Dunbar. But, I have plenty of nice neighbors, and I enjoy helping the children."

Reg stared into her green eyes. "I take it you are a widow."

"Yes, for over twenty years now. I have one son who lives in Key West and has never married. How about you?"

"I divorced twice, both long ago. Three adult children who live in Raleigh, North Carolina, Miami, Florida, and Castle Rock, Colorado. All doing fine, with, if I remember correctly, eight grandchildren. I thought that I would be fine living alone, but sometimes I do get lonely. Maybe, that's just me getting old." Reg sighed.

"Reg, I don't think it has to do with getting old. I'm an optimist. I keep thinking that I will meet the right person. I still think that I can find a companion who I can trust and share with."

"Mee Maw, I got to get back to a class. I'll drop you off at your car. I'll give you a call as soon as I have finished reading all the files. It's been a real pleasure to meet you.

CHAPTER 31
Dysfunctionality, April 28

David sat at the head of the long mahogany table in the MagnaMeta conference room. Along one side of the table was a trio of accountants from MagnaMeta's accounting firm, Shillington and Roberts. "Guys, I have just concluded the meeting with the board of MagnaMeta. That meeting lasted over four hours. So, it's already been a very long day for me. But, I understand you have concerns about our work on the financials. So, let me hear your questions, so that we can get out of here."

The leader of the accountants turned to each of his two colleagues and nodded at them. "I'm Frank Babidge, I am head of auditing for Shillington and Roberts. On my right is Justin Rice, who is a finance forensic specialist with the firm, and to my left is Anthony Princisi, the lead auditor on the MagnaMeta contract."

"Sounds like you have the A team here. Let's hear your concerns."

"The principals at our firm are very concerned over this debacle and, of course, the potential liability that we may be exposed to as a result. Several of the board members have complained to us about DRPearl's role in the matter and, frankly, what you have said about the company. On April 26, for example, two days ago, there was an article in the Washington Post that heavily criticized the management of MagnaMeta, and by inference, Shillington and Roberts."

"I haven't spoken to the media and never will. So, I don't know their sources and will not comment on the accuracy of the reporting. So, are you here representing MagnaMeta or Shillington and Roberts?" David snuck at glance at his watch.

"Both, really. What I would like to know is how you came to be the investigator, if you will, on MagnaMeta's accounts."

"My firm has the security clearance necessary to do the investigation, the computer skills, and the financial acumen to get the job done. I understand that Shillington and Roberts is a respected accounting firm. The choice to hire my firm was made at the highest national security level. Beyond that, I will not go."

Anthony Princisi cleared his throat. "The report that you gave to the board was devastating, for example, that there are no funds with which to pay employees or contractual obligations. But, you did not speak of the responsibility for this disaster beyond mentioning Miss DeLorme and her criminal associates. Will your final report speak to this?"

"Of course it will. And I think that Shillington and Roberts, MagnaMeta's board, and its top management all should be held accountable for the mess that happened on your watch."

Princisi slumped back in his chair. "I see."

"I have detailed my best financial analyst, Yacob Fleischmeister, to work full-time on the MagnaMeta case until we can securely transfer all the computer and storage files. DRPearl will do a full accounting for Homeland Security, which has taken the lead role in this matter. I expect another contract from Homeland Security to pay us for our services and the bankruptcy attorneys. Beyond that, I am not willing, at this time, to go. In the future, please direct your inquiries to Yacob Fleischmeister. I really have to go." David shook their hands and left them huddled together as he departed.

Back in the office, he sorted through a pile of yellow phone messages. He decided to return the call of Douglas Antonopoulos first. "Hi Doug, what can I do for you?"

"Thanks for returning my call, David. I know that you briefed my, excuse me, MagnaMeta's board. Not one person, except for you, has returned my calls."

"Well, Doug, hopefully that will pass. When all the dust settles, I think you'll be in a better place."

A short, not quite stifled gasp came out of Antonopoulos. "I sure hope that you are right, David. What I needed to tell you is that after several confrontations at my front door, on the street, and many more while at the gym, shopping and elsewhere, even church, in addition to the threats delivered by email and telephone, I have reluctantly concluded that my wife and I and our four children need to get out of town, so we'll temporarily relocate to Greece. As you may know, I am a third-generation Greek from a diner-owning family in Pittsburgh. I have some distant cousins in Greece, and we need to get a breather, away from all this pain and suffering."

"Gosh, I certainly understand. Please stay in touch. There may be some questions still that need to be answered. Godspeed."

David walked upstairs to Alice's office. "Hi, Alice, you got any pressing issues for me before I go see Dingfelder?"

"Not really. The financials are looking good at the moment, so we have a decent cushion for a change. Go ahead and see what Dingfelder wants; get that over with. His office has been calling two or three times a week since you went to work full-time on MagnaMeta." Alice flipped a notebook page over and glanced at it before looking up again at David.

"Thanks, Alice. I knew I didn't have to worry about things here while I was gone. Thank the rest of the team for me. We'll all celebrate sometime soon."

David, freshly showered and wearing his best suit, was met in the lobby by Dingfelder's executive assistant, a striking brunette in exquisite shape, who he estimated to be about six feet tall. She motioned for him to follow her.

"Mr. Pearl, we are so glad that you can finally meet with Deputy Secretary Dingfelder. I'm his confidential assistant, Wendy Sutton. We know how busy you are. How are you doing, taking care of yourself while you worked those fifteen hour days?"

"As good as can be expected under the circumstances, but I hope to resume running someday soon. You look very fit. I'm sure you know how hard it is to maintain a regular fitness schedule with the work schedules that we have."

"I agree. I've had this job for three years, so I know that the choices are killer: personal life, workouts, or work, and sometimes it's just work and none of the other."

The elevator reached Dingfelder's floor, and the two of them stepped out into the reception area.

"It seems that everyone has left already. "I was hoping to start doctoral work at Johns Hopkins, but I can see now that was a fantasy."

"If you can juggle all four of those priorities, please let me know how you do it." Wendy touched David's elbow to gently direct him into Dingfelder's office.

Dingfelder met him at the door, put a hairy hand on his shoulder, and with that pressure directed him into a conversational grouping in front of his massive desk. CNN was reporting the day's news on the monitor behind his desk. A metal cart stood beside the desk, holding numerous red-bound folders.

Dingfelder dropped himself into a leather recliner. "David, everyone in town really appreciates the heroic work that you've done with MagnaMeta. We all realize what incredible stress you've been under. You need to duck out of town for a few days and get some rest." Dingfelder's eyes were in constant motion from the television, to Wendy Sutton, to the file in his hand, and then back to David.

"I'm afraid there is to be no rest for the weary, Burt. I know you're right, but at this point, I can't get to sleep when I try. There are just too many loose ends and questions flying around in my brain." At that moment, David's brain was still bouncing from one topic or thought to another in a seemingly random pattern. Only great effort, on his part, allowed him to concentrate on the moment.

Burt Dingfelder smiled, and his eyes focused with affection upon David. "David, we are getting nowhere fast on the murder of Cardiff Shapiro. The FBI says that it looks like a contract killing. The police have exhausted all leads. The State Department Security Service has examined everything that he was working on. There is nothing in the files that gives any additional leads. In fact, there is nothing in the files that would indicate anything other than many other nations' leaders in foreign relations would be pleased to buy Cardiff a cup of coffee, if he was still alive. What we need is a security think tank, such as your firm, to examine the case file, get us some leads, and hang onto developing the case until the killer is found. More importantly, we need to find the killer's motivation. Just like we need to find the reasons for and the ramifications resulting from the MagnaMeta collapse. The vice-president personally asked me to talk to you and get your thoughts."

David was instantly, fully alert at the mention of the vice-president. "My thoughts, Burt, are as follows: MagnaMeta's collapse has cost my firm over $200,000 for our prior work that is not billable. My firm billed another $300,000 for our efforts in closing it down. We have assumed responsibility for all of MagnaMeta's current deliverables. Our other pre-existing work is barely above our internal control points on our process charts. My best financial analyst is worn to a frazzle. We don't need any more work. Second, I, personally, have a great interest in finding MagnaMeta's missing analyst, Yvonne DeLorme. But at this moment, my firm simply doesn't have the time, the resources, or the energy to do so. So, my advice is keep on doing what you're doing, and I'll lend all the moral support that I can muster."

Dingfelder frowned, pursed his lips, made eye contact briefly with Wendy, and leaned forward. "David, I realize that you are exhausted. We all know that. I'm afraid that I've been given no options regarding the absolute national security interest in retaining your firm. You set the timeline. You set the budget. You can even define the deliverables for us. What we are facing is a stonewall—no, make that a steel wall. The other firms in the business are not action-oriented like DRPearl. Or, they can't be trusted on a matter like this for one reason or another. The vice-president chairs the National Security Council, as you know. This work is the highest priority for the president. And, frankly, I can't take no for an answer."

David sat in silence for a few moments before he responded. David could not see a way out. His key staff was already working seventy-eighty hours a week. Chasing down leads in the murder of Cardiff Shapiro would be yet another, perhaps, blind alley to travel down. He was disgusted, but ever so reluctantly decided to comply because he couldn't see a way out. "Okay, Burt, I'll have the proposal to you in two weeks."

"I think you better make that four or five days, my friend. Any questions?"

David's eyes widened. "Who has the complete files, the FBI or State?"

"Neither one. I have the complete files right here. There are computer disks for all of this, of course. When we get the contract signed, you'll have a great responsibility in maintaining their security. Now, please get out of here, and get some sleep."

CHAPTER 32
For the Sake of Money, April 29

David had arranged to meet Yacob Fleischmeister in his office at 6:45 AM on June 5. For David, who usually slept upstairs on the third floor, getting to the office early was no problem. Yacob, on the other hand, lived in Fairfax, Virginia, to provide a house in a decent suburb for his three children, when it was his turn to have them. Coordinating this with two different mothers, he once explained to David, had sharply enhanced his listening, anger-management, and time-management skills. Yacob had to take the Metro subway into the District, change trains, and still had to walk two blocks to get to the office. Jacob walked in five minutes late.

Jacob slurped his coffee and bit into a bagel while he perused his notes.

"Jacob, how does the MagnaMeta project stand? What do we still owe the bankruptcy court?" David's tired, watery eyes focused wearily on Yacob.

"Not much, just the closing, final financial statements, which the accounting firm is working on. I put a little bonus in the contract for them, enough to keep their attention, so I think that we should get them the first week of May. I'll be glad when we can clear out the financial aspects of it. But, as you know, the intelligence angles are myriad. I need help on those." Jacob talked while seated at the edge of his chair. When he finished talking, he returned to his coffee and bagel. This process would be religiously repeated every time he finished a comment to David.

Before David could open his mouth to ask his next question, Odette came through the door. "I'm sorry, Jacob, but I think David needs to see this." She hustled over to David, and shoved some papers under his face. She put a hand down on top of his desk and peered over his right shoulder, revealing to Jacob the majority of her breasts. Jacob watched and quietly nibbled on his onion bagel.

When David looked up after a few seconds of reading the top page, Yacob asked, "You want me to leave, boss?" David shook his head.

"Odette, make sure that I have this right. This woman, Olympia Oblinger, sent me an email through the company website saying that I sexually abused her, stole all of her cash, and left her a note saying that my firm would make good her loss? And, this was last night in Beirut? That son of a bitch Nicolaos Polopolis must be in action on the ground in Lebanon. Odette, call the U.S. Embassy, Lebanese Customs, and the Greek Embassy in Beirut, and see what you can find out about our lover boy. I had a feeling the son of a bitch wasn't going back to Greece."

"Will do. Now, David, the calls are backing up on you. The National Security Administration wants to meet with you today, as soon as possible. Burt Dingfelder wants you to call immediately. Anthony Ritzenheim says call; it's urgent. Zoe wants you to call. And last, but certainly not least, that esteemed motherfucker, Nicolaos Polopolis, is holding on line two."

"Odette, transfer Nico first. Call Zoe and see if you can take a message or a subject, and tell her it doesn't look like I can get back to her until late this afternoon. Yacob, stick around, but we may have to continue this some other time."

David picked up the phone and forced his voice to sound cheerful, "Nicolaos, what a surprise! How nice of you to call. What have you been up to?"

"No need to be sarcastic, David. I've been running ever since I landed here. You know that bombs went off in Beirut last night, and I heard shots being fired this morning? This place is deadly."

"I'm not being sarcastic. Here, let me read you a little email I got this morning." David read him the email from Olympia Oblinger. "Nicolaos, whatever shall I tell Olympia?"

"That had to be done, David. I had to escape customs. They wouldn't honor my visa and were grilling me for hours. So, I ran away and have been running ever since I escaped from their custody. But I had to leave my wallet, cell phone, suitcase, and golf clubs in customs at the airport."

"So, therefore you were forced to debauch this woman and steal her money. I can see that." Odette rolled her eyes at David as he stated the facts. Yacob smiled, but his attention was fully directed to his bagel.

"David, I'm giving you a courtesy call. I was temporarily inconvenienced, so I did what I had to do."

"I really don't think so. You just like being a pain in the ass. What are you doing in Lebanon? And how did you lose your money?"

"I had a problem at the airport. Customs wasn't going to let me enter the country. It will take me a while to get more cash, so all I have to live on for the moment is Olympia's cash."

"Poor, poor baby, you've lost your golf clubs, too. Listen to me, Nicolaos. Are you listening?"

"Of course," Nicolaos said.

"How much money did you relieve Miss Olympia of?"

"Twenty-five thousand Lebanese pounds, plus or minus."

"Okay, I'll have Odette arrange to reimburse her and provide some extra funds for her trouble." He nodded to Odette, and she went off to complete the task. Yacob opened his laptop computer, clicked through some screens, and then brought it over so David could look at it.

"David, I need money to rent an apartment, get a cell phone, new clothes, and some golf clubs."

David studied the computer screen, which was a map of Beirut with arrows applied by Frankie Ballinger, pointing to sites where suspicious phone calls had been made or received. "I don't think so, Nico. Please stop harassing me. I'll make a report of contact and send it to the US state department and the Greek embassy. They'll help you out."

"Don't mess around, David. I have no ID," Polopolis was pleading. Odette returned to the office.

"You created the problem, and you'll solve it or not. I think I'll bring charges in Lebanon, so that will give you something else to think about."

Polopolis snorted. "Fuck you, AMF."

"Well, I guess Nico didn't want to talk anymore. Odette, wait up for a second." Her cherubic face appeared once again in the doorway. "Please get Abdul for me. I need to see if he can take a little trip for the company."

David then returned to his desk, picked up the phone, and punched in Tony Ritzenheim's number. "Hi, Ritz, yeah, we are still ahead of the bad guys. Listen, before we get to the reason you called, I need some background information on why Dingfelder has given me five days to put a proposal together on the Cardiff Shapiro case."

"David, you seem to be the man on the hottest seat in town at the moment." Ritzenheim's voice was matter of fact, but cheerful.

"Thanks, Tony. It's feeling real hot at the moment. I wish the money would flow half as well as the workload is flowing, but that's my problem. Why do all the high potentates of intelligence suddenly want DRPearl to take over the investigation on Cardiff Shapiro?"

"The Cardiff Shapiro case is going nowhere. I think the studs at the White House think that a private operator will cut the corners and eliminate the legal niceties to get to the killer and the reason why. They are tired of all the lack of progress and excuses, frankly. So, I'd call the pressure on you the result of a confluence of events, David. You are intimately involved in MagnaMeta. You have expertise in dealing with the Greeks and the Greek underworld. The intelligence powers that be want to get you involved in what is rapidly becoming the hottest, literally, issue in the world, finding the smugglers who were dealing the radioactive cargo on board the Ileana Iazarou. So, that's the next shoe to drop, so I wanted to give you a head's up. If they can get you on board, then they won't have to spend time bringing any other potential contractors up to speed. They have already agreed to sole source your company, if you agree to the job."

"Okay, then what's that job, exactly, dare I ask?"

"Well, you read the Washington Post article, so that's the nucleus, if you will pardon the word, of your task. Our intelligence operatives know that several governments and the bad guys desperately want to find the captain who left the ship in Tripoli after he became suspicious the authorities were onto him. Undoubtedly, he had help from the crew, who were almost certainly getting paid under the table to secure their cooperation in the smuggling operation. So, your next contract will be to find Captain Moschos and fill in all the blanks."

David sighed audibly. "I'm with you so far."

Odette stuck her head inside the door. David asked Ritzenheim to wait. "What do you need, Odette?"

"I have Robert Woggins on hold, on line two. He's demanding to talk to you. I have Neal Walters, the DC cop, holding on line four, and I have Harry Markos holding on line five. They all say it's urgent." Odette was calm, assured, and smiling.

"Odette, would you mind getting me another cup of coffee? And tell Abdul to get ready to go to Lebanon. And, make travel arrangements for us both."

"I already talked to Abdul. We will have you ready to go before you're ready to go," Odette teased.

201

"Tony, I have to take two calls very quickly. Can you hold?" David got a reluctant yes. He punched line four.

"Neal, what's happening, buddy?"

"David, I got bad news. Taz has been shot up bad. He's in the Washington VA hospital in surgery as we speak." Neal's voice sounded extremely tired and on the verge of tears.

David threw his head back against the chair and pounded his desk once. "I am so sorry, Neal. What happened?"

"We were out in the northeast, between two blocks of row houses, trying to find a suspect when a sniper parked at the end of the street fired three shots at us and then backed out into traffic and was gone. Taz squeezed off a few rounds. I'm sure I hit the car once or twice, but Taz took the automatic rifle fire. He's got two bullets in the chest and one in the shoulder. He's critical. I thought you'd like to know."

David's body shuddered. "Jesus, I'm sorry, Neal. I'll be there as soon as I can." David hung up and took Harry Markos's call, but a bad feeling lingered.

"Have you found Polopolis yet?" Markos demanded.

"Harry, yes, we've located him. He's not in Greece, and he's not here." David gazed at the ceiling, his mind running through the pressures now stacking up on him. He had already filled a yellow sheet full of notes and was starting on the second. His biggest worry now was who shot Taz and why? He had to force himself to listen to Harry Markos.

"What about that Greek freighter captain? I'm feeling a lot of heat over this."

"Well, you should be, but we are not yet looking for him. When and if we learn something and if we can share that information, I'll give you a call, Harry. Why are you looking for the freighter captain?" Markos did not respond to David's question. "I have to go." David clicked off.

"Tony, sorry about that. A friend has been shot and is being operated on right now."

"Anyone I know?"

"No, he's a DC detective. He was at the wedding. You may remember him. Tough, smart, and always on the ball. I think I'm in shock."

"Oh yeah, too bad. I hope he recovers. Let me finish my answer to your question. I have to hustle. I'm due for a meeting with the Secretary in five minutes. There are several intelligence agencies in Europe and the Middle East banging around in regard to this Ileana Iazarou incident. So, the Greek government has pressured our State Department to come up with something to cover their ass. The crew of the Ileana Iazarou got antsy and took a dim view of being held at sea with radiation leaking from a steel crate stowed on deck. So, during the night, they dropped it into the sea. This happened while the Greek navy had supposedly secured the ship, and so they own that part of the mess. The first officer, engineer, and first mate are now under arrest, and the freighter is now docked indefinitely in port. So, to sum up, Moschos needs to be found so that the police agencies can track the radiation back to the source. If the tracks can be determined, I should say. So, there's a lot riding on you. Your firm has the most expertise in this matter, so you're getting the deal."

"Wow, thanks, Tony. Let me call the state department and get the ball rolling. Be safe."

"You too, David. Keep me posted."

David next called his contact at the state department. Abdul came into his office as the Deputy Secretary of the State Department was picking up. David motioned him to sit down.

"Hi, Amos. Sorry it's taken me so long to get back to you. It's been busy around here this morning." David lifted his cup and motioned to Abdul to please get him a refill. Abdul happily obliged.

"David, good to hear from you. I wanted to brief you before you go over to the National Security Administration. It's a matter of international concern."

"I'm listening. What do you have?"

"Listen, I know your plate is full. The Med situation is heating up. The United Nations may get involved. Russia is not commenting on anything, which is strange, and I think implicates them, in all probability. The environmentalists are having a major spitting contest with several governments, including the US. There's been a call by the President to the Russian Prime Minister, directly, about this, but so far zilch."

"I see. I'll call NSA and set up the meeting right now. Thanks, Amos."

As soon as David concluded, Odette appeared in the doorway again. "It's Woggins. He won't take no for an answer."

"Tell him if he wants to talk to me, he can meet me in the surgery waiting room at the VA Medical Center. And, call the Administrative Directorate at NSA, and get an appointment for me to meet with her today, if at all possible."

Pulling into the VA Medical Center grounds, David parked in the only available visitor space, while other cars continued to circle the lot. The medical center structure looked like a series of buildings slammed together as if the initial building was way too small from the start, so add-ons sprouted every year or two. Inside the lobby, he found a policeman and asked for directions. The officer walked him to the OR suite. David found the surgery waiting room filled with people uncomfortably waiting: sleeping, or with their heads down, or quietly talking, or watching whatever monotony filled the television screen. The room was cramped and messy. Neal Walters was among those sleeping. David gently jostled Neal's shoulder. The detective was instantly alert.

"Hey, Neal, what can you tell me about Taz?"

"Good to see you, David. Thanks for coming." Neal rose to his feet, put a hand on the back of David's arm, and guided him out into the hallway. "The nurses tell me that Taz is fighting for his life, but they're cautiously optimistic. Whatever the fuck that means? He's out of surgery and is in the recovery room. I'm waiting until they get him into a room, so I can call his family. Most of them live in Baltimore. He has a couple of kids, two brothers and a sister up there. I told them not to come until I had something definite on him."

"Neal, you look completely worn out."

"For sure, David. I have briefed what seems like the entire DC police department, at least all of the brass. Internal Affairs was here, and they want to grill both of us. We are both on desk duty until they rule on the shootings. What were we supposed to do, just stay in the line of fire until we both died of lead poisoning?"

"That's a mandatory investigation, Neal. This will blow over. You'll be back on the streets in no time."

"Man, I don't know if I want to be back on the streets. If I do, I need to get my nerve back. I think I'm quitting. I really do."

"Go home and get some sleep, Neal. Things will look a lot better tomorrow. I mean it. I'll stay. When Taz gets out of the recovery room, I'll call you."

"Thanks, brother. At least Taz is here with his comrades in arms. I'm telling you, he loves this place." Neal handed David his business card after writing his personal cell phone number on the back. David watched him walk down the long, brilliantly lit corridor. As Neal was getting on the elevator, Woggins came striding out.

David stood waiting in the corridor for a moment, then turned and walked to the nursing station. He told the nurse and administrative clerk that he was replacing Detective Neal Walters in the wait on a report on Taz Washington. He gave them his name. The clerk wrote it down and smiled. David turned to face Woggins.

David extended his hand, and this time Woggins took it.

"How's your friend doing?"

"He's in the recovery room. He's fighting for his life, supposedly."

"Tough duty, being a cop in DC."

"He's a tough hombre. He'll survive."

"Good. I wanted to talk to you about the Shapiro case." Woggins waited politely this time for David to respond.

"Okay, I can't say anything about it, so what I can tell you?" David kept his voice light and unofficial. He assumed Woggins was under intense pressure as a result of the failure to find Shapiro's killer.

"The pressure is on. Our leads have all been run to the ground, and we have come up with nothing. I heard through the rumor mill that you might be getting a contract to develop leads in the case through some kind of fucking meta-analysis or some shit like that. I'd like to work with you."

"We haven't started our work yet, Robert. And, the contract requires clearance only for State and NSA officials. Work your end to get clearance, and I'll work with you. Otherwise, my hands are tied."

"I'll do it. I understand." Woggins smiled at David warmly, shook his hand, and walked briskly back down the hall to the elevator.

CHAPTER 33
Campaign Brain, April 30 and May 1

David and Abdul were patiently waiting in the customs line at the airport, in Lebanon, at 11:40 PM. Their place at the end of the line hadn't moved much since they got in it. David looked at Abdul and grinned.

"Abdul, you seem to be a patient traveler. You're taking all this in stride. You look peaceful and relaxed."

"I am, not much you can do about the bureaucracy. Security will always be vigilant in Lebanon."

"I'm calling the office. It looks like we'll be in this line for awhile." David listened to the phone intently and was surprised when Odette picked up without his hearing a ring. "Hi, Odette. Abdul and I are standing in a long line in customs, in Lebanon. What's going on? Just give me a general sense of things. I'm in a crowd."

Odette sounded like her usual, cheerful self. "David, it's fine here, busy. Everyone is keeping on, keeping on with the workload."

"Very good. Let me talk with Alice and then anyone who needs to talk to me next."

"Good morning, David. Where are we on the exactly global grid this morning?" Alice sounded aloof and maybe a little angry.

"Alice, you sound a little hostile this morning. Listen, Abdul and I are at the airport in Lebanon, so we have definitely gone global. How are you?""

"I'm doing alright. I'm in kind of a nervous fidget about workload. We have two critical contracts pending. You know the ones with NSA and State. Have you started assigning staff to these? With Abdul and you there, we'll need to maximize our resources here."

"Yeah, Gao, Frankie, and I talked briefly last night. We'll get on top of it. Don't worry. Oh, Odette needs to talk to you again. We'll send you an encrypted update before we leave the office today."

Odette's voice came back on the phone. She made a huffy sigh. "David, I have Dan Casteel on the phone. He's a campaign manager for the Maryland Republican Senatorial candidate, Ansel Tritt. He's demanding to speak to you right now. If you have a few minutes, maybe you can handle it."

"Put him on. Hello, this is David Pearl. What can I do for you?"

"Hello, Pearl. You can join forces with the Tritt campaign, that's what you can do. We need to vet some of our people and some of their people, if you know what I mean?" Casteel's voice rang with a nasal shrillness.

"I'm awfully sorry, Dan. I can't do that."

"Why the fuck not, Pearl? Ansel Tritt is going to be the next Senator from Maryland, and he can be a powerful help or not. That's up to you." Casteel snarled.

"That's not the business we're in, Dan. We have no expertise in background checking, and right now we're up to our eyeballs in work."

"Now, David, the next Senator from Maryland and I have heard so much about DRPearl, it would be mutually beneficial if we joined forces and presented a united front to the voters. We want you on the Tritt team."

"Sorry, Dan, we're not into politics. If we needed the money, and we don't, your job would still be outside of our expertise. We would have to charge a lot more than the organizations who do that, the ones you can find all over Washington."

"That's not the point. You don't want to help. I can understand that. You know that politicians have memories like elephants, don't you? We don't ever forget our friends who could help the team, but don't."

"I hope we're still friends. I wish you the very best in the campaign, but I also hope you remember we are an intelligence and security operation, one of the best. Anything else?"

"No, thanks a lot." Casteel's voice was terse and edgy.

David paused to jot down the time, purpose and date of the call for the record. If there was any kickback from his refusal to join the campaign, he would have the note in the file.

Odette came back on the line. "David, you have two more callers who say it's urgent you call them today, Doug Antonopoulos and Frank Fulton from WaveLinks. Neither one wanted to give me a subject. That's all; good luck hunting, and we miss you already."

David chuckled before thanking Odette and concluding the call.

David knew that Antonopoulos was living off investments and had little chance of getting a job in intelligence, let alone an executive job. He called him first. The line at customs had inched forward slowly for about five feet.

"It's been very quiet, David. You find out who your friends are. You are a true friend because you returned my call. I really appreciate that. I wanted you to know that my family and I are home. The kids just raised hell about being away from their friends. I'm at my wit's end. Frankly, they want me out of the house." Antonopoulos weary voice cracked and paused as if he was on the verge of losing control.

"I can imagine what you and your family are going through. Doug. What can I do for you?" David would have liked a long conversation out of sympathy with the defeated and jobless Antonopoulos, but this was simply not the time.

"I need to get out of the house. I need to have an adult, non-spousal conversation. I need something to take my mind off my misery. I guess I need a shoulder to cry on at the moment."

David was interrupted by Abdul motioning him to move forward in the line. Antonopoulos sounded close to desperation. His lack of oversight, failure to implement vigilant computer security, lack of internal controls, failure to analyze internal risk, and horrible personnel vetting were all the direct fault of others in his organization, but Antonopoulos was the visible leader, accountable for it all. He had become a public, horrible example for every executive in the intelligence or security business.

"Doug, I'm in Lebanon on the moment. Why don't you go to the office in the morning and start working on getting your clearance reestablished. Odette will keep you busy. She'll find something for you to do. It will be clerical, but sometimes monotony is good for clearing the mind."

"Are you kidding me, David? I was simply angling for a lunch date. I'll be there in the morning and buy lunch for everybody. Thank you so much."

"Doug, we usually get lunch from Chung's Buddha Belly. It's at the end of the block where the office is located. Tell them that I sent you. Oh, and get plenty of Walnut Chicken. That's Alice's favorite. See you soon."

David told Abdul to text a message to Odette and Alice about Antonopoulos. "I've got one more call to make. Thanks."

The voice of Fulton, the pompous Chief Operating officer from DRPearl's competitor, WaveLinks, squealed with irritation and arrogance.

"Pearl, I hear you're rolling in the gold nuggets over there. You've got lots of contracts and fantastic goodwill with the current administration."

"Work life is good, but overloaded at the moment, Frank. What can I do for you?"

"You can share your bountiful good luck, Pearl. Sometimes we contractors have to scratch one another's backs. Business over here is a little slow. The navy is getting cut out of the intelligence business. The current administration is focused on the ground game and not keeping its eyes on the prize elsewhere. We need enough subcontract work, candidly, to tide us over until we can redirect the administration's interest to what we see as the priorities. And really, what I hear about the latest contracts, concerns stuff that is right up our alley. You know that as well as I."

"I'm sorry to hear about your business, Frank. Alice and I will review our contracts and performance next week, and if there's anything we can outsource, we'll do it."

"That's great, Pearl." Frank Fulton hung up abruptly.

Abdul pushed their bags forward again. "Now, I'm getting another call. I'm ready to throw this phone in a trash can."

Abdul smiled. "We won't be far away from the ocean in a few minutes. Why don't you wait until then? It'll be far more satisfying. That should calm your nerves. Everything about the Mediterranean is serene and beautiful, as far as I am concerned."

Eyes suddenly widened, David shot a look of surprise toward Abdul's face. "Abdul, it's the office of a Congressman Eugeniades."

"Hi, this is David Pearl."

"Pearl, listen, I want to come over next week and get a briefing from your firm. How can that be arranged?"

"It depends on what you're interested in, sir. And, right now, I'm not sure when I'll be back in town."

"What do you mean?"

"It means that I'm on assignment in Lebanon, and when I get back to Washington, whether I can brief you or not depends on your clearance and what you would like to be briefed on. Depending on that, you would have to be cleared by the appropriate department: Defense, State, Homeland Security, or NSA. And, you would need the House Intelligence Oversight Committee to clear you, as well."

"You've got to be kidding me. Can't we simply have a little fireside chat?"

"We don't have a fireside, Congressman, but we can chat all that you want to. I'm just saying we can't release any confidential or secret information about any of our contracts. I can listen, of course, and I can tell you how my firm does its work, but that's about it."

"I don't think I can get the Intelligence Committee Chairman to agree to it. He's an asshole, even if he is in my party. I'll try. My secretary will call you next week. Why don't we plan on you coming over to my office, then?"

"It would be my pleasure, sir." The Congressman abruptly hung up. David sent a text message to Odette to get background on Congressman Eugeniades. David and Abdul finally arrived at the customs table where they handed over their passports, had their luggage searched, and were given forms to fill out. At 12:30 AM, they were passed through to the door that led to the rest of Lebanon.

Outside, the intermingled smells of the night desert and sea washed over them, and the bright airport streets lights illuminated them. David's secure phone rang. "Hi Alice, what do you have for me?"

"I thought you should know this. One of our analysts, Ali Nassar who covers Yemen and Saudi Arabia, says that a website with news in Sana'a, Yemen, the capital, reports a body being found in the bay of Al Hudaydah. The body has tentatively been identified by Interpol as Andreas Moschos."

"Okay, ask Nassar to get all the information on the death as humanly possible." David said.

"Sure. Maybe we should send Ali to Yemen. He's got a lot of drive and savvy."

"Okay, and ask him to give the information to Frankie, so she can put that information in the computer." David stared at the phone momentarily before continuing. "Alice, I know I'm asking the impossible, but see if you can find Frankie some help, and tell her investigators to apply logic, you know my philosophy, so get all the damn facts on Beirut and Yemen that she can. We need to do that, follow the trail; be the trackers from hell. We must use our collective imaginations, define a workable hypothesis, and then try to tear it apart. We must discover the choices not made and why not. If doing all these correlations doesn't help us this time, then it will for the next time. These smuggling gangs reputedly have three or four hundred, loosely affiliated members, most of them with real jobs, who participate when summoned by the masterminds. That's who we need to get, the masterminds that lead each criminal network and the corrupt officials."

Alice waited for a moment before she responded. "David, you are preaching to the choir. We are already on it. Please be careful."

"Yeah, I know it, Alice. I'm overtired, and I apologize. Bye," David slumped back into the cab's backrest. "Okay, Abdul, now I'm getting a text from Odette." David read the message: "Eugeniades, two term republican, retired navy captain, armed services committee. All right, my dear comrade Frank Fulton must have put Eugeniades on our case, Abdul. I'm turning the phones off. I have to attend to some real work here. I need to get some rest before anyone else calls." They laughed.

CHAPTER 34
Love Is All It Is, May 1

Mee Maw and her beau, Reggie Roach, were lying in bed on Sunday morning. In the distance, they could hear church bells calling the obedient. Mee Maw didn't go to church anymore. She loved the traditions and the fellowship, but the sermonizing often didn't sit right to her.

The small grouping of homes on the ridge where Mee Maw lived was surrounded by forest, grass, and late spring flowers. The houses, mostly small, with two or three bedrooms and full basements, were past middle age, but almost all were well maintained. On this Sunday morning, she could hear a few lawn mowers in the distance, birds singing, hammers and saws sounded from far away, and cars moving down the hill to their occupants' chosen house of worship.

Mee Maw quietly got out of bed, put on her housecoat, and went to the kitchen to start coffee brewing. She felt comforted by the scene outside her dining room window, tree trunks spiking upward into varying shades of lush green, sunlight filtering through the leaves. She went to the front door and waited while one of her neighbors from further up the ridge drove slowly by on their way to church. Then, she darted out to pick up the Charleston Gazette.

Reg had settled himself into the kitchen chair nearest to the stove. Mee Maw took her usual place on the opposite side. She removed the plastic wrapper from the Sunday newspaper and pushed the paper over to Reggie. He continued smiling. "I guess it's not the New York Times, is it?"

"No doubt about it, Reg. You can use my computer to check on the news. Most of it doesn't get to the Gazette, I'm afraid."

Reggie reached for her hand, drew it to him, and gently kissed the back of it. "You are an amazing woman, Margaret. I wish I had met you about fifty years ago."

"But, we didn't. Our lives would sure have been different. We found each other now, and that's the main thing. I thought in retirement that I could read, and quilt, and be content. But, I hadn't bargained on meeting a seventy year old professor who has such charm and wit."

Mee Maw poured Reg another cup of coffee. She glanced at the headlines. "Reg, I know you wanted to talk about our project, so tell me what you've come up with."

"Margaret, is there anything that happens that you miss out on? I don't think so." Reggie laughed. His head gently bobbed.

"I'm not nosey. I just am a good observer of human nature and curious about almost everything. Thirty-three years as a teacher and principal will give you those skills if you don't have them in the first place. And now, I have the Internet, which is an incredible resource, but not one agency has responded appropriately to my concern. I have even sent letters to my congressman and the two senators. In response, I got nice polite letters saying that they would look into it, but I doubt they did. Of course, they wouldn't tell me if they were investigating Nevzlin."

Reggie looked down and then turned to look out the window where, in the sunny morning light, there was now a large, buff Labrador out in the backyard placidly sniffing around. "I know, Mee Maw, a simple citizen without direct access to someone in authority is simply not going to be heard. That's just a fact of life. It's not personal. I have talked to my friend, Coopersmith, at George Washington University in DC. He's a Russian language professor. We often collaborate on research. So, he and I brainstormed a bit on where we should go with the information that we have discovered."

MeeMaw set up abruptly, her back stiffened and her eyes wide "When were you going to tell me about that, Reg? I'm dying to know."

"I'm not being deliberately slow. My students frequently tell me on the end of the semester, professor assessment questionnaires that I am slow to get to the point, and I suppose I am. But, here's the story. Your neighbor, Nevzlin, is employed as a Russian translator. He is gainfully and legally employed. It looks like he gets fed information, data, and communications from wiretaps or wireless interceptions, one would hope, by virtue of the consent and agreement of our federal government. We don't have enough to tell, really, what he might be up to in regard to his official job. He translates. All of the conversations in regard to that job appear to be benign, but quite possibly are in some kind of code, about which my friends in the math department have suspicions, but do not yet have an answer. Many of those translated conversations are from or to email accounts that I haven't been able to trace to the real identities of the owners. I don't have the skill set, but given the content of the messages and the use of codes, the owners could be diplomats and counselors of the Russian Embassy in Washington. Furthermore, I doubt the company he works for, InfoSystel, knows about those contacts. InfoSystel is a highly secretive operation, obtaining communications from sources for the government. I think this job is legit, but he has a clear conflict of interest between his job and his other correspondents."

"Okay, Reg, a conflict of interest isn't legit, is it?"

Reg smiled at her, his demeanor and quiet calmness providing a steady state of reassurance. "No, and what else doesn't appear to be legit is this export-import business, the European Design Systems. Nevzlin gets gifts from this firm like the Harry & David gift box. He apparently flies to New York on occasion, based on extrapolation from the two credit card statements that you reconstructed. We could surmise this is what Nevzlin doesn't want you or anyone else to know about. There are also long exchanges with various people in this firm that range from idle chitchat about hockey to overt political statements. Nevzlin is a great admirer of Putin and states frequently his agreement with Putin's policies and strong, domineering attitude toward the U.S."

"Okay, so how do I do research on this European Design Systems?"

"Well, Margaret, you don't. Allow me to deconstruct what we know and identify what appear to be gaps or incongruities with our Victor Nevzlin. Incongruity number one is what's he doing in Dunbar, West Virginia? Based upon his interests in mother Russia and the fact that his employer, InfoSysTel, is based in Vienna, Virginia, which is just outside of Washington, DC. So, his being here is inexplicable based on this contradiction. There is no discernable reason why he's here and not in New York or Washington. The second incongruity is that from all currently available evidence, he has made no attempts to make friends, start a family, join the Moose, or socialize in any way. Therefore, the man's social needs—and he must have them—must be being satisfied on these long weekends that you spoke to me about. The third incongruity or gap is the playful, and I'd say loving, emails between Victor and one Dimitria Debresky, mostly in Russian and in coded language. One would want to be with one's loved one. That's usually how it works. What is holding our boy in Dunbar, West Virginia? Fourth incongruity conjecture: Given Nevzlin's dislike of the neighborhood, what's keeping him in it? When one can't move, or for example, one can't leave the state, or one has to report to a probation or parole officer every so often, then one's movements are restricted. Why then, is Nevzlin's residence restricted? I think it must be, has to be, a legal requirement of some sort. My next door neighbor, the law professor and dear friend, is mulling that one over. Our fifth incongruity, for the moment, is when one is proficient in Russian and one is far away from one's homeland, one probably would seek out other Russian émigrés. I checked the web, and lo and behold, there is a Russian-American Friendship Society in Charleston, West Virginia, just a hop, skip, and jump away from us here in Dunbar. I called the Russian-American Friendship Association, and after some small talk, the nice lady who coordinates affairs for the Friendship association volunteered that they had no members in Dunbar. I offered to come speak to their group some time, and she was positively thrilled!" Reggie paused and sipped from his now cold coffee. Mee Maw poured him another cupful.

"And, the sixth and last incongruity is the fact that Nevzlin disappears from view when one looks back to about seven and a half years ago. There's no way you or I could get information beyond that point. Someone else, like a top security cleared firm or the CIA, could find that out."

"I can see I brought my little issue to the right man, Reg."

"And, I bless the day you became annoyed with Mr. Nevzlin. You have brightened my life."

"I was beginning to obsess about Nevzlin. Without you, I'd have probably done something crazy." Mee Maw gazed into his blue eyes.

"Margaret, I adore you, and I have enjoyed delving into this puzzle you brought me. Now, for next steps."

"What can I do?"

"Relax. We don't know what we have here, Margaret. We can afford to be cautious, don't you think?"

"Sure, but you've done all the work. I think your analysis will open the eyes of the authorities. Maybe not the FBI. I've given up on them."

"I have given that some thought. I think there's a better way to approach the FBI."

"Okay, but hurry up. I want to take you for a hike at the Kanawa State Forest. It's gorgeous this time of year."

"Sounds like a fine idea. Before I lose the thread, let me finish. My friend at George Washington University has a colleague who is a consultant for some companies engaged in communications 'research,' or as I would put it, intelligence gathering, with a mission to prevent terrorism in all its ugly facets. So, my GWU friend asked him who would be interested in this little situation of ours. He surprised me with a company's name, not an agency or a CIA official. He said to write it up and send it to DRPearl Inc., an up and coming intelligence and security firm in Washington, DC. This Middle East expert says he has met the owner, the CEO, and believes he is an open-minded and responsive person. So, my dear Margaret McKay, you package this up and mail it to DRPearl Inc., and then wait to see what happens. From what my friend says, someone from the firm will definitely be in touch."

"Ah, Reg, you've been such a find! Let's go get ready for that hike."

Chapter 35
Game On, May 8

Nicolaos had already spotted David and Abdul. Nicolaos was wearing a brown pinstriped business suit and carried a folded up newspaper that he frequently pushed in front of his face. He stayed hidden and away from the line of sight of the café where Abdul and David sat. Having followed Yvonne DeLorme for two days, he usually stayed twenty to thirty feet behind the slowly walking woman whose maroon dress stretched too tightly over newly acquired weight. Nicolaos scanned the crowds and the people who were in cars or out on the sidewalk, standing around. Then, he jogged across the street and fell in behind DeLorme, carefully keeping several people between him and her and, wherever possible, using cars or people as screens from the prying eyes of David Pearl. Several times, Nicolaos had to stop, pretend to window shop, or read his newspaper. She strolled in a wavy pattern down the sidewalk. When he closed the distance between them, he could hear audible breaths of exertion. He pressed Yvonne in the middle of her back, turned to her ear, and whispered to her to walk away with him. She glanced at him, but continued walking until she reached an ATM. The moment she finished her cash withdrawal, he hustled her away through the crowds and away from her seaside apartment.

DeLorme lagged and coughed and sputtered complaints at Nicolaos. He slowed, put his arm around her, and slowly they walked, the crowds passing them on the left, often having to step out into the street. Nicolaos's mind was calm, his determination constant; even so he continuously glanced around to scan the people and movement behind them. After a few more minutes walking, he steered her into a bar and settled her into a booth with tall backrests. He watched her chest heave and her fingers nervously clutching her bag. He would let her rest for a few minutes, while he watched the front door of the bar. After ordering beers, Nicolaos reached for her hand, pulled it closer to him and smiled at her.

"You are safe now, Yvonne. You were being watched by the secret service of Lebanon. We need to move quickly before they realize what happened. They'll soon spread the net wider, if they haven't already." Nicolaos sipped his beer.

"Nico, what are you doing in Lebanon?" DeLorme nervously kept her hands around the glass.

"Protecting you. I represent a law firm in Washington, DC that has an interest in keeping you away from the authorities, so I have been asked to get you away from the dangers here in Lebanon. This place isn't secure. If you can walk, I think we better start moving.

Yvonne slumped down in the booth. "None of this was supposed to happen." She didn't quite manage to stifle a sob.

Thirty minutes after they entered the bar, just before noon, Nicolaos negotiated Yvonne out the back door, tipping the waiter handsomely for his kindness in telling them about the rear exit and his promise to forget they were ever there. "I have another appointment. We'll catch a cab to get there. Don't worry." He escorted Yvonne into the middle of the back seat and sat beside her. Before they got to the destination, she had fallen asleep. A small stream of saliva dribbled from the corner of her mouth.

They were now in the outer, southern suburbs of Beirut. The cab driver slowed the car and glanced back at Nicolaos inquiringly as if to ask if this was the location that he desired. Nicolaos nodded. His destination was a mall built in the characteristic manner of the casbah. The mall was faintly pink on the outside and a yellowish cream color throughout the interior. Graceful arches were prominent in the interior, and the three golden domes dominated the outside. Rows of small slit windows were visible just below the roofline.

The cab driver dropped them off in front of the main entrance, a circular drive in front of a large half circular glass wall with automatic doors set into its middle. Nicolaos quickly paid the cab driver and then steered Yvonne toward a beauty shop. After a brief inquiry, Nicolaos saw Yvonne settled into a chair for a wash, haircut, and coloring. Nicolaos told her to wait there for him.

Nicolaos walked outside into the parking lot hidden behind a high stone and masonry wall from the street. He walked the sidewalk that ran alongside the mall, looking for the contact. Spotting a dust-covered, white minivan, he approached cautiously. He found the driver asleep in the front seat. Since the driver's window was rolled down, Nicolaos reached through the window and shook the man awake. The man was dark, sweaty, and had a two or three day's growth of beard. "Get in." The man pointed toward the front passenger seat. The man's pungent, unwashed odor filled the van.

As Nicolaos settled himself in the van, he scanned behind him using the rearview mirror. He decided that scene in front of the storefronts was ordinary. "I am Abraham." Nicolaos used the code phrase in English that his Greek gang contacts in Athens had ordered him to use.

"You are the Greek? Call me Nazz." The slovenly man spoke English with a severe Arabic accent.

"Very good, Nazz, I can't waste time. Let me see the goods."

"We must crawl into the cargo space. I don't want to be seen anymore than I absolutely have to, Abraham. There are too many prying eyes about. With us in Lebanon, it could be the police, it could be the Israelis, or it could be Hezbollah, or it could be the fucking Syrians, or it could be someone trying for some quick money. I must pay Hezbollah, but sometimes even that is not enough to have security."

Nicolaos crawled through the opening between the front seats, parting the heavy curtains that shielded the cargo area. As his eyes adjusted to the darkness, Nazz turned on his flashlight. The golf clubs were immediately visible, as was the heavily taped, greasy and worn cardboard box.

"I asked for new clubs!" Nicolaos pounded the side of the truck.

"Lower your voice or I drive away. This is not Greece, my friend. It's Lebanon. The clubs are as good as new." Nazz's eyes narrowed and his forehead wrinkled in deep crevices in concert with his hearing this outburst. He covered Nicolaos's fist with his hand and raised a finger in front of his mouth. "Do not raise your voice again. In Lebanon, everyone is nervous and worried, so anything could make them call the police. We must be extremely cautious, invisible, and anonymous." Nazz paused to listen to the sounds coming from outside the van. "I caution you that there are many predators throughout Lebanon hoping to make a score. Do exactly as I say."

Nicolaos studied the golf clubs, then the bag, and finally opened the pockets of the bag. "I can't use this. It belongs to Dr. Eman Alhadi. The balls and the bag have his name on them. He's a member of the Golf Club of Lebanon, which is one of the few places to play. They would be easily recognizable. Your men need to go to a pro shop and steal new equipment, understand, Nazz?"

"I still want to be paid."

"Not for the clubs; my order was specific." Nicolaos turned his attention to the documents and identification. As he carefully studied each one, he nodded his approval. Next, Nazz handed him a bone-handled hunting knife, which he used to open the greasy cardboard box. Inside, wrapped in heavy plastic, was a shoebox-sized bundle of U.S. currency. He nodded his approval. For the final item, he looked directly at Nazz.

Nazz stared directly back at Nicolaos. "No more, Abraham, until I receive payment."

Nicolaos paused to consider the arrangement. After staring hard into Nazz's black eyes, he tore into the heavily taped box, counted out four thousand U.S. dollars in one hundred dollar bills, and handed it to Nazz. Nazz counted it slowly and carefully.

"The man you are looking for lives at this address." Nazz handed Nicolaos a dirty business card with dark pencil marks, giving the address. "The man is not there. He left two weeks ago. We do not know where he is. Call me in two or three days. My sources should know by then if this Moschos has left the country or not."

"You call me when you get the new golf clubs." Nicolaos climbed into the front seat, opened the door, and didn't look back.

Nicolaos found Yvonne sitting just inside the beauty shop. "Come on, Yvonne. We need to get going." Pulling her along, clutching the greasy box in the other hand, Nicolaos found a cab driver at the curb of the busy street.

"Where to?" The cab driver was a young man with a practiced and constant suspicion.

"The Hotel Intercontinental." Nicolaos reached his hand over for Yvonne's, but she removed it almost as quickly as he touched it.

Arriving at the hotel, Nicolaos paid the driver and guided Yvonne into the lobby, where he paid for two nights in cash.

Nicolaos directed Yvonne into the elevator, to the fifteenth floor, then down the long corridor to their corner suite. He gently pushed her inside. Once inside, he turned on the radio. Lebanese rock music filled the room. He stepped into the bathroom to relieve himself. Back in the room, he found her standing in front of the window gazing out to the shoreline. He pulled her away from the window and pulled the drapes. "Yvonne, please don't park yourself in front of any window. I'm trying to keep you safe."

He directed her to the sofa where they sat, turned in each other's direction. "Yvonne, we need to talk. You need to tell me where the money is, and who is helping you here. Otherwise, I won't be able to protect you."

"Really, Nico, I don't feel like talking. I have made a few friends who would help me in an emergency."

Nicolaos smiled. "I need to bring you up to date. The emergency is here and now. Every police agency in this part of the world, the US, and Interpol are looking for you. I represent your best and only chance to get out of Lebanon to someplace safer."

Yvonne's pale, fleshy face frowned. "I don't want your help, Nico. All you have is words. If I trust and am wrong, I'm a dead woman."

"Trust me. I am your last, best hope. There are lots of people here in Beirut looking for you. If you stay, it's only a matter of time."

"What are you talking about?" Her brown eyes widened in surprise and turned back to the window, her arms suddenly clasping tightly to her waist.

"Yvonne Delorme is dead and gone forever. I have secured a new identity for you. I will get you out of the country and away from the people who collaborated with you. They are not your friends. You know, the losses of money and intelligence security were enormous. MagnaMeta is no more. Not only are the security breaches of grave concern to the US, your investors and collaborators don't care how they get their share. They just want it."

Delorme's head dipped downward. "I see."

"Yvonne, I am worried. You are in a very dark place. Do you take any meds?" Nicolaos was planning, anticipating contingencies, and assessing what would work best for him.

"Yes, I have always been depressive, but nothing like the last two weeks. Blood pressure and birth control. I've been taking my meds." She closed her eyes and bit her lower lip.

"You want to see a doctor?"

"No. I want to lead a quiet life without hard work or stress, somewhere I can walk on the beach without a care or worry."

"Where would that be?"

"Mexico, I think."

"We'd better be moving along in that direction. You should move your money to Banco Santander. They have branches here and in Mexico and many other countries. I think you should not go back to your apartment. If the Lebanese don't have it covered, somebody else will."

Nicolaos's cell phone rang. He clicked it open. Abdul's voice rang out. "Where are you? Turn yourself in before we find you." Nicolaos terminated the call without speaking.

"Who was that? Are they here?" Her high pitched, near wail caused Nico to turn immediately in her direction.

"A former associate, Abdul, wants to talk to me, but I don't want to talk to him. That tells me that I need to get a new cell phone. The US satellites can pick up any conversation and trace a call within minutes. I'm going to buy a new cell phone right now. You going to be okay?"

"Yeah, get me some gin and tonic."

Nicolaos stepped away from her and out of the room, taking both keys to the room. When he reached the lobby, he stopped near the line of guests waiting to check in and searched the lobby, looking for anyone who might be there looking for Yvonne or him. First he went to his contact to obtain a new cell phone and calling card, then purchased a large metal briefcase for his cash, and finally went to the liquor store. When he returned, without speaking, he went to the bar and fixed a gin and tonic for her.

"That drink smells good." She was sitting in the same spot on the sofa, but now leaning back into the corner of the arm and backrest.

Nicolaos was studying the false identities provided by Nazz. He glanced at her for a moment.

"Why don't you want one?"

"I have too much work to do. First thing, we need to get your money moved to Mexico. Second, we need a new identity for you." He handed her an Egyptian passport and other documents identifying her as Abedeh Haneef. "Check these out. I can't see any flaw in them."

Yvonne looked at the passport and documents. "I think this will work. My ancestry is mostly Lebanese-American." She got up and fixed herself another gin and tonic.

"Okay, call the bank. Set up an appointment for us to transfer the funds." Yvonne called the bank on Nicolaos's new cell phone.

The meeting at the bank took less than an hour. When they got back to the hotel, Nicolaos settled her onto the sofa again and made her another gin and tonic. When she fell asleep, Nicolaos loaded the briefcase with the cash from the cardboard box and the documents from Banco Santander.

Then he walked out. On the sidewalk, he called Jose and told him where Yvonne DeLorme could be found.

Nicolaos walked casually in the direction of the sea. On the sidewalk that fronted the buildings that faced out to the Mediterranean, he turned into the Holiday Inn. Once safely inside his room, he put the briefcase down and studied his new identity once again, Abdulla Haneef. His plan was to find a way to get safely to Spain and move the funds once again, but this time without his "wife," Abedeh. Her death certificate was included in his documents.

Nicolaos impulsively tried a travel agent on Minet el-Hosn Street. The lively, young woman with large, friendly, dark brown eyes gave Nicolaos a curious stare. "Abdulla, let me remind you of the intense security at the airport. I don't think you look enough like the guy in the picture, and you sure don't sound like an Arab to me. If you want a ticket, I'll sell it, but I think your best move is to get new ID." Her nametag read 'Salwa.'

Nicolaos looked back into her questioning eyes, while smiling broadly. "Salwa, of course, you are right. I wonder if you know of a better way for me to get home?"

She eyed the tall, tanned man in front of her. "Ship out on a fishing vessel and prepare to pay dearly."

"I'll take that ticket and be on my way. Thanks so much."

Chapter 36
Evolving Events, May 13

David Pearl rolled off his twin bed and hit the floor with a thud. Alice Boggs opened the bedroom door and strode in. David managed to grab a sheet just in time to cover himself as she entered the room. She was smiling, and her eyes darted from spot to spot in the room, as always not missing anything. David coughed deeply, bringing a mouthful of phlegm he reluctantly swallowed.

"Are you okay, David? We got a staff meeting, your in box is overflowing, and you have calls to return on this fine spring day, in DC."

"No, not okay. I have a bad cold. I didn't get much sleep on the flight back here, plus too many late hours, and too much stress, I suppose." David paused to blow his nose. "I'm still pissed off about missing Polopolis and DeLorme in Beirut. The bastard's quite stealthy, I'll give him that. But, I think his luck is going to run out, sooner or later. Alice, I'll be up and around in a few minutes."

David took more than a few minutes. His congested head and chest slowed his every move. His brain was full of conflicting thoughts: going back to bed, going to the walk-in clinic, or keep forging ahead. But, he decided he had no choice with his workload at crisis levels. Finally, he got dressed, leaving the tie hanging loosely around his neck. He chugged the last remnants of cold medicine and went downstairs, slowly.

Alice, Gao, and Odette were waiting for him in the kitchen. Gao handed David a cup of green tea, which he sipped carefully, pausing frequently to pull the bits of tea leaves off his tongue. Odette held out a mug of coffee, which he also accepted. David motioned for all three of them to follow him into his office.

"Good morning, folks. I'm going to try to make it through the day. You know my tale of woe. I'm sick, I think in part, because Nicolaos got to Yvonne DeLorme first. We know he bought a plane ticket, but didn't get on that flight. Jose and Abdul are canvassing the waterfront, checking with every police agency in an attempt to find him. Neither the Greek nor the US embassy has heard from him. The US has convinced Interpol to issue a warrant. I'll probably go back as soon as a real lead emerges." David stopped to blow his nose. "Now, who wants to go first?" David took another sip of green tea. He didn't really like it, but Gao had convinced him of its medicinal value and health benefits.

Alice stood gazing intently at him. He hoped that he didn't look as bad as he felt. "David, if you don't mind me saying so, I think you should go back to bed."

"Overruled, what do you have for me?"

"We have a number of transmittals you should sign today, for a large stack of interim contract deliverables. Jose reports that DeLorme is now awaiting extradition. Abdul and Jose are still searching out leads on Polopolis. Antonopoulos and Ali are now on their way to join them. You owe Captain Fulton from WaveLinks a call. All our other work is under assigned control limits at the moment. I'll let Gao tell you about his work."

Gao smiled and took a deep breath. "David, I have seen scalded dogs that look better than you do."

David laughed and tipped his head slightly to the left. "That's really bad, Gao. Just when I was beginning to think that the Chinese didn't eat dogs."

"Trust me, they don't in this country. Ready? The Greek smuggling gangs are like a Chinese menu." Everyone laughed. "This gang Moschos was in is a large organization, with maybe two or three hundred members. They use lots of banks, but most financial transactions seem to be in and out of Lebanon. They have lots of possible combinations in doing their work, so we are tracking them using cell phone chain analysis. I have created a program that will demonstrate in a spider type web, or network, the most prominent hubs. These central hubs use combinations, one from Column A, another from Column B. Sometimes different gang members are drafted for the soup or salad. The combinations of individuals changes all the time, but we are focusing on the hubs."

"Good work. I think I understand." David pitched into a coughing fit for several seconds. The group eyed each other nervously.

"I have uploaded the 3-D matrix program for Jacob so that we can visualize the correlations. I am looking at ways to automatically upload the data, but haven't settled on a means yet." Gao looked apologetic.

David spit into his trash can.

"Gao," said Alice, "Be sure to make those tables sequential and as neat and clear as possible for the deliverables report. They are very impressive, even though we all know they are actually preliminary work to get the necessary intelligence, for which the primary question is, 'who should we be chasing.' You'll have to label the charts very carefully, so our clients will hopefully be impressed."

Gao smiled and nodded. "David, I am working on something else. I have constructed what I call an expected ratio for all the Middle Eastern countries, plus Greece. I think that by using econometrics to determine, from the base data, what a particular country is producing and has in reserve, such as oil and gas and cash and equivalents. Then, when I get their actual reports, I can then give you probabilities as to where the underground cash is coming from."

"From illegal sales of gas and oil, you mean?"

Gao smiled broadly. "That's right. Follow the money."

David blew his nose before replying. "Okay, if there's nothing else, let's get going. Odette, if you would please go to the drug store and buy another bottle of cold medicine, I would be very grateful. No, buy two bottles." David opened his wallet and handed her a twenty.

The three vanished from his office quickly, and David began to review his emails.

Not a moment later, Alice rang on the intercom. She said the CEO of Halliburton was on hold on line two. David picked up.

"David Pearl, is that you? You don't sound like yourself."

"Yes, Mr. Tobin, I have a bad cold. How are you?"

"Fit as a fiddle. Listen, I'll go right to the point. I have a VP for operations job open. I fired the last guy for doing too much guesswork. I was talking to my friend, Vice-President Cheney, and he mentioned you as the best in the intelligence operations business. What about it?"

"Thank you so much, sir. I really am comfortable running my own company, but I am thrilled and humbled by the offer, sir. I am sure that you will find somebody excellent."

"Well, do you have any goddamn ideas, Pearl?"

"No, I can't think of anybody off the top of my head. But, I'll talk it over with my key staff and see if we can come up with some names for you."

"That would be fine, David. How is that dumb son of bitch, Antonopoulos? What do you hear about him? We had a contract with his firm, and I would sincerely like to wring that SOB's neck."

"I'm afraid there's already a long line waiting to wring his sorry neck, sir. I have been asked to take on Antonopoulos by Homeland Security in order to keep him available for questioning. So, he's on assignment now in Lebanon at this very moment. He just got sucked into a confluence of events, I think, though he was definitely negligent. We're putting his security clearance to work, but nothing mission critical, of course. We're monitoring him carefully, as a favor to the Homeland Security."

"Yeah, I think you better monitor him carefully. Don't tell him I called. I'm having our attorneys file against him personally for the losses we incurred. Maybe next time I'm in Washington, I'll come over and kick his ass. I gotta go, Pearl, but if you change your mind in the next day or two, just let me know."

David, for a moment, thought about Nicolaos in Lebanon and his other lesser distraction, Antonopoulos. He realized he didn't help himself at all if the word got back to the Vice-President about his new association with Antonopoulos.

Next, David called Captain Fulton at WaveLinks. "We've really searched, Frank. We just haven't found anything that can be compartmentalized for a subcontract."

"Oh, come off it, David. You know the next time you're in the desert, I'll have the canteen."

"I'm sorry it didn't work out. All our subcontracts prevent us from re-subbing."

"Don't forget our many political contacts. We'll be back on top soon." David made a note for the file, but for the moment decided to let it end there.

David walked to the kitchen for more coffee. He heard the heavy thumping of feet pounding down the stairs. He knew those heavy steps belonged, almost certainly, to Yacob.

Odette yelled from her perch at the front of the building. "Bonjour, I got your medicine, David. Abdul and Jose are on line three. Yacob is joining you for the call." David returned to his office and sat down. Yacob was quickly in his usual seat, next to the small end table upon which rested an additional speaker phone.

"Hello, Abdul and Jose. How goes it?" He was eager for news from or of Nicolaos.

"Hi, David, Abdul here. Jose is with me. We are using the encrypted cell phone from our room in the hotel. We haven't found Polopolis. This afternoon, Jose and I will go back to the neighborhood cafés along the sea and look around. We are also going to the travel agency that sold him the ticket. We think that we have made contact with Hezbollah. They want money for 'research,' as they call it, but I think they definitely were aware of Nicolaos, from our contact's reaction. We will work on that today, as well."

"Good. Yacob, why don't you bring them up to date on Andreas Moschos?" David watched Yacob flick through the pages of his notebook to find the right page.

"Antonopoulos and Ali are on a slow bus ride to join you in Beirut. Here is what they learned about the late, unlamented Andreas Moschos. Yemen is a hell-hole, poverty stricken, the poorest Arab country, by far. Moschos got drilled in the back of the head with two, .22 caliber, hollow point bullets at close range, then he went for his swim. It appears that Moschos was traveling with a man called Damon. Damon skipped out, apparently on a boat with the name of Kirie Pondiki; that's Greek for Mister Mouse."

David cleared his throat. "So, be on the lookout for that boat, Kirie Pondiki. It's probably a yacht."

Abdul barked. "Got it. What else?"

"Here's the thing. Ali has gotten Moschos's keys. It's a key ring with house, lock, or maybe trunk keys. So, we need to figure out what the keys are for."

Abdul responded, "We'll find a locksmith to see if we can get a head's up about that. David, you sound terrible. We will await the arrival of Antonopoulos and our good buddy, Ali."

"I will have Gao send you, via email, some corporate names from banking transactions that we have identified as suspicious. See what you can find out about them. Anything else?"

"I agree we need to start looking at companies, shipping and trading are at the top of our list. Polopolis must have connections somewhere here in Beirut. If Gao could just email us the corporate names and any cell phone contacts, we could get a lead on Polopolis. Everyone here is very alert, very afraid of the Syrians, the Israelis, Hezbollah, you name it. But, we are confident that we will find our Nico."

Yacob trundled back up the stairs to his office. David wanted to take a nap, but instead began reviewing the contract deliverables, taking notes on points that he wanted to follow up on, and signing transmittals. His chest ached, and his watery eyes required the continued use of tissues. Suddenly, he looked up toward the ceiling before hitting the intercom. "Odette, book me on a flight back to Lebanon in three days, as early as possible on May 24."

"You got it, mon patron."

He put his head down on the desk and was quickly asleep.

Chapter 37
Cold Call, May 20

David heard the knock at the front door at 6:35 AM. He slowly got up from his desk and went to the front door. Peering through the peephole, he saw Demetrios standing outside with a smile, holding the Washington Post. David was pleased to see him, but he was still blowing his nose, trying to manage his hacking cough, and constantly watering eyes. Demetrios couldn't quite stifle his laugh as he saw how miserable his friend was looking, but he quickly apologized. Once back in his office, David ordered his friend to sit down. Demetrios handed over the newspaper.

Demetrios settled into the chair, his hair unkempt as usual. "David, I bring some confusing news." Demetrios slumped in the chair. His eyes looked directly at David. His lips were a straight, tense line.

"Demetrios, let me have it. News is news. I don't shoot the messenger."

"You really don't look so good. Are you sure you want to sit here listening to me?"

"I am sure. If it wasn't you, it'd be someone or something else."

"Yeah, I understand that. Your friendship means a lot more to me than our professional relationship. You know what I'm saying?" Demetrios's hand that held the mug was slightly shaking. He set down the mug, emblazoned with gold letters reading 'US Navy,' on the side table.

"Did you have another late night at Stoney's?"

"No, not late by my standards, and I got some good news, my friend, I'm finally going home for three weeks. It's been a long haul."

"I know it's been tough on you, Demetrios. We have fulfilled all our contracts with your embassy and have received positive feedback. So, I thought maybe your workload was getting more controllable, leveling off maybe." David popped a cough lozenge into his mouth, paused for it to control the cough he felt coming on, but lost the battle. As he started coughing, he motioned to Demetrios to bear with him.

"Sorry, every time I think I should be getting better, it seems to get worse."

"Chicken soup and rest, David, nothing else will work."

"I know you're right, Demetrios, but time and work just won't allow me to rest. I can't say that I am sleeping that well when I do lie down. I cough the night away until I pass out."

"All of the reports on the various investigations have come in. I have heard some very favorable comments about your deliverables, by the way. The administrative officer has completely revamped computer security. Everyone in the embassy is having their friends and neighbors checked and rechecked. I wanted to talk to you about the Greek State Security reports. I was allowed to sit and read them in the presence of a senior investigator. The bastards videotaped the entire three hours that it took for me to review them. I wasn't allowed a pen or paper. And, they wouldn't permit questions. So, what I will be telling you is A, from memory and B, totally confidential." Demetrios was now sitting up straight and alert.

"Okay, let's have the bad news. I take it there's some bad news somewhere in the reports?"

"You take that correctly. Nothing about you, directly, or your firm. The bad news concerns Zoe."

David was instantly alert. "What about Zoe?"

"If her resignation had not already been approved, she would have been fired or worse. If this affair wasn't a can of worms before, it sure is now." Demetrios sputtered the words out, turning his eyes toward the floor.

"Fired, what on earth for?" David felt a surge of anger, but he felt so bad, it quickly dissipated.

"As a result of an unauthorized misadventure that resulted in the death of Antonis Pelakanos."

David's mouth opened. His head leaned to the right, His right hand, which was holding a cup of coffee, let it drop to the desk top. Moments passed between the two men without another word. His eyes closed, and he rocked back in his chair.

Demetrios ran to the kitchen, returning with a handful of paper towels. As he swabbed the desk, he leaned forward David. "David, can I get you something?"

David slumped forward, looking wildly around the room, and after a few moments, stood up, paced to the office door, and came back to his desk, picking up his coffee mug. He walked to the kitchen and filled his cup, then went out through the backdoor. Demetrios followed him. David marched across the backyard, went through the gate in the backyard fence, and proceeded into the alley. David walked three blocks. At a small park, he settled onto a park bench. David drank his coffee and stared off into the distance.

David watched Demetrios come into the park and followed him as he walked a perimeter around the park, before settling onto a bench where he kept his eyes on David. David only briefly glanced at Demetrios, sitting on a far bench, before he let his eyes close, and he became lost in thought. David sat for thirty-five minutes before becoming uncomfortable on the bench, but throughout that time he felt a myriad of emotions: sorry for being betrayed, anger, a new and sudden recognition of a profound sense of loss, and a sudden inability to see his way forward.

A DC police car, with its sirens and lights on, pulled to an abrupt stop on the south side street of the park. The two police officers ran into a small convenience store next to the entrance to a six-story office building. Five minutes later, they came out with a suspect in handcuffs. They walked him to the back seat and shoved him roughly in. The taller officer went back into the shop. The shorter kept his eyes on the suspect in the back seat. From where he stood, David could hear the suspect yelling, "I ain't done nothin." The suspect repeated his mantra several times to no avail.

The shouting brought David to his feet, and as soon as he stood, Demetrius reacted by quickly walking to him. "In my past life, patrolling the streets of Rhodes, I might have been that arresting officer."

"I need to figure out what happened with Zoe." David started walking in the direction of the office but hung a right and entered Chung's Buddha Belly, instead. Demetrios stayed at his side.

The owner, Vern Chung, had a prominent nose and dark eyes set slightly too far apart on his face. This gave him a look of being slightly not-too-smart. David suspected that Vern had long ago learned to use this to his advantage and had developed a quick and easy sense of humor to go along with it. "Vern, I need a quart of chicken soup."

"You look very, very sick, my friend." Vern's eyes were full of concern.

"I know it." David turned around to see Demetrios with his back to the counter, carefully observing the world outside the windows of Buddha Belly.

"You want noodle or rice?"

"Rice."

Vern returned after a few minutes, bringing out the soup. David attempted to pay. Vern shook his head. "On the house, my friend."

David knew he would pay Vern one way or another sometime in the future, and that probably Vern knew this, as well. The two men walked slowly back to the office. As they entered, Odette confronted David.

"David, where have you been? You're scaring us. Woggins called. The contract manager at Nanotech called. You look terrible, David. And, Alice has gone out somewhere and hasn't called. I think you should lie down."

"Me too, but I'm not going to. I'm going to finish meeting with Demetrios. Call Alice, and if need be, go get her."

As David and Demetrios settled back into their chairs, David sighed. "Fill me in, before I go knock myself unconscious with cold medicine."

Demetrios grimaced. "I'm sorry to be the one to tell you all of this, David. The report said that Zoe was assigned to a team watching Polopolis, and she was posted inside his house. Her partner was outside patrolling the neighborhood and was probably watching you. The embassy knew nothing about Greek security service personnel being there. When you made moves like you were going inside the house, he called her. Of course, Pelakanos was already inside the house. Zoe was frightened and possibly in sudden concern for her life. In any event, she got the jump on Pelakanos. She testified that Pelakanos was completely surprised when she punched him. Then, she jabbed him hard in the throat and forced the box cutter out of his hand. She then sliced his throat. Greek security states in their report that her actions are not justifiable. For example, she could have held him after she had disarmed him. The investigators couldn't understand or agree to her argument that it was self-defense. They ruled that it was manslaughter. Yet, in addition to the box cutter, Pelakanos was carrying a switchblade knife in his back pocket and a Berretta holstered on his belt. And, he was known to Greek police as a stone cold killer. Her partner called for backup, but Greek security was not in a position to provide it. I think she thought she better take him out, in case there was more than one intruder, and escape. So she went out the back door in a controlled panic. She ran across the backyard, jumped the fence, and zigzagged through three backyards until she came to a side street. Then she jogged out of the neighborhood, before calling her partner. She was afraid of what she had tumbled onto." Demetrios paused and drank some green tea.

"So, the investigators thought that Zoe overreacted and used poor judgment."

"That's right, and the murder is still under investigation by the DC cops, who are suspicious of a cover up, but they got murders galore to investigate, so the case will hopefully fade into the back recesses of their files. The Greeks have not applied diplomatic immunity to Zoe. She's back in Greece assigned to Security Headquarters, so my guess is she remains in a kind of legal limbo. Now, for Polopolis. He's been officially terminated from the Greek Department of State. They think that he's fairly harmless at this point. I agree he's a whimsical kind of character, but we know he's lied, stolen, and committed fraud. They've washed their hands of him, but that doesn't mean he's not still trouble."

David closed his eyes and put his hands together as if in prayer. "That's funny, Demetrios, because Polopolis has gone off the radar in Beirut. What I want is to find him and get him arrested. He did lead us to Yvonne DeLorme but not before he stole most of her ill-gotten funds. The U.S. filed for her extradition two days ago."

"She's that missing analyst who broke the bank at MagnaMeta?"

"The very one. Jose, Abdul, Doug, and Ali are all in Beirut looking for Polopolis. So, the Greek government can now have plausible deniability, whatever Polopolis does?"

"At this point, unless you can make a case, I don't think the Greek administration is interested in Polopolis. He or his criminal associates may have something on somebody in the government. Listen, David, I am truly sorry to be the one to tell about Zoe. I hope it won't change a thing between the two of you. She's a fine woman who got herself into a situation that she possibly mishandled, but it could have happened to anyone." Demetrios rose slowly and went out the door. David watched him until he reached the door, but called him back.

"Demetrios, I know that you are very worried about me. And frankly, I'm worried too. I'm sicker than a dog, and I should really wait until I'm back to normal before deciding for sure about Zoe. It's a hard fact to absorb about someone you love. I can understand her actions in defending herself, but I cannot see why she never told me. I wish Zoe had confided in me, but I won't lose Zoe over it." Demetrios stood in the doorway listening, and before he left, he managed a weak smile in acknowledgement of David's words.

David stared out the door for a few seconds after Demetrios left. He wondered if Demetrios might be withholding something else. He coughed, a lung clearing cough that resulted in a mouthful of mucus. He spat the mouthful into the trashcan and covered it with the classified ads of the day's Washington Post.

Chapter 38
Meltdown, May 23

Abdul met David as he cleared customs in Beirut. David was still sick, felt utterly exhausted, but had achieved a sort of steady fog shrouded frame of mind where he could function.

Abdul, good to see you. Any news on Polopolis" David cleared his throat.

Abdul shrugged and frowned. "Nothing. But, here's the thing. I didn't want to talk to you about it until you got settled in. But I am sick and tired of looking for Polopolis. In Beirut, everyone is suspicious, and any situation can turn violent in a split second. We need someone on the inside from the police or the judiciary to make progress. And, my girlfriend is giving me a hard time. My parents think I am wasting my time. I really need to go home."

"Let me see what the situation is first. I don't see why you can't go home. We really need more help back in the office."

David's secure cell phone chirped. Odette skipped the formalities. "David, Woggins is here. He says it's important. He needs to talk to you."

"David paused, looked out the cab window at the apartment buildings lining this neighborhood street for a moment before responding. "Yeah, sure, put him on."

"David, I've been immersed in this Shapiro case for days. I've been reading and rereading the reports, the interviews, everything that's in the files. I think we missed something."

"Yacob is handing the matter for the firm, Woggins. Why don't you talk to him?"

"No, thanks. I know you have confidence in him, but I don't. I need to tell you about this, and what you do with the information is your business." David stayed silent.

"Here's the deal. After reading everything in our inventory, I began to think that Shapiro's murder was somehow personal. So, I went back to interview the wife. I went over all of his possessions. I talked to her for hours about personal stuff, and finally she went to find his small, leather date book. She couldn't find it. Then, she remembered that he sometimes took it with him to the gym. We didn't find it on him or in his locker. So, we need to find the date book. I asked his wife what happened to his old date books. She took me to a small closet off the family room, and there, on the top shelf, were about thirty years worth of his old date books. Each one contained a calendar year, date by date, with Shapiro's writing on nearly every page. Most of his notes are lists of actions he wanted to take, phone calls, to do lists, that kind of thing. Cross checking these notebooks against his office calendar, I can see that when he got to the office, he would transfer these to his official calendar, not always, but most of the time." Woggins paused.

"Good work, Woggins, no—great work. That's a promising lead. You have something to search for, and now we need a place to search. The police searched all the trash at the gym and the immediate vicinity, so maybe, possibly, the killer kept the notebook."

"That's right. I went to the gym last night and talked to Tabitha Plante, the woman who discovered Shapiro's body. I asked her about the notebook. She said that she had seen Shapiro before that night with a notebook. He would be jogging along, then apparently have a thought, get his notebook out, and write something down. So, it seems like he definitely had the notebook on him at all times." David thought that Woggins sounded a little too pleased with himself. If it were he, he'd probably be criticizing himself for overlooking the detail in the first place.

"That's a great pickup, Robert. As soon as you can, get copies of the notebooks over to the office. The guys in the back room will work over the dates, issues, comments, and create a time line. Thanks again."

David and Abdul arrived at the Intercontinental Hotel and checked in. Jose and Abdul were in David's room waiting while he got ready. David asked Jose Gonzalez to monitor his calls while he was in the shower.

When David walked back into the room, Jose pointed at the cell phone and said, "Yacob, hold a minute. David's just now available."

David put it on speaker. "Yacob, thanks for calling. What have you got?"

"I have a little mystery package from West Virginia. It's a file, really, I have labeled the Meltdown. I'm trying to sort through it, but I thought I should get some guidance from you. The package is from a Mrs. Margaret McKay in Dunbar, West Virginia. She's feuding with her neighbor, a Russian man named Viktor Nevzlin. Viktor pops up on the radar screen about seven, eight years ago. Prior to that Viktor is completely invisible. I'm not sure about Mrs. McKay, but there is something about her story that sounds like something we ought to pursue to some extent."

David was immediately amused and intrigued. "I think we should run this down too, Yacob. So, what do you need from me?"

"I need to start melting this information down. I think we should find out who Viktor Nevzlin really is. Could you do me the favor of running his name by your associates in high places? I think Viktor needs to come in out of the cold." They both laughed.

"I'll do that. That's a good code name for this file, Meltdown. Now tell me about lost radioactive material."

"The trail leads to the Greek port of Piraeus. Our man, Nicolaos, made calls to Greece. The area code includes the port of Piraeus. The shipping company, Nikolaou Kasos, is headquartered there. I think we should send someone to Piraeus to have boots on the ground there. That way, we should be able follow-up on the Greek gangsters who we have learned about, like this character, Damon."

"Yacob, I think first we identify all of the gang's leaders, then we'll track them down."

"Right, and for that, we need a consultant who can tell us about the local Greek police, for example, someone who understands not only the language, but who can research backgrounds and maybe do some tactical stuff for us."

"Ah, good point, Yacob. The only boots on the ground we have at the moment are here in Lebanon, so that intelligence gathering in Greece will have to wait. Let's review the bidding. Yacob has connected Nicolaos to phone numbers registered to the area code that includes the Greek port of Piraeus. We know the Ileana Iazarou not only made port there on its last cruise, but that's where the ship is being held for the foreseeable future. I'm guessing it wouldn't be too hard to track down the first officer/police informant, and some of the crew. So, Yacob has a good point, and I think that we need to focus on Pireaus and Beirut. We have the calls made by the late captain Moschos. Some of the telephone numbers match up to the numbers we already had for the gang."

Yacob hesitated before he responded. "We will follow-up on our end, David, but I'm still thinking about a team in Pireaus. Somebody to hang out in the bars, pick up on the waterfront gossip. How about Zoe?"

David sat quietly, mulling this thought over. "I'd have to vote against that. She's not yet a free agent. She wouldn't fit in on the waterfront. I talked to her briefly yesterday, and she seemed content to sit on the sidelines until she's civilian again. And Yacob, she stood out in the crowd in Montreal. She would certainly never blend in on the Greek waterfront. I'll talk to her again, probably this evening; maybe she has a relative or knows someone who could do it."

Abdul interjected. "That may be stretching our net a little thin. I think that's introducing an unknown into another unknown. Better to use one of our guys."

Yacob suddenly sounded very anxious. "I think I agree with Abdul, David. I think we should only rely on known quantities. Look at what we are dealing with in Nicolaos Polopolis. So, using Zoe or one of her relatives is a bad idea. I get it."

"David, if you don't mind another interruption, I think that of the known quantities, it has to be Antonopoulos. He's quick, and he's a solid person with basic good sense. More importantly, I don't think that anyone would take him for a spy." When Abdul finished, he settled himself into a cushioned love seat and shot a glance at Jose.

"He'd hardly blend in on the waterfront. What's his cover? And he doesn't speak Greek. We'd definitely have to find somebody to go with him."

Yacob's voice and tone grew lower and more deliberate. "I agree that Antonopoulos shouldn't go alone, but with help, maybe he could pass as a shipping executive or attorney from the U.S., looking into settling damage claims, something like that."

"I have to think about that. As of right now, I am out of options. Antonopoulos goes to Greece, but he definitely needs a strong backup. Abdul will shortly be on his way back to Washington. So, who do we have?"

"I think it gets us back to the unknown. We have analysts, not field operatives. We cannot afford to take any one of them off what they are currently doing either, not if we want to meet our deliverable schedule.

Maybe, you should have that talk with Zoe. Antonopoulos would require a leader, someone who could initiate action and take care of the both of them."

"Okay, point noted. I will talk to Zoe this evening. What else, Yacob?"

"Another angle to consider for Antonopoulos: that customer list you lifted from Harry Markos's office, it includes the shipping company, Nikolaou Kasos. Our guy, Nicolaos, is directly related to the family that owns and operates this shipping company. So, I think that Antonopoulos could focus on the shipping company, while his new associate focuses on the waterfront. That way, Antonopoulos could possibly contribute and be of some assistance to whoever we find to work the waterfront."

"That's right. Have you gotten the background on Congressman Eugeniades?"

"I got my new guy, Stanley Berwick, working on that."

"Well, let's see if we can get connections between Eugeniades, Moschos, Polopolis, and the shipping company. Or, at the very least see what his connections are in Greece and the Middle East? I think plotting these connections might have the plot points of this network looking like a spider diagram." David stood at the window, gazing out toward the Mediterranean.

Alice joined the conversation. "Are you sure about researching Eungeniades, David? Just because Congressman Eugeniades is in WaveLinks's pocket, doesn't mean he's engaging in any criminal activity. And, if he ever found out, there'd sure be hell to pay."

"I know that. It's a hunch, a gut instinct if you will. We are planning the future course of this investigation, and I don't want to leave any of our players off the board without carefully examining their means and motives. Possibly, we cannot know with absolute certainty about all the criminal activity of the individuals linked to the gang that stole the radioactive material. Maybe it's a tangent, but if there is linkage, then we would have a best seller of a report."

As Yacob was beginning a comment, Alice cut him off. "I just don't think pursuing that angle is prudent, David. Prudence and caution are mandated in this case. We cannot be found out to be checking up on a sitting congressman."

"I assume we will operate with discretion and prudence at all times." David understood Alice's point and was glad she made it, for the benefit of the others listening.

Alice immediately responded. "I know that. The question is, what does the Greek gang think and do, given that multiple police agencies are already looking for the source of the radioactive material and for those who moved it? I think that means we investigate, but with our caution flag flying at all times."

Yacob answered, "Do what the Israelis just did. After patiently waiting through weeks of random rocket attacks from the Gaza strip, they moved with overwhelming force against the Palestinian Hamas organization in the Gaza strip. I think it's a new definition of insanity: firing rockets every day into your enemy's heartland and expecting nothing to happen in response."

"We lack the Israelis' firepower. I see your point, Yacob, about overwhelming firepower. Target all the players at the same time, but resources just don't permit it. Stealth and cunning will have to be our values. Still, I think Alice raises a good cautionary point. We need to keep the Greek government on our side. We cannot survive public accusations from Congress. I will talk to Ambassador Gliniadakis and to Virgil Moody over at the State Department. That's all for now, folks. Thanks, Alice and Jacob. We need to get our feet out of the hotel and onto the ground." Yacob laughed. The men in the hotel room chuckled and began to get ready to hit the streets of Beirut.

Chapter 39
Culture, Cunning, and Stealth, May 25

David called Zoe early in the morning. Dawn was just beginning in Beirut. The two of them had talked at least once, every day, in the three days since David had learned of Zoe's responsibility in the death of the Greek thug, Antonis Pelekanos, but he had yet to bring it up. Before his team met to decide their tactics for the day, David decided that he had better clear the air between them. "Hi, baby, I'm sorry for calling so early, but we are going to have a busy day."

"That's fine. I was about to get out of bed anyway. Mother's started the coffee, and I can smell that she's got something baking. How are you?"

David pursed his lips. "I'm good. I wondered if you were getting any closer to being cleared by the Greek government?"

Her voice instantly sounded more pitched in tone, along with a step up in volume. "They seem to be in the report writing mode, David. Their questions are now infrequent, but they are still holding up the effective date of my resignation."

"So what's their report going to say, and when do they tell you it will be ready?"

Zoe's voice dropped in register and slowed down. "David, the report is written. I am deemed to have used unprofessional conduct and will be dismissed from the Greek State security service any day now. I'm so sorry, I just couldn't bring myself to tell you."

"That's another lie, Zoe. How do you think I should feel?"

A moment of silence ensued, followed by a sudden gasp erupting from Zoe. "I'm so sorry, David. I have thought and thought about telling you, but I was afraid. I'm sorry. I realized that I was in trouble, and ran when I should have stayed with the body."

"I'm sorry you didn't feel like you could tell me, Zoe. I really am. You may be deemed a security risk by the US. I will absolutely have to disclose this to the State Department and Homeland Security."

"I knew you would be hurt, but I loved you so much. I couldn't bear the thought that you would leave me. I'm sorry." A silence fell between them.

"I feel stabbed in the back again. I know I'm tired and sick, but I need to do some thinking about our relationship. Another long pause ensued. David sighed deeply. "I need a recommendation from you. I've got to get someone in Greece who can go to Pireaus for us. We need somebody tough, a native Greek speaker who can work the waterfront for us."

"David, all I can be is sorry. I don't want to have my heart broken, as well. But, I understand, at least a little, how much I have hurt you. Let's leave it at that for now. Whatever else I may have done, it was in the line of duty."

"Your actions put me in a tight place. Do I tell my friends, the DC investigating officers?"

Zoe sighed deeply, and her voice cracked. "Please don't. I realize I have compromised you in many ways. I can't regret it anymore than I do."

"What about someone to help us in Pireaus?" David's voice was taut and staccato.

Before Zoe answered, David heard her blow her nose. "I have the perfect person, my cousin, Peter Diamondis. He's out of work. He's an artist, a self taught mechanic, an army veteran, and carpenter, almost a Jack-of-all-trades. He's a rough looking, thirty-two, but very intelligent."

"Sounds like someone who can do what we need done. Talk to him and fax his information over here to the hotel to the attention of Jose. I want as little as possible documented that associates me with this place. I have to go. I love you."

David, Jose, and Abdul went out to the Corniche, the broad sidewalk along the Mediterranean. David wanted them to show him around.

Later that afternoon, Odette called David. "There is a sweet little dame waiting on the reception couch. She says she has an important message for you. She asked me to remind you that you two first met in Rome." Odette giggled.

David locked eyes with Jose, and they both grinned. "Fine, ask her to wait for two minutes, please. Get Alice to talk with her. And, call me back as soon as Alice figures out what happened." David, Jose, and Abdul had spread out along the Corniche. David sat at the southernmost end, wearing a baseball cap and dark sunglasses. He had been sitting there for fifteen minutes when his encoded cell phone rang.

"Hi, David, I just had a nice chat with the nicest lady. Can you talk?"

"Yes, I can, Alice. I'm waiting to hear from Ali and Antonopoulos. What did you find out?"

"This slender woman of about sixty-five, who is aging very gracefully, tells me her name is Tootsie Wong, from Orlando, Florida. She tells me that she met you first in Rome, at the airport, and then again at her daughter's home in Beirut."

"Oh dear, let me guess. She means Polopolis."

"That's affirmative. She described the man she met, and it's definitely Polopolis. I told her that a former associate has regretfully used your name in the past, and I showed her your picture, so she was assured that she had been duped. She met a man at the Rome airport who identified himself as David Pearl. They had a nice chat. After a few days, this man called and asked if he could come over. She was puzzled about how he got her number, but agreed. Well, he was so personable with her and her family when he got there. He brought flowers, wine, and chocolates. They sat and talked about Lebanon until midnight. Anyway, before he left that night, he handed her an envelope and told her if there was any way she could personally bring this to his office, he would very much appreciate it."

David turned around and checked out the people getting off a bus. "I can't wait to hear this."

Alice laughed. "Well, actually, it's quite interesting. The envelope is addressed to 'David Pearl, CEO.' She arranged her flight so that she would have time to come here to the office before her Orlando connection departed."

"I see. What's in that that envelope?"

"The contents are photographs with annotations, in writing, as to identities and places."

David had an elbow on his thigh, and he slouched over, but continued to carefully examine every person who passed his position. "Where is Tootsie now?"

"I sent her on her way. I will send her a bouquet in the next couple of days with a note. I told her we do security work around the world and apologized profusely for our former associate involving her in his activities. She seemed satisfied with that."

"Okay, tell her in the note that if our former associate ever contacts her again to call the office, at once. Oh yeah, tell her to check her bank account and to definitely change the password. Now tell me about the contents."

"It appears that Nicolaos has been working on covering his backside. Yacob just joined me. I asked him to join us, so he could begin studying this stuff immediately."

"That's right, Alice. Hi. Yacob."

Alice paused briefly. "The first page identifies the twelve photographs. Photo #1 is Andreas Moschos sitting in a cyber café. Photo #2 is identified as Yvonne DeLorme standing at an ATM. Photos # 3, 4, and 5 are of a man identified as Karolas Damon. On these, the setting is identified as the La Paillotte Restaurant, located along the Corniche, in Beirut. Seated next to Damon is a man that Nicolaos identifies as Julian Farkis. Photos 6 and 7 are a commercial building on Minet el-Hosn Street, in Beirut. Nicolaos wrote, in his shaky penmanship, that an office inside this building is the cover for various financial transactions for the gangsters associated with Damon. Photo 8 is of Abdul and Jose standing on a street corner trying to look like tourists. Photo 9 is of Tootsie Wong and her daughter's family. Photos 10, 11, and 12 were of Ionnis, 'Ike,' Zisis. Nicolaos wrote that he thought there were contacts between Zisis and Damon, but offered no evidence. According to the annotation, Zisis stays at the exclusive Le Meridien Commodore Hotel."

David leaned back on the concrete bench. "Nico has presented us with good leads or pure bullshit. We have to run these leads down and fast. I wonder if he's settling some old scores or simply muddying the water. We have to find out what his game is."

"The note addressed to you simply says that he tried to leave Lebanon three times, but was afraid he couldn't get through customs. One time, he narrowly escaped being arrested. He is requesting a boat, so he can leave without going through customs. He adds that he is in danger. And, he has written on the back of one picture of Damon that Damon suspects him of playing both sides, which sounds like what Nicolaos would do."

"Alice, this is our connection between the Zisises and the smuggling ring. Jacob, let's get our analysts, there, on this right now, find the registry for the power boat, Mister Mouse. That misguided asshole may have outsmarted himself this time. Fax those pictures to us right away. Once a rat, always a rat."

CHAPTER 40
Port of Pireaus Pitfalls, May 30

Peter Diamondis met Douglas Antonopoulos in a small efficiency apartment located near the port of Pireaus.

Antonopoulos looked around, over, and to the sides of Peter. "Come in. I need to talk to you."

"Sure, I'd like to get briefed. I want to get started right away." Peter's round, plain face showed a toothy smile.

"I think it's all wrong. I think this gang is already onto me. I am just a liability now. I'm going to call David right now and tell him that we should go home. It's too dangerous here."

"Go ahead. Call him, but I just got here. I talked to David yesterday afternoon; he didn't mention anything about shutting down this operation." Peter walked to the window, pulled the curtains slightly open, and looked around outside.

Antonopoulos held his cell phone to his ear. He walked to the curtains and pulled them closed.

"Yeah, David, Peter Diamondis has shown up. I have to tell you that I have no confidence in this operation. I think we are going to get killed."

"What's happened there? Did the gang find you out? You've only been there for two days."

"It's my gut feeling. I think we should go home." Antonopoulos stood, slender and tall, leaning against the wall, avoiding eye contact with Peter.

"Let me talk to Peter." Antonopoulos handed the phone to Peter. Peter put the phone on speaker.

"Yes, David, Antonopoulos seems to think there is danger here, but I just got here. I want to do this job. I'll protect him."

"What about the financial records? Is Antonopoulos studying the records of Nikolaou Kasos?"

Peter looked at Antonopoulos seeking an answer.

"I have looked at them." Antonopoulos's voice answered flatly, without a trace of enthusiasm.

"Alright, no good deed goes unpunished. Doug, you need to do more than look at them. Get an outline of the company's officers, board members, customers, state of finances . . . anything that might give us a clue. From this moment on, Peter, you are in charge. I'll get you help as soon as I can. I think that you should pay a visit to the Ileana Iazarou and see what you can find out."

"Thanks a lot, David. I think you're going to find out that I'm right." Antonopoulos abruptly sat down on the bed.

"I'm going to start work then. If you need me, call." Peter went outside and headed for the bars nearest the port.

After checking out several bars, Peter walked into one where he found a matronly bartender, sat down, and chatted with her at length. Only after Peter had polished off several beers did the sixtyish, bottle blonde seem relaxed enough with Peter to start revealing the harbor's dirt, politics, and gossip. When she got onto the subject of the Ileana Iazarou, he let her carry on until she dropped the name of the bar where the crew usually hung out. He tipped her generously, gave her a pat on the back of her hand and a wink.

He went straight to Yianni's bar. The front was glass with numerous spots of dirt and grease and a tired looking neon sign flashing the bar's name. He sat down at the bar, passed twenty Euros to the bar man for alerting him when the crew of the Ileana Iazarou came in. Peter waited for an hour before the bar man nodded at him as a group of seamen walked in the door. He got up and sat down with the men, uninvited. "Gentlemen, I'm buying, so order up, please."

"Who are you?" A skinny sailor, with a dark scar across his forehead that ran into his shaved head, asked. He held off on shaking Peter's proffered hand.

"I'm Peter Diamondis. I'm a writer for The Greek Business Journal. I'm interested in checking out your former ship, Ileana Iazarou. I want to hear your stories, but what I really need is access to that ship."

The men tensed immediately, looking at each other and around the bar. The skinny one was rising up off the bench when an older sailor put a hand on his shoulder to get him to sit back down. "You'll keep us out of it, right? All of us are barred, now, from shipping out until all of the fucking investigations are over. All we did aboard was protect ourselves from the Greek navy and the radiation, and now we're getting punished for it." The older sailor spoke with a guttural, smoky voice. His black eyes never left Peter's face.

"You shall remain nameless, my friends, and once my story is filed, my notes shall be burned, so no one can trace the story back to any of you. Fair enough?" Peter continued smiling at the men.

A short man still in a black pea jacket reached into a pocket and pulled out a set of keys. He threw these at Peter who captured them in one hand. "Thanks, sailor."

The man in the pea jacket showed a mouth full of decayed teeth. "I'm Kosimido, I was a mechanic on board. I somehow forgot to turn these keys in. You might find them useful, especially if you decide to steal something." The group laughed.

"Thanks, Kosimido. If I find anything marketable, I'll be back to share the proceeds with you guys." Peter pulled some more Euros out of his front pocket and stood. "Have a good evening."

Peter went back to the cheap apartment. Antonopoulos lay on one bed, snoring gently. Peter shook him awake. After giving Antonopoulos careful and deliberate instructions, the two men dressed in dark clothes and athletic training shoes. They then slipped out of the apartment and walked casually down to the port.

Cargo containers were stacked and lined up in places ready to be loaded. Huge cranes and heavy-duty trucks moved cargo. Bright lights covered the working areas of the port. Using fake ID's, they readily passed through the first line of security for the Kasos shipping line. Peter led the way to a chain link fence enclosure where various pieces of equipment used to facilitate the handling of freight were enclosed. Using one of the Ileana Iazarou keys, they were quickly inside. Peter pulled out binoculars to study the ship. He noted the security guards, speaking softly as he discovered each one.

Antonopoulos sat on a crate in the dark. "Peter, we don't have to do this. And, we need back up. Why don't we think about it?"

For several moments, Peter did not respond. When he did, it was a whisper. "Keep your voice down. All you have to do is watch my back. Simply remember: you are a physics professor who has been asked to consult on the radiation, so stay in role, please."

"From the reports that I have read, there is nothing radioactive on that ship."

"I doubt if security has read those reports or believed them if they did. They crew sure doesn't believe it. Come on, there's a group of men moving toward the Ileana Iazarou."

"Please, Peter, let's go back."

"No, this is the chance to get into the captain's cabin and search it." Diamondis stared at Antonopoulos who simply shrugged his shoulders.

"I'm not ready. I'm tired. I could make a mistake."

"You aren't nearly as tired as I am. Shut-the-fuck-up."

They were now passing a group of sailors walking in the opposite direction. Peter greeted them heartily in Greek, and they reciprocated.

Reaching the gangway to the Ileana Iazarou, Peter hunched over, taking long strides to get up the gangway and pushing Antonopoulos ahead of him. He scanned constantly above, to the left and right, and at his watch. He lifted and shoved Antonopoulos over the chain that barred entry at the ship's main deck level. He grabbed Antonopoulos's arm and pulled him into the dark shadow provided by a closed freight cargo hold. Just as quickly, he pulled Antonopoulos to the metal surface of the deck and lay down beside him. Peter listened for the guard who paced from the middle of the ship to the back. Peter studied his watch. When precisely one minute had passed, he jumped up and pulled Antonopoulos to his feet. In a crouch, he sprinted to the superstructure of the bridge. Antonopoulos followed at a walk, already gasping and breathing hard. Peter studied his watch, and when the next critical moment had passed, he physically directed Antonopoulos up a steel catwalk to the second level of the bridge. Once there, he used the ship's keys on the door. On the fourth try, he got the door open and shoved Antonopoulos through the opening.

Having memorized the layout of the ship, from information supplied by Yacob back in the Washington office, Peter knew exactly where he was and where the captain's cabin was located. Peter paused briefly before looking around the corner, but he heard nothing. The two men moved silently past the galley and up an open, steel staircase. At the next level up, the personal officers' cabins were situated along a narrow passageway. In the dark, operating by memory, Peter went directly to the door of the captain's cabin. In seconds, he found the appropriate key and opened the door, closed it as quickly, and stood there listening for any suspicious sounds. He flipped the light switch, found a bath towel, and wedged it under the door.

"I thought you were a carpenter and artist, not a cat burglar." Antonopoulos had settled himself on the bed, stretching his full length. Breathing hard and sweaty pale, his hands were folded over his heart.

Peter gave Antonopoulos a quick glance. "I am determined to succeed in whatever I do. Now please, no more talking." Peter opened drawers, pulled out clothes, and searched each item carefully before neatly replacing it. From the left side of the room, he worked his way to the right of the built-in wardrobe and closets.

Peter worked quickly and with compulsive thoroughness. He stuck his head into every opening. He looked at the underside of every space and eventually discovered some photographs. He glanced at each picture before carefully placing it inside a side pocket of his backpack. When he was finished with the rest of the room, he turned his attention to the bed where Antonopoulos was asleep. Peter roughly shook Antonopoulos's shoulder.

Antonopoulos abruptly sat up and pushed Peter's hand away. "What the fuck?"

"Get out of bed. I need to search it." Peter assisted Antonopoulos into a sitting position on the floor. Antonopoulos sat with his back against the wall, pale and gazing blankly at Peter. Peter, with deliberate speed, searched the bed linen, the pillowcases, the mattress, the box spring, and then he slid under the bed. With his hand, he both looked at and felt every surface. When he had finished, he went back to the left bottom corner of the bed where the leg was welded to the frame. He carefully removed a piece of clear packing tape stuck to the inside corner. Under the tape was a 3X5 yellow, lined index card. He scooted out from under the bed.

Unfolding the card, he found that it contained, in tiny, meticulous handwriting, a list of numbers. Some were definitely Greek telephone numbers. Others appeared to be bank accounts. And some were other identifiers with only a single Greek word to distinguish the number. Peter carefully put the card with the photographs.

"Let's go. Peter pulled Antonopoulos to his feet, marched him to the door, and turned out the light. He threw the towel on the bed. He listened carefully before gradually opening the door. They went back the way that they had come.

Peter made Antonopoulos go down the steel ladder first. On the deck, Peter kept Antonopoulos in front of him. The security guard on the harbor side was at the far end of the ship. Peter helped Antonopoulos over the chain at the top of the gangway.

Suddenly, halfway down the gangway, Peter stopped as a voice on a loudspeaker boomed out, "Stop! You are trespassing!" Echoes reverberated as Peter hustled Antonopoulos faster down the gangway.

"Stop right there!" The loudspeaker squawked metallically.

At the bottom of the gangway, three armed guards emerged from the shadows, manhandling Peter and Antonopoulos onto the pavement, where they were forced to kneel and were roughly frisked. Antonopoulos's hands began to shake. He placed them under his thighs.

A short man wearing the uniform of the security firm suddenly appeared from the entrance to the gangway. He was slender, dark, and had the beginning of grey in his closely cropped hair. He confidently walked to where Peter and Antonopoulos sat. One of the guards handed him their passports.

In Greek, the security leader asked what their business was. The man had a jacket on with two stars on each shoulder epaulet.

Peter looked up at him. "We are working for the shipping company, Nikolaou Kasos. We were hired to check the radiation situation on board." Peter's voice was confident. Antonopoulos fidgeted and stared at the ground.

"Bullshit." This time the word was in English. The leader switched back to Greek. "I'll make a call to find out what the boss wants to do with you."

Peter slowly whispered the translation to Antonopoulos. In a minute, the security leader was back in front of Peter. He kneeled down to eye level with Peter. "The vice president wants to meet you. He'll deal with you personally. Get up and into the car."

Antonopoulos and Peter settled into the backseat. Antonopoulos grumbled, muttering under his breath. Peter tried the door and found it locked. When the car stopped, they found themselves outside an eight-story office building. They were quickly escorted inside and led to an elevator where they rode to the fourth floor. The security leader told them to go right, and he followed them halfway down the hall, where he told them to stop. Peter saw that this office was identified by a sign "VP, Operations, Julian Farkis." Once inside the office, Peter saw a slender man with black hair swept back on his head, and wearing heavy black frame glasses, standing behind an oak desk.

"Come on in, gentlemen. Sit down. I'm Julian Farkis. I have fresh coffee for you." Farkis dismissed the security leader with a casual, "I can take it from here, thanks."

Farkis poured coffee for each of them. He then went back to his desk where he studied a document for a few seconds before picking up the backpack. "You have binoculars and a few hand tools in this backpack. Did you leave something on the ship? Maybe like a video camera? I doubt that either of you could find radiation without any equipment. Who are you working for?"

"We were hired by Nikolaou Kasos shipping." Peter said.

"No you weren't. I work for Nikolaou Kasos shipping. What were you looking for on the Ileana Iazarou?"

"We were scouting the location to see what would be involved in getting our equipment on board." Peter and Farkis were speaking directly to each other in Greek. Farkis seemed to have lost interest in the backpack.

"Who ordered you to examine the Ileana Iazarou?" Farkis sat down and stared at Peter.

"Nicolaos Polopolis." Peter maintained his casual facial expression.

Farkis's eyes widened, and then nearly instantly the lids narrowed to slits.

"Nicolaos, eh? Why in hell would Nicolaos Polopolis be concerned about radiation levels aboard our vessel?"

"Polopolis told us he is on the board of directors authorized to do an independent examination."

"Polopolis is only an investor. He's not on the board. He doesn't represent shit." Farkis picked up a ballpoint pen and began tapping it on top of his desk.

Peter shrugged and drank some coffee. Antonopoulos, however, got up, walked over to Farkis and gently touched the hand that Farkis was using to tap on the desk.

Farkis jerked his hand away. "Don't touch me, you fucking faggot." Antonopoulos smiled and gestured that he was sorry.

"Is your friend a deaf mute?"

"He doesn't speak Greek, and he isn't feeling well."

"And yet, his passport identifies him as Douglas Antonopoulos, and you tell me he's working as a radiation consultant here in Greece. But, he has no identification to show that's a radiation expert. In fact, his corporate

ID says that he's a security and intelligence consultant for company called DRPearl, Inc. You are lying."

Peter shot a disbelieving glance at Antonopoulos. Farkis stood and walked to his office window, where he stood looking out while he waited for an answer. Antonopoulos sat slouched back in his chair, smiling gamely despite having no idea about what was going on.

Peter stood, stretched, and took a deep breath.

"What are you doing?" Farkis wheeled around and started back toward Peter.

"I think we should leave. I know you must have far more important things to be doing." Peter grabbed the backpack and the ID's and headed for the door, stopping only when he realized that Antonopoulos hadn't moved.

"Are you staying here, Doug?" Only then did Antonopoulos begin to get up out of the chair.

Farkis came over to Peter and got in his face. "I'm calling the cops. Stay right here, you slimy prick."

"Get the fuck out of my face." Peter pressed a palm against Farkis's chest and shoved. Farkis went flying backwards, grabbing at a chair and missing before falling to the floor. When Antonopoulos finally made it through the door, Peter slammed it shut behind him.

Antonopoulos and Peter were waiting for the elevator when Farkis burst out into the hallway holding a nine-millimeter Berretta. "I suggest you wait in my office until the police get here."

"That's funny. I thought we were US citizens being held against our will. We have an appointment with our embassy, and I don't think you'll shoot us right outside of your own office." Peter shoved Antonopoulos into the elevator. On the ground floor, they walked past the security guard and were quickly outside. They kept a brisk pace back toward the apartment. After a seven block walk, during which Peter circled back three times to check if they were being followed, Peter ushered Antonopoulos into their apartment.

Peter stood at the window, carefully watching the street. After a few minutes, he turned around to find Antonopoulos slumped down in the desk chair, his face in a dark frown. Peter sat down in the armchair and glanced at the front page of the newspaper he had picked up on their way back to the apartment, and then began leafing through the newspaper. Suddenly he stopped, his eyes drawn to a picture and caption on page

5, Metropolitan Section. He folded the paper and shoved it over to Antonopoulos.

"What's this?" Antonopoulos's voice was barely audible, without a note of curiosity or interest.

"It's a picture of U.S. Congressman Odell Eugeniades. It says that he is here as part of a congressional fact-finding investigation looking into the matter of the Ileana Iazarou. They are having a closed door meeting with the Greek police and maritime authorities in the auditorium of the port authority, this afternoon. We are going to be there."

Antonopoulos looked away from Peter. "I can't go. I'm not feeling very well."

Peter looked at Antonopoulos intently. "Okay, I can do it by myself. When Farkis found your company ID, I thought we were done for. Don't carry your real ID when we are working. Honestly, I feel better about working alone than having you with me. You are a completely liability as far as I can tell."

"No need to be belligerent. I'm sorry, so what does this picture mean?"

"It means that Farkis didn't call the police or attempt to hold us, because he didn't want a stink while the US Congressional members were in town. I think we should call David with this news."

Antonopoulos nodded and shrugged.

Peter placed the call. "Hi, David, something's come up here. First, we have identified Farkis. He's the VP of Operations for Nikolaou Kasos shipping."

"That's great, Peter. How's Doug?"

"He says he's not feeling very well. I'll send you a full report as soon as possible on encrypted email, but the important thing, for now, is that Congressman Odell Eugeniades is here as part of an investigation into the radioactive material that had been aboard the Ileana Iazarou."

"Wow, you've already stumbled onto one of the gang's leaders and Eugeniades. Get some pictures of Eugeniades and whoever he's with. Follow him, be careful, but don't make contact. Send me what you have as soon as possible. When you have a chance, look around the port for the yacht, Kirie Pondiki. It's one hundred sixty-one feet long, three levels, with a flying bridge, white with blue trim, registered to the Nikolaou Kasos shipping line. We'll fax you a picture today. Anything else?"

"Thanks for having confidence in me, David. I will keep you informed."

Antonopoulos was sweating profusely. Peter changed clothes, taking the pictures and note card out of the backpack and stuck them in the top of one of the black socks that he was wearing. When he reentered the bedroom, he found Antonopoulos lying on the bed. "Do you need to go to the hospital?"

"I don't think so. I just need to get some rest. I'll be fine, really."

"If you need help, call me. I really need to get to the port authority."

Peter walked three blocks before grabbing a cab. As soon as he was dropped off, Peter walked around the port authority building and through its public areas. He read the posted notices pinned to the official port authority bulletin board. He studied the crowd milling around in public lobby. Suddenly, he spotted Farkis.

Farkis entered the port authority building through the front entrance. He was trailed by two men in casual attire. One of them looked like the short security leader from the Ileana Iazarou. Farkis walked through the crowd to an unmarked door at the back of the lobby, followed by the two men. Farkis rapped the door with his knuckles, and the three men were immediately given entry. Peter slowly, cautiously moved outside. In front of the building was a street with heavy traffic and spaces for taxis and buses to pull over. Across the street was a small park with benches. Beyond the park were the brilliant blue waters of the Sardonic Gulf. Peter stopped at a kiosk and bought a disposable camera. At another store, he purchased an Olympiacos basketball team cap. He moved around, sitting on benches now and then, and moving always with an eye on the front of the port authority building. After a two hour wait, he observed Farkis and his entourage coming out of the building. Just behind him was another group, with the Congressman in its middle.

Peter raced to the small building that housed a tourist, rental shop half a block away. He rented a scooter. He adroitly maneuvered the scooter into the traffic, which was moving sluggishly in the late afternoon. Darting in and around cars, Peter quickly caught up to the limousines. The limousines stopped at the front of the Nicolaou Kasos Shipping Company building. He immediately took several photographs. After the assemblage had disappeared into the building, Peter found a spot down the street where he could wait and watch.

An hour passed, and dusk began to settle in over the area. Street lights came on. In a small tavern, diagonally across the street, Peter ordered a lamb pita and a beer. He sat outside at the tavern's sidewalk cafe. Before he could finish his pita, the congressman came out. A black limousine whisked him away. An hour later, Farkis came out alone, headed in the opposite direction and entered a parking garage. Peter hurriedly paid and sallied forth down the street to the parking garage. He couldn't locate Farkis.

After he returned the motor scooter, Peter walked back to the apartment. He found the door slightly ajar. He pushed the door open cautiously while remaining slightly outside the apartment. From where he stood, he could see that the contents of the apartment had been rifled through, with clothing strewn about. Peter cautiously stepped into the apartment, but left the door open. Antonopoulos was sprawled on the bed, naked, on his back. Peter checked his pulse. He was dead and cold. Then, Peter surveyed the kitchen, the bathroom, and the closets. He sighed and dialed David Pearl.

"Hi, Peter, what do you have?"

"I have Antonopoulos dead in bed."

David gasped. "You've got to be kidding."

"No, he's dead. He has two red marks in the middle of the chest about an inch apart, with some yellowish bruising. Looks like he got tasered. I was out at the port authority, and maintaining surveillance on Farkis and the congressman, and when I got back, I found him."

"Are you okay?"

"I'm not really sure."

"Take a picture of Antonopoulos. Call the police and an ambulance. Wait for them to arrive and request an autopsy. I'll call his wife. Son of a bitch, I guess I'd better call the State Department too. When the police and the body are gone, get the hell out of there. Get away from there. Find another place to stay. Let us know when you have settled in somewhere safe, and stay there. Don't stick your face or neck out anymore until further notice."

CHAPTER 41
The Drudgery of Searching, June 1

David listened patiently to Alice. "Really, David, you're missing too many meetings. You know how important face time is in Washington. A few of our contract officers are demanding an audience with you. It seems to me when they find themselves with nothing they want to be doing, they ask for a meeting. But seriously, you have no business being away for so long."

David looked out the hotel window, visualizing himself out on the Mediterranean in one of those sailboats. "I hear you, Alice. I'll give it two or three more days. Taz is a fixture on the cornice. Ali has developed relationships with bartenders, clerks, and policemen all over downtown Beirut. I think Polopolis is still here."

"You got no evidence of that. Come home, or let me come to Beirut, and I'll look for Polopolis."

"Very funny, Alice, but you are where you need to be. Listen, Jose is on the other line. Go ahead and set up appointments for next week. I'll come home no later than this weekend." Alice hung up abruptly.

"Jose, what do you have?" David turned his attention to the long yellow legal pad in front of him on which he had one long column for a to do list, and on the other, a long list of people and places in Beirut that they had yet to check out.

"Ali is telling me that a security guard friend of his has identified Polopolis. Thinks he saw him yesterday going into a bar."

"Let's check out the bar. Meet me in the lobby."

Ali was the first arrival. David watched him as Ali stepped confidently, smiling and nodding to the staff in the lobby. Ali went to the bellman and whispered something to him, at which the bellman laughed loudly.

"Ali, what's this bar you want to check out?"

"It's actually a restaurant and bar called La Paillotte. It's at the south end of Minet el-Hosn. We ought to get moving. One of my sources says that Polopolis checks in there from time to time."

The four men walked briskly down the cornice. Taz pointed out to the others the security professionals along the way. "I can spot a cop at a hundred yards. The ones here are mostly very fit men and women, not usually the sort to be lounging at the beachfront. They sit or stand with little interest in each other. They have earphones. Or, they drive by slowly, studying the crowds, the cars, and the bars."

"Who provides all this security? It must cost a fortune." David kept his eyes straight ahead.

"It wouldn't be politically correct to try and find out. I think some are from the government of Lebanon, some from the City of Beirut; some are hired by business groups, and maybe, possibly, some from the various political factions. Lebanon prides itself on being a business and banking capitol, so it behooves the powers that be to maintain the peace, at least where the tourists and business people are concerned."

"Taz, are you sure you're okay?"

Taz grinned at David. "I won't push it. The disability retirement has left me with a shoulder that aches constantly, but my conditioning is otherwise good. Plus, I'd like to figure out who shot me before I go home. I don't want to be constantly looking over my shoulder there."

They reached the restaurant. La Paillotte was dingy on the outside and dark on the inside. The aroma of fish and vegetables, grilling, pervaded the small dining room. They picked a table in the middle so that they could cover every angle of the restaurant.

The waiter appeared, poised with pen and an order pad. Ali ordered for them in Arabic, the catch of the day grilled and draft beer. David pulled a file from the leather portfolio he carried. "I want all of you to study these pictures again. These were the pictures that Polopolis had taken in La Paillotte."

After their food was served, a tall, swarthy man wearing a tropical shirt with palm trees and dancing sailfish, in green and blue, came and stood at a corner of the table between where David and Jose sat. He stood there with a stern look on his face.

Ali smiled at the man and spoke to him quietly. "Hello, my friend, what can we do for you?"

"You can tell me who you are looking for." The man's voice was deep and menacing.

Ali continued smiling. "We are eating lunch. We aren't looking for anyone." Taz, meanwhile, kept surveying the room, suspecting the man interrupting them would have a backup.

"I don't believe you. I saw the pictures. Give them to me." The man bent over the table, reaching for David's file.

"No, the pictures are none of your business, my friend." Jose used his official Marine voice, a voice that could be acquired only through the experience of having issued and received hundreds of orders and ass-chewings.

The man continued to hold his hand out, but his gaze shifted to Jose. "I'm not your friend. I want the pictures. I am security here."

Jose motioned to the waiter who had served them. The waiter did not budge. "I'm with you on the 'we're not friends' bit. Why don't you go get the manager?"

"For you, I am the manager. For the last time, let me have those pictures." The man reached across the table and grabbed the front of Jose's shirt. The cloth began to tear as the man attempted to lift Jose off his chair. Taz delivered a blow to the man's side, knocking him to floor, dazed. Taz then grabbed the man's wrist and used all of his leverage to slam the man's elbow into the floor. The pop from the bone breaking was loud. Everyone in the restaurant had stopped what he or she was doing and watched, except for the backup. This man, short and squat, stepped a few feet out from the bar where he had been sitting, and drew out a black matté Kimber 10 Eclipse. Before the squat man could issue a threat, Jose disarmed him. Jose delivered several hard blows to the man's face. When the man fell to his knees, Jose kneed the man in the forehead.

The tall thug now lay on his back, his wide open and fearful eyes staring at Taz who stood over him. "Who are you mother fuckers?"

Sirens began to sound in the distance. Taz searched the man, relieving him of a Leatherman tool, a set of brass knuckles, and his wallet. Taz took the man's ID and put the wallet back in his pocket.

"You tell the police we are the good guys." David touched Taz's arm to pull him away. "Let's get out of here."

Outside on the sidewalk, the four men casually ambled along the Corniche. "Guys, I think that tells us the Greek gangsters own and operate that bar. I want you to focus on the marinas and the keys. I think when we find the boat or whatever those keys open, then we'll find Polopolis. I will go back to the suite and pack. I have been away from the office for too long. So, the marinas, whatever the keys unlock, and Polopolis, in that order."

As David waited in the gate, he typed in his journal. Last night's nightmare involved his falling down flight after flight of endless stairs in some unidentifiable building. He just fell, trying desperately to stop falling, lost in a kind of vacuum. He never landed or got hurt, just the sense of flailing, unable to resist or change his downward flight.

CHAPTER 42
Nocturnal Interludes, June 3 through 5

At 10 PM on a Wednesday night, Mee Maw answered her phone. She had been sitting at her oak kitchen table, sipping hot chocolate, and reading a suspense novel.

"Hello, Margaret McKay?"

"Yes, that's me. Who am I talking to?" Mee Maw pulled her housecoat more tightly across her chest and, as was her habit, she looked out the kitchen window into the darkness of night.

"I'm FBI Special Agent, Robert Woggins. You sent a file to DRPearl Inc., in Washington, DC. After analyzing that file, they referred the matter to the authorities—which is me. I am working on a case that may be related to the material you provided DRPearl." Woggins paused.

"Oh, I see, Agent Woggins. I totally gave up on the FBI a long time ago. I guess this DRPearl has some clout. What can I do for you?" Her voice soared as she spoke before finally finishing with a giggle.

"You can provide me with a bedroom and cover for a few days. If you agree, my partner and I will be dropped off at your front door in thirty minutes."

"Does this have to do with my neighbor, Victor Nevzlin?"

"Yes, it does."

"I'll be waiting for you."

Thirty minutes later, Mee Maw heard a vehicle pull up in her driveway. She heard the doors close, and seconds later there was a knock on her door. Two men dressed in blue jeans, tan work shirts, and boots quickly entered the house. They carried three large Army camouflage duffle bags. They both were carrying lightweight black parkas, black fatigue pants, and shirts.

"Hi, Mrs. McKay, I'm Special Agent Robert Woggins." Mee Maw sized him up with a quick appraisal: Woggins would have been a very good student, dogged and determined, but his original, small stature was now filled out with heavy, muscular shoulders and big thighs. "This is Agent Svidler. Let's get this stuff into your spare bedroom, and then we can talk in the kitchen." Mee Maw led the men to the second bedroom.

"I'm afraid that you won't be too comfortable in here, but make yourselves at home."

"Not a problem, Mrs. McKay."

"Call me Mee Maw, please."

"We'll do that too, Mee Maw. Now, let's get into the kitchen. You got any coffee?"

"No, but I can sure make a fresh pot. Just takes a few seconds."

"Thanks. Before you get started on that, let me turn out this light, so that my partner can slip outside." Agent Svidler pulled on a black nylon hood and night vision goggles before stepping out on the back porch and then quickly into the night.

Woggins and Mee Maw sat at the kitchen table. Woggins held a mug of coffee in both hands, his elbows on the tabletop. "Mee Maw, thanks again for your hospitality, especially on such short notice. Please don't tell anyone who we are or what we are doing. Are you planning to have any visitors over the next three or four days?"

'This weekend, I'm planning on having my friend, Reg, over."

"Please cancel. At this time we don't know exactly how long we will need to be here. But, otherwise, go about your business as normally as possible."

Mee Maw cocked her head at his comment about Reg. "I guess it's not too high a price to pay after waiting for so long." She smiled at Woggins, but knew she could trust Reg and would tell him everything.

An hour and half after Svidler had gone out into the darkness, he tapped lightly on the back door. When Woggins turned out the light, Svidler reentered the kitchen. He gratefully accepted a cup of coffee. Mee Maw excused herself and went to bed.

Mee Maw got up at 5 AM to find Woggins asleep in the second bedroom. Svidler was in the kitchen with a large, soft-back book that he only occasionally glanced at. He more frequently went to the window and stared out at Nevzlin's house, with a long-range, hunting scope.

It was two nights later, at precisely 1:45 AM that the FBI plan was put into action. Mee Maw suspected that something was about to happen. So, she went to bed early and woke up at 1:00 AM and couldn't go back to sleep. She put on her pink, heavy, cotton housecoat and her pink, bunny rabbit slippers and went out into the kitchen. Woggins and Svidler were standing at the window in the dark. She went out into the living room and sat in her favorite chair and read her current library book, Rules of Deception, by Christopher Reich.

Mee Maw sat up alertly as Svidler pulled the curtain open slightly and watched as three cargo vans raced by her house in quick succession. She then padded back into the kitchen, standing at the backdoor with the lights out and the curtain pulled slightly open. The vans had come to a stop at Nevzlin's house. Agents jumped, carrying automatic pistols, wary and alert, from the vans as soon as each one reached a full stop. The men were dressed in black with tight stocking caps pulled low over their heads and black grease paint under their eyes and on their cheeks. As soon as the vans stopped, Woggins and Svidler went out the back door. The two men ran toward Nevzlin's house. As they reached the back door, Svidler broke the glass in the storm door and quickly unlocked the back door. A small battering ram opened the front door just seconds later. Five of the men entered the house. Mee Maw could see lettering on the backs of their jackets spelling out 'Special Agent' in capital letters. Others had spread out across the yard, one at the far corner of the garage and others in the yard, where they stood as shadows in the darkness.

Mee Maw stood transfixed, staring at the scene with her small binoculars. She watched as the room lights went on in succession, and then as quickly were dark again. Thirty minutes later, agents led Nevzlin to a van. Nevzlin wore shackles on his hands and feet, attached to each other by a small chain. An Agent pushed Nevzlin into the van. Nevzlin was stoic, not smiling, not showing fear, just his usual intensity. Three agents then got into the van and drove off with Nevzlin.

Mee Maw made herself a full pot of coffee and munched on a handful of granola. But she mainly studied the activity at Nevzlin's house. Agents carried boxes out to the vans. Computers were the next to go. When the first van was crammed full, it left with two agents. An unmarked, late model, Lexus SUV pulled up, and two men in dark suits went inside the house. Just before dawn, Woggins and Svidler came back through the back door. They gratefully accepted Mee Maw's coffee and slices of her chocolate crunch coffee cake.

Woggins sat at the kitchen table, slouching over his coffee. "Mee Maw, you have done the nation a great service. You may never know how much you helped the FBI. Nevzlin, not his real name by the way, will never take another breath out of confinement. Unfortunately, I can't divulge any more information."

"Agent Woggins, I knew he was up to no good. He certainly won't be missed around here."

Svidler came back into the room. "Bob, our ride is here."

Woggins smiled at that. "Mee Maw, please don't tell anyone, including your neighbors, what happened or even that we were here. We don't want any information leaking out that could be of assistance to our enemies. Eventually, there will be trials, but the trials, in all probability, will not be public. We thank you again, but I must take all the files."

Mee Maw led Woggins into her bedroom. She pointed at the two cardboard boxes at the top of her closet. He grabbed one and directed Svidler to get the other one. Woggins squeezed her hand, and then departed with Svidler.

CHAPTER 43
Feedback Loop, June 7

Aroused from a tension filled nightmare about a tall woman refusing to let him into his own office, David groggily sat up and answered his phone. The caller was Ritzenheim. "David, I have some news that you'll want to hear. It's important. I'm sorry. I know I probably woke you up."

"Yeah, Ritz, but that's okay. I'm always ready for news. There's always noise throughout the night around here anyway, so I wasn't sleeping that soundly."

"You really scored big-time with that information from the West Virginia grandmother, David. You have been the prime topic of conversation at the National Security Committee and the NSA."

David smiled with genuine pleasure. "Thanks, Ritz. It's a direct result of having a flat organization with no organizational silos, other than those required by contracts. But, it pleases me to no end that the matter ended successfully."

Ritzenheim coughed. "David, I have to tell you, I get to deal with a lot of creeps around town and have to make nice with them. It does me so much good to see someone I sensed had all the right tools and abilities to be successful in the intelligence business, becoming widely acknowledged as the best. Keep it up, and you'll be a legend in your own time."

"I'm sure I'm blushing. I couldn't have done much without your support and more importantly, advice, Ritz. I mean that."

David listened as Ritzenheim took a sip of something. "Damn, that's good scotch, the devil's own precious nectar. Before I get sidetracked again, let me tell you the gory details, and then let you get back to sleep."

"Sounds good." David sat on the side of the bed, typing notes into his encrypted laptop as Ritz continued talking. Later, he would add the nightmare about the tall woman into his personal journal.

266

"The FBI gets inside the house without a hitch, except that Nevzlin is out of bed in a fighting mood. The first agent gets kicked in the face, breaking his jaw. The second gets his nose busted and some eye damage, but manages to knock Nevzlin to the floor, where three more agents fall on top of him. In the process of getting Nevzlin under control, he gets three ribs broken, three fingers broken, and a fractured skull. He's recovering without complications at the moment." Ritzenheim laughed.

David made a silent prayer of thanks. "I wish I could have been there."

"You and me both. This Nevzlin is tough. He'll make a quick recovery. The son of a bitch was a Russian spy who defected ten years ago. At that time of what I call the euphoria and enlightenment still going on about the end of the cold war, and the breakup of the Soviet Union, there was a strong attitude that with the Russian bear in decline, putting this former spy into our very own witness protection program would be the very best possible thing. The CIA thought he had completely cooperated, and that their debriefing of him was successful. So, the Department of Justice signs on to that. The former Boris Ignatieff becomes Viktor Nevzlin. Then about five years ago, because he's become so giddy about Putin, he approaches a former girlfriend in Manhattan and re-ups as a spy. The son of a gun is translating lots of stuff for InfoSystel, a lot of which is highly classified. The simple folks at InfoSystel claim they monitored him, gave him a lie detector test every six months, and that he did good work. Well, when the FBI invaded the design store, they found lots of encoded material, enough to suggest that Nevzlin's work was appreciated greatly. And they found something else. Cardiff Shapiro's notebook."

"He's the SOB who murdered Shapiro, without a doubt. We dodged a bullet. If that Mee Maw hadn't been on Nevzlin's case and sent her files to us, Cardiff's murder would never have been solved."

"No shit, David. It seems that Shapiro made tiny little notes in his planner/calendar. Even his notes that were purely personal were often written in his own personal code. Our guys are still trying to break it down. I will take the small liberty of bringing you a copy of the planner as soon as I possibly can." He heard the trill of ice cubs rattling in Ritzenheim's glass.

David stood up and walked to the window, pulling the drapes open a crack. "No wonder the top intelligence officials and national security advisors are so pleased."

"There's a mountain of stuff, yet, that still needs to be analyzed, but it was definitely a home run for the good guys. Now, here's the part where it gets interesting. While Nevzlin didn't have Shapiro's calendar on him, it turns out that when he defected, he mentioned that he assassinated two of our CIA station chiefs, along with some other 'business' people who had somehow run afoul of the Russian bear. So, it stands to reason that he's the killer."

"Oh my God, and all of this can be blamed on the CIA and this administration if it ever gets out."

"It won't get out, God forbid. The Russian Prime Minister has already called in our ambassador in Moscow for an ass-chewing, and we have sent three of their New York Counselor political attachés home. This will remain a closet affair that no one in the public will ever know about. Someday, twenty years from now, when someone like me writes their memoirs, maybe the truth will be told."

After concluding the call with Ritzenheim, David placed a call to Robert Woggins's home number. A teenaged male with a squeaky voice answered the phone. David asked for his father.

When Woggins got on the line, David quickly reassured him that this call was personal. "I just want to tell you that you did some great work, and I am very proud of your work, Robert."

"Thanks a lot, David. It's my great honor, really, should give the old career a big boost. I really appreciate being able to work with you. It's definitely been a win-win."

"I think it's a win for a grateful nation. I had a thought I wanted to share with you that might help pin the tail on the donkey."

"What's that?"

"Did you get the toiletries?"

"Toiletries from the recovery site? I'll have to check the inventory."

"You may recall that the witness, the actuary Jasper Reinking, who was mugged before Cardiff was murdered, claimed that his mugger had an unusual smell about him."

"Oh, shit, that's right."

"You did great work, Robert, just close that loose end if you will. Thanks again." David terminated the call. David then texted a note to Odette, which asked her to order the largest gift basket available from Harry & David and send it to a Mrs. Margaret McKay, 11 Briarwood Road, Dunbar, West Virginia, 25064.

Chapter 44
Radiant Recordkeeping, June 9

Yacob sat in the conference room, slouching in the chair and doodling on the pad of paper in front of him. The dark recesses under Yacob's red, watery eyes revealed fatigue and stress. Alice sat across from him, but did not look at him. She studied a report that was due out to TechPro. She methodically read, pausing briefly to make pencil notes in the margins.

Settled into a chair at the conference room table, David looked expectantly at Yacob. "Let's get this thing started, Yacob. What do you have?"

"My analysts with the erudite, technical assistance of Gao have broken the Shapiro code. The first twelve letters of the alphabet begin on the right side of the top row of the standard keyboard. In other words, a is the = sign, b is the—sign, c is the 0, and so on. The next ten letters of the alphabet are from the bottom row, and are also backwards, so the letter m is the / mark, n is the period, o is the comma, et cetera. The last four letters of the alphabet are w, x, y and z. Because z and x have already been used, Shapiro used capital Z's and X's for them. And he used numbers for the most common words like 'and,' 'a,' 'the,' etc."

"Shapiro must have had a brilliant mind to do all of this from memory." Alice raised her eyebrows in admiration.

"The notebooks are filled with this code. Woggins told us that there's at least twenty years of notebooks. So, my guess is he could write quickly and fluently in this code. He was a very smart guy, so like skilled typists who don't ever look at the keyboard, Shapiro probably wrote in his code as fast as he could print out the words normally."

"So, what did he write that is of interest to us?" David paused to take a long sip of coffee and with his peripheral vision watched Odette sashaying back and forth outside the open door.

"Gao set us up a word searchable spreadsheet. A lot of the code was strictly personal. Remembering to make reservations for his anniversary, things like that. Thanks to Gao, that's twenty-three per cent of the total, coded entries. Another fifty-one per cent of the entries are of historical interest. This includes the key agreements at meetings, issues that he was working on, and personnel issues at the office. You talk about a person paying attention to details; well, this guy was that in spades. That leaves us with thirty-six per cent of coded messages that fall into three categories: one category is messages that we don't know anything or enough about to know whether the message is meaningful to us or not. This is about a third of the thirty-six per cent. I have printouts for you both. If you could give the printouts a quick read, annotate any observations you have, and get it back to me, we may be able to make an informed decision on some of these messages. And we have to decide if we want to release all the messages to the State Department for review, I think."

"Alice, you agree to that, right?" David was already studying his message list.

"Oh, absolutely, David, these messages may be very important, but just not germane for our purposes."

"Thanks. All of the other messages, except for two, appear to be time-limited or scheduling matters that also don't pertain to what we are working on. But again, we need a careful review by other, more expert eyes to make sure of that." Yacob handed over another list to each of them.

"So, that gets us down to two messages. The first is dated November 21, 2007. Checking back through his official calendar, we learn that Shapiro attends a reception in honor of the appointment of the new Ambassador from the Republic of Georgia. In Shapiro's notes, Miss Natia Ratiani is credited with telling him of a missing shipment of radioactive, fissionable material from a Russian stockpile. Now, this is from reading the note: the commander in charge of the stockpile accepted a large sum of money from certain Greek parties who arranged to secure the material and transport it out of Russia. The shipment was driven through the Republic of Georgia, and ultimately to Greece, for delivery to Yemen, and then to be reloaded aboard another ship for final delivery to Iran. This Greek gang, Stella, used its allies in Albania for that."

"So, who is this Ratiani person?" Alice asked, sitting up straighter.

"Natia Ratiani is the first political counselor for the Georgian Embassy here in Washington."

"Do we know her source?" David exchanged an approving glance with Alice.

"We have no idea, but we must protect her identity. Her name doesn't go into any written report. David, you should whisper it in the Secretary of State's ear. She may be a player for Georgia's security apparatus. She may have been playing Shapiro in order to make trouble for Mother Russia. We don't know, and maybe we never will. But, the CIA or the State Department has to follow-up." Yacob caught a piercing glance from Alice, but chose to ignore it.

"And the second message?" Alice was now at the edge of her seat. David saw her eyes sparkling in anticipation. David looked down at his tie, straightened it, and tried to control his own eagerness and a scratchy throat to learn what it was.

Yacob paused momentarily. "The second message is also from Natia Ratiani. We don't know the setting, only the date that the coded message was placed in Shapiro's notebook, December 14. This message warned Shapiro that the Russian Embassy had somehow compromised the telephones in the Georgian Embassy in Washington. During a single phone conversation, Ratiani mentioned to the Georgian ambassador that the U.S. State Department Undersecretary, Cardiff Shapiro, was following up on the missing, fissionable material. The Russians' interception of internal, Georgian Embassy messages didn't last long, maybe thirty-six hours, but long enough for Cardiff Shapiro's name to be connected to the missing radioactive material. My guys think that the Russians immediately thought that they could add a layer of smoke, blaming the government of Georgia in this matter, just in case their cover got blown. They are the 800-pound gorilla standing at the border of Georgia and probably have many, many spies in high places in the Georgian government. And, frankly, the Georgians just aren't as concerned about terrorism being directed at them by a dirty bomb as they probably should be. They wake up every morning and stare into the eyes of their terrorist threat, Mother Russia. Therefore, to the Russians the problem would be Cardiff Shapiro. And so they acted quickly. Cardiff Shapiro was dead less than twenty-four hours later. The notebook was found at the European Designs firm in New York. I think that's enough to connect Nevzlin to Shapiro."

Alice spoke up. "That's great, Yacob. Please rush a draft report of this to me and David. David, I think we should waste no time in getting this report to the Secretary of State. I'll ask Odette to get you an appointment as soon as possible. We shall say it's urgent." She got up and left the room. David thanked Yacob for his work, then went to his desk and began to return telephone calls.

CHAPTER 45
Discovery, June 9

Taz, Ali, and Jose sat in the outdoor café of the Moevenpick Hotel in Beirut, a perch which afforded them an excellent place to observe the boats in the hotel's own marina, the last marina on their list. For days now, the trio had searched the Lebanese, online listings for boats and ships in port and checked the available registries for large cabin cruisers entering or leaving port. They had also pounded the concrete sidewalks and piers for hours every day.

Jose was sipping his fourth cup of café Americano when a person's movement in the passing montage, on the park adjacent to the marina, caught his eye. He tapped Taz and pointed in the direction. Taz turned in that direction immediately.

"It's Nicolaos." Taz lurched out of his chair, ran in a smooth, contained lope, and leaped the iron railing, dropping cat-like onto the sidewalk. He sprinted across the street. A cab driver, pulling into a spot to await fares from the hotel, swerved to narrowly avoid a collision with Taz, slamming his brakes. The middle-aged driver screamed an Arabic obscenity while pumping an open palm up and down. Before the cab driver could resume his attempt to park, he was startled by Jose sprinting across in front of his cab. The man then placed his head on the steering wheel in order to regain his composure.

The waiter soon ambled over to Ali who had watched his friends' departure with a sudden desire to run after them.

"Please get our bill."

"Yes, sir, of course." The waiter disappeared, and Ali's frustration grew from waiting behind while his friends were chasing Polopolis. The waiter finally reappeared.

"Here's your bill, sir."

"Here, this should cover it." Ali handed him enough Lebanese pounds to cover the tab and provide for a ten percent tip. The man looked at the money and counted it slowly.

"Do you need change, sir?" Ali ignored the man and raced out of the café hoping to catch up to Taz and Jose. He ran out of the restaurant, choosing to go through the immense pool area to get a better view down the hotel's entryway.

Out on the sidewalk that laced around and through the marina, Ali caught sight of a large powerboat entering the marina. The crew was preparing to dock the ship. One stood on the prow and another paced the lower deck. Both gazed to the opening the captain maneuvered toward.

Ali immediately changed course. The power-boat had three decks, a fly bridge, and seemed to be approximately the right length they were looking for. Ali stopped and began walking into the marina. He slowed down before he got into the vicinity of the boat, giving every appearance of being a tourist enjoying a walk by the water. Ali walked past the boat, strolling to the end of the dock. Then, he turned and walked back with his eyes riveted on the back of the boat. In a few more steps, he was able to read the lettering on the stern: Kirie Pondiki, Pireaus, Greece. Ali walked more briskly, but avoided eye contact with the two crewmen and the captain who were now standing on the fly bridge in conversation.

As soon as he reached a point slightly beyond the hotel, Ali began to sprint. He had tried calling Jose's cell phone, but Jose did not respond. As he sped along the waterfront street, he carefully studied the view in front of him, but could see nothing out of the ordinary. Passing the first side street, he glanced up, and there about a half a block away were three police cars, an ambulance, and small crowd gathered to watch whatever was happening. Ali turned in that direction.

Ali found Nicolaos being loaded into the ambulance by two emergency medical technicians. Taz was sitting on the curb with his hands cuffed behind him. Jose was sitting in the back of the one of the police cars. A police sergeant and plain-clothes detective stood in the middle of the street, apparently discussing the charges. Ali got David on the phone and briefed him.

"Ali, stick with Nicolaos. I will call the American Embassy to get Taz and Jose out of jail." As David was speaking, Ali saw Taz being loaded into a police car. Yet another policeman got into the back of the ambulance with Nicolaos.

"Okay, David, they are being taken away. And one more thing, the Kirie Pondiki is docked in the Moevenpick Hotel's marina."

"Son of a bitch, you find the boat, and suddenly all we got at the moment, Ali, is you. I'll see what we can come up with. You find Nicolaos, and stay with him." David's voice stopped for a moment. "Please remember how tricky Nicolaos can be. Call me, Ali, on the hour. I'll find you backup, some way, somehow. Get going."

Ali went down to the crowd and asked in Arabic what hospital the patient might be going to and what police facility the two men arrested would be taken to.

An elderly man standing nearest to Ali responded quietly in carefully phrased English. "Be careful, young man. You speak excellent Arabic, but not with a Lebanese accent. You could find yourself in a world of trouble for less." The man's suit was neatly pressed, but worn and old, but he presented himself with a professional stature and demeanor.

"I am grateful, sir. My friends and I are here on business, not politics."

"That doesn't matter. Your friend, the injured one, is almost certainly being taken to the American University of Beirut Medical Center. As for the other two, get a lawyer."

"Do you know of a good one?"

"Yes, he's at the firm where I once worked. Aziz Al-Mustakbal. Follow me; it's not far. I will introduce you."

As they walked haltingly, due to the old man's use of a cane, down the block to the next intersection, the old man told Ali about his long career as a lawyer. Introducing himself as Assaad Rahim, he politely inquired as to Ali's business. Ali smiled at Assaad. "I'll tell you later."

Reaching a ten story, blue-gray glass building, Assaad Rahim led them inside, where he went straight to the elevator. The security guard received a smile and nod from Assaad. They rode the elevator to the fifth floor, where a receptionist greeted them. She politely listened to the old man's story, got them coffee, and then disappeared. In fifteen minutes, a tall, distinguished Arab man with a shoulder stoop greeted Ali warmly. Then, he hugged and kissed the old man on both cheeks.

"Ali, you made a very good friend this morning. Assaad Rahim has been my mentor for over thirty-five years. I would cut off my hand for this man." The attorney had a desk piled with legal briefs in tan, bound-at-the-top file folders. His suit was a classic cut, tailored precisely for his height and angular figure.

"Thanks so much, Mr. Al-Mustakbal."

"Call me Aziz. What can I do for you?" Ali went through the story, giving names and telephone numbers for Taz, Jose, and DRPearl Inc.

"You also want me to represent this third man, Nicolaos?" Aziz listened quietly as Ali told the story of Nicolaos, his aliases, and his irresponsible behaviors.

"Okay, so Nicolaos is on his own. I will get one of my staff attorneys on this right now. Now, I suggest that you take my friend, Assaad, out to lunch, some place very nice. You are very lucky to have made such a friend."

Back out on the sidewalk, Ali suggested a cab ride to the American University of Beirut Medical Center. The old man readily agreed.

The American University Hospital of Beirut is a huge modern structure of an all glass exterior and a concrete and structural, steel interior. As they walked into the lobby and studied the directory, Ali could see that every possible specialty and subspecialty was represented. The atrium lobby was bustling with doctors, nurses, and countless others emerging from one corridor or another and then quickly disappearing down a different corridor or behind doors that lined all the corridors. Ali found the ER, and they went there, stopping at an information desk to see if they could find Nicolaos.

The older woman listened while Ali told her the story of the accident and that he was looking for his friend, Nicolaos Polopolis. The woman looked at a list on the counter in front of her and shook her head. "I'm sorry," she said.

Assaad took over the conversation. "Are there any patients who have arrived in the last hour from the vicinity where the accident occurred, perhaps with the name David Pearl or Abdullah Haneef?"

The woman immediately bowed her head to check for those names.

"Yes, Abdullah Haneef is listed as being in the ER." She smiled at Assaad. Assaad reached for her hand, brought it to his lips, and kissed it.

In the ER, there was constant movement, conversation, and noise. Ali slipped behind an empty computer, found that it had been left on and went to the ER listing for patients. Abdullah Haneef was listed as having been discharged. His examining physician was listed as George Zeh. He went to the nursing station and asked to speak to Dr. Zeh.

Ali and Assaad sat down in the immediate vicinity of the nursing desk. After fifteen minutes, a slender, pale man with a head full of bushy black and grey hair came striding out toward them. He stopped at the nurse's desk. The nurse pointed out the two men.

Dr. Zeh strode over to them. "I understand that you would like to know of your friend Abdullah's condition and whereabouts at the moment."

Both Ali and Assaad stood up, nodded, and shook Dr. Zeh's hand.

"What is your relationship to Abdullah?" Dr. Zeh asked.

"We are his friends, and we represent his employer."

"I find it curious that someone with an Arabic name cannot speak a word of Arabic. You Americans can be quite obtuse and confusing." Dr. Zeh's eyes fixed upon Ali.

Ali shrugged and gave the doctor a sheepish look. "Abdullah is an alias that our friend adopted. His real name is Nicolaos Polopolis and he is Greek."

"I'll make a note of that. Your friend, whatever his name is, almost certainly has a ruptured ACL, that's a primary ligament behind the knee. He needs for the swelling to go down before he can have surgery. But, his larger problem is that the national police came and arrested him. I suggest calling the embassy and get them to intervene." Dr. Zeh went striding away from them. Ali and Assaad looked at each other.

"Mr. Assaad, I think it's time that we did lunch."

Ali led Assaad outside, where the two men jumped into a cab. Ali suggested that they dine at the Restaurant Mediterranee at the Moevenpick Hotel. During the ride, Ali called David.

"Yes, sir, I hired an attorney, Aziz Al-Mustakbal, to represent Jose and Taz. He's assigned an attorney to work on their cases." He provided David with the telephone number and email address.

"Thanks for that, Ali. Now, I have already contacted the U.S. embassy. I got mostly lip service, but we should get some support from them. What else?"

"We've contacted the municipal police, by phone, from the hospital just a few minutes ago. The municipal police told me Taz tackled Nicolaos from behind, as they were both running. Taz came down on Polopolis's right leg. His knee buckled, and he apparently ruptured a ligament in the hard landing while they struggled. Jose arrived and punched out Nicolaos. Taz and Jose were attempting to haul Nicolaos away when the police arrived."

"OK, so the police may drop charges if Nicolaos refuses to make a formal complaint. I'd better call the Greek Embassy. Maybe they can get Nico into their custody. What do you have on the keys?" As Ali was listening, the cab dropped them off at the front entrance of the Moevenpick Hotel.

"Nothing yet, I am going to tackle that next. There are some storage facilities, but because of bombings in Lebanon, they all have very high security. Oh, and I almost forgot: the Mister Mouse is still docked at the Moevenpick Marina." Ali slapped his forehead. Assaad smiled at his new friend's youthful enthusiasm.

"Keep your eyes on the boat. I'll see if I can get you some help from the American Embassy. Failing that, I will see if Mr. Al-Mustakbal knows of someone who can assist us."

"I think we need more help. I have a Lebanese friend, Assaad Rahim, who helped me with the lawyer. I can use him, but I still need more help. Assaad knows the lay of the land, the local political conditions, and who's who in Beirut."

"Consider that done. As soon as you can, get me an update on that boat." Ali agreed and quietly snapped his cell phone closed. He looked at Assaad who smiled and motioned that they were nearing the hotel.

The cab arrived at the Hotel Moevenpick. Assaad told Ali to tip the man generously. The two men conferred in order to get the payment correct. They thanked the driver profusely.

Assaad said, on their way into the hotel, "I hope our expressions of gratitude and the handsome gratuity will protect us, so the driver does not report the conversation to police intelligence."

Ali turned to Assaad at that comment, eyebrows arched and mouth open in deep appreciation of the older man's wisdom. Assaad shrugged.

Ali and Assaad waited at the impressively decorated restaurant on the second floor. Ali tipped the maitre d' fifty dollars for a table next to a window. They quickly ordered. After a couple of mouthfuls of the salmon, Assaad looked up at Ali. "Ali, I overheard your comments about lockers. The hostels, or at least most of them, have lockers. Of course, they inspect everything that goes into the lockers."

Ali smiled, but looked out at the vivid, blue Mediterranean Sea. "I had such good luck in meeting you, Assaad. I will make sure that you are compensated for your efforts."

Assaad shrugged. "The good fortune was richly mutual, my young friend. It has been an excellent adventure for an old man. My wife died years ago. Our only child chose to study medicine in the U.S. He's a surgeon who works at Johns Hopkins. He's busy with his work and his own family. Sometimes, my old law firm and my friend, Aziz, will throw a little work my way or invite me to a lecture." Assaad pulled out a well-worn wallet, opened it to a picture of his son, and handed it over to Ali.

"When we are done with lunch, I think that you should stay at the marina to keep an eye on the Kirie Pondiki, and I will go see if these keys fit any of those hostel lockers." Ali jotted down the names of the hostels that Assaad remembered and asked the waiter for a phone book to get the rest of them.

The taxi dropped off Ali at the third hostel, the B & B Meharma, on the Rue Cheik el Ghabie. After checking the first two hostels, Ali knew his low key, friendly approach was working. A young, pale woman worked the front desk. She wore a white scarf around her head, and her nametag identified her as Hoda. She kept her eyes mostly downcast and spoke in a soft voice. Ali told the young woman his story. As he talked, several young, German men wandered boisterously out of the hostel, into the bright sunlight.

"They made so much noise last night, Ali. I don't think that anyone got any sleep. Let's go to the lockers, then." Hoda came around from behind the counter as she spoke to Ali.

Her green-grey eyes sparkled as she walked through shafts of light that filtered in from the glass door and interior courtyard windows.

The two of them walked past several dormitory-like rooms, each sleeping eight. Past a row of single bedrooms, at the back of the building, were the storage rooms and the locker room. Hoda stopped in front of the door and waited. Ali quickly realized he should try the keys on this door. On the second try of the five keys, the door opened. Inside the locker room were standard, metal lockers arrayed in three sizes. To the right of the room were small lockers that could only hold a football or handbag and not much else. Along the front of the room and along the left side were lockers about two and half feet high and ten inches across. The back of the room held the largest lockers, about seven feet tall and twelve inches across. In the middle of the room were two wooden benches.

Hoda moved to the center of the room. "Our guests often change clothes and keep their camping gear or cold weather gear in here. I remember the man whose keys you have. He was older, and although he took one of our private rooms, I don't think that he actually slept there. His identification said that he was a sailor named Daoud. When he disappeared after a few days, I wondered about his lockers, but he paid for as much time as we permit, three months. I stood here and watched him put his stuff in the lockers. That's one of our security requirements. "Her eyes connected with Ali's, but quickly darted away, and she backed away from him by up a couple of steps.

"Hoda, can you point me in the general direction of the lockers Daoud used?"

Hoda quickly pointed to the half lockers along the front wall.

"I checked the log. It's these three lockers on the bottom row." Hoda darted to the vicinity of the three lockers, pointed them out, and backed quickly away. "Ali, I will wait outside in the hall. I need to watch the front desk, just in case."

Ali opened the first locker. A computer, a small duffel bag, and ship captain's hat were in this locker. The duffel bag held some personal items: family pictures, letters, post cards, copies of emails, and financial records. Ali loaded the computer into the duffel bag. After checking the liner for anything that Moschos might have stowed in it, he threw the captain's hat into the waste bin. The next locker contained a black wool pea jacket, a briefcase, and an accordion file filled with papers. Ali used one of the smallest of the available keys on the briefcase and was successful in getting it opened. He gasped at the sight of the briefcase crammed full of U.S. currency. He checked the pockets in the pea jacket and found nothing, so he left the jacket on the bench. The third locker held a Glock pistol. He put this in the duffel. Ali grabbed duffel bag, briefcase, and accordion file and left the room.

"I left the keys in the locker, Hoda. Thanks again."

Hoda was pacing in the hall, but abruptly stopped when she saw him. Ali kept walking. She turned around and jogged toward the front counter.

She picked up the phone and motioned for Ali to stop. "I think that I should call the police."

So unexpected and sudden was her declaration, Ali immediately stopped and looked at her with wide eyes and a face draining of color. "Please don't," Ali pleaded. "I work for a private company that has been hired to trace this man, whose real name is Moschos. This matter will be handled between the U.S. government and the Lebanese government, I promise."

"No, I'm calling the police. Just set that down over here and wait. I think I might be in trouble. If the police are involved, then I'll be safe."

"This is secret and confidential. I would never do anything to cause you harm, Hoda. You have my word." For a brief microsecond, their eyes connected. Ali saw her body stiffen, and she glanced around nervously.

"I can't believe you. I need to protect this business. The police could shut us down for harboring a terrorist."

"I'm sorry, I can't wait. Here, take this for your trouble." Ali pushed a handful of Lebanese pound notes into her hands, then rushed out into the street to find a cab.

CHAPTER 46
Waiting and Watching at the Marina, June 9

Assaad sat stoically on a concrete bench with the best view of the Kirie Pondiki. He smiled at those strolling past, and sometimes they said "hello" or smiled back. He occasionally got up and stretched, walked to the bathroom, or sat for a few minutes in the pool area. Assaad went to the hotel's gift shop and purchased an Arabic version of Time magazine. He settled himself back on the bench. At dusk, he continued his vigil, carefully scanning the boats, but always focused on the Kirie Pondiki. After the sun had disappeared over the horizon, his phone rang. It was Ali.

"Assaad, my magnificent friend, I am delayed at the U.S. embassy. David and the U.S. Deputy Secretary of State have been in lengthy discussions with the ambassador. I think we are finally getting to a point where they will provide some assistance to us. Your protégé, Aziz, is making good progress in getting Jose and Taz released. Maybe a few more hours, and then they will be expelled from the country and escorted to the airport. They will fly to Greece to continue our investigations there. Please be patient. I will call again as soon as I am through here, hopefully with someone from the embassy assigned to assist us."

Assaad smiled. "I am here for you, Ali. This will make a fine story to tell my friends at the café. I am well. You take your time. No one has come to the boat or left it. The sunset was infinitely glorious." They ended the call. In a few moments, Assaad was sleeping on the bench, his head gently nodding toward his chest with each breath.

An hour after the phone conversation between Ali and Assaad, Assaad was gently awakened by a toggling of his right shoulder. His eyes opened to see two policemen standing in front of him. The two officers were in the familiar, dark blue trousers, white tunics, and plastic brim, white hats of the city's police. Assaad had his ready smile on his face, and the two officers were warmly smiling back at him.

"The restaurant manager was concerned about you, sir. Are you all right?"

"Yes, indeed, I am. It was a long day, and I was enjoying the sunset. I must have nodded off." Assaad stood up, shook their hands vigorously, and wandered down the sidewalk just outside the fence of the marina. The police watched him for a few minutes and then turned around and departed the grounds of the Hotel Moevenpick.

Assaad waited at the far end of the marina for five minutes. Then, he returned to his bench, but was startled to see the Mister Mouse was now being resupplied. The crew was loading boxes and stowing them in the interior of the boat. Assaad called Ali.

"Assaad, what's happening?"

"The crew is loading the boat. I think they may be getting ready to leave." Assaad had begun to pace the sidewalk edging the marina.

"Okay, take some pictures. Try to get each member of the crew in at least one frame. I'm coming back to the Moevenpick. The embassy will be sending someone to assist us. Thanks, Assaad, you have truly been a lifesaver."

Assaad continued to walk up and down the sidewalk, taking pictures every few minutes. He pretended to be closely examining a yacht with a for sale sign at the far end of the marina. As he reentered the pool area, two men wearing the hotel's front desk uniform stopped him. The one with the heavily pockmarked face grabbed the camera, his cell phone, and his magazine. The other one put his hand roughly upon Assaad's shoulder. Then, the pockmarked one insisted on taking him to their office. The two guards escorted Assaad through a back door to the hotel and then down a flight of stairs to the basement.

Assad felt strangely calm and fully cooperated with the two security guards. He smiled and was relieved he was taking this matter with grace and dignity. Of course, he fully expected to be released in a few minutes. After all, he was a person of some repute in the city.

Light was shining from the security office's door into the dimly lit corridor. They led Assaad to the security officer on duty, a thin-faced man whose nametag read, 'Sergeant Jazzar.' Sergeant Jazzar's reading glasses perched on the very end of his nose, and his lips moved as he read and checked Assaad's identification slowly and carefully. Finally, Jazzar waved the two guards away. A moment later, the telephone on the desk rang. The security officer responded, 'Jazzar.' Jazzar's dark forehead wrinkled as he listened for a moment and then left, motioning with his hand for Assaad to stay where he was. So Assaad sat, noting the time, and waited for twenty minutes. Then, he began to look through the files in the security office. He found two that would be of interest, possibly, to Ali. So, he placed these files in the back of his pants and tucked his shirt back in over them. Then, with his camera, cell phone, and magazine, he slowly walked out of the office, studied the possible exits, before taking the stairs he thought would lead him outside by the motor entrance. Once inside the stairwell, he thought he might have heard a muffled shout.

Assaad stayed in the shadow of the entrance to hotel parking, alternating from just inside the entranceway to a tall hedge that bordered the landscaping in front of the hotel. From this last vantage point, he watched as an official US embassy car pulled up.

Ali arrived with the embassy's chief of security, who was dressed in a tan suit, blue shirt, and red tie. The man's head was shaved, and fat bulged at the back of his neck, shoulders, and hips. Ali walked at his side as they entered the lobby. Assaad followed them. When Ali saw him, he smiled broadly and touched the old man's shoulder. "Assaad, this is Rob Skinner, the Assistant Chief of Security at the embassy. Rob, this is my friend, Assaad Rahim."

Rob Skinner only briefly made eye contact, did not smile, and dropped Assaad's hand almost as soon as he touched it. In a few minutes, a lean and wiry man with a broad, plain face walked up to Assaad. Trailing the wiry man was Jazzar. The three security officials stood in front of Assaad and Jazzar and started talking loudly and repeatedly pointing at Assaad.

Ali interrupted. "Excuse me, do you know when the Kirie Pondiki will be leaving the marina?"

The lean and wiry man stared at Ali with a smirk on his face. "Your friend there, the old coot, was being detained in my office. We can't have him around here sleeping on benches, wandering around. If anything happened to him, we'd probably get sued. I am Ibrahim Tawk, Chief of Security for Moevenpick. You and your friend will leave the premises, or we will have the police arrest you for loitering."

"I see you know my associate here, Rob Skinner from the US embassy. I'm Ali Nassar. Assaad and I work for a U.S. firm called DRPearl Inc. We are at the hotel to meet people of interest to our security work."

Ibrahim Tawk leaned in closer to Ali, and his face displayed a drawn and serious demeanor. "It would have been nice if you had checked in with me, Ali. Lebanon can be very deadly. I would have objected to your 'security' arrangements at Hotel Moevenpick. We are very careful, even, as to what groups we allow to use our conference rooms."

"I apologize. We didn't think that there was any danger involved. We are not armed. We are a professional organization."

"I don't have time," Tawk interrupted. "I'm not going to help you do anything that might result in unpleasantness for one of our customers. So, leave the premises right now."

Skinner and Tawk walked away from Ali and Assaad, but Ali kept an observant eye on them while they chatted. Skinner lit a cigarette and offered one to Tawk, who readily accepted.

Ali switched to Arabic, asking Assaad if he was all right. "Yes, Ali, I am fine. I made some important discoveries while in the office. We need to go to my apartment. And, we need to send Mr. Skinner back to the embassy."

"Why is that, Assaad?"

"Because I don't trust either Tawk or Skinner."

"Okay, I can see that. Let's get out of here." The two men quickly headed for the cab stand. Tawk motioned for Jazzar to follow them.

"Yes. I will tell the cab driver to take me to the general area of my apartment. We need to change clothes. I don't want Tawk to find out where I live. He will almost certainly question the cab driver the next time he sees him. If not he's making an attempt to follow us right now."

"Why do we have to change clothes?"

"Because we must go to the Casino Du Liban to find the people that you are looking for. The casino requires a proper tie and jacket."

CHAPTER 47
Rendezvous With Force, June 10

David slept fitfully until he became aware of the incessant chirping of his cell phone. In an attempt to reach the phone, he succeeded only in knocking it to the floor. He sat up on the bed and felt around the floor with his left foot. Locating the cell phone, he bent over and picked it up.

"David, this is Peter Diamondis."

"Yeah, Peter. What is going on?"

"I have a problem. Taz has decided to stay in Beirut. He says he met a woman, and he's staying there to romance her."

"What? When did he have time to meet the woman of his dreams?"

"I don't know. While he was looking for Nicolaos, I suppose. But that's not really the big issue."

"Really? What is the big issue, then?"

"Zoe is coming here to Pireaus."

"How did that happen? I talked to her four hours ago, and she said nothing about joining you in Pireaus." David rubbed his forehead. "What motivated her decision?" David turned on the lamp next to his twin bed. He could hear the continuous ringing of the office phone, two floors below, and wondered who was supposed to provide the overnight coverage for the office. He slowly lifted himself off the bed and went to the bathroom, with the cell phone stuck between his shoulder and ear.

"I was assaulted last night. I went out to make the rounds of the marina. When I was about a block from the marina, three guys jumped me, knocked the crap out of me, and told me to go home. A good Samaritan took me to the ER. I got twelve stitches above my left eye through the eyebrow and four more in my chin. I didn't know about any health insurance, David, so I called Zoe. She gave me the insurance carrier information. But, she said she was tired of waiting around and insisted that she would come here to protect me. I had changed apartments, but the gang must have been watching me all the time. Jose is here, and he's as tough as they come, but he doesn't speak Greek, and the new apartment is probably being watched. And if it is, Jose might be next."

David made his way down to the reception area. "All right, Peter, hold on. I have to answer another phone." He reached for the office phone and quickly said, "This is DRPearl Inc. How may I help you?"

"David, this is Ali. I have located Julian Farkis and Karolas Damon."

"Where are you, Ali?"

"We are at the Casino Du Liban, north of Beirut."

"Okay, stick with them. I will notify the Justice Department and the CIA. Who's with you?"

"My friend, Assaad, learned the hotel was providing transportation for Farkis and Damon, and a couple of other people, from the Kirie Pondiki to the casino. This casino has no hotel."

"What are they doing now?"

"They just returned to the craps table after they finished dinner. Uh oh, hotel security is pushing me out of the casino, David. Call attorney, Aziz, please." After those words, someone else spoke into the cell phone.

"Who is this?" The man's voice sounded angry and urgent.

"My name is David Pearl. What happened to Ali?"

"David Pearl? Your friend is being arrested for stalking one of our guests. I would urge you to stop harassing them." The phone call was abruptly cut off.

David set down the phone, sighed, and shook his head in impatient disbelief at this latest bad news. He redialed. "Peter, are you still there?"

"Yes, I am."

"Let me speak with Jose." There was a pause while Peter gave the phone to Jose. "Jose, how bad off is Peter?"

"I'd say he should stay on the bench for at least a couple of days. He's also got a chipped tooth, so he needs to go to the dentist to get that fixed."

"Anything else?"

"Yes, we got the autopsy results. Antonopoulos died of a heart attack. He had bad coronary artery disease. He was tasered, which probably initiated the heart attack, but he was a dead man walking before that."

"Well, maybe that helps to explain why he was essentially just going through the motions with MagnaMeta management. I could see he was having trouble concentrating, and the last couple of times I talked to him, he sounded defeated and disheartened. I want you to wait for Zoe; don't go back to that apartment. Go to Athens, or better yet, take a cruise. Just get out of there."

"Yes, I understand. Are there any developments on your end?"

"Yes, the materials that Ali discovered in the hostel are a gold mine of information. The office techno-gnomes are working feverishly to run down all the bank accounts, the telephone numbers, and determine what the other numbers indicate. The State Department is working with the Department of Justice to bring Interpol into the case. It should be a few days before the gang starts getting arrested. Please, get somewhere safe, and then, call in."

Odette came into the kitchen and began making coffee.

"I need you to get me the first available flight to Beirut," he said. "And I need to talk to Alice the minute she gets in." Odette responded with a brief smile and wiggled the fingers of one hand at him.

David returned upstairs to shower and pack. When he returned to the office, he found Alice waiting for him in his office with a concerned look on her face.

"Alice, I need you to run the office for a few days. To make a long story short, Zoe has decided to go to Pireaus. Apparently, she's finally gotten a termination clearance from her bosses at Greek security. Peter Diamondis is recovering from a severe beating. He was being followed by the gangsters. Ali has been arrested in Beirut, but before that happened, he located Farkis and Damon. I am fresh out of ideas about who to send other than me. I can work with private security in Lebanon and Greece to wrap up our work."

A brief look of affection passed over Alice's face, her body stiffened, and then her worried face returned. "David, please be careful. Jacob hasn't finished analyzing the Moschos materials. It could be very dangerous in Greece."

"I think it will be very dangerous, but I need to get Ali out of Beirut. So, I need to go to Beirut first. We should all be back before the news of the indictments and arrests leaks out. I think we should sign off on the radiation source contracts and declare victory. The State Department will follow up with the Georgian embassy for the actual name of the Russian general involved in the theft of the radioactive material and the arms."

The office phone rang. Odette answered and turned to David. "It's Acting Secretary of State, Virgil Moody."

"Yes, Mr. Secretary. This is David Pearl."

"Good, David, I wanted to speak with you about the situation in Greece. There have been formal complaints to the embassy about your people—break-ins, burglaries, stalkings, assaults, et cetera. I wonder if you could explain or reassure me that these reports are overblown."

"I'm bringing my assets home as soon as possible, sir. But, it is they who have been attacked, stalked, and assaulted. You will get a copy of our final report on the radiation incident, as well as what we have discovered about the Greek gang's involvement in smuggling."

"Good, you can't get your people out of Greece soon enough. I also have Representative Eugeniades complaining to me about someone following him when he was in Greece, and he's saying that the U.S. government is playing favorites with you having so many high value contracts."

"We've done good work, sir. I think you know that."

"I'm just saying I am caught between two external forces, David. I know there are extenuating circumstances, and I know the quality of your work. We are all appreciative of that. Anything new on the Cardiff Shapiro case?"

"Yes, sir, we are finalizing our report. The State Department should have it in a matter of hours." David briefed Virgil Moody on the details of Viktor Nevzlin. David quickly clicked through each of the salient points on the murder of Cardiff Shapiro.

"A grandmother in West Virginia, heh? I can't wait to read about her. I'll look for that report. Thanks, David. Let me know when your assets are out of Greece."

"I will. One of them, Douglas Antonopoulos, is on his way home already in a casket. We feel confident he was murdered, but the death certificate called the death a heart attack."

"Oh my God, I'm sorry to hear that. That poor bastard sure had a run of bad luck."

"Another asset spent the evening in the ER getting his face stitched up. But, he'll be okay."

"I'm sorry. I have to go, David. Let me know what happens."

David clicked off. David sat for a moment with a red face and a rising tide of bile. With his jaw clenched, he dialed Peter Diamandis.

"Peter, is Zoe there, yet?"

"Yes, you want to talk to her?"

"I most definitely do."

When Zoe came on the line, she sounded tired. "Hi, David. Please do not worry about me. We are on board the ferry to Crete. We should be there in two or three hours."

"I am most definitely worried, Zoe. The threats have reached the US Department of State, and so, onto me. You should consider yourself as definitely not safe, so please be very careful. I think that we might be getting set up. Please, darling, please, take care of yourself. Keep Peter or Jose with you at all times."

"I will. We will take every precaution. I love you, baby."

"I love you too. I will see you in two or three days." David unlocked the door and grabbed his suitcase, heading for the front door.

Odette and Alice were waiting for him, along with the cab Odette had called. Alice hugged and gently kissed his cheek. She had tears in her eyes. "We are all so worried, David. Please be careful."

"I will, Alice. Zoe, Peter, and Jose are on a ship headed for Crete. I will keep you informed as events happen, but expect a call at least once a day. If I can get Ali sprung, we will go to Crete, join up with the rest of them, and fly back home."

Alice smiled gamely and gave his hand a squeeze.

Odette had carried his bag out to the stoop. She embraced him, and he returned the hug. "Don't worry," he told her, and wished he could heed his own advice.

Chapter 48
A Maris Breakdown, June 11 and 12

The metallic, grey cab, with a small dome Taxi sign on the roof, but no other visible markings, dropped Zoe, Peter, and Jose off at the front entrance of the Heraklion Maris Hotel. Jose waited outside because he was certain they were being watched while aboard the Knossos Palace ferry. He stood partially hidden behind a pillar at the far edge of the hotel's circular drive. After a few moments, he spotted a cab pulling up to the curb, across the street, and two men exiting. He recognized them from the ferry as they looked at the hotel, nodded at each other, and walked into a bar on the corner the block.

Jose rejoined Zoe and Peter who were waiting for him in the lobby. They had taken two adjacent rooms on the top floor. Once inside the rooms, they opened the connecting door. Zoe stood outside on the small balcony. After a brief stop in the restroom, Jose joined Peter and Zoe out there.

"We were followed. The two thugs I recognized from the ferry are in that corner bar over there." Jose pointed toward it. "I think I should case the neighborhood. Get a feel for the territory."

Jose looked at the Mediterranean and took a deep breath. "We can wait for them to find us, or we can get rid of them first."

Peter, still showing the effects of the beating, looked at Jose. "I think you're right. I had much rather take the offensive, than be a sitting duck like the last time."

"Me, too. I'll check out the bar. Wait five minutes, and then, join me there." Jose waited until he saw Peter walking toward him, and then he entered the Kokkini tavern.

Jose settled into a booth where he could study the two gangsters. When Peter walked through the dark glass door a few minutes later, the bartender turned in his direction, his eyes following Peter until he sat down with Jose. The bartender frowned briefly in their direction, then went back to work pouring beer. His face had the sea weathered look of a dedicated fisherman. The bar was festooned with pictures of fishing boats and fishing gear: oars, part of nets, fishing line, and floats. Peter and Jose sat quietly in a booth near the two men. Before they could be served, the two men turned their heads to stare at Jose and Peter.

Jose got up first and went to their table, where he spoke softly. "I think you two are following my friends and me." The two men grinned and shrugged. Peter moved to their table and sat down across from the older of the two men. The young one, thin and wiry, with scaly skin on the backs of his hands, and the expectant look of the perpetual underling, nervously glanced at the older man. The older man stared at Peter. Peter stared back. The older man took a long gulp of beer, settled the beer glass back down, and continued to glare.

"I will try again. What are you doing following my friends and me?" Peter smiled the barest of smiles, full of menace and confidence.

"I don't know what you are talking about. Leave us alone." The older man answered in a tone that made his response sound like an order he expected to be obeyed.

"I can't do that," Peter said.

The older man had angry, reddened eyes and a wart-like growth at the end of his nose. He stared at Peter. "You better leave us the fuck alone." The man's harsh, guttural Greek sounded of the waterfront in Pireaus.

"I'll leave you alone as soon as you tell me who you are working for and what you are doing following us." The older man's hands knotted into fists, and he banged the table hard, making the beer glasses jump and some of the amber liquid spill out. The bar maid hustled over to wipe up and provide more napkins.

"Is there a problem here? If there is, you guys need to take it outside." The bartender stayed behind the bar, and spoke in a calm but insistent voice.

"This asshole is bothering my friend and me." Peter kept his eyes on the man sitting across from him.

"I have contacted the police. They should be here shortly. We don't want any trouble." The bartender's voice was calm.

The older man slid out of the booth and stood up. Jose stayed where he was. The man reached over, grabbed Peter's arm with both hands, and pulled him to his feet. The younger man slid out, but remained beside the table and in front of Peter.

"I guess you didn't learn your lesson back in Pireaus, did you?"

"I guess not. Here, I'll give you another chance to do the job right, but you don't have all your buddies with you now." Peter braced himself for a blow that never arrived. Jose had ambled into the walkway space between the tables and booths, as if he was going to the men's room, but he suddenly stopped to deck the older man with a hard, straight right to his temple. The man fell across the table and then, rolled onto the floor. His knees crumpled as his body's momentum took him to the floor, and his head sounded like a dropped melon as it hit the floor.

Jose bent to collect the man's wallet. He looked at the driver's license only long enough to try to read the name. When the younger man lunged toward Jose, Peter's elbow pounded into his rib cage. This was followed, quickly, by a hard, double fisted chop to the man's neck. And, as the man was falling, Peter brought his knee up into the man's face. Blood cascaded downward from his nose, and bright droplets of blood flew out in a red spray. The man dropped partly on top of and partly beside his associate. Jose slipped the driver's license into his pocket.

Jose and Peter quickly conferred. Peter handed the bartender a U.S. hundred-dollar bill and asked him about a rear entrance. The bartender quickly obliged by pointing straight back and moving quickly in that direction. He escorted them through a storeroom, packed haphazardly, with cases of food in cans, open boxes of kitchen and dining room supplies, and bags of trash. The bartender, with an anxious look, quickly led them out the rear delivery door.

Outside, Peter told the bartender he would call later in the evening to make sure that all the damages had been covered. As soon as the door closed behind them, they sprinted away down the alley. The sirens were getting near. They made their way back to the Maris Hotel, Peter striding ahead and Jose meandering behind him.

At 9:00 PM, Jose asked Peter to phone the Kokkini tavern. The bartender answered. "Yeah, hi Peter. The police took the two men away. They looked around, asked a few questions, and then left. Yeah, no problem, man."

Jose spent much of the evening sending a long email to David about the day's events, Zoe's sudden bad mood, and his assessment that the trio should be changing their location soon.

Peter and Jose were asleep in their room when, at 2:00 AM, Zoe woke up screaming. "I can't breathe, call an ambulance." She wept and spoke rapidly in Greek in a weeping, gasping voice. Peter awoke instantly and pounded on the connecting door until Zoe was able to get it open. When his efforts to console her failed, he dialed the emergency number. Jose paced, looking anxiously at Zoe, uncertain as to what was going on with her and struggling with his own nerves. His hands shook as he punched David Pearl's telephone number on his cell.

"Hurry up! I can't stand this pressure anymore." Zoe's voice was too loud and now frantic.

"The ambulance is on its way, Zoe."

"David, sorry to call you with bad news. It's Zoe. She's having some kind of breakdown. She says she can't breathe." Jose held the phone to Zoe's ear. He could hear David tell her he loved her and he would be there as fast as he possibly could. Jose reassured David that Zoe would get his and Peter's undivided attention.

The hotel's front desk manager called the room. Jose picked up the phone. "Our friend is having a difficult time. She needs to see a doctor. We called the emergency number. Please get them up here as soon as possible." He hung up.

The ambulance crew arrived shortly thereafter, and ran straight to Zoe. The two women fluttered about her, taking her pulse, speaking soothingly to her, listening to her heart and lungs, and telling her to stay calm. In less than a minute, one of them peeled off, ran to the hallway, and returned with a wheelchair, and quickly loaded her in. Zoe shook and moaned, her hands tightly wrapped around her torso. Jose and Peter followed closely behind. They rode with her to the hospital.

Peter and Jose paced in the hallway outside the hospital's emergency room. Peter called numerous relatives in Greece and spoke for seven minutes to Zoe's mother, whose sobbing Jose could clearly hear, although he was standing five feet away.

"Are you her husband?" The psychiatrist's black eyes were vibrant and riveted upon Jose. Jose shook his head and indicated that Peter was the one she should talk to. Peter translated.

"I am her cousin, Peter Diamondis. Jose is a work associate and personal friend. Her husband is in Lebanon, trying desperately to get here as soon as possible." The physician disinterestedly shook Peter's hand.

"Well, Zoe Pearl is sedated. I think that perhaps recent stress has caused her to have a panic attack. I have written a prescription, but she should seek ongoing mental health care. Apparently, she hasn't been sleeping, so she is exhausted. You can go see her now, but keep the visit short. If there are no unforeseen developments, she'll be able to go home in a day or two." The psychiatrist turned on his heels and walked briskly away. Jose texted the news to David.

Peter called Zoe's parents. "It's Peter. I'm afraid that I have some bad news. Zoe has been admitted to the hospital."

At first, there was a moment of silence, followed by intermittent sobs from her mother. Her father finally gasped. Peter translated for Jose. "They want to know what happened to Zoe."

"I'm telling them she had some kind of breakdown and that she said she wasn't sleeping and seemed depressed."

"Oh no, they want to come to Heraklion. Her father is very concerned and I can't seem to reassure him." Jose shook his head at Peter who immediately smiled in acknowledgement of the impossibility of her parents getting there before they would need to leave.

David listened to Peter with a growing sense of worry. Peter's stress level increased the clipped tones of his voice. "I discouraged her parents from coming here. We might have to change plans. Hopefully, she'll bounce back. She's tough and resilient. Let me call you tomorrow."

"Alright, as soon as you talk to Zoe in the morning, call me. Thanks, Peter, I'm glad you are with her. Tell her we love her and will see her as soon as I possibly can."

CHAPTER 49
A Prayer Offered, June 3

David arrived at the Beirut airport twenty hours after he had departed his office. He was anxious about potential difficulties that he faced and was over-tired. He hadn't been able to sleep at all on the flight. After he cleared customs, he spotted an elderly man standing just past the doorway to the main terminal. The man wore a tweed sport coat over baggy, blue, cotton pants. The man caught David's attention and motioned for him to come over. David initially feared a con game of some sort or an offer of some illegal service.

"Dear Sir, I am Assaad Rahim. I think that you are David Pearl." Assaad stuck his hand out, and David grasped it firmly.

"Yes, I am. I am most pleased to meet you. Any news on Ali?"

"No, nothing yet, but Aziz is diligent. Don't worry. Let's go out this way to the cab stand, David. There are many sinister eyes here in Beirut and especially at the airport. Security is tight all the time. But, I fear that the police may be looking for me and perhaps you, as well." Assaad gently gripped David's elbow and led him to an unmarked door. This door led to a stairwell and a long corridor of private offices. Through another beige metal door, and they were outside, standing under the departures canopy.

"I haven't picked up my bag, Assaad."

"Most assuredly the gangs and police are watching the baggage area. I will send a friend to pick it up later."

"Who are these people who you think are watching for me?"

"I think that the most dangerous are elements of the state security apparatus. We have many currents in the political stream here. And, to paraphrase your American saying, very few are singing from the same hymnal."

David laughed, but tension rode just beneath the humor.

"There are only two people in the line for cabs. Let's go quickly, David."

They jogged across the lane of incoming traffic and darted to the taxi stand.

Their cab driver was a middle-aged, angry-looking man named Farouche. Assaad gave the driver an address close to the law offices of Aziz Al-Mustakbal.

In the law office of Aziz Al-Mustakbal, the receptionist directed them to the red leather armchairs in Aziz's office. "Mr. Al-Mustakbal has been urgently summoned to a phone call. If you will please wait, I can get you some tea or coffee?" Assaad asked for coffee, and David, still tired and dehydrated, requested water. While they waited, Assaad quietly attempted to bring David up to speed on events. Too exhausted to listen, David fell asleep, and Assaad did not wake him.

Forty-five minutes after they were seated in his office, Al-Mustakbal arrived. The tall, slightly stooped, Al-Mustakbal smiled broadly when he saw his old friend, Aziz.

Assaad gently woke David, helping him to his feet. David stretched and remained standing. He shook hands with Al-Mustakbal. Freshly awake, David studied the walls, which were covered with the numerous awards, photographs, and certificates prominently displayed on the dark paneling. Aziz stood at his desk, flipping through message slips.

"Mister Pearl, welcome to Beirut. What do you think of our fair city?"

"From what little I have seen Mr. Al-Mustakbal, it's beautiful. It's hard to imagine that some people want to plant bombs in it."

"Yes, it can be very dangerous; we must all watch out for the dangers. But, with Allah's blessings, we can survive. And, please call me Aziz. I must tell you: the news about your Nicolaos is not good. He doesn't have an attorney. The Greek embassy has turned their back on him. However, Ali should be released today. Unfortunately, both men have been severely beaten. The U.S. embassy has intervened in both cases. I have personally spoken to the ambassador. I have two private detectives watching Farkis and Damon. We have pictures of the people they are with." Al-Mustakbal handed the photos to David. David sat up, alarmed at the familiar face.

"Oh, my God, this is Ike Zisis, his wife, Stella, and a Washington-based attorney, Harry Markos. I don't recognize the other two, but this is fantastic. We need all the pictures you can get. Are these from a digital camera?"

Aziz handed a flash drive to David. "Yes, of course. You can send these to your offices right now, if you so desire." Aziz pointed to the computer on the credenza behind his desk. David went right over to it, logged on, and scanned in the photos and emailed them to Jacob Fleischmeister and Alice Boggs, with instructions to send them on to the acting Secretary of State, Virgil Moody, and the State Department official assigned to the case, Liesl Kremer. When he finished, he tried to jump up out of Aziz's chair, but Aziz pointed back to the chair. "Please, stay seated, David."

David slumped back into the chair. Al-Mustakbal now slowly paced through the room. "David, I have assigned one of my staff attorneys to go to the jail where our friend, Ali, is being held. We have purchased a small bond, and he should be free at 4:00 this afternoon. Our attorney will bring him back here, unless you have a better place to rendezvous."

"I don't, and thank you so much. What are the issues with Nicolaos?"

Al-Mustakbal stopped pacing for a moment, frowned, and scratched the thick slate grey and black thatch of hair on his head. "The troubles are myriad, complex, and very serious. His elopement from Lebanese customs leaves him in a very bad place. That makes our state attorneys think he is guilty of various misdemeanors, and they want to hold him until they can make a stronger case."

"Well, he's definitely guilty of evasion, stupidity, and craziness."

"At the very least, I have been working with the Lebanese Department of State to convince them to extradite him to Greece. I think that would be in everyone's best interest. If you could contact your sources in the U.S. government to support this, then we could possibly get him out of here in a few days."

"Have you talked to him or Ali?"

"Yes, both of them, in person. As I have already mentioned, they have been badly beaten. When they get to wherever they are going, they need to get extensive check-ups. Ali is fit and has bounced back mentally. Nicolaos is another matter entirely. He can hardly speak, is very angry, and I think, depressed. I'm quite angry about it and intend to pursue the matter to the extent of my personal leeway. I say that because I really don't know who, in the government, ordered the beatings or allowed the beatings to happen. Here, one must always be testing the political winds. So, we will proceed cautiously."

Aziz sat down beside Assaad and whispered to him. "At morning prayers, I prayed for both Ali and Nicolaos. I think that their bruises are both physical and spiritual."

"I shall pray for them also, Aziz." Assaad reached his hand to Aziz and very gently touched the top of his hand.

"Assaad, you stay safe. I do not want them to do the same to you. Why don't you go visit your son, the surgeon, in America? Seriously, I think that would be prudent and for the best. I must leave you now. I have a court appearance that I must attend to. David, wait here for Ali. My secretary is working on your travel arrangements to Crete."

Chapter 50
Peripheral Damage, June 4

Frankie Ballinger paced the hallway outside of Yacob Fleischmeister's office. Yacob saw her pass the door to his office several times, but he wasn't annoyed. The spirited, young woman often displayed her nervous energy when she had something on her mind, but she had a style and direct manner that he admired. Yacob was being briefed by Gao on the probable sources of the cash that Moschos had been smuggling. As Gao left the room, Yacob ushered the young woman into his office. He sat her down in the only armchair that could fit into his office.

He sat down and smiled at her. When she didn't say anything, Jacob motioned to her to begin. "Please relax, Frankie. We already shot a messenger this week, so the quota is filled." She grinned.

Her green eyes flared momentarily, as she prepared to speak. "I thought this news couldn't wait. I spotted a story in the Athens daily newspaper, the Kathimerini. I have gone weeks at a time reading these various publications and not seen anything of value, but I think this connects to some of what we have been working on." Her hands were tightly clasped in her lap.

"Go ahead, Frankie. Please proceed. You just rediscovered the fundamental truth of intelligence work—weeks of tedium and then a discovery that helps tell the tale."

"Okay then, a small story about the torture and murder of an Alexandros Stratakis," she said.

Yacob was instantly alert. He began to type an email to David and Alice, as Frankie spoke softly, reading from her notes.

"I'll give you the gist of it. Port of Pireaus police and state authorities reported the murder of Alexandros Stratakis. According to Police Chief Athanassios, the body was found face down in a dinghy, floating along the northern shore of the Pireaus Bay. Stratakis's body showed evidence of having been beaten and tortured. Stratakis was the first officer of the Ileana

Iazarou, the Kasos line freighter caught smuggling by the Greek Navy. The ship is still under guard in the port. Stratakis, as you will remember, worked undercover at the time for the Greek National Police." She paused to flip the page.

"The ship's captain, who abandoned the Ileana Iazarou in Tripoli, Lebanon, was found murdered in the Sudanese port of Al Hudaydah. Federal police spokesman, Theo Kavvada, stated Interpol was investigating Moschos's death, and there are no leads at this time in Stratakis's death.'" Frankie stopped reading and looked up at Jacob with her penetrating, green eyes.

"That was a good pickup, Frankie." Jacob stared back at her.

"Do you want to hear my analysis?"

"I sure do."

Frankie at last relaxed, and stated her analysis calmly, without the aid of notes. "The two murders are connected through their prior association, and various published Greek investigations have firmly established that large scale smuggling through Greece, by land, air, and sea, is an ongoing criminal activity. Intelligence sources within the Greek Federal Police report that several gangs are actively involved in this criminal activity. The so-called 'Ajax gang' has affiliates in Turkey, Lebanon, Cypress, Corsica, Marseilles, Sicily, Naples, the US, and Europe. Other gangs are identified either by code names assigned to them by police or are the names by which the lower level members refer to their organizations. These include: Stella, Pondikya (the mice), AKA Athens-Coffee-Underground), and the so-called Greek mafia. These groups have specializations and form ever-mutating alliances. They take their illegal funds and push them into legal businesses such as cafés, shops, shopping centers, construction, and Greek restaurants throughout the world." Frankie again paused to make eye contact.

"I think that's enough, Frankie. Get your report scanned into the computer database, and let's see if we get any more hits."

CHAPTER 51
A Reunion, June 5

David, Assaad, and Ali arrived by chartered powerboat. The captain pulled the boat alongside the marina's dock and snuggled alongside it only long enough to drop off the three of them and their luggage. Then, the boat did a pirouette and turned its prow back toward the western coast of Crete, beginning its return voyage to Beirut. As the charter boat passed in the channel between the island of Dia and the mainland, a sleek powerboat, with a fly bridge, passed it. The men standing at the wheel of each boat made eye contact and saluted the other.

David, Assaad, and Ali arrived by cab at the Maris Hotel. Assaad's appearance was neat and trim. He had catnapped on the boat. He was cheerful, continuously pointing out history and geography throughout the journey. David and Ali had been restless throughout the trip. The group drew stares from the front desk staff and the others in the lobby as they quick-stepped to the elevator. Ali had five days' growth of beard that failed to cover the cuts and bruises on his face, and David had three. Ali was still hurting from being beaten in jail, tired, stiff, and anxious.

In the room, David crawled into the bed with Zoe. She wrinkled her nose and squeezed David with her left arm.

"How are you doing, Zoe?"

"I wish I knew the answer to that. I don't feel like my old self. I don't like how the medications make me feel. I hate it here, but I am so glad to be out of that hospital. Twenty hours as a patient there would be enough to make one depressed if they weren't already. I don't know where I want to go. I . . . hope now that you are here, I'll feel better." Zoe was now sitting up in the bed, propped by three pillows. David snuggled beside her until she fell asleep. He carefully got off the bed and went outside on the balcony.

A floral arrangement from Zoe's parents sat on the glass coffee table. A wine and cheese basket from DRPearl Inc., along with a faxed card, signed by all of the staff back in Washington, rested on the small, round table in the living area of the suite.

David sat at the wrought iron table, peeling an orange. From time to time, Jose would go out on the balcony and look around. "Peter is watching the hotel from the lobby. He's a good man, David. We should keep him on the team."

Assaad sat in the room with Zoe reading, but watched her closely and periodically checked on Jose, David and Zoe. David watched the old man briefly and smiled at his attentiveness and concern for his new friends.

Jose's attention became riveted on the street below. "Son of a bitch, Peter is running toward the Kokkini bar." Jose dialed his number, but Peter didn't answer. "He disappeared into the bar. Answer your phone, Peter. Geez, I'm not believing this."

David stood and caught a brief glimpse of Peter coming out of the Kokkinni's door. "What's the problem, I wonder?"

Jose's cell phone finally chirped about five minutes later. "Peter, what's happening?"

Peter's voice was almost inaudible. "Can you hear me?"

"Barely."

"I'm in a cab. I'm following two men I recognized from the photographs Assaad took of the Kirie Pondiki. The men were talking to the front desk staff at the Maris. When they left, I followed them. As they got into their car, I had to jump inside the Kokkini to avoid being seen. We have just arrived at the Venetian Port. That's the marina in the harbor."

"Thanks, Peter. We are on our way."

Assaad and David followed Jose out the door, scrambling to keep up with Jose. Assaad clutched his book and ignored Jose's demand that he stay at the hotel.

Outside, Jose yelled at the waiting cab driver. "As fast as possible, get us to the Venetian Port." The driver nodded, and the car was moving before Assaad had managed to close the car door. David sat in the middle seat. The driver maneuvered through the streets, drawing a few horn blasts. When the car roared up at the main entrance to the Venetian Port, Jose stood with the door open and watched as Peter was running away from the marina toward the main ferry port. Jose stayed on his side of the street to observe the situation. Shortly afterward, he saw the three men who were following Peter.

"Do you see that man running? Catch up to him. We need to get him into the cab." As the cab driver pulled alongside Peter, Jose yelled at him. Peter had sweat on his brow and a sudden grin on his lips, as he felt the surprise of sudden safety. Jose turned to see the three men, who had been gaining on Peter, stop and gesture pointedly in the direction of the cab.

"Please just drive away and show us the sights of Heraklion. Preferably those as far from the port as possible." Jose looked to David for confirmation of his directive to the cab driver and got it.

The driver, a slender, middle-aged man with an untrimmed moustache and heavy growth of a black beard, smiled at Jose and nodded. "You don't want your friends back there to catch up to you?" The man's hearty laugh filled the cab.

"No, we don't. Those guys are gangsters." Jose spoke, leaning forward, trying to get a better look at the driver. Peter was still regaining his breath and studying the traffic behind the cab. Assaad grinned, his eyes taking in all of the excitement.

"You are English?" The driver asked.

"No, my friend, I am Mexican-American. My friend is Greek. What is your name?" Jose continuously looked around, in front and behind the cab, searching for possible trouble.

"They call me Zeno. I'll be happy to be your guide."

"A tour guide. That would be great, Zeno. David, what do you think? I think we need to get out of town fast." Zeno waved his hand in acknowledgment.

David glanced at Jose. "Absolutely right. Crete is too dangerous. I think we are in danger. Peter, call Zoe and Ali right now. Tell them to pack up and check out and grab a cab to the airport.

Peter instantly had his cell phone out and called. "I'm listening to a lot of rings. Jose, why don't you call Ali. Surely one of them will wake up. Oh, Zoe, hi. You need to alert Ali. Check out right now, and take a cab to the airport. We will meet you there."

A minute's pause while Peter took a deep breath and resumed speaking in a sudden burst of words. "Our lives are in danger. The Greek gang nearly caught Peter at the marina. I think they will be there at any moment. So get going, please. Oh good, Ali is up and about. Seriously, Zoe, you need to be out of there in just a few minutes."

Zeno turned the cab toward the airport. "Change of plans, heh? We are ten minutes from the airport."

David patted Assaad's shoulder. "You up for some more excitement?"

Assaad smiled. "More fun than I have had in years. I'm already working on a plan."

Zeno stopped suddenly at a stoplight. "There's policeman over there. No sense in compounding your problems. You will have to come back to see all the architectural influences that have made their mark on Heraklion. We have them all: Venetian, Turkish, Greek, Byzantine. Here's my card, send your friends." Zeno thought for a minute. "And now, we have the English. They are moving to Crete by the thousands."

CHAPTER 52
The First Argument, June 6

The rented Ford SUV was traveling hard and fast along the western coast of Crete, moving toward the city of Chamia. David and Zoe sat in the first back seat. Ali and Assaad sat in the second bench seat. Peter drove, and Jose rode shotgun. For the first twenty minutes, they rode in silence.

Assaad smiled and his voice reflected his joy in this new adventure. "We are about to leave Heraklion, which is one of sixteen prefectures, or states, in Greece and one of four in Crete.

David concentrated on reading messages saved on his laptop. Zoe stared out at the passing scenery. Ali slept.

Assaad was chatting on the phone with his friend, Aziz Al-Mustakbal. When he hung up, Assaad turned to David. "David, if you agree, here is the plan. Al-Mustakbal has volunteered to charter an airplane to fly to Chamia, Crete, to pick us up. From there, the charter will fly us to Rome, where we get a commercial flight to Dulles International."

"Sounds like a plan, Assaad. Give Aziz the go ahead."

"Very good, and I will visit my son and grandchildren." Assaad called Aziz and spoke to him in a whisper. He clicked the phone off and turned back to David.

"These mountains are beautiful, Crete is so ruggedly beautiful. I think I'll try to talk my son into a vacation here."

For a few moments, everyone in the van was quiet. Zoe suddenly turned to David with a frown and anger in her tone. "Seriously David, we need to find a place to live. I need to get my family to visit. We can't stay in that stupid townhouse. Are you listening to me?" Zoe had not bothered with makeup or a shower. Her hair wasn't combed. She had no makeup on and smelled far too strongly of her perfume.

"I'm sorry, Zoe. I didn't plan on the Greek mafia taking such an interest in us. Nobody planned for you to go to Pireaus. You picked the ferry to Crete. I haven't had the time to find a house or an apartment. It will come in time."

"You know what I mean."

"Right, so why don't we just focus on staying safe and worry about life in the US when we get there?" David stopped reading emails and reports on his laptop and closed it.

"I can't focus on anything else. I'm sorry." Zoe started to cry.

"I'm sorry, baby. When we get back home, my parents will help us look for a place. They have friends in the real estate business."

"You don't mean it." Tears continued to course down Zoe's cheeks.

Before David could respond, his cell phone rang. As he clicked it open, he automatically put the phone on speaker. He didn't want to have to repeat the conversation.

"David, its Alice. We have a big storm brewing." Alice was using her most official and urgent tone of voice.

"We are at this very minute trying to stay ahead of the storm we have here."

"I think that we are talking about different storms."

"Okay, we have multiple storms. Go ahead."

"I'll run down my list so that I don't miss anything. First, the biggest storm: Gao's expected-to-actual ratio report has ruffled feathers in State and at the CIA. They don't debate the analysis or the formulas, just the conclusions. Their first objection seems to be that the magnitude of oil being smuggled out of Iraq is unbelievable. I should add this revelation is very politically incorrect at this time, and our assertion that the Greek and Albanian, and probably Turk, criminals are responsible for oil being lost to the legal, commercial channels also flies in the face of the administration's desire to believe that everything is getting better in the Middle East."

"What else, Alice?" David smiled lovingly at Zoe, hoping his other concerns didn't show in his eyes.

"The other part of Gao's report that they don't like is the assertion that Saudi Arabians claim to have oil fields and reserves they really don't have. Gao has gone over the numbers with me repeatedly, and I think they are right. But, the problem, here again, is that this is very unwelcome news for the administration and, if true, is bad news for the US. If the top officials in Saudi are not involved in the scam, then they are mistakenly counting on reserves that aren't there. But, our analysis can't identify which fields are not there or over estimated. And if the report got out, it would be fresh ammunition for the environmentalists, the natural gas lobby, and the Democrats."

"So, Alice, the administration is denying our findings in our report?"

"Not only denying the findings, denying us payment until they can get all of their questions answered, but the fun doesn't stop there. They want to see you now. They want to get you under oath. What they really want to do is to force you to pull back the report and deliver unto them some whitewashed report. Then, the world, as it exists in their minds, would be spinning as it should be through the universe and not wobbling all over the fucking place."

"Oh, my God—and there's more?" David's voice betrayed his rising concern. He looked over at Zoe. She still had tears running down her face.

"Oh yeah, there's more. Your good friend, Congressman Eugeniades, managed somehow to convince the House Intelligence Committee Chairman to issue you a subpoena in order to compel your testimony before the committee. I called the ranking staffer, and he claimed to know nothing about it, and that may be true, but I doubt it. I suggest you call Ritzenheim to see if he can find out from his own sources. I have asked our attorney to try to have it quashed, but in the meantime, you may be detained when you arrive back in the U.S. By the way, what is your estimated time of arrival back here?"

"Three days, four at the max. We have an exit plan lined up, and we're on the road, making good progress toward it. We can't travel too fast with Ali hurting and Zoe exhausted. I will call Ritz, but I know nothing about any of this. The only possible link I can see is that Eugeniades found out that Peter Diamondis photographed him with people we believe are leaders in the Greek mafia. Have you heard anything about that from Justice?"

"I'll make a note to call them, David. My spies tell me that the Department of Justice task force has developed a bad case of the stalls, accompanied by frequent memory loss. I haven't been able to find out why. You can ask Ritz about that, too while you're at it. But, you should be pleased to know that our Frankie Ballinger has made another connection. One of the men photographed with Eugeniades is Julian Farkis. So, we do have him directly linked to Eugeniades."

"That helps explain the gang's deviant interest in us, then. They stumbled onto Peter and may suspect either he witnessed the two of them together or got a photo. What else, then?" David peered out at the passing landscape, wishing that they had time to stop to enjoy the vistas and places they were passing. He looked over at Zoe. She was looking at him with eyes full of tears.

"Acting Secretary Moody wants to meet with you. He wants to be briefed by you personally, but at least his secretary is pleasant about it."

"What else?"

"Harry Markos calls every day with threats of lawsuits. He claims you two had a deal and you reneged. He says he's ready to go public. I think he wants Nicolaos's and your dicks shellacked, made into a trophy to hang on his office wall, or maybe it's his living room."

"I know you won't tell him anything, and I damn sure won't. What about Nicolaos?"

"The Greek government finally has decided to throw every conceivable charge against him. The U.S. is half-heartedly trying to get him extradited to face charges here. Yvonne DeLorme has applied for lower bail and is either threatening to sue or actually suing Nicolaos and the Nikolaou Kasos Shipping Line for legal fees, pain, suffering, and damages. But, she's still in Federal lock-up awaiting trial. Nicolaos is in jail in Athens, being held without bail. That is, that's where he's at right now. He spent three days in the hospital recovering from the beatings that he received in Lebanon."

"It's good to know he's safe and secure."

"Everyone here is willing to take the bet that he won't be safe or secure for long, David. Our Nicolaos is too sneaky and crazy to remain in custody for long. I'll tell everyone you'll be back in three days and ready to set things right." David thanked her and speed dialed Tony Ritzenheim's number.

"Hi, Tony, this is David."

"Where the fuck are you?"

"On highway 65 in Crete, presently in Rethymno Province, about to enter Chamia Province."

"That's good. . . . How's everyone? . . . Is everyone okay?" Ritzenheim sounded distracted, pausing more between words than usual.

"For the most part. Ali is recovering, but still hurting. Zoe is exhausted. The rest of us are just tired and cranky. Why is everyone in Washington so anxious to talk to me?"

Ritzenheim's voice lowered. "David, your report assessment on the Middle East reached the vice-president. He ranted at the National Security

Committee meeting for forty-five minutes about what a misguided, misbegotten, ignorant ass of a son of a bitch you are. And, your company is even worse."

David paused while his anger welled up inside, his face turned a blush pink, and his right hand turned into a fist. "Just a few weeks ago, he was trying to enlist me to go to work at his former firm. What a turnaround! I'm sure he doesn't want that report leaking out. Why is Greek Congressman Eugeniades on my case?"

"The Greeks have major problems with smuggling into their own country. They got into the European Union, some think, only by cooking the books. The government and especially the new ambassador here in Washington, Eleni Zographos, are putting the pressure on all of their friends on the Hill and in the administration to downplay the Greek mafia angle. And, there are still a lot of countries, including some in the Middle East, very upset about that radioactive material being lost at the bottom of the Mediterranean, and they are shouting their expectations that the US of A will sort it all out. But unofficially, the Greek government doesn't want it sorted out. They want it to go away."

"I see. So the truth will not set them free, but instead make certain high ranking officials squirm and do their best to avoid having to face the facts."

"You got it, my friend. The veep is a sterling asshole on the best of days. I have heard that the VP reads all the cabinet secretaries' and deputies' emails. He gets them on a blind-copy basis and gets transcripts of their official calls, monitors their travel, so none of them have much spine to disagree about anything." Ritzenheim paused.

"So, what should I do now?"

"Come home. The subpoena will get quashed. The veep doesn't want you under oath in front of a Congressional committee. I think you may be getting surveillance from the CIA or some of our other cloak and dagger types. However, you should worry about the Greek mafia. You're a huge liability for them. Come home, get in your bunker, and stay there until the vice-president's attention gets diverted to something else. Oh yes, and one more thing, tighten your belt. You won't be getting any more contracts from this administration. Hunker down. Give me a call when you're back in town."

"Thanks, Tony. We'll see you soon." David ended the call and briefly placed his head in his hands, massaging his forehead and temples. David's anger slowly gave way to his usual, fierce determination to succeed.

Peter passed a truck, narrowly making it back into the right lane in time to avert a collision. Ali slept.

Assaad turned his head toward David. "Our charter has landed safely at the Chamia airport. They suggest we make all due speed."

"Thanks, Assaad. Peter did you hear that?"

Peter yelled back. "Going as fast as possible. Given the conditions, we are making good time."

Zoe shot a stern glance at David. She closed her eyes. Her face was pale, her feet were curled under her, and she finally fell asleep.

"Boss, I have an idea." Jose was grinning.

"Let's hear it, Jose."

"I think that you should call the Maris Hotel back in Heraklion and ask if there has been anybody looking for us or if you have any messages. I was thinking about Ritz telling us that the CIA was probably looking for us. Maybe we could steer them toward the Greeks who are looking for us."

"Devious, Jose. I'll do it." David laughed, shifted slightly to get his cell phone, and made the call.

"Hello, this is Aphrodite Philippidou, front desk supervisor. How may I help you?"

"This is David Pearl. I thought I recognized your voice. Aphrodite, I was wondering if anyone has tried to get a message to me or was trying to find me. We left in sort of a hurry this morning."

"Mr. Pearl, as a matter of fact, there were some gentlemen looking for you about thirty minutes ago. Three Americans who said they were friends of yours."

"Did they leave a business card or a number where I could reach them?"

"Yes, they gave me a card. Hold on. Let me see if I can find it. Yes, here it is." Sophia read off the number slowly as David wrote it down, while he held the cell phone between his ear and shoulder.

"Thank you so very much, Aphrodite."

"Have a safe trip, and don't forget to come back and stay with us again."

David dialed the number slowly, anxiously trying to anticipate who might answer and what the situation might be. "Hello, this is David Pearl. You wanted to talk to me?"

"Yes, David, my name is Sam Solmssen. I am with the U.S. embassy in Athens. I was directed to provide you with security, but you left Heraklion before we could meet up."

"I'm sorry. We're headed home to Washington."

"DC?" Solmssen's voice was firmly authoritative.

"That's correct."

"Where are you now?"

"I'm not going to answer that. There have been threats against us, and I really don't know for sure who you are or who might be listening."

"I understand. Is there anything that we can do to help you?"

"As a matter of fact, there is. A yacht moored in the Venetian Port is owned by Greek gangsters who have been chasing us. We did some work connecting them to some fairly serious crimes. I understand Interpol has entered the investigation against them. The yacht's name is the Kirie Pondiki. That name on the stern is written in the Greek alphabet. There are several Greek gangsters on that ship. If you would, go down there and talk to them. See what it is that they want with me. They've beaten up two of my staff, chased one down the street by the ferry port, and have previously accosted other people on my staff. And, we will press charges if that's necessary."

"Talk to them, you say?"

"Right, just talk to them, see if you can scare them off of us, or at least get a phone number out of them. Tell them I will call them and straighten things out with them if they will give me a chance. That will really help possibly get them off my back. As far as I know, they could be following me right now."

"All right, Mr. Pearl, we'll have a chat with them. Please stay in touch." Solmssen hung up.

"Jose, let's find that airport and get out of here, please. I'm getting tired of Crete."

CHAPTER 53
The Entanglement, June 6

The three CIA operatives walked three blocks from their hotel to the Venetian Port. Sam Solmssen, a muscular blonde with a crew cut and athletic build, led the other two into the marina, where they began to look for the Kirie Pondiki. They wore suit pants and dress shirts opened at the collar, and they drew suspicious stares from a number of people in the marina.

Solmssen turned to watch an unmarked police car as it stopped and off-loaded three men. Attired in casual clothes, these men blended right in with the pedestrians on the street as well as those aboard ships moored in the harbor. The three men walked casually along the pier, stopping to look closely at different boats and chatting among themselves. Solmssen and his two operatives then stood about one hundred feet further down the pier. As he was trained to do, he memorized the features of the group. The apparent leader wore a simple, sky blue, open-collared shirt over dark brown trousers. Of the remaining two men, the short one with the shaved head had the burly look of a wrestler, moved with a self assured grace. He wore a green dress shirt over tan pants that showed many wrinkles, formed from his muscular movements, and pants that were stretched tight over his lower torso. The third, a slender man with a fair complexion and black rimmed glasses, moved in his black, silk shirt ahead of the other two and seemed to wear a perpetual smile. Solmssen turned away from them, and his team continued on looking for Kirie Pondiki.

The CIA operatives finally zeroed in on the Kirie Pondiki. The long, elegant, and sleek vessel had glare reflecting off its many chrome and metal finishes. The three men stood looking at it for a moment. Then they spread out. Solmssen went to the gangway.

Solmssen yelled. "Hello, on board there. We need to talk to your captain." Solmssen looked around, adjusting his wraparound sunglasses as he did so, and stepped aboard.

Solmssen watched a crew member hustle into the main cabin. Another looked up and stared at him with a sullen resentment. Solmssen stepped over the ship's rail and stood on the deck. His two companions followed him on board. A moon-faced man with a white shirt came out of the cabin and directly faced Solmssen. His shirt bore the insignia, an anchor entwined with chains, with a single star above it, indicating he was the ship's captain, and he wore a white hat with much gold embroidery on it.

"What's your business?" The captain asked.

"We would like to talk to the owner of this vessel." Solmssen calmly stared at the captain.

"I'm the captain. You can talk to me."

"No, I can't, but I can wait for the owner." Solmssen smiled at the captain, his muscular arms now at his side. He turned to look the boat over. As he turned, he motioned for the nearest agent to cover his back and started walking toward the cabin.

The captain grabbed him by the arm, causing Solmssen to stop abruptly. Solmssen slowly removed his sunglasses and stared at the hand that touched him.

"Who the fuck are you, and what are you doing on my ship?"

"I'm Sam Solmssen with the auditing firm of Patterson and Fugate. We are verifying assets of the shipping firm, Nikolaou Kasos. What's your name?"

"I am the captain of this ship, Doukag Roussopoulos. I am asking you to get off my ship right now."

"My associates and I aren't leaving until we do our inspection audit." Solmssen inched closer toward the moon-faced man. Roussopoulos loosened his grip on Solmssen.

"That's too bad because that's not going to happen. I can give you an appointment for some other time." The captain backed slightly away from Solmssen, but kept a hard stare on him.

"We do these audits unannounced. It works a lot better that way." Solmssen's eyes were steady, and he maintained his calm demeanor.

"My orders are clear. No audits, inspections, or any other official business without the owner's direction, Sam. Georgie, call the harbor police. I've had enough of this asshole." He spoke in Greek. The youngest CIA operative, the one with a bull neck and the hardened hands, now stood immediately behind Solmssen and quickly translated for him.

Soon, three men Solmssen had previously observed arrived at the side of the boat. They quickly boarded the boat, with the third CIA man moving into a defensive position near them. The man wearing the blue shirt jumped onto the deck. His long arms casually at his side as his dark eyes surveyed the situation.

Sam Solmssen was turning toward them, when he was pushed into the side of the cabin. His arms were pulled behind him, and metal handcuffs were slapped on his wrists. The man in the sky blue shirt then turned to the captain, speaking to him in Greek. "You are under arrest. Sit down, and shut up."

A crew member tried to run into the cabin, but the wrestler type in the green shirt tackled him, manhandled him onto the deck, and placed handcuffs on him. The third of the new arrivals, a grey-haired man with black-rimmed glasses, pulled a Berretta out from the waistband of his open collared, black shirt. "I am Federal Police Inspector Bersimis. Stay calm. Be safe, and most of all, please cooperate." He said this first in Greek and then in English. Off in the distance, a siren sounded.

Solmssen's two associates were shoved toward him and directed to sit down beside him. The man in the green shirt flew up the external ladder to the fly bridge. Federal Inspector Bersimis opened his cell phone, hit the redial button, and began to quietly talk. The man in the sky blue shirt kept his Berretta in hand at his side and cautiously entered the cabin.

Two uniformed Heraklion police officers walked up to the Kirie Pondiki. Before they could speak, the wrestler yelled down to them in Greek. The police officers climbed up to the fly bridge. The wrestler then entered the ship's interior from the fly bridge.

The bull-necked CIA operative translated for Solmssen, then slowly and cautiously removed his cell phone and contacted the embassy. The phone was answered immediately by the officer of the day. His hands concealed the cell phone, which was held directly in front of his mouth. The CIA operative spoke in a whisper. "This is Jennings. Solmssen, Sollazo, and I are being detained on the Greek registered ship, the Kirie Pondiki. We are in the Venetian Port in Heraklion. The Greek National Police are on board."

The slender agent in the black shirt noticed the conversation. He strode over, grabbed the cell phone, and threw it out into the glimmering waters of the Venetian Port. Solmssen maintained his stoic smile. His eyes did a continuous sweep of the Kirie Pondiki, the pier, and the other boats, nearby. Slowly, the thought began to dawn on him that perhaps David Pearl had set him up or, at best, given him incomplete information.

A heavy thud came from inside the boat. Some yelling in Greek was followed by two gunshots. The police officers on the fly bridge immediately drew their pistols. The senior of the two began quietly talking on his radio. On The 25th of August Street, more police cars arrived, braking to screeching halts. The officers inside those cars exited quickly, trotting down the marina's sidewalk toward the Kirie Pondiki. Each one jogged with a hand on the pistol butt that rode on the right side of the police tool belt. An ambulance pulled up and backed up to the marina's walkway.

Greek Federal Agent Bersimis came back out on deck. He gestured to the new arrivals of police that two of them should remain with the detainees on deck. He took two other police officers and reentered the cabin. More shouting in Greek with loud, crude phrases erupted from the ship's interior. Then, a few moments of quiet ensued, followed by the first prisoner emerging onto the main deck. This one was an older man with a trickle of blood coming from the corner of his mouth. The man spit on one of the policemen, and the officers manhandled the man onto the pier.

Solmssen's phone chirped its ring tone. The CIA operative who spoke Greek politely asked the policemen if he could answer the phone. Both of the officers out on the deck nodded agreement. Jennings got up, fished around in Solmssen's shirt pocket, and answered the call.

"This is Jennings. Yes, sir. I don't know. We are still being detained at the moment. The Greek Federal Police and the Heraklion police are on board." The Heraklion police officer took the cell phone, listened for a microsecond, and asked the speaker to identify himself.

Solmssen was close enough to be able to hear the reply. "This is the American Embassy in Athens. Three of the men you are holding; Solmssen, Jennings, and Sollazo, are U.S. diplomats entitled to diplomatic protection and have immunity. Please release them." The police officer took the phone away from his ear, looking at it as if it were an alien being, and tossed it over his shoulder into the glistening blue waters of the Venetian Port.

The ambulance medics brought the stretcher on board and awkwardly maneuvered it into the cabin. As the door opened, someone could be heard yelling something in Greek. Jennings translated for the other two operatives. "I want my attorney, right now." The two Heraklion policemen smiled at each other.

The short National Police officer in the green shirt came out of the cabin next. He was dragging a man of approximately sixty, pulling him along by the handcuffs that bound his hands. The National Police officer assisted the pot-bellied, heavy breathing man over onto the walkway, marching him away to the area where the police cars were assembled.

A Heraklion police officer and two paramedics struggled with the wheeled stretcher. As they attempted to get it through the cabin door, the man on the stretcher growled in pain until the stretcher and its patient cleared the entry. Blood seeped from the man on the stretcher through the bath towel that had been placed over a wound in the front left shoulder. The paramedics lifted the stretcher over the railing to the pier and quickly pushed him away toward the waiting ambulance. In two minutes, Solmssen watched as the two policemen carried another man out onto the deck. As gently as they could, they carried the man, who wore shorts and a t-shirt emblazoned with the Washington Wizards' logo, to the rail and then lifted him over the side.

Three other men were brought out onto the deck and hustled away. They were younger than the first two, with blank expressions. Then, a quiet, two-hour period ensued. The remaining Heraklion police officers and the Greek National Police stood around, looking at each other, sometimes laughing and chatting. Once in a while, one of them would smoke a cigarette. Attempts by the U.S. operatives to get a response to their questions failed. Dusk fell on the Venetian Port. The prying eyes had long ago stopped looking at the activities occurring on the deck of the Kirie Pondiki. Solmssen began to plot how he would return the favor to David Pearl. He and his team patiently waited their release, Solmssen was confident that he could easily identify the men taken away by the police, and he mentally worked on his explanation for getting into this completely unnecessary entanglement.

CHAPTER 54
Argument, Appeasement, and Advocacy, June 7

Once at the Rome International Airport, the Pearl group slowly cleared customs. David was at the end of the line, but once he made it beyond the exit door, David saw Burt Dingfelder, the Deputy Director of Homeland Security waiting for them. Standing slightly behind him was Liesl Kremer from the State Department.

"Hi, David, how are you?" Dingfelder stuck out his hand, and David grasped it. "The State Department chartered a jet to pick up your group. Besides Liesl, who I think you've met, Anastasios Dimantidis, the Greek Embassy in Washington's chief military attaché, is waiting on the plane."

"Thanks, Burt. We are most grateful for a more comfortable ride. We are all tired, for a fact. Just lead us to it."

During the long walk to the private terminal, David noticed the group was silent, his comrades exhausted and focused on getting to the next pit stop. The Gulfstream G550, 19 passenger jet had a metal stair way up against its open door. The co-pilot assisted and welcomed each of them.

Once everyone was on board, Liesl Kremer made an announcement. "I know you are all beat, but I need to individually interview every member of the Pearl group. You will sign a statement that you will never divulge any information about the interview to anyone. Anastasios Dimanitidis wants to interview you concerning your actions while in Crete, on a purely voluntary basis, of course. But, the State Department hopes you will cooperate. Welcome home."

After takeoff, the group settled into a routine befitting a long flight. In the forward cabin, Zoe slept fitfully on the divan. David sat facing forward in one of the captain's chairs that were part of the airplane's internal seating design. Opposite him was Burt Dingfelder. The two of them kept a nearly continuous stream of conversation going. Dingfelder, during this conversation, variously checked his email on his cell phone, read hard copy reports, or worked on crossword puzzles.

When Zoe woke up after a nap of forty-five minutes, she called David over. "David, I know I'm tired, but I am not feeling any better at all. I think I should go back to Greece." Her blue, satin blouse had kept its shape but now had spotting on the front, and her light blue pants were wrinkled and dirty. Her face was still without makeup, very pale, with redness around her eyes.

"If that's what you need to do, I will support you in whatever you want, and if that means getting you back to Greece, so be it."

"I think that's it; you haven't supported me." Her voice was matter-of-fact; and her tone was quiet, but resolved.

David's head slumped as his mind raced for an explanation, a clue, any possible cause for this sudden turn in her attitude. "Zoe, I love you. I feel like I have supported you. I know I've been busy, preoccupied by events out of my control."

"Stop right there. You'll always be busy. Why don't you go back and talk to Dingfelder. I want to be alone." Tears rolled down her cheeks.

"Please don't do this. You're tired. We all are."

Zoe slowly turned her head up to look at David, now standing a few feet away. "I'm sure. I'm searching for something that used to be there, and I don't know what it is. I want to be alone. Please just go."

Jose worked in the galley. First, he baked peanut butter oatmeal cookies. He kept the coffee pot brewing fresh coffee, and he fixed cocktails for anybody that wanted them. After he had fully explored the pantry, he began to prepare arroz con pollo.

Burt Dingfelder chatted about the not-too-distant closing of the Bush administration in Washington. "At the end of the Bush administration, things will change for you, David. You may not believe that now, but you do excellent work, and your business will resume. In fact, if a Democrat wins, you may even do better."

"What will happen to you, Burt?"

"I'll have to go to work, David. I hate the sound of that. But, some lobbyist or law firm will want me for their letterhead, and to impress clients, and to be a rainmaker, bring in the big bucks. Do lunch with prospective clients, that sort of thing. One of the think tanks is also a possibility. I wanted to come out to meet you in Rome so that I could talk to you about your future."

"I sure appreciate that. I still don't understand why the administration turned on me so viciously." David sipped his coffee.

"They don't like bad news. They only want news that will support the re-election of Republicans and fits neatly into their predetermination of results for their own strategies. You know that I am a big supporter of yours, always will be. The value of your work is unparalleled in the intelligence business." Dingfelder looked down at his crossword puzzle and printed in an answer.

David realized what Dingfelder might be hinting at. "I wish that I could give you a job, Burt, but we are definitely facing some seriously bleak financials at the moment. Cutbacks in staff will definitely be coming."

Dingfelder briefly frowned. "I understand and really do appreciate the problem and the irony of what's happening to you. It's simply a reprisal for telling the truth or an educated opinion about what appears to be reality, I should say. Getting a job is not a problem. I'll get a job somewhere. I don't want one, but I'll get one. I have to maintain my wife's standard of living, or I'll suffer for it. The job isn't the issue."

"So what is the issue?" David stared out the window for a second and then turned his attention back to Dingfelder.

"The issues are survival in the short run, set your firm up for the long run, and have as much fun as possible all the time." Dingfelder laughed. "The US is better for you being in the intelligence business, so I offer my personal philosophy of working successfully in the DC arena."

"I'm going to check on Zoe." David walked toward Zoe, passing the co-pilot walking in the opposite direction. He knelt beside her, watching her breath for several moments before he returned to his place opposite Dingfelder.

Dingfelder wrote a word into the crossword puzzle he was working on, then looked up at David. "David, the co-pilot, who is really CIA, reports to me that we left the Chamis airport just before four gangsters arrived looking for you."

"So, we were being followed. What happened, anything?"

"The CIA, and we suspect the Greek State Security, got plenty of pictures, made some ID's, and one or the other or both are now following the gangsters, who are heading back to Heraklion, where as it happens there was a little situation." Dingfelder laughed and stayed silent while Jose poured a fresh cup of coffee for David. Dingfelder sipped at his gin and tonic.

"What little situation?" David became very alert, preparing himself for what possibly could be more bad news.

"According to the CIA, thanks to a tip from you apparently, a CIA team went aboard a yacht moored in the marina there. After they got on board, the Greek Security Service stormed the yacht catching some Greek gangsters who were having a summit conference with their lawyer, one Harry Markos. In the ensuing fracas, Markos took two bullets in the shoulder. Julian Farkas, Ike Zisis, and Karolas Damon, along with some underlings, were arrested."

"So, how pissed is the CIA?"

"Very. They think you deliberately set them up and put their team into harm's way." Dingfelder sipped at his gin and tonic.

"Okay, the administration, the Greek gang, and the CIA have me at the top of their enemies list."

"I'd say that's a safe bet. Do you still have the NSA contract?"

"Sure, Burt. We have thirty full-time positions there. They work directly for NSA, so there isn't a means by which I could influence their work in an evil or misguided sort of way. That's probably why the contract hasn't been canceled. I can shift some of my other staff over there, when and if there is some turnover. But, we can't wait long. With every other contract being terminated, we have very little wiggle room. Alice has hired two contract attorneys to do battle, and we may eventually get some money out of the CIA, Homeland Security, Justice, and Defense. But, we have started getting our subcontracts canceled, as well."

"Yeah, I heard that, and am truly sorry for it. The fucking Bush administration is all about intimidation. The spastic logic of their thinking is if you bring them problems, they'll take it out on you. All they want are solutions that must fit into their predetermined public political positions. Distorting or covering up the facts means nothing to them. They see any truth or reality that doesn't fit their political framework as devious, directly opposed to their own strategies, and wrong."

"Burt, I understand how I became such a wrong-doer in their eyes."

"So, tell me. I have an idea, but let me hear it." Dingfelder sat still, completely dedicating himself to David's story.

"First, DRPearl outed Nevzlin."

"Affirmative. The word in the inner sanctums is that Putin was directly negotiating with his pal, Bush, to exchange Nevzlin. In return, Putin promised to go easy on the U.S. and the Georgians and quit supplying Iran with nuclear equipment and advice."

David took a sip of his now cold coffee. "The US could still send Nevzlin back to Russia. I think it would be criminal to do so, but some pretext could be ginned up, but the Israelis smelled the deal out. They made a few well-placed phone calls. I think that Bush was still considering the swap, but couldn't figure out a way to keep the Israelis from retaliating. Bush wanted to go out on a huge swell of goodwill that would result from getting the signed treaties with Russia, Georgia, Iran, and control of nuclear weapons. And Nevzlin would soon be forgotten, simply repatriated, unofficially, at some point in the future, another problem swept under the rug."

Dingfelder finished his gin and tonic, grinning broadly at David. "Sure, and for what its worth, it makes me sick too."

"As it would for everyone with a penchant for rational thought. I imagine the death knell for Cardiff Shapiro was sealed at the highest levels in Russia. The problem, as they saw it, was Cardiff Shapiro. They concluded that Shapiro had deduced, from a conversation with the Russian vice-premier, that the questions and concerns about the security of Russian radioactive materials were valid. As soon as the Russians learned the Georgian Deputy had passed on to Cardiff the source of the radioactive material, they knew they had to take Cardiff out and quickly. Shapiro set up a meeting with the CIA Director and Energy Department secretary, but the meeting never took place. Oh, and by the way, the vice premier, Roman Brezovsky, suddenly retired and disappeared shortly after his conversation with Shapiro."

"Okay, hang on to your thoughts, David, while I go get a refill." Dingfelder was back in two minutes. "David, give me the rest of your assessment of why Bush and Cheney are so unhappy with DRPearl."

"Pissing off the Greek prime minister by revealing the connections between the Russian missing radioactive material, the business with Nicolaos Polopolis, and the Greek mafia involvement with the ship that resulted in the radioactive material resting at the bottom of the Med. My spies tell me the Greek prime minister summoned our ambassador in and gave him a spitting fit of rage over what he called 'the unverified allegations about Greek government complicity in smuggling the stuff.' He may be simply acting on orders from their Prime Minister, who may well be just another one of those who want to sweep the bad news under the rug rather than deal with it. The fact that my firm was single sourced to do the investigations is a mere trifle; now it is far beyond being an inconvenient truth. It's a singularly hot political issue, and DRPearl is accused of wrongdoing."

"Wrong? What's wrong got to do with anything? It's not wrong, but the Greeks reached out to Congressman Eugeniades. Eugeniades complained to the president. The president thought he needed Eugeniades for support on various appropriation votes and so was happy to oblige him by telling Cheney to put the word out that all of your contracts were to be terminated. Simple GOP politics, that's all."

"Would that they cared about the truth? You know that we have firm, photographic evidence Eugeniades met with members of the Greek mafia. I suppose that no one cares about that now."

"Save it for Eugeniades's next campaign. All of this really doesn't amount to much. It's a confluence of events. In time, you and your firm will be rehabilitated and you can resume business as usual." Burt reached over to pat David gently on the back of his hand.

Zoe woke up and sat up on the divan. She went to the restroom in the galley, briefly consulting with Jose about the arroz con pollo, and strolled back through the first cabin. When she returned, Burt Dingfelder excused himself and went to the second cabin where Ali, Assaad, Anastasios Dimantidis, and Peter Diamondis were playing poker. Dingfelder bought into the game.

David reached for Zoe's hand as she sat down opposite him. "How are you feeling, babe?" She pulled her hand away.

"Shitty. I want a home, and I'm beginning to think more and more that's back in Greece. We need to talk."

"Okay, let's talk."

"I don't think that you love me anymore. I don't know what has happened between us. It's not my fault my job made me kill a gangster. I'm off the hook, officially."

"I love you totally, completely, all the time, and forever. I am not angry about anything. There's a lot of pressure on me and the company right now. I have a lot of things on my mind."

"I should be the first thing on your mind." Zoe sat with her arms wrapped around herself and slightly bent forward.

"You are first in my heart, but I have to make a living, and sometimes times get tough. Right now, we are in the midst of very tough economic times."

"You neglected me." Zoe began to cry. Jose hustled through from the galley pushing a cart carrying the arroz con pollo, several cold beers, and corn chips for the guys playing poker.

"Whatever I did, I'm sorry. I will make it up to you. I don't understand your change of heart. I really don't. Can't we talk about?"

"I have this sadness, and I'm not sure that I will ever know what you really think about me." Tears softly rolled down Zoe's cheeks.

"We can work on that, baby. Washington's got fine physicians and health facilities. We'll get you checked out. You have been through an ordeal."

"I don't want to face your parents or your employees. I think everyone on this plane knows what I did, and I don't think I can't ever live it down. I need some quiet time by myself, not with some shrink." Zoe had stopped crying and now had a look of fierce determination on her face.

"My parents don't know anything about your career or what you did. I love you, and that's enough for them. But, in the short run, we have to live somewhere. The firm is facing some financial difficulties, and I need all of my savings to keep things afloat. So, that limits the alternatives."

"Oh, that's great. How about me? We need a place of our own."

"When the financial situation changes for the firm, we will get our own place."

"So, you'll be spending all our money propping up the firm. You could easily get a job from someone else. You had that offer from Halliburton."

"I don't want to work for some other firm. This is a temporary downturn. I don't want to lay anyone off if I can possibly avoid it." David looked directly into her eyes, trying to see some compassion or understanding, but her eyes looked cold and distant.

"Why don't you cut salaries or put them on furloughs? I have to find some peace and get myself together. I need my own place and space." Zoe's voice trailed off into a whisper.

"I'm not cutting salaries. Most of my staff could go out in today's intelligence market and get a job immediately. I cut my salary."

"You cut your own salary? Why on earth?" Zoe's stared at David in disbelief.

"Because it was the right thing to do. My company will survive and thrive in the future."

"You are just doing this to get me to leave you, David. You resent me now for some reason. I can't figure it out."

"That's complete nonsense!" David shouted. His body stiffened, and he suddenly realized that there was nowhere to go, nowhere to run, nowhere to hide. He instantly regretted shouting, nervously checking to see if anyone reacted to his loudness. He wanted to get away from her and her moody anger, but he sat there and stared back at her before finally speaking. "I know what you've done. I'm not happy you didn't trust me enough to tell me everything, but I still love you and always will."

"I was scared, David. I made mistakes and ran." Her voice sounded with an urgency that quickly ran down into tears. David dropped his head and stared for a few moments at the carpeting between his knees.

Zoe got up out of her chair, came over to David, sat in his lap, held him in her arms, and sobbed. Her tears rolled off her face onto his shirt. David suddenly felt very doubtful about the future with Zoe. What had been a world of optimistic possibilities was turning into a very small place filled with uncertainty.

Chapter 55
Homecoming Hype, June 8

The Gulfstream jet landed smoothly, almost imperceptively, at Andrews Air Force Base in Maryland. The airport terminal was mostly empty, but the tarmac was filled with parked airplanes. The State Department had already cleared them through customs. The empty corridors had been silent until their entourage entered. Now their echoing footsteps, their rolling bags, and even their quiet conversations intruded.

The young airmen hustled them through the complex politely, and in some cases, assisting them with their luggage. David thought they must look ragged and wrinkled to these very fit and polished young men and women. Outside, hired cars, black limos, and one mini-van awaited them. Standing before them on the sidewalk were the waiting drivers, along with Ben Pearl. A brief, intense chattering arose among them as they neared their transportation. David said goodbye to everyone at least once. He was so happy to be home. He thought for a moment of falling to the filthy, concrete, arrival platform for a welcome home kiss.

Ben Pearl, David's father, waited patiently, leaning on a new minivan. David had called his father as the Gulfstream jet taxied to its assigned parking space. Ben hugged everyone. Then, he loaded all the gear of Peter Diamondis, David, and Zoe. They stepped into the minivan and were quickly off for the close-in suburb of Silver Spring, Maryland.

*　*　*

Anastasios Dimantidis went immediately to the driver of his awaiting limo, the one with the diplomatic plates. He recognized the man from embassy security, but simply handed over his bag and jumped into the back seat. Anastasios nodded off on the ride to his condo, on Connecticut Avenue, in DC. Once inside his condo, he went to his secure computer and sent emails to the Greek ambassador, Harry Markos, and Congressman Eugeniades that summarized the journey and its conclusion. He included David's parents' names, as well as their address in Silver Spring.

*   *   *

David's mother, Alexis Pearl, had generated a computer banner, 'Welcome David & Zoe.' Ben took pictures of the homecoming. Alexis jumped, bounced, and danced around. David knew that as her only child, his homecoming was such a thrill she couldn't contain herself, Ben Pearl directed everyone to his or her bedrooms. Peter Diamondis got the bedroom in the basement, cleared of its clutter only hours before his arrival. Ben, Alexis, David, and Zoe talked for an hour over Alexis's ranch omelets, bacon, and English muffins. Zoe was very quiet and soon retired in moody silence to David's old bedroom.

At 1:30 AM, David went for a two-mile run, followed by a long hot shower. Then, he cautiously positioned himself beside Zoe and listened to the little noises that she made while she slept, trying to imagine that somehow their relationship could get back to where it had once been. He fell into a black hole of deep sleep. He got up at 6 AM, kissed Zoe as she slept, went into the kitchen where he kissed his mom, and then headed for the office.

CHAPTER 56
Damned with Disapproval, June 10

David's early arrival did not result in his being able to sit in his chair, quietly catching up on emails and the hardcopies that filled his in-box. Odette met him at the door with a long, warm, enthusiastic hug. When he finally disentangled from her, he saw tears dripping down her cheeks.

"David, I thought we would never see you again." Odette clutched a tissue in her hand that she used to blow her nose and blot the tears from her eyes.

"Odette, with any luck, I'll live to be a hundred. Are you going to be okay?"

Odette finally smiled. "I think so. I just worried about you so much."

As they walked to the kitchen, Odette grabbed David's mug and poured his coffee. He kissed her on the check and instantly regretted it when she clasped her hands around his hand holding the hot coffee. "I really need to get to the office, Odette."

"You've got visitors in the office. Taz was already here when I arrived. Alice is in your office, too."

David walked into his office. Alice stood, and the two of them embraced. Then, he turned to Taz, who was also now standing. The two men hugged each other. Taz reluctantly sat down. Taz's face sagged with sadness. His usual solid, resilient, confident, often cocky, emotional state was clearly missing, replaced by a downcast embarrassment and shame.

"Taz, what brings you back to town?" David asked.

Taz slumped down into the chair even more. His butt now rested on the outer edge of the wingback chair.

"The woman I loved told me she didn't feel the same way about me. She wouldn't even agree to a date. She said she was just a friendly person.

I fucked up. I let the team down at a bad time. There's no fool like an old, middle-aged one. I'm sorry." Taz shook his head back and forth.

"Yes, it was a bad time. So, now you want your job back?"

"Yes, please, David. I need to do something. I belong here and want to be here."

"You know Antonopoulos was killed in Greece, and Peter Diamandis was damn near beaten to death. Ali and Nicolaos were arrested and beaten in Lebanon. We really needed you."

"I know. I'm sorry. I should have been there." Taz was solemn.

Alice was sitting primly in the other wingback chair with her legs crossed. Seven inches of paperwork were poised on her thigh. "David, I told Taz that under our present financial circumstances, we could not hire him back."

David looked directly at Taz. "And, I agree completely. Taz, our current financial picture simply does not allow for new hires. We will be lucky to hold onto the employees we have. I am sorry that your dream romance didn't work out."

"You don't have to pay me, David. I'll work as a volunteer. Just give me an assignment, and you'll never hear a word of complaint out of me."

Alice glared at Taz. David needed to start digging into the mountain of paperwork stacked up in his in-box. "Okay, Taz, you're a volunteer. Now, go see Odette. You'll be assigned to her until we can get our finances improved or can think of a better assignment."

Taz smiled. "Thank you!" he said, then jumped to his feet and raced out of the room.

"Okay, Alice, what do you have?"

"I have a hard time figuring out a place to start, David. So, since everything seems to be critically important these days, I'll start with Frankie. Frankie Ballinger has zeroed in on Crete for the last week. She's made friends with the police under the guise of her being a criminology researcher at Georgetown University. In this way, she verified that Harry Markos was shot in a Greek police action in the Venetian Port on the afternoon that you flew out of Crete. No charges were filed against him because he claimed legal immunity and was given it. But Harry spent two days in the hospital, and he's now winging his way back home. Farkis and Damon are in jail awaiting indictment. The Greeks are in the process of filing claim to the Mister Mouse and have seized it."

David leaned back in his chair and stretched his arms over his head. "Before you continue, tell me about our two contract lawyers."

"They both were really desperate for jobs. Legal work is slow around town, and they recently graduated from George Mason University and passed the bar in Virginia and DC. I have them in our lease space at Tech World, working ten hours a day with Suzy Stordahl. They're learning. Suzy is cracking the whip, but both of them are very motivated. We should have our first demands for penalty payments out at the end of this week."

"That's good. I need to slip over there sometime to meet them."

Alice glanced down at the speaking points list that topped her pile of paper. "The bad news is the NSA is sending its inspector general auditing and compliance team to visit us again. The good news is that we don't have that much ongoing work, but that's also bad news."

"Just another Valentine from Vice-President Cheney."

"Yeah, really. Our next item is our dear friend at WaveLinks, retired Navy Captain Frank Fulton, wants to contract with us for our formulas, algorithms, and all the work files for intelligence gathering and analysis on the radiation misadventure."

"Tell him to go fuck himself. No, better yet, I'll tell him."

"It's easy money, $1.5 million." Alice smiled as she studied her list.

"It would have to be $1.5 billion for me to contract with that motherfucker. Just another gambit to put us out of business, Alice. Please continue."

"An up-and-coming web development company wants us to provide security for their confidential information, physical assets, and intellectual property. They do business worldwide, David. I talked to their chief operating officer, and it sounds like something we could do. They want us to submit a proposal."

"I like it. Let's do it."

Alice's cell phone began its dance across the side table, vibrating enthusiastically. Alice briefly reddened and then grabbed her phone, turning it off in one swift movement. "I'm still hearing whispers of our having a leak. I've gone over the entire office again and had our communications security firm back to go over the entire place; despite our budget problems, we need to get our communications security reputation reestablished somehow."

"Yeah, I didn't hear a word about this from Dingfelder or Liesl Kremer with State. Let's put Frankie on reviewing everyone's emails and the phone logs. I can't imagine there are any slipups there, but let's check it all again. I'll call around with my contacts and tell them we had a little problem, long ago solved."

Alice's face tightened, and her eyes drilled into David's like a high school principal staring down her favorite bad boy. "Too many people seem to think they know our business. The current administration is extremely good at keeping the public and the media in the dark, but they love to gossip. I think you should call Ritzenheim and ask him. I went to that Washington Area Integrated Intelligence and Security meeting for you last week. For one thing, Fulton never said hello or acknowledged my presence in any way. For another, the CIA public affairs person, while otherwise studiously avoiding me, passed me a note saying that DRPearl Inc. needs to quit telling their internal business all over town. We are now being labeled as a security risk. Our secrets are safe, but what's being talked about is the personal stuff, none of it news at all."

"Right, Jesus. Those gangsters of Uncle Ike had us bugged in the kitchen for a few weeks. But, it's the gift that keeps on giving. Let's put Taz to work on security. I want him here all night and all weekend. We need to have someone in this building 24/7. Make a list of all the security actions we've taken to protect our information, including the checking and rechecking. Its just a matter of time before someone official wants to investigate us."

"Consider that done." Alice rifled through the papers perched on her thigh and pulled out a document contained in a yellow, plastic sleeve. "Now, let me bring you up to date on our dear friend, Nicolaos Polopolis. Nico was, as you already know, badly beaten in Lebanon. When he got to Greece, he was thrown directly into prison. The next morning, the jailers found him on the floor unconscious. The cellmate was thrown into solitary confinement for not reporting Nico's condition, but he denied having anything to do with Nico being unconscious. So, Nico was taken to the hospital and examined. He got a full workup. Nico was found to have broken ribs and several hairline fractures in his face, some internal bleeding, and a collapsed lung. Nico was admitted and sometime during the night, he escaped and hasn't been found."

"What in the hell is with that guy, Alice?"

"I'm not a psychologist, but I'm thinking that potty training didn't go well for him." They both laughed.

"What else?"

"Mrs. Cardiff Shapiro, one of her sons, and their high-priced Washington lawyer are on your schedule for this afternoon. Mrs. Shapiro has brought suit against the U.S. and the Alexandria Health and Fitness Center for not maintaining adequate security for Cardiff."

"Good for her. Why does she want to see me?"

"Ideally, she wants you to name some names. She's getting stonewalled from Justice and the Department of State. Her fancy pants lawyer would be willing to lay some serious funds on you for your cooperation."

"Well, that certainly is an entertaining thought. We'd get paid, be on the side of justice, and get some sweet revenge. I'll think it over, but I think we should do it."

"Got work to do, David. I'll get on with it if you don't mind." Alice stood, straightened her skirt, and walked out the door.

David closed the door and assiduously applied himself to the stack of documentation needing his attention. The work required dragged David through the day. At 7 PM, he finished reading his company secure email, when the phone rang. With great reluctance, David picked up the phone. It was Ritzenheim.

"Meet me at the place where your reception was held, David. I'll be there in fifteen minutes." Immediately after saying that, Ritzenheim terminated the phone call. David called his parents' house.

"Hi, Mom. How is everybody?" His mother sounded cheerful as usual.

"Everybody is fine. Peter and Zoe went for a long walk this afternoon. Everybody seems to be in good spirits."

"Is Zoe available?"

"Not just now, sugar. She's taking a shower."

"Tell her I love her and that I'll be home late. Love you, too."

CHAPTER 57

Loose Lips, the evening of June 11 and the early morning of June 12

Tony Ritzenheim sat in the darkest corner of Stoney's bar. He nursed a double Johnny Walker Black whiskey. David spotted him as soon as he walked in, paused only to wave to the crew at the bar, slap a young waiter on the back, and then slid into the booth across from Ritz.

"Hi, Ritz. You look like you're carrying the weight of the world on your shoulders. Confess your sins, my brother. It'll do you no harm." Ritzenheim smiled, his shoulders moving up and down as he silently laughed.

Ritz sat up and smiled. "David, you are one in a fucking million. You got the whole fucking administration dumping on you, and you still have a sense of humor."

"I owe it all to my boyish charm. I'm feeling the heat, Ritz, for a fact."

"Can you ride out the storm?"

"Which one? The cancellation of all our contracts, except one, or the irrational anger that my wife is feeling toward me? Or the death of Antonopoulos, the beatings of my staff, or the latest escape of Nicolaos Polopolis? He's gone missing from the hospital in Greece and has so far eluded the police. I could use some closure on all of these."

"I am sorry to hear about Zoe. And all the rest, too, for that matter."

"Thanks, I hope she perks up now that nobody's in danger. It's good having Peter Diamondis, her cousin, around, though. He's very good to Zoe and a tough SOB. I feel better that he's with her." David took a sip of his beer.

"'I'll add Zoe to my prayers. You've both been under a lot of stress."

"So, Tony, why the rendezvous? You look like something's on your mind."

"Yes, I've got things on my mind. I damn near resigned today. But, knowing I needed to chill myself down some, I called an old friend. He joined me for lunch at the Chop House and told me that I shouldn't deprive the government of the opportunity to fire me." The two men laughed.

"They can't let you go. You are much too valuable, Tony. You shouldn't let the bastards get to you." The two men smiled at each other.

"I sure wish that the bosses at Homeland Security all felt that way. These fucking, rigid ideologues are in place to advance the political aspirations of their party and not much else. Every night, they pray that there won't be another terrorist attack, and every day they take credit for there not being another terrorist attack."

The two men were interrupted by a thirty-something, slightly overweight woman with a yellowish mop of hair. "Hi guys. I have something very special with me I think you'd be very interested in." She pointed to the younger woman standing at her side. The young woman had shaggy blonde hair, an open and plain face, and a voluptuous figure readily displayed in her too tight, mauve skirt and pink blouse. The young woman smiled broadly and didn't bother to adjust her miniskirt, which had risen up enough to expose her lack of underpants. Then, she twisted forward to reveal an abundance of cleavage.

"No thanks. Please leave us alone. We aren't interested." Ritzenheim's voice conveyed his hostility at being interrupted.

"You'll think about her later tonight, guys, and you'll be sorry." The older woman steered her protégée toward a table of men sitting at a table at the front window.

When he was sure that the two were out of hearing range, David frowned. "Not as sorry as we'd be if we took you up on the offer."

"I'll cut to the chase. I tried to get Homeland Security not to cut your contracts, David. I really did. But, the Secretary and Deputy all march to the beat of the administration, and to them it's a nitpicking little detail, not worth worrying themselves about. I even got our general counsel to advise them not to default your contracts. But, to no avail." Ritzenheim stopped and held up his glass, signaling the bartender for another round.

Ritzenheim picked up his discussion. "They lay out the broad guidelines at the top, while demanding immediate, complete execution and no negative feedback. The administration's internal organizational communication runs to the policy/political staff from the White House and OMB. From there, the message is delivered to the agency head, more often to a confidential assistant, maybe a chief of staff. The further down the executive order, or the simple, expressed desire goes, the more it becomes a canonical law, until it hits those who are running programs, but these people have learned to stifle their dissent and shut off their brains because input is not desired or, fuck it, tolerated."

"Tony, I know you tried. You can't stop every bad move by the Secretary or anyone else. I appreciate your efforts. You couldn't have done more."

Tony frowned, as though that wasn't good enough for him. "This contracting business of yours gets punished because the vice-president expressed some unhappiness in some staff meeting about the outcomes you delivered. He seems to have wished out loud that you should find out the harsh realities of the business world the hard way. Probably within minutes, his fury is over and has been replaced by the usual sour taste in his mouth. Still, he knows his outburst will make you sweat, but actual pain will be even better. He is, however, unaware that one of the young gunslingers at his staff meeting has already begun to rattle cages across Washington. The young gunslinger only wants a notch on the handle of his professional resumé, his Colt .45, if you will. He wants to build his rep, have something to show that he's a real Washington political operative. So, the word goes out: cancel the Pearl contracts. Contracting officers get the message through the political channels. The operating guys and gals will learn of the business eventually, but they are too busy to sort out things at the immediate time of the threat. The contracting managers are also too busy, and the latent hostility that they feel toward the contractors, in general, enables them to cancel the contracts without any heartburn, upset stomach, or even a headache. Then, back up the chain goes the message: we've all done good."

"Jesus, Tony, you can't let this crap get to you like this. Now I am worried about you."

"The silver lining, David, is that you and I are both survivors." Ritz stood suddenly. "And now I'm going home." David hugged him before walking back out into the night and the office.

At the desk the next morning at 7:05, David read the Washington Post business section, which printed a small notice among many contracts being bid, awarded, completed, or canceled: "Homeland Security and NSA cancel contracts with DRPearl Inc over allegations of nonperformance. The company declined comment citing pending litigation. Sources in the industry not authorized to speak for their company blamed the administration's lack of strategic focus for the abrupt move."

CHAPTER 58
A Conundrum, June 14

David went for a morning run through his old Silver Spring neighborhood. He ran down his parents' street, Sherwood Forest Drive, and angled through two side streets to reach Northwest Branch Park. Once there, he hit the familiar trails that he had been running since junior high. He knew every bend, rise, and dip on these highly trafficked paths. The coolness of this morning encouraged him to sprint, every so often. He was thinking that tomorrow, he should go in the opposite direction, over to Paint Branch Park.

David ran up a hill on a long, well-worn path heading toward the southern end of the park. He saw movement at the top of the hill where the trail went through a cluster of mostly oak and ash trees. As he ran, he decided to detour around the trees. Just as he turned from the trail to the grassy area of the park, a man stepped out into the open. "Hey buddy, help me out here. I'm lost."

David knew that he just heard a ruse, but he kept calm. "Stay on the trail. You'll find your way out."

The man pulled a pistol and leveled it at David. "Right now." The man was thickset and smiling, which produced deep fissures in his forehead and cheeks. His broad, long teeth, barely grayish white were the central point in a rounded head, set on a seemingly invisible neck.

David stopped and walked over to the man who wore suit pants, dress shoes, and a white shirt. David now noticed someone else who stood back in the shadows of the trees. David walked up to the first man.

"We need to talk. Let's get some privacy." The man spoke slowly, seemingly pausing to punctuate after each word.

"No, I'm staying right here." David looked at the second man, who wore a lightweight, blue jacket, blue, oxford shirt, and sandals, but whose face stayed in shadow. David turned his head toward the middle of the large grassy area. The man's eyes followed his. David kicked the man's gun hand, sending the gun flying. David grabbed weapon, protected it to his side, and held up his other hand to stop the man's movement toward him.

David heard the sounds of more people walking toward them. He put the pistol in his waistband. "Tell your friend to come out of the woods. We can talk right here."

"Pearl, we have been sent by an old friend of yours, Mr. Markos. We were with him in Heraklion, where he was shot in the shoulder by the Greek police. Mr. Markos does not appreciate the fact that you put the CIA and the Greek police onto him." The man in the blue jacket slowly walked toward them.

"You can tell Mr. Markos that I didn't put anyone onto him, nor was I anywhere near Heraklion."

"He won't believe that. Why don't I start over? We have reliable information that you told US agents where Mr. Markos was." The man sounded calm and assured. His English was not very good. The man in the blue jacket's face was leathery, with a heavy beard still showing under where he had shaved. He was five or six inches shorter than David, muscular through the chest and arms, set atop slender legs.

David kept his hand on the pistol, anger rising up in him. "Listen to me. I will talk slowly so that you can understand. Fuck Markos. Fuck you. You all need to get out of my life. Tell Mr. Markos I hold his future in my hands, and so, he needs to be very careful. Now, get lost." David turned away.

"I don't like that answer. Your answer will be very troubling to Mr. Markos." The man with the muscular chest puffed out the words. "You will regret messing with Mr. Markos."

David took a deep breath. "Tell Markos to leave me alone."

"We understand each other. This is your last warning." The man in the blue jacket yelled after David, in a hoarse, raspy voice. When David was far enough away, he turned his head slightly to see them standing there looking at each other. Then, they slowly walked away, winding their way through the park.

David jogged back to his parent's house. Zoe was awake, sitting at the kitchen table, drinking coffee. She didn't look up at him. He kissed her on the cheek because she didn't turn her face toward him. When he was dressed for work, he asked his father to drop him off at the Metro station.

As he rode into DC, he studied the financials that Fleischmeister had sent him over the long weekend.

Alice was waiting for him when he got to the office. "David, let's go over the financials again. We are skating on some thin ice. Everyone appreciates the sacrifices you're making. I am more comfortable if we talk about our finances every day. I don't want to miss anything. With the one NSA contract, where we are renting out analyst bodies, we can probably scrape by for another six months, but anything out of the ordinary could sink us."

"Yeah, I'm with you on a daily budget discussion. Since the administration has another year to remain in office, we have to pay for the operational blood and guts, and not much else."

Alice stood, softly smiling. "I knew that's what you'd say. I'll have the corporate security proposal to you this afternoon."

At 1 PM, David huddled with Ali and Jose. "This is what I need you to do. Ali will rent a truck and have professional, magnetic lettering made, which you will attach to the sides of the truck, just before you arrive at our target. Some generic sounding company name like Two Men and a Truck. He will also rent a 1,500-square-foot, storage space in Alexandria. Jose, you go to Arlington to visit the temporary labor force office, and hire three laborers, preferably ones that don't speak English. The temporaries have to be ready to be picked up at 10:30 tonight. Are we okay, so far?"

Ali nodded. Jose grinned. "Sounds like a caper. I'm all in."

"Fantastic. Next, Jose will visit the moving supplies store in Fairfax where he will purchase unassembled cardboard boxes, tape, packing paper, and two hand carts for moving appliances and boxes. Frankie will prepare IDs and documentation for you. All right? Get going, guys."

Next, David met with Frankie. "Frankie, we're engaging in what Jose is calling a caper. I need your assistance. I'd like you to organize and supervise the removal of all the furniture and files from Markos's law offices. You'll need to develop orders for the property management company that manages the building to allow the movers into the building at 11 PM and to open the Markos offices. Call the property manager; use your most officious voice to complete the arrangements. I'm pretty sure that you can find the signature of Markos's administrative officer in our files, and if so, just transpose his signature onto the needed requisition."

Frankie grinned. "It is a caper, and I must say, a pleasant diversion."

At 3 PM, Odette bounced into the office with her hair cut short and a dramatic blouse of grey and silver. She brought David a new stack of documents for his inbox and took away those that he had read, initialed and/or approved. "David, Alice and I are doing Happy Hour at the Sofitel. Why don't you join us? You need a break."

"I gotta pass on that. I'm working on a top secret project that goes down tonight." He left the office at 3 PM and was at his parent's house by 4:15.

David took his father out on the back deck. "Dad, do you still have your shotgun and revolver?" David asked as nonchalantly as possible.

"I sure do. Is there a problem?"

"I've received some threats, Dad. I want you and mom to be safe."

Ben Pearl furrowed his brows. "Son, are you in trouble?"

"No. But I've been threatened, and most of our work is very sensitive. I simply want to take some precautions."

"I'll check the weapons right after dinner. Your mother is making chicken parmagiana, one of your all-time favorites. Is this about Zoe?"

"No, dad, it isn't. She hasn't been well. These threats have arisen because of some of our work. Let's leave it at that." After dinner, David went to the living room with his laptop and called the police department, requesting increased patrols for the next week for his parents' house. Then, he read and sent emails until midnight. When he had finished, he went into the bedroom he and Zoe were sharing, and kissed her on her lips. She seemed to remain soundly asleep. He stripped down to his boxer shorts and got into bed.

At 1:30 AM, David heard the soft music of "Zorba the Greek" sounding Zoe's ring tone. Zoe immediately grabbed the phone and left the bedroom. David silently followed her. He found her sitting at the back of the house in the family room. Her voice was deliberately low. David listened from the kitchen.

"He's fine." There followed what sounded to David like a man's voice, but it was too low for him to be certain.

"I love you, and I want to be with you." Zoe's voice trailed off into tears. "I know. I know. I will. I'm trying. I really am." David quick-footed it back to his spot in bed. He heard the sounds of the ice water dispenser on the refrigerator being used, and then within five minutes, Zoe was back in bed beside him. His rising anger made him sure she would be able to tell he wasn't asleep. He knew that if he confronted her now, the ensuing argument would wake his parents and most of the neighbors. He fought the anger and the thought this romance was coming to an unseemly end. After thirty minutes of mental 'what ifs,' and unable to bear the thought of listening to more of her lies, or even her touching him, he went to the living room and settled down on the sofa.

David woke up at 5 AM. His cell phone alarm woke him. He slipped into his running clothes and ran out into the early morning predawn. He ran under control, and before he left Sherwood Forest Drive, he made sure that there were no Greeks waiting in parked cars. Then, he ran the same route that he had run the morning before, except this time he was particularly cautious at those places where the trees hugged the trail. The run was, fortunately, uneventful, except for painful, worrying doubts about Zoe.

Back home once again, David sat down at the kitchen table with Peter. His mom was making omelets.

Peter sat at the table dressed in a shirt and tie, both of which he wore awkwardly. "I told your mom I can eat cereal. I am developing a habit for her omelets though." Peter laughed and then asked, "Are you sure it's okay for me to go to work with you today, David?"

"I'm positive Peter. We need extra security anyway. You can meet everyone. We have two guys who will have to go home early. They were on assignment all night." David looked at his cell phone. The agreed-upon text message from Jose was there, "One small step for humankind." David smiled.

David read the Washington Post, as the two men sat side by side on the Metro train. "Peter, do you think Zoe is okay? Is something bothering her?"

Peter looked at David with deep concern etched on his coarse features. "I worry about her, too. I asked her about it two days ago. All she would say is that she's confused about the direction of her life. Sometimes, she said the smoky confusion has so clouded her thinking, she was afraid that she would suffocate in it."

"I wonder what that means. I am beyond worried. I need to find out what's going on with her for sure. I'm going to talk to her tonight." David went back to pretending to read the paper. Peter studied the commuters on the train.

At 10:30 AM, Odette rang David on the intercom to tell him that Harry Markos was holding on line three. "Tell him I'm still tied up."

At 1 PM, Odette rang David on the intercom to tell him that Zoe wanted to talk to him. He picked up the phone. Without any introduction or other formalities, Zoe simply said, "I want you to meet me at the National Gallery of Art at two o'clock. Can you do that?" David said, of course.

At 2 PM, David walked through the main entrance of the National Gallery. He wandered around in front of the gift shop for five minutes before Zoe entered. She looked as perfectly beautiful as the first time he saw her. Her soft brown hair encircled a classically perfect face, and her curves were accented by a warm chocolate brown pant suit. Already some heads of the men traversing the lobby had turned in her direction. David hurried to her, but stopped abruptly about two feet away. Zoe began to cry.

When David moved to comfort her by touching her shoulder, Zoe turned her head away. She pulled on his hand to follow her outside. "I am in a hopeless state, David. I can't go on this way. I know you love me. I know I love you. But, right now I need to go back to Greece where maybe I'll find some peace of mind. Every time I close my eyes I see the man I killed. I killed him because I knew that he would kill me if I didn't. I felt better when I was in Greece. Goodbye." Zoe turned around and got into a cab that was idling beside the sidewalk.

David stared in the direction of Ronald Reagan National Airport for a long time. Then, he found a bench on the mall, and he sat there for an hour, lost in thought. Sometimes, he tearfully shook his head as if to shake loose some thought. As dusk fell, he made his way to the nearest Metro station.

CHAPTER 59
Down and Dirty, June 14 and June 15

David wandered down the mall, all the way to the Lincoln Memorial. Once there, he slowly climbed the steps to the statue of Lincoln. He stared into the great President's face for some time, slowly regaining his grip on his emotions and thoughts. The tourists around him laughed and oohed and aahed over the statue and the great president's words chiseled on the sides of the memorial. But he felt emotionally empty; his own thoughts focused on the beautiful Greek woman who had just left him. David wondered if he would ever find peace in his heart again. After several minutes, he turned around and walked away from the Memorial. He found himself passing through the Viet Nam Veteran Memorial. Thinking about the enormous loss for the many represented on that wall, in his comparatively lesser loss, he found some hope in his heart to carry on.

Back out on Constitutional Avenue, he hailed a cab. Sitting in the back seat, he told the driver to take him to the headquarters of Homeland Security, and then he dialed the number for the direct line to Tony Ritzenheim. "Can I come to talk to you?"

"Of course."

David signed the security log at the desk in the lobby, the guard confirmed the visit with Ritzenheim's secretary, and then David walked to the elevator bank.

Ritzenheim waited in front of the elevators for David. "Hey, Tony, thanks for seeing me. I really need to talk to somebody who cares." Ritzenheim put his hand on David's shoulder, gently directing him toward his office.

David slumped into the sofa. The green and tan, weaved, cloth sofa was wedged into the entire wall space on one side of Ritzenheim's office. A table sat in front of the large window. A silver laptop rested on top of the table on the otherwise bare surface. Ritzenheim's books, files, and journals were stuck into the bookcases in disorder and more were stacked on the credenza next to the office door.

David fought back the tears welling in his eyes. He held his breath to stifle a shudder. His hand reached into a pants pocket and pulled out a tissue. He blew his nose and wiped his eyes.

"So, my dear friend, did you get the license plate number of the truck that hit you?" Neither man laughed.

After a lengthy pause, David lifted his head. "No need, the truck was driven by my wife, Ritz."

"What?"

David looked at his watch. "Three hours ago, she told me that she was leaving me to go back to Greece. She is right now, at this very time, on an airplane flying to Athens."

"I am so sorry, man. That is so unbelievably shitty! Has Zoe lost her mind?"

"She was definitely unhappy with me about work, the present state of my finances, and not being sensitive to her needs, but I thought that she loved me and we would work through the issues. I really did."

Ritzenheim stared at his friend. "I'm appalled and stunned. If you weren't sitting there telling me this, I wouldn't believe it."

"Well, it's the truth."

"What a damn shame! Well, there's only one thing a man can and should do at a moment like this. We're going to get ripped, my friend."

A grim smile came to David's face. "Now, that's a good idea."

"Is there anything else Uncle Ritz can do to make this better?"

"You can be my advisor and counselor in this. You've been through a divorce twice. Help me to prepare." David lifted one of the coffee table type books off the top of the credenza, scanning the book's cover and looking somewhat perplexed. "You can help me get through this. I know I need to calm down and start making plans. I should be focusing on work with all the problems that have been thrown my way, but I know me, and I know getting divorced is going to be job one."

"That's exactly right. The first time I pretended that my work wouldn't suffer, and the work would get me through the pain and suffering, but that turned out to be completely foolish."

David was still focused on the book he held in his hand. "I didn't know you fished."

"I don't any more. Went a few times long, long ago. None of my ex-wives approved of me fly-fishing. Perhaps because I used it as an excuse for drinking and getting some quiet time away from them." Ritzenheim forced a laugh. The intercom buzzed from its place on the third shelf of the bookcase. He punched the button and listened. With a trigger finger twirling, he silently invited David to listen.

After a few moments of listening to Dingfelder, Ritzenheim said, "Yes, Burt, I totally agree with you. Let's not change the fucking color threat level scheme. For God's sake, it's a fucking joke already. What we need is some academic to come up with a scientific study that validates a ranking system like the ones for earthquakes or hurricanes. We should get a proposal on the street. Should have done that already. Listen, I'll work on it, Burt. Now, I have our mutual friend, David Pearl, here in the office."

"David, what's shaking?"

"Too much to talk about over the phone, Burt."

"Burt, he'll tell you all about it tonight at poker. Maybe have a few libations while we're at it. Okay, see you at my place."

Ritzenheim turned to David after hanging up. "The bad news is that I have a new thankless task to do for Homeland Security. The good news is Dingfelder will party with us. We'll go to my condominium in Georgetown. We'll stop at the liquor store to get the necessary supplies. If you get too drunk to go home, I have plenty of bunk space. Come on. We've kept democracy safe for another week. Let's get the fuck out of here."

Ritzenheim led David down to the third subbasement level. Once there, he retrieved his silver Mercedes Benz convertible coupe.

David smiled in admiration of the car. "Great set of wheels, Ritz, I imagine you can really seduce the women with a vehicle built for romance like this."

Ritzenheim shook his head. "It doesn't work like that. They see me before they see the car, so the results are less than satisfactory."

When they got to the Georgetown Liquor store, Ritzenheim parked illegally in a bus stop and ignored the dirty looks from the waiting passengers. He quickly came out with two cardboard boxes and a clerk carrying a third.

Back in the vehicle, Ritzenheim did a U-turn to a chorus of horn blasts, then drove over the C&O canal and into a driveway that led into a parking garage with tight, compartmentalized, and numbered spaces one level below ground level. David carried two boxes of liquor, beer, and mixers. Once inside the condo, Ritzenheim pointed to the couch, and David obediently plopped on it. He took off his suit jacket and tie, folded each neatly, and placed them on the floor beside the couch. Then, he took off his dress shoes and placed them beside the jacket and tie.

Ritzenheim put ice cubes into a crystal tumbler, filled it with single malt scotch and walked it over to David. He then opened the brie and gorgonzola cheese and served them on a tray. Hearing the sound of the front door buzzer, he stepped to the door.

Ritzenheim checked through the peep hole. Burt Dingfelder stood in the middle of the door. He was holding two canvas bags and immediately entered when Ritzenheim stood by the door, bowed, and waved with his right arm for Dingfelder to enter. Right behind Dingfelder were two men. The first was over six feet tall with a ruddy, reddish face. He was wearing a tailored suit of dark grey with bold cream pin stripes. Behind him was a slightly shorter and somewhat younger man. This man was very fit with slightly blonde hair cropped short in the style the military call 'sidewalls'.

David remained on the sofa, silently sipping his drink. He watched the men follow Dingfelder into the kitchen. From the kitchen came loud, boisterous talk with Ritzenheim and Dingfelder loudly accusing each other of sucking up to the Secretary to the detriment of progress, justice, and the American way.

When the noises had quieted somewhat, David called the office, after seeing that the office had called him numerous times while his cell phone had been turned off. He hit redial, and on the third ring, Odette picked up. "Where have you been? Are you all right? We are so worried." Odette's words were almost sobbed.

"Yes, Odette, I think I'm okay. I had a bad shock, but I am recovering I think." His voice sounded tired and unenthusiastic.

"What happened? Is it about Zoe?" Odette's voice was returning to its normal state, but her concern sounded earnest to David.

"Yes, but I'm not ready to talk about it yet. I'm in good hands at the moment getting much needed emotional therapy. I've got to go, Odette. I really appreciate your loyalty and concern. That means so much." David clicked off and clicked the number for his parents.

David watched Ritzenheim, who was in the process of setting up a folding poker table. David silently held out his glass as Ritzenheim walked by. Ritzenheim refilled it with an ice cube and scotch and promptly returned it to David's waiting hand.

He sipped the scotch and saw that the group had settled around the poker table. Ritzenheim motioned for him to join them.

David grabbed his drink and slowly made his way to the open dining room chair at the poker table. He carefully sat himself down.

"David, I would like you to meet Mike Finegan and Percy Moreland. Guys, meet David Pearl. David is the most capable intelligence operative and leader in Washington. Mike is the toughest SOB divorce lawyer in town, and Percy is a staff attorney in his firm." David shook their hands and gave a two handed shake to Burt Dingfelder.

"These guys are part of my Thursday evening poker group. The other two are former classmates of Percy's at Maryland who couldn't be with us this evening. They actually have a life." The men all laughed, Dingfelder the loudest, and David hardly at all.

David sensed that Finegan was sizing him up. He looked into Finegan's steely blue eyes. Finally, Finegan smiled. His smile brought the man's otherwise turned down lip corners into a multi-dimpled grin. "David, I understand you need a good divorce lawyer. Some advice I give for free. Such as, I urge you to file as quickly as possible. I know the emotional state you must be in, but act now, save yourself time and money later." Dingfelder slowly dealt out the cards. Finegan paused to examine his first three cards.

Dingfelder finished dealing out the first five cards. Finegan glanced at the last card and looked at David. "I handled the last two divorces of Ritz here. He didn't follow my advice the first time, and it cost him a lot of money."

Finegan laughed. Ritzenheim grunted. Moreland laughed too loudly and inappropriately at Ritz's misfortune.

Dingfelder spoke, "First, we'll play a little five card, deuces wild. David, we ante a dollar. Our limit is three raises with no raises above ten dollars. We try to keep this a friendly little game."

"Mike, I will take your advice and your counsel. What do you need in the way of a retainer?" Before Finegan could answer, a loud pounding commenced on the door. Ritzenheim rushed to the foyer closet where he pulled out a 9 millimeter Beretta from a cardboard shoebox that sat on the floor behind and under the coats. He chambered a round. He cautiously moved to the door and peeked through the peephole. "We got a male, dressed in a business suit, red in the face and breathing hard."

He checked back with the group. No one responded, so he turned back to the door. "Tell me who you are, and what the fuck you want?" Finegan stood and pulled his Walther SP22-M4 from his left pants pocket and positioned himself behind and to the left of Ritzenheim. Finegan dropped to one knee. He flicked on the laser sight. The red line made contact at the doorknob. Finegan held the molded and flared grip in a strong, practiced position.

"This is Harry Markos. I'm looking for David Pearl. Tell him that I have his loyal assistant, Alice Boggs."

"Who else is with you? You didn't get Alice here without assistance."

"My security team."

"Tell them to get lost." There was a pause. Murmuring could be heard coming from beyond the door. David calmly observed the scene and sipped his scotch. Dingfelder was in the kitchen. He had selected a meat cleaver and was now standing patiently behind the counter waiting for events to unfold. Percy stood apprehensively in the hall that ran from the living room to the two bedrooms.

"My guys left. Please open the door. I need to talk to Pearl. I am unarmed. Alice thought she knew where David would be. We are worried about him. One way or the other, I am going to talk to Pearl. Please, let's just do this nice and easy." Markos's voice was hoarse and pleading.

Ritzenheim looked at David who nodded his agreement. "Okay, Harry, We are armed. I am going to open the door nice and easy. Don't fuck this up." He slowly pulled the door open, stood to one side of the door, holding his pistol at his side. Finegan didn't move, remaining in the shooter's position. His pistol now aimed at the middle of Markos's chest. Markos held up his hands, his eyes wide and his mouth open. He walked slowly toward David. Markos made eye contact with David, and he pushed Alice ahead with his left arm.

"Harry, long time, no see. What brings you out away from your coven?" David had enough whisky on board to be unconcerned. Just one more problem to contend with. He slowly got up from his chair, went to Alice and hugged her. He gently stroked her back with his right hand and knocked Markos's arm away from her with the other. She clung to David and flicked a middle finger at Markos. Ritzenheim tenderly dislodged her from David and led her into the kitchen. She made herself a double gin and tonic, brought it back to the poker table. She moved a dining room chair to a place beside where David had been sitting. Percy was now sitting at the poker table, nervously stacking and restacking his chips.

Markos was directed by Finegan to sit on the sofa. Finegan pulled the cushioned armchair to a position directly in front of Markos. He held his pistol in a firm grip and kept it aimed at Markos.

Markos hesitantly began speaking. "David, I am in a bad, bad way. I think you stole my office files, furniture, and equipment. I've gone to the police, but they haven't got a clue. They think it's hilarious that I lost my entire office. The night security provided authentic looking forgeries that only someone with your resources could have produced. Somehow the video from the security cameras is missing. So, I am asking you for a good deed, a favor. I'm going to be losing clients over this mess. Uncle Ike has threatened my life. So, please help me. I could even get disbarred."

David smiled at Markos. "I find your sudden humility to be surprising. Harry, my firm and I have experienced a lot of shit that derives directly from you and/or your uncle. My office was bugged. My staff and I have been assaulted. I was threatened, once again, by your thugs two days ago. Now, I didn't take your office files and computers, but I know who did. The nice man who may have knowledge of the location of your firm's files and other assets is a businessman like you and Uncle Ike. He will want some cash and some guarantees. If you can convincingly provide these, I think I can talk him into parting with some of his investment."

"Some of his investment? Are you kidding? I'm sick of this bullshit, David. I need those files. We've already had to postpone some court cases." Markos's voice was frantic.

"I'm not playing around here, Harry. You can fish, or you can cut bait. Either way is going to hurt. And either way is fine with me."

"What are you talking about for God's sake? What do I have to do to get my files back?" Markos emitted a heavy sob. "The word is getting out on the street. One of the partners from a firm in the building called to ask me if my firm was going paperless, for God's sake." Finegan and Moreland chuckled at this.

Alice grabbed David's arm and pressed it to her chest. "This son of a bitch was waiting outside the office when I came out. His so-called security men grabbed me and threw me into the backseat of Harry's Mercedes limousine. I want to file charges. I was assaulted and kidnapped. They threatened me into telling them where I thought you would be. I'm sorry." She clung to David.

David calmly turned to Alice and kissed the top of her head, then turned back to Markos. "Well, see there, Harry, the price of poker is going to go up. Think of this as a long-term financial settlement like a divorce. You had better be serious about paying up, even to the extent of making some financial sacrifices, or you could wind up in jail or lose your coveted reputation among your low life associates."

"No, fuck no, David. Listen to me. I am desperate. I'm rapidly running out of excuses and time. You are putting me out of business. Some of my clients won't hesitate to kill me if I can't represent them and can't return their files." Markos dropped his head into his hands, his body tensed, and rocked back and forth.

"Harry, this is purely a business deal. My friend will return whatever you need when you need it, but Alice has been abused and hurt, as have I. My life has been threatened, Harry, threatened by your associates. I am so worried about my family and friends getting hurt . . ." David paused to stroke the back of Alice's head. "So I need insurance. My friend wants to know, for sure, that his investment is solid because he cares about me, and he wants to make certain that my firm, my employees, and my family don't have to worry about you and your thugs anymore. Oh, and I need you and your friends in Washington, like Eugeniades, to stop spreading the news about what a screw-up I am and what crappy work DRPearl, Inc does. Do I make myself clear?"

"Yeah, yeah, I understand I'm getting screwed. What a mess." Harry reached into his jacket pocket and pulled out a checkbook." I need the hard copy files labeled Giatrakis Shipping and at least two of the computers. How much for that?"

"My friend will want one hundred thousand. That's just to cover expenses, you understand. Don't forget about those guarantees, will you, Harry? How about drafting something up in the way of a contractual agreement and getting it to me next week? Oh, we'll download the files from the two computers before returning them." Alice rested her hand on David's thigh and stared at Markos.

Harry Markos wrote out the check, in agonizing deliberation. His hand was shaking visibly. When Markos had finished writing, he held out the check. Finegan took it, rising out of the chair with the pistol still firmly gripped at his side. Finegan studied the check briefly, then walked it over to David and placed it in front of him.

Markos sunk back into the sofa. "I fucking guarantee your safety. I will tell Uncle Ike to leave your firm alone. You know that Ike has suffered tremendous losses because of you."

"Tell Ike that if I think he's interfering in my affairs again, even a sniff, our little deal will be off, and you can explain to the judges how you lost all of your clients' files. Tell him all about your losses. Explain to him that the security of my firm and my family means everything to me. This time, things are much different. We are in a bad business environment. And for DRPearl Inc., you and your Uncle are vulnerabilities that will be controlled. It's all simple risk management, Harry."

"How soon can I get that file and my computers?"

"On Monday afternoon. My investor is a busy, busy man." A loud banging on the door startled everyone. Ritzenheim moved to the side of the door with his pistol out.

"What do you want?" Ritzenheim moved his pistol into a two handed grip and aimed it about five feet above the transom.

"Harry, you in there? Are you okay?" The man's husky voice sounded like the voice of a heavy smoker, thick and coarse.

"Yeah, I'm okay. I'm coming out. We're leaving." Harry stood with the help of a hand placed on the arm of the sofa to push him up. Harry glared momentarily at David and then at Finegan, walked slowly to the door, which Ritzenheim held open for him. The thug outside had disappeared from view. Harry walked out into the Washington DC, humid evening, Ritzenheim and Finegan watched, peering carefully around the door jam. They followed him until they saw Markos get into the elevator.

The men rejoined David and Alice at the poker table. Ritzenheim invited Alice to play. She declined, keeping her arm on David's thigh and her shoulder gently touching his. David was comforted by Alice's nearness and by the ritual of playing poker. The play, the soft gentle touch of Alice and her familiar smell, and the scotch all combined to take David to a better place.

By 1 AM, David was overly drunk and realized it. Alice had to be helped to her feet. Dingfelder hugged Alice and assisted her into the spare bedroom. David followed, after shaking everyone's hand and telling Finegan that he would be calling him on Monday. Ritzenheim cleared the table, cashing everyone out. Finegan was the big winner.

Chapter 60
Destiny, June 20

David was sitting at his desk, trolling through his emails, looking at the latest email from Markos. Markos wants to make a final settlement for the rest of his files, computers, and peripherals. I'll have to think about that. A loud knock on the door interrupted him.

"Oh, hi, Odette. What've you got for me?" David looked up and smiled at Odette.

"A bicycle messenger just delivered this. He told me that I had to hand it unopened to David Pearl, personally. No one else. So, here it is." She walked to the front of his desk and handed it to him.

"How's the new romance going?"

Odette blushed, but grinned. "Merci, mon chef. It's going great. I think Percy and I will make a great team. I just have to convince him of that."

David watched her leave the room. He reached for his pen-knife and sliced up the heavy, padded, manila envelope. Protected inside by two sheets of stiff cardboard were five 8X10 glossy photographs. David turned to the one on top. A few moments passed as David refocused on the photograph. After several seconds passed, he realized the pictures were of Polopolis and Zoe in bed. Both of them bloody, mangled, and dead. He checked the mailing address. There was none, only the postmark indicated that it originated in Athens, Greece. He put a hand over his eyes to hide the tears rolling down his cheeks.

When his tears stopped, he blew his nose, and called Alice. "Alice, as the Chief Operating Officer for DRPearl Inc., I think we should put our heads together for a little strategic kanoodling at your place."

"You are so fresh, but smart and strategic, too. I'll grab us a cab."